*Gambling Rogues,
The Rush for Gold,
And a Woman Whose
Price was Beyond Passion!*

She was the daughter of an English king. From London and Paris where she lived the glittering life of a demimondaine, mistress to Dexter Roark, darkly handsome and mysterious international financier, to the storm-tossed nights of her passage round Cape Horn, and finally to the American land where gold dust sparkled amid the rough-hewn longings of men taming our last frontier in California—Poppy could not forget her past . . . and the man whose embrace tore her passion loose and held it gently.

TRUE SUMMERS
Poppy

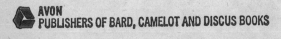

AVON
PUBLISHERS OF BARD, CAMELOT AND DISCUS BOOKS

To V. J. H.
with
Gratitude for
Faith, Hope, and Charity

POPPY is an original publication of Avon Books. This work has never before appeared in book form.

AVON BOOKS
A division of
The Hearst Corporation
959 Eighth Avenue
New York, New York 10019

First Avon Printing, August, 1978

AVON TRADEMARK REG. U.S. PAT. OFF. AND IN
OTHER COUNTRIES, MARCA REGISTRADA,
HECHO EN U.S.A.

Printed in the U.S.A.

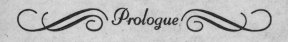

Prologue

London 1833

SHE was born impetuous and with no regard for rank or propriety. At her first public appearance two weeks after the birth, she dribbled on the royal waistcoat and batted the regal nose with a clenched fist.

Though a fond father many times over, William set her beside her mother on the gold brocade chaise longue. He had ten other acknowledged bastards, but this was his young mistress's child, and the girl looked more beautiful than ever, with her violet eyes shining and her golden hair tumbling down around a bosom more luminously white than the creamy satin of her peignoir.

"I thought I'd name her Violet," Daisy Smith said, handing the baby to the wet nurse.

"Violet? She's red as a beet."

"That's usual."

"Look at that hair."

"I suppose there's Poppy."

"Suitable," William said. "Suitable."

The next day the rubies, in a velvet case tactfully unmarked by his crest, were delivered by a gentleman in black, his livery discreetly plain, to the small cottage on Pallminster Lane. Their disappearance from the royal treasure chests caused such criticism at a politically crucial time, that William dared make no settlement on the baby, let alone ennoble her as he had his other children. He was King of England, but the treasury was low, and in a last flare-up of his Stuart blood to

3

prove he could rule supreme, he began to realize he had overreached himself. Though he had formed a ministry around Sir Robert Peel, the Parliament was determined to teach him that his powers were limited.

He made promises to Daisy for the future. The child would need a large dowry to make anything like an appropriate marriage. The bluff sailor king meant his promises.

He was fond of the child and liked to watch her splashing in her bath. He laughed as heartily as she when the nursemaid was drenched. Later, when she could toddle, her habit of darting from behind doors and wrapping herself around his ankles was taken beamingly as affection. He was much too solid on his feet to trip and fall with a satisfying thud as the butcher's boy and the scullery maid did. She was a mischief, he admitted, but high spirits did a beautiful girl no harm, and her wide-set, amethyst eyes were exceptional. She should do well on the marriage market, for Daisy had a practical head on her lovely shoulders, and could guide her.

Still, the King was not a young man, and this surprising proof of virility in his old age may have given him a false sense of immortality. The political battles were wearing, though the people did not lose their affection for the sailor king, and the defeats made him cautious. He procrastinated, and the general debility that killed him struck before Poppy's dowry was arranged.

Because all his children were illegitimate, his niece Victoria became Queen. Poppy was left the nameless bastard of a beautiful demimondaine without a protector.

Part One

England
April-September 1851

Chapter One

THE Crystal Palace, a blazing arc of glass rising like a fountain from the green turf of the park, shimmered in the late April sunlight. Outside, great dray horses hauled wagons heaped with bales and packing cases of exhibition materials yet to be arranged. The opening was only two days away, and sweating laborers unloaded the cases outside the doors while bearded, frock-coated bobbies patrolled to keep order.

Standing on tiptoe among the pushing crowd, as close as the bobbies would let anyone get, Poppy Smith tried to see through the glass. Painters still were working inside, and red carpets hung from the girders. She was sure the elm trees in there had grown in the last two weeks, enormous trees right inside the building and beautiful now that the birds were no longer perching in them and making a nuisance on everything around. The Duke of Wellington had solved that for the Queen as he had solved so many worries. "Try sparrow hawks, ma'am," he had said.

Poppy drew a long, ecstatic breath. The Great Exhibition was going to be the most wonderful thing that had ever happened in London or even all England. Paxton, who had grown the giant lily in a glass house for the Duke of Devonshire, and Albert the Good, the Prince Consort, had raised this shining pavilion. It was almost as if they had waved a wand over the park this winter, and it had sprung up like a fairy arcade of bright streets and sunlit spaces. Now all the countries of the world were sending their most advanced and

7

best products. Everything a manufactory could make or hands could fashion would be on display inside the Palace.

Poppy jabbed an elbow into the side of the fat woman who was trying to push her off the little mound on which she stood. She anchored herself more firmly by digging into the turf the small green parasol that matched the stripe of her plaid street attire. Then she felt the empty space beside her and turned uneasily, amethyst eyes narrowing as she looked around. Andy had slipped away, and she knew what he was trying to do. He was determined to get inside, and if the bobbies caught and held him, as they surely would, they both would be in terrible trouble. When Daisy had given them their season tickets, she had said they must never come here without telling her. They had not told her. Worse, when the Reverend Dr. Minton, who had been their tutor these last two years, had dozed off after morning tea, for he was elderly and often weary from reading late into the night, they had slipped out of his rooms and run away without a word to anyone. Andy detested Julius Caesar, Poppy abhorred mathematics, and the Exhibition beckoned.

"My brother," Poppy murmured.

"That way," the fat woman said, pointing toward the Palace, and pushed triumphantly up on the mound.

Poppy debated shoving back, as any right-thinking Londoner was obligated to do, and then shouldered and wriggled her way through the crowd to the front. She would not have been surprised to see Andy right under the hoofs of the dray horses or hiding behind one of the bales, waiting his chance to slip up to the doors, but she could not see his halo of golden curls anywhere.

She looked toward the small hill where pickpockets were supposed to congregate, but even Andy would have better sense than to go there. Then, in a small group of trees to her right, she caught a glint of gold as high as a man's elbow. Edging along in front of the crowd, murmuring apologies, she rehearsed a tirade and discarded it. Instead she would threaten not to help him with his lessons for a week. That would keep him docile.

At the edge of the trees, she stopped, stiffening. Andy was talking, his deceptively angelic face tilted up, to a big man. Poppy did not like the man's looks. She did not like his full, damp underlip or his moist, protruding eyes. She did not like his fancy embroidered waistcoat and ruffled shirt—they were not only old-fashioned but in bad taste. Especially she did not like the way his plump, ringed hand was fondling Andy's shoulder.

Poppy had heard about such men from Daisy. Daisy had grown up in the country, during the frank Georgian era, and she could be a blunt-spoken woman. She had warned them both. Andy was a fool.

Poppy did not run, but she quickly arrived beside them with a busy rustle of her underskirts. "Andy, we've got to go. Come on."

He raised limpid blue eyes. "We can't go home yet, or Daisy will know we slipped away from The Rev."

How much had he told the man? At the least that they were unchaperoned and would not be missed for hours. "It's hot. I want to find a water ice seller," she said.

"So you're the sister, miss?" The man's voice was unpleasantly soft. "I was just telling the young man that I have a marvelous toy train I'd like him to see. I live just over there. You can come with us."

"No. No. Andy, come on."

"I want to see the train."

Poppy felt her face getting red. How could any London boy, eight, almost nine, be so stupid? "No. Come with me. Now."

"You'd enjoy the train, too." The man's hand clamped on her arm like a steel band. "I have a friend I'll ask to join us. I know he'd like to meet you."

Did he think they were going to walk meekly into some locked, shuttered place to be chloroformed and raped? "Let me go," Poppy hissed, digging in her heels.

He had Andy's arm in his other hand. "Come sweetly

9

now. It's just across the road." He jerked her arm up behind her.

She gasped and tried to raise her parasol, but he twisted her arm high, turning her until she bent half double, her face crushed against his waistcoat. She kicked futilely, and he twisted her arm higher. She gulped down nausea, wondering if her arm had been dislocated.

"Sweetly, softly," he whispered. "Quiet now. We'll have a water ice there, and I've some tin soldiers to show the boy, too."

"Trouble?" a deep voice inquired.

"My sister's children up from the country," the man said hastily. "I brought them up for the Exhibition as a treat, but it's spoiled they are, ripe spoiled."

"Not yet. Let them go, Archie. You don't remember me, but I was there when you had that little trouble in Dorset last year."

The man's hand loosened like magic, and he fell back. Poppy staggered against a tree, eyes closed, gasping for breath. A bobby, a bobby had saved them. And caught them too, but that was better than this monster.

"Go play with your tin soldiers, Archie," the deep voice said. "And don't forget again that people know you and your special little tastes."

As Poppy opened her eyes, the plump man turned with a whip of his coattails and scurried off among the trees. Her eyes purple dark, she stared at the stranger who stood leaning indolently on his cane beside Andy. He was not a bobby, and she knew she had never seen him before. She would not have forgotten him. He was subtly different from anyone she had ever known. He was impeccably dressed in a short, dark-gray coat with lighter gray trousers and a fawn waistcoat. The excellent tailoring almost concealed that his shoulders were too broad and his hips too narrow. The gold head on his cane was just a touch too heavy. His black hair was a shade too short, and his neat sideburns led to the merest thread of a mustache. His skin was bronzed, but it was not the weathered coloring of a hunting man. His face

10

was too lean and strong-jawed to be completely handsome, but everything about him proclaimed a gentleman of wealth and good taste. Yet something about him was not English. Perhaps it was his eyes—of a strange, changing color like the stone they called a cat's-eye.

"Are you here with your mother or an escort?" he asked. Then he read the guilt in their faces. "So you're alone? I'll take you home."

"Please, sir, it's all right. We have our fare for the horsecab," Andy piped up.

"I'll take you home."

Daisy would not be leaving Pallminster Lane for her daily drive in the park for another hour. They dared not return so early. Poppy swallowed hard and said in her sweetest tone, "We thank you, sir, but our mother does not allow us to ride in a carriage with a strange man." For a moment, the cool eyes looked so hot she thought she had gone too far and he would answer with a scathing reminder of his timely rescue.

Instead he smiled. "Naturally not. I'll put you in a cab and pay the driver and come along behind you."

"You are too kind, sir," Poppy refused.

Andy seemed to have taken one of his inexplicable likings to the stranger. He slipped a hand into his and confided, "We can't go home yet, you see, but we'll be all right."

"So that's the way of it."

Andy nodded, looking up worshipfully. "You wouldn't happen to know how to get us inside, would you, sir?"

Then it sounded, Daisy's shriek. She worked hard at her genteel manners, though she was not one to worry if people said there was a hint of the vulgar about her. But when she was shocked, she turned pure country woman. Her shriek split the air.

"My children! Andy! Poppy! What are you doing over there?"

Poppy and Andy looked at each other, white faced. Daisy, too, had been unable to resist an impulsive visit to the Exhibition. They consulted silently over what explanation they could give for their presence and knew there was none. They could not say The Rev had let them go early or even that he had dozed off and they had slipped away to spare him. Daisy would ask him, and he would promptly tell her the whole. Twice lately he had wakened after a short time and found them gone. A short walk could have been their excuse when they returned, but they had not returned at all, either day. Even the second time, he had not told Daisy, but he had warned them he was too old and tired to stay to teach pupils who did not wish to learn when he had a son with a country parish who had offered him a home. Now Daisy had caught them, and The Rev would say the third time was too much.

"Oh, he's gone," Andy wailed. "The grand gentleman is gone."

Poppy could not think how he could have slipped away so quickly and quietly, but he was gone. "Thank goodness for that," she said crisply. "Now don't you dare mention him—or that train and toy soldier man, Andy. Don't you dare. At least Daisy can't punish us for something she'll never know."

"Would he have told on us?" Andy cried, disappointed.

"With bells on and fireworks," Poppy swore. She added darkly, "He had a foreign look about him."

Chapter Two

THE terrifying thing was that Daisy made no threats. As they had guessed, unable to resist the final bustle before the opening of the Exhibition herself, she had started her drive early. Now she had Peters turn her carriage straight around and take them all home. She sent word by Peters that Mr. Hammett, who had been her gentleman for the last year, was not to call that evening. She told Poppy and Andrew to go to their rooms and stay there. Mrs. Peters would bring them bread and butter and broth on a tray and that was all they were to expect. She left to see the Reverend Dr. Minton.

Sitting in her sewing chair in front of her room's unlit fireplace, Poppy knew she was in the worst trouble of her life. She loved her home, the little cottage on Pallminster Lane. It had three bedrooms upstairs, the parlor and dining room down, and a kitchen that looked out on the small enclosed garden toward the carriage house, which had rooms for Peters and Mrs. Peters above. She would have enjoyed her lessons with The Rev, but Andy was no scholar. The Rev thought any boy was as bright as a girl twice his age, so he set them the same tasks. Even at the hardest of those in mathematics, she had to hold back so Andy would not seem a dullard and be in trouble.

Looking at her pretty, glazed pink tile fireplace, she thought it would break her heart to leave her home and London. Probably Daisy would try to find boarding schools that would accept them, even if their mother was of a known profession. But she had tried before and failed. So the worst that could happen would be a terribly strict tutor who used the cane freely. She would probably take away their season tickets to the Exhibition and their spending money, too. She might even say Poppy was to have no new summer dresses. What worse could she do?

Daisy had always sworn she would never apprentice them. They were too well-bred for any work of that type. They could do better. She thought she might get Andy into the Civil Service when he was old enough, provided she could find the right gentleman to make a strong recommendation. Poppy was to marry. Beauty was better than any dowry, Daisy sniffed, and as to how Poppy was to meet proper young men with honorable intentions, time would take care of that.

Poppy was not so sure. She had no school friends to invite her to small dances to meet their brothers, and Daisy's friends did not have sons who were eligible. The one man who hinted he might make an offer, she had regarded with horror. He was one of Mr. Hammett's friends and nearly as old and much fatter. Daisy said that he had buried two wives and had any number of half-wild children hidden away in some country house and that he was frantic to find somebody to care for them, a woman obligated to stay regardless. Mr. Hammett did not like to be reminded Daisy had two large children on the premises, so he urged the match.

Poppy often marveled at Daisy. She could change a gentleman's frowns to smiles as easily as she twisted a tendril of golden hair into a curl around her finger. She never lost her wits or control of her tongue. She did not say she owned the cottage. She did not say removing Poppy would still leave Andy. She simply murmured that Mr. Hammett's friend was a fine, upstanding gentleman but Poppy was still a schoolroom miss and perhaps not simple but awkward in her ways. The gentleman had commiserated with her, left, and not returned. Surely Daisy would not change her mind about him now.

Poppy jumped to her feet. Daisy was back. She could hear her voice downstairs. Now she would learn the worst. Or maybe it would be better if Daisy waited until after she had eaten and was not so cross.

Daisy did not send for her or for Andy that night or the next morning. Noon was striking on the parlor mantel clock before Mrs. Peters came puffing up to say Poppy was wanted downstairs.

Daisy was standing in the center of the parlor, wearing her black dress with the thin white stripe, and that was bad. She wore it only when she went to the bank on business or sallied out to dispute with a tradesman over a bill that seemed too large. The black dress meant serious trouble.

"Dr. Minton is through with you, going to his son in the country, and I'm rusticating you and Andy with Gramps," Daisy announced.

Poppy stared at the beautiful, golden-haired woman who was her mother and still looked no more than thirty. Rusticating? That was what they did to university men who got into scrapes. Daisy had talked to The Rev, and he was a university man. To him, that would have seemed a suitable punishment. But rusticating with Gramps? The Rev simply had not known.

"With the man who sold you for ten pounds?" Poppy gasped.

"Certainly he sold me for ten pounds. I'll tell it any day because girls were bringing only five pounds those hard times. Still do, even now. So I was a ten-pound virgin and proud my pa thought enough of me to do it and make a good arrangement. I'll always be grateful for it."

"Proud of the ten pounds maybe," Poppy whispered. "But grateful?"

"Sit down. You and I are going to have a little talk. It's only fair to Gramps you should know how things were before you go there. And maybe, too, it will make you appreciate what you've had here."

"We didn't get into any trouble or do anything bad."

"Not yet. And you'll not be spoiled if I can help it,

15

the same as my pa saved me from being spoiled. So sit down and keep your feet together and your hands in your lap the way you've been taught to do while I'm speaking."

She had never seen Daisy in such a temper. "Yes, ma'am," she whispered and sat down.

"Now you mustn't expect too much when you get there, though things are easy now compared to when I was a child," Daisy said, pacing the floor. "Then there were twelve of us living in that two-room cottage. We had a smithy and a garden, a few fruit trees, and a bit of pasture for the cows and chickens. But even with the smithy, that didn't feed us. From the time we were seven or eight, we were all out working at whatever came to hand—rough work, field work—for a few pence a week. Those were cold and hungry times, and I suppose we were lucky, for we owned the cottage, and the fields were healthy work. If there'd been factories or coal mines near, we might have ended in them, and those are a hard life and short. Then the older ones started growing up and could get away.

"The oldest, Nellie, went into service, and she was lucky to get on in a big house, so she had a bed in a dormitory and hot meals and two uniforms a year and a bit of cash in her hand at the end to send home. Nellie's done well. She's an upstairs maid now. Nellie was plain and common-sensical, but poor Allie was always dreaming, and she got in trouble and would not stay to face it. She ran off and nobody knows what happened to her. The river, mayhap, or a house or it could be anything else. Josie, Tom, and Will all died young and nobody had the heart to grieve much. Davvy went for a seaman, and Dan'l got taken on at the stables up at the manor. Dorcas married, and it was a misery, the same as our folks or worse, even today. Then there was Barney, the oldest boy, and that was the trouble. He was a mean one. Still is. Finally Pa said Barney could have the place but only after he was gone, and Pa drove him off. He got taken on as a laborer with a cottage and garden space on a farm on the other side of the village. He married, but his wife has it hard, and everybody says it is a mercy the children never live long.

"I was the last, and my folks were at their wits' end. I was as common-sensical as Nellie, but with my looks no woman was going to have me in her house with men-folks around, not in good service. A couple of men made offers for me, but Pa wanted a better life for me than he'd given Ma. But Barney kept coming around, begging for this and that, hanging around, hanging around, and he would not let me be. My folks weren't going to have me spoiled and by my own brother. I was thirteen and full grown, but I was the last, and things were easier. So it wasn't a matter of eating dinner that day to get me placed.

"The Colonel was visiting at the manor and saw me and came around to make an offer. He was a retired Army man, with a scarred face and a limp, and he put his terms plain and clear. He liked young girls, and he liked to have them first, as so many gentlemen do, but some only for the once. The Colonel never kept them long. But neither did he turn them out when he was finished, though that's the common thing and no one would have said a word to him. He set his girls up in a decent place, he paid the rent ahead, and gave them cash to see them through until they made a new connec-tion—if they had the sense to use their chance. If not, of course they ended on the street. Then he offered Pa ten pounds."

Daisy's face lit up, and she sank down into the chair across the hearth from Poppy. "I was a ten-pound girl and in hard times. I knew then, and the folks knew, too, that I would be all right. The Colonel was not a patient man, and I could not call him kindly or say I ever could like him, but he was fair. I ate good food and wore pretty clothes and had as sweet a pair of rooms as any-body could want in London. When the Colonel got to hungering for a new one, he told me straight and kept his word. He paid a quarter's rent ahead, gave me another ten pounds, and let me keep the clothes and trinkets I had.

"Now, he had kept me to himself, and I was young and green from the country. I was timid, knowing that. But I kept my wits about me. I didn't know where the gentry went or how to meet them without picking them up on the street and making myself cheap. But I let myself be seen, and I didn't jump at the first offer I had. I never even considered I might go on the streets or end up in a house. A few gentlemen had seen me with the Colonel, and when they saw me without, word got around. By the time the ten pounds were gone, I had a new connection. That gentleman taught me about London, the people, and the different places—where to avoid the rough ones and where the gentry went. When William saw me, strolling in the park, I was on the arm of a gentleman and had on as pretty a walking costume as any woman could wear. Blue, it was, with a white satin stripe and a bonnet with a double-fluted edge and velvet ribbons floating to my waist.

"He was a fine gentleman, your father, lovable. He set me up in this house, but he wasn't a young man. We both knew someday I had to make a life for myself, but I would be all right. By the time he died, I was not twenty yet, and I was one of the beauties. Not one of the first ones, with my pictures on sale and all, but I was pretty as any picture, and my next gentleman was as sweet a boy as I ever knew. We were happy, Poppy, we were happy as a pair of lambs in a spring meadow all those years. And he was good to you, too. When his family made him marry, and he went back to the West Country, I couldn't settle. It's a wonder I didn't end up between the hammer and the anvil."

"That was when you got Andy?"

"Not from him. My next was a manufacturing gentleman from Manchester who came in occasionally to see about loans in the city. In and out, he was, but I wasn't ready to settle, either. He never grudged what he spent, but the times he was gone—well, I was lonely, and we never fixed it as a permanent connection. So when I met this lovely young cavalry boy in the park, on leave he was for just a few weeks, I fair lost my head for a while.

Oh, it was lucky the manufacturing gentleman was a long time away just then, but that's the reason I've never been sure about Andy. To be truthful, I never thought the officer gave me his right name. Some will do that when they're on leave and running free. So I just called the baby Andrew, meaning manly, because they were both good men, but I've never been sure which it was. After he arrived, my manufacturing gentleman left. I always thought maybe he had too many babies at home and didn't enjoy another one. I knew I had to face up to my responsibilities. Mr. Manwitter was just the right man for me at that time. He thought my being settled here in this house proved I was settled, not flighty, and he could not tolerate a flighty female."

"I remember you yawning behind your fan."

"I wore mitts too. Gave me an excuse to put my hand to my face and flirt with them. He was such a serious man. But he was the one who made me take the bank notes from under the carpets, the gold from where I had it hid under the loose tile on my bedroom hearth, and the trashy trinkets out of my powder box. He got them all together, not the rubies or my diamond earrings or the gold bracelets or the other things I wear, of course, and took me to the bank. I did as they told me, bought the freehold here and let them invest the rest in four percents. From that day, I've never had a real worry that I wouldn't have a roof over my head or would go hungry."

"I couldn't find a fan big enough to yawn behind, with a man that serious," Poppy cried.

"You could learn the lesson he taught me," Daisy said severely. "It's not enough to be provident today, you've got to be wise for tomorrow, too. Oh, dear, oh, my, but he was a provident man himself."

"You were certainly unsettled when he left."

"Why shouldn't I have been?" Daisy cried, her cheeks rosy with remembered indignation. "Here we'd been cozy as two birds on a high roost all those years and then that wife of his got to acting up. I think that was the reason he valued me so high, we were easy together. He'd married above him, and she made him feel it. When she finally heard about me, she went to her family, and they all crashed down on him together. He sold to the Royal Navy, you know, brass fittings and things. What that family did was ask him how many orders he thought he'd get if our dear queen ever heard about me and his leaving his wife alone so much. Now he was between the hammer and the anvil."

"If you understood, why did you get all in a flutter and go running off to Paris after he left?"

"I said he was a provident man. He'd given me a proper allowance, paid on the dot every quarter, to run this house the way he liked. But when he left, he said getting the bank to take me as a client and his advice on the investments were my settlement. Not one penny in cash did he give me more."

"He was no gentleman," Poppy cried hotly.

"He did as he saw right. Still, none of my other gentlemen ever did a thing like that. I thought if it could happen once, maybe times were changing. I'd heard how high and handsome those Paris beauties were flying, and I thought I'd better find out for myself if I'd have it finer over there. Besides I was unsettled in my mind." Daisy pursed her rosy lips in a kitten's hiss of contempt and shook her golden head. "High and handsome it was, but when I saw those *grand horizontals,* as they call them, and the way they live and throw their money around, I tell you I was fair disgusted. They'd break themselves, they would, for a dress for a grand ball or a costume for the races or a necklace they fancied. There they were, laying around half the day and letting their servants steal them blind because they were too lazy to care. Oh, I don't grudge the year we spent there because you children did learn a nice French, proper accent and all, but I came back knowing England and the English ways were best. Maybe our dear queen would be shocked at the likes of me, but she knows how to run her house and raise her family, and what's good enough for her is good enough for me," Daisy finished breathlessly.

"Andy and I used to put it in our prayers every night for you to decide to bring us home," Poppy confided. "Even if the Queen doesn't like dancing and balls the way she used to and the Court is getting so proper."

Daisy's charming, girlish smile flashed. "Were you wishing for the old days? They weren't so good, I've heard, miss. Oh, we've had our high steppers, on the throne and off. But the days are gone when Nell Gwyn could roll down her carriage window and call out, 'I am the Protestant whore, good people,' and be cheered for it. Even *she* had her troubles getting her king to set her up proper in her own house and provide for her children as was right. No, these are the good times, and we're lucky to live in them." Her face sobered. "So don't you go thinking I'll let you do anything but what your father wanted for you, marry a respectable man. Now you go upstairs and pack and help Andy do the same. I'm putting you both on the train tonight and sending you to Pa."

"We don't know him, he doesn't know us," Poppy cried in a panic.

"He's expecting you. Dr. Minton had a friend who was traveling that way last night, and he took a message to be passed along. It's all arranged."

"For how long?"

"Until I can make suitable arrangements here. That may take a while so don't go counting the hours."

"You wouldn't—that man—Mr. Hammett's friend," Poppy began and could not put the thought into words.

Daisy understood. "Not unless you drive me desperate, miss, and sometimes I've thought you would."

21

Chapter Three

$\mathcal{P}$OPPY knew she would not have hated the country so much if Andy had not been so wildly happy and she had not been such a failure. She could not do one thing right.

Daisy put them on the train herself and watched until it pulled out. Poppy could remember the trip only as a bad dream. The second-class car had no heat or lighting or glass to protect them from the soot flying back from the engine. She and Andy huddled together on the bare board seat, their feet on the single portmanteau holding the old clothes Daisy had said were good enough for the country. They were terrified by the burly, rough-spoken countrymen around them, who spoke in accents they could hardly understand. They were too frightened to eat the parcel of food Daisy had given them, sure it would be snatched away. Besides, Gramps might not have enough food for them when they arrived. Andy was certain they would have to sleep on straw on the floor. Poppy knew they would wade through mud outside and share the house with pigs and chickens.

Gramps proved to be a red-faced, jovial man, as big as Granma was small and quiet. Seeing her, Poppy understood why Gramps had wanted an easier life for his beautiful daughter. Granma's face was a fine-featured mask of wrinkles, and her mouth looked like a nutcracker due to the loss of her teeth. Her hands were gnarled and swollen with hard work, and her body was thin and bent. She looked twenty years older than her husband and wanted only to slip away and nap every chance she could find.

The tiny thatched cottage was as clean as scrubbing could make it. The mattresses were straw, but the mended sheets were fine linen. Poppy recognized them as some Daisy must have sent when they became too shabby for Pallminster Lane. Flowers grew around the door and bordered the path leading to the smithy. The three pigs and the dozen chickens were in pens between the kitchen garden and the orchard. The two cows had a small pasture.

Andy took one look at the smithy, and, giving a whoop, ran out there. He watched Gramps shoeing a big farm horse. After that, he could hardly be dragged away to eat or sleep. He did not listen when Gramps roared with laughter and said he was the worst smith in four counties and only worked the forge because it was the family trade and he had inherited it. He got only the poorest work, shoeing farm horses brought in because he was cheap or mending broken rakes, hinges, or whatever oddments came his way.

Andy, blue eyes shining, pounced on a hammer small enough for him to handle and, day after day, hung over the anvil, heating and pounding every piece of old metal he could find.

Poppy was less successful at finding something to do. She tried to weed the kitchen garden. She did learn that if the tiny roots were orange or red, she had pulled carrots or beets, food for next winter, and hastily thrust them back. At the end of a week, Granma said it was lucky she had saved back some seed. She planted again and forbade Poppy to set foot in the place. Once, only once, Poppy brought in an armload of lovely blossoms from the orchard to decorate the house. Gramps beat her with them, not hard and smiling cheerfully, then explained each blossom would have been a fruit. She stayed out of the orchard after that.

She carried scraps to the pigs and chickens. She thought the pigs quite amiable but she took the chickens in strong aversion. Nothing could have gotten her in the pen with the nasty pecking things that might fly at her. She drove the cows in from the pasture and tried to milk them, but she got only half as much as Gramps or Granma, so she was not allowed to do that, either. She would not go near the forge because of the way the farmers stared at her and the remarks they passed. The washing, cleaning, and cooking in the tiny cottage were soon finished.

She watched Granma churning by the open door. "I could learn to do that."

"I know you could, child. There's nothing wrong with your head. Daisy says you're better with the books than Andy."

"When did she tell you that?"

"She told Nellie. The family takes her to London when they open their house every year. And Davvy gets into port now and again." Smile lines crinkled around Granma's eyes, age-washed to the palest blue. "Daisy's fond of her family, she is, now Barney's not making her life a misery. He ain't been near any of us for years now. Of course she's never made us known to you because it wasn't fitting."

"You're our family, too."

"Not fitting," Granma repeated firmly. "You're a king's daughter, and Andy's a gentleman's son. Your lives will run on a different path than ours, and you can thank the heavens for it."

"We're here, and Daisy was glad to send us."

"We're glad to have you," Granma said placidly. "Good blood is wild blood sometimes when it's young. You'll settle soon."

Poppy looked down rebelliously at her idle hands. She did not have even a deck of cards to amuse her. "You still could teach me to churn."

"I trade my butter for winter feed for the cows and people like my churning. I make good sweet butter." Granma's face softened. "You'll never need to know hard work like this, child. Your mother's raised you proper for a proper marriage, and a gentleman might not be happy to have his wife know rough work."

24

"Maybe I'll never marry with no dowry."

"Now it'll work out. T'ain't reasonable to expect Daisy to sell the rubies for that. Things like those rubies go down in a family. Your girl, when you have one, will get them."

Poppy moved her shoulders, fighting the intolerable feeling of being bound in idleness in a cage that would open only to release her into another cage as tightly closed and barred. In desperation, because in London she despised nothing more, she suggested, "Daisy had a friend show me how to work in Berlin wool. If I had some, I could make a chair seat."

"Now, you're not to go to the village except with us on a Sunday, straight to church and back, and you know it." Again Granma softened. "Why don't you go for a walk in the woods? Squire keeps it for hunting and fishing, but nobody will think you're a poacher or mind if you pick a few wild flowers. You'll be safe enough. People is frighted of the Squire. He had a young man visiting, relative of his wife, thought he could throw one of the lasses down in the hay field and take her. Squire beat him near to death with his riding crop."

Poppy had looked at the well-kept woods, glimpsed the glades and paths that stretched from behind Gramps's place to the manor house barely visible on a faraway hill. She had thought that would be even more forbidden than the village.

She was thoughtful as she walked out of the cottage and wandered aimlessly through the woods. She had always accepted that her mother wanted them to call her Daisy, because then people often assumed they were her younger sister and brother until they knew them better. That made things easier, though none of the gentlemen had ever objected to them until Mr. Hammett. It made him feel old to be reminded Daisy had two large children. She realized suddenly that Daisy had always looked forward to the day when she and Andy would live quite separately from her. Daisy was a good mother, but she did not dote and sacrifice herself. She must be counting the time until she could be free of responsibility for them.

Poppy shivered. She would not marry someone like Mr. Hammett's friend. Then what was she to do? She would simply have to wait and seize an opportunity when it came along.

London was opportunity. London had everything. When they returned there, she would begin to investigate immediately. Meanwhile the woods were deep and pleasant.

On the third day, she found the stream. She ran and plunged her arms into the sunlit, limpid water beyond the rippling verge. Deep, deep, the center was deep enough for swimming. She looked around her and laughed aloud. That weeping willow with branches sweeping all around it to the ground might have been planted there as a dressing room. When she swept the branches aside and crept in on the moss-covered ground, she was in a little house almost high enough for her to stand.

She tore off her clothes and plunged into the water. Only when she was back in the willow shelter, teeth chattering but skin tingling, did she realize she had no way to dry herself. Would Granma notice if she came back with only two petticoats under her cotton dress? Never. She dried herself and left the wet petticoat hanging inside on a branch. Enough breeze and sun crept through to dry it for the next day.

That night Poppy was thoughtful. Some of the paths looked as if they were used for riding, with branches cut back for the riders' safety. Tomorrow she would explore deeper toward the manor house.

Because, though Granma and Gramps would never guess it, she could both ride and swim. Once, years before, when Daisy was between permanent gentlemen, a lovely man had taken them all to the seashore for a month. Daisy had had to duck in and out of a bathhouse rolled into the water, but the children had been allowed to swim naked and free. The lovely man, in a suit that covered him from neck to elbows to below the knees, took them out beyond the waves and taught them swimming strokes and how to kick. That wonderful, free feeling with the water all around her intoxicated Poppy. Whenever they had dragged her out, blue-lipped and prickly-skinned, she screamed and screamed, until the gentleman thought of bribing her with a ride on the ponies that trudged up and down the sand. Poppy had a vague idea the lovely gentleman had been a school-master who genuinely loved children and fortunately one with private means. When he disappeared at the end of the month, giving Daisy a charming opal and pearl ring, Poppy swam fearlessly and could ride the largest ponies, not much smaller than a real horse. Even Andy could paddle alone and keep his balance in a saddle.

Now she was sure that where there was swimming, there must be riding. All over the country, horses were left running free in pastures. She only had to locate one.

After four days of searching, she found the pasture at the far end of the woods. She had been looking too close to the manor. This pasture, watered by a branch of the stream which ran through one corner, was obviously for horses that were seldom taken into the stables. Two of the horses were too old for riding, two were colts, one limped, one was a plow horse, but the sorrel was perfect. She hung over the fence, eyes shining. The sorrel was a small horse with white feet and a gentle look. She was not young, but she was spirited and had a lively gait. Poppy yearned to ride the little mare. There was her horse, and over there was a gate leading to the woods.

That evening she found an old bridle hanging for-gotten in the smithy and smuggled it out, hidden in the folds of her skirt. When she cleared the table after tea, she filled her handkerchief with sugar.

The sorrel was a coquette, but on the third day Poppy got the bridle on her and led her through the gate and mounted there. "Keep your knees in," the lovely gentleman had instructed. "Knees and hands are everything." Who needed a saddle? A couple of times she slipped off when the sorrel jumped playfully at a shadow, but she simply led her back to the gate and mounted again.

By the end of the week, the sorrel knew her and would come prancing and shaking her head, pretending to shy, but waiting for her. Once or twice Poppy saw that grain had been thrown into the pasture, but that must have been done early in the day. She refused to worry, for she never saw anybody near the place. So she would ride to the stream, tie the horse while she swam, and then dress and ride back again to the pasture.

If she smelled faintly of horse when she got home, so did Andy and Gramps, and nobody noticed. Granma said she had never seen a girl so hard on her clothes, she might as well sleep in them, but that was all. Nobody seemed aware the sun was burning her hair a brighter red-gold and that her skin was warmly creamy all over.

One day she swam longer than usual. Tomorrow was Sunday, and by the time they returned from church, it was always too late to slip away, a day lost. She paddled and kicked, rolling and twisting and whirling in the water that tickled her skin like champagne, only sorry she had to be careful not to wet her hair so Granma would not suspect.

"So this is where you bring Penny?"

Poppy shrieked and dived, coming up behind a rock out in the middle of the stream. She brushed her soaking hair out of her eyes and, peering over the rock, saw a tall masculine figure, blackened to a silhouette by the sun in her eyes, standing on the bank.

"Come back here, you thief."

She quavered, "I never stole a penny in my life."

"Coppery Penny," he said impatiently, and his voice was young. "My horse. My first horse after I got too big for a pony. And you do steal her. You've had her out every day since I got home. I went to the pasture, and she wasn't there, and in the morning I could tell she'd been ridden. You didn't wipe her down. Her coat's a disgrace."

"I didn't have a cloth or comb," Poppy said and shrieked again as something brushed her bare thigh, and a shadow darted past her in the water. "Oooh. Go away. Go away this instant. I've got to come out."

"Come, then. Besides, you turned her out warm without a rug over her. She's not a young horse. She's my horse, and I won't have her mistreated."

The monster fish was close again. "Go away. Go away. I didn't mistreat her. I didn't hurt her."

"I don't think you know how to treat a good horse."

That was too much. This was no London blood who would regard a country girl like any other chance-met animal, something to be used and thrown away without a thought or qualm. This was a young man, little older than herself. "You don't know how to treat a lady. Go away and give me a chance to get out of here."

"Aren't you a child?"

"I am not. My clothes are in under that willow tree, and I want them."

The silhouette retreated slightly. "You're not supposed to be in that stream either, frightening the fish."

"Then let me get out."

"All right. All right. But I've got Penny, and we'll be over behind that oak."

Poppy scrambled up the bank, into the shelter of the tree, and hurriedly put on her clothes. Rubbing her dripping hair with the damp petticoat, she realized she did not have a comb. One look and Granma would know.

"Are you ready?"

Poppy stepped out of the shelter of the willow. "Do you have a comb?"

"Of course not. What is this?"

He came close, leading Penny, and stood looking at her. He was a tall, handsome young man with hair the color of strong tea and bright gray eyes set far apart in a strong, square face. His country clothes were worn, but Poppy knew good boots and tailoring when she saw them.

"You must be the Squire's son."

"Of course."

"Home from school?"

"For the long vacation."

Poppy knew a weeping woman or a frightened woman made a gentleman uncomfortable, and a gentleman could not like a woman who made him uncomfortable.

So she smiled dazzlingly and said, "What are you going to do? Because I'm going to be in trouble enough at home about this," and she touched her wet, tangled hair.

He stared, his eyes widening as he looked at her from small feet to glowing face and shining hair. "Home? Who are you?"

"The smith's granddaughter," Poppy said discreetly.

"Oh, one of those." He must know of cousins living nearby. "What are you doing here?"

"My brother and I are here for the summer, and I didn't have anything to do." Poppy widened her eyes and drooped her mouth. "I didn't mean any harm. I thought nobody minded. A few times I did think I heard the gamekeeper in the woods, but he always seemed to veer away from me."

"Orders. My father'd rather have poachers scared off than caught. Costs too much to support their families after."

Poppy laughed. "Are you scaring me off?"

"No," he said slowly. "No, I'm not scaring you off. I don't have much to do during the holidays myself. And it's not much fun riding alone."

"I won't be able to get away tomorrow," Poppy said and fingered her tumbled curls. "Maybe never again."

"I know." He plunged a hand in the pocket of his tweed jacket. "Penny's coat is so rough I brought her comb. Could you use that?"

"I could use anything," Poppy rejoiced.

They met almost every day at the willow. Edmund Chalmers found a small saddle he had used as a boy and brought it and found a branch strong enough to hold it. He would ride his horse from the stable, get Penny from the pasture, and meet Poppy by the stream. He worried about the saddle, but Poppy assured him she saw no reason women had to ride sidesaddle. He showed her the proper way to hold the bridle, how to signal the horse, and how to judge the gaits. Before, she had ridden for the pure joy of action and motion, but Edmund showed her it could be an art and one at which she could excel.

Day by day, he brought more things to the willow tree. He brought rugs, pillows, and a picnic basket with cutlery, dishes, glasses. Every day he brought a large lunch he had had Cook put up for him. Shyly, he brought a silver-mounted comb, towels, and scented soap so Poppy could freshen up before she went home. The willow began to resemble a small summer house by the stream.

They rode and picnicked and then, Edmund leading Penny back to the pasture, they would part to go home for their evening meals. On a few occasions, when Edmund had to pay calls with his mother and sisters, Poppy went alone to the willow house and swam all afternoon. Other days she did not miss the water. Edmund and the rides and the lunches were enough.

If they had not ridden too far and long, after they had eaten the cold chicken and ham and cheese and pasties and thick slices of bread and the buns and rich, fruit-filled tarts and sipped wine cooled in the stream, they would stretch out on the rugs. Warmed by the sun, soothed by the soft summer breeze, they talked the afternoons away. Poppy guessed Edmund had been so much at school that he did not know the country people well and assumed she was the daughter of one of the smith's children who had gone into good service and therefore would travel with the family. She would not risk telling him about Daisy, but she still could talk about France, the summer at the seashore, and seeing

31

the Crystal Palace, and mourn the wonders she was missing at the Exhibition. Edmund was happy at Oxford, but once he took his gentlemanly degree, he had no wish to study further. He thought his father would let him take the grand tour, and then he would return and try to interest the Squire in some of the new scientific methods of farming. He was quietly content with the prospect.

Under the muted talk ran another silent, powerful conversation. As the days went on, it grew more open. It was in Edmund's fingers brushing her breast, smoothing the thin material of her dress over her thighs, lingering to follow the neckline of her gown. It was in Poppy's breath warm against his cheek as she talked, her head resting on his shoulder, in her hands learning to know the smooth rippling muscles she could feel even through his jacket.

They were in no haste, but the summer was young and sweet, and their veins ran hot, young blood. One day before she knew what was happening, she found herself flat on the rug with Edmund bending over her, his lips greedy and his hands impatient at the buttons of her bodice. She reached up to pull him closer, eyes closing, lips parting, whole body softening. Then Edmund's horse stamped, and Penny nickered impatiently. The spell was broken.

Poppy sat up, brushing the tumbled, disheveled hair out of her eyes. "Oh, Edmund, no, no."

"We mustn't," he said and jumped up and ran to lean his head against a tree and pound at the bark with angry fists.

Poppy wept that night, softly, so nobody in the little two-room cottage would know. She could not give him up. She could not stop seeing him. Her lips knew his, her body knew his touch. Her ears knew the sound of his voice, her eyes the exact way his hair curled around the crown of his head, her fingers the strong muscles of his young body. She moaned and turned her hot face deeper into the pillow. She had to see him. She had to be with him. He was happiness and ecstasy and warmth.

Without him, she was weak, and lost in a desolate world that held nothing.

If she went on seeing him, she knew what would happen. He could not marry her, nobody needed to tell her that. She did not want her young life ruined, to become spoiled goods no decent man would want. Yet she was too weak to give him up and knew Edmund was not old enough or strong enough to make the break with her himself.

They tortured themselves there under the willow tree. They swore they would not, they must not, and tore themselves out of each other's arms and parted in agony. They knew this must stop, yet they met again each day. Finally one afternoon Poppy sank back with a sob and blindly drew Edmund to her, knowing she had lost her battle and that the end must be tragedy, yet without the strength to do anything but kiss him more deeply and hold him close.

A voice roared, "There they are, at it like they are every day. I told you, Marster, I told you how it was, and now tell me you can't believe it of your boy. Tell me your own eyes are lying now."

Poppy recoiled and flung herself away and up, on her feet with one lithe motion. She stared incredulously at the bluff, hearty man with eyes so like Edmund's that he had to be the Squire and at the roughly dressed man beside him, dangling an ax from one huge brown hand. She shrieked at the sight and jumped to the brink of the stream and teetered there.

"Don't be a fool, girl," the Squire growled. "The ax is for the tree." He looked at the clutter on the ground and peered through parted branches at the things inside the willow. "Quite a little dollhouse you have here. Any treasures you want before we cut it down? All right, Gallens, chop it fine. Edmund, take the horses back where they belong. I'll escort your young acquaintance to the smithy."

"Oh, no," Poppy whispered.

"Oh, yes," the Squire said. He grasped her wrist and

started through the woods, leaving her to stumble along beside him.

Running, shaking, Poppy panted, "We didn't—we hadn't—we were just—we went riding."

"Only on horseback, I hope for your sake," the Squire said bluntly. "You're the whore's daughter, aren't you?"

"I'm—" Poppy began. Then she tightened her lips and said with as much dignity as she could manage while being dragged along at a half run, "I'm Poppy Smith."

Edmund had not come with them. He had not protested. He had not even spoken. Poppy blinked tears from her eyes and tried to straighten her dress and smooth her hair with her free hand. The way through the woods had never seemed so short. In no time, she could hear the light tapping of Andy's hammer on the anvil.

"Smith," Squire roared, and Gramps came popping out of the smithy door. "Smith, here's your granddaughter. Best send her back to London before she causes trouble here."

Gramps ducked his head. "What's she been doing, Squire?"

"Riding my horses for one thing. And you can hope that's the only thing. I found her with my son."

Andy popped out of the door, hammer swinging from one hand, a white-hot horseshoe in tongs in the other. "What's that you're saying about Poppy?" He drew back the arm holding the tongs.

"Boy," Gramps growled and chopped his hand down on Andy's elbow, sending the tongs and white-hot iron flying. "Sorry, Squire, he's just a child."

"Have you money enough for their fares on the railroad?" Squire asked, reaching for his pocket.

Poppy's face flamed. "We've the money. We don't need anything of yours."

"Keep that in mind and don't come back," Squire said. He turned away on his heel and strode off.

They were on their way back to London before dark.

Chapter Four

$\mathcal{P}$OPPY was as restless as a bird in springtime. The Queen's weather was holding, and all London basked under the August sun. Peters had taken Daisy to drive in her carriage in the park as usual, although one of the papers had printed that it was as shocking for members of the demimonde to appear there as it would be for gentlemen to smoke, especially at the fashionable hours of five to seven. The Queen herself, with Albert, often appeared at that time, as did the Duke of Wellington. Daisy tossed her head, said the Great Exhibition should prove the world was changing like lightning every day, and went off to join the gentlemen on horseback and the ladies in their carriages to be stared at by the common people hanging on the railings.

The cottage on Pallminster Lane was too small and too quiet to contain Poppy's energy. She peered out at the tiny garden between the cottage and the carriage house, but she had watered the red and white geraniums and brushed the London soot from the brick walks before the afternoon heat struck down. She drifted back to the bow window in the parlor and pushed aside the red brocade overcurtain and lace undercurtain and peered through the gauze. A butcher boy, standing up in his little cart, was shrieking impudence at a beer wagon. Out of sight around the corner, a flower girl called, "Sweet flowers, sweet flowers, a'blowing and a'growing." Farther away, an oyster vendor shouted his wares. Nothing moved on Pallminster Lane. The ladies had retired to their rooms to rest before they dressed for dinner, and the gentlemen had not yet returned from offices, businesses, coffee shops, or their clubs.

She drifted over to the fireplace and put two small sticks on the glowing embers, for the brick cottage held the damp even in midsummer. She considered the mantel with its gold-looped and fringed red velvet draping and the silver, gilt, and china ornaments grouped around the ornate clock. She wandered to the mirror over the tufted loveseat and considered her new cream-and bronze-striped afternoon frock. The ruffles around the bodice and on the elbow-length sleeves set off her glowing skin, and the color emphasized the red-gold of her hair and the brilliant amethyst of her eyes. The new slippers of satin and bronze kid were as pretty as they were tight.

She listened to the house. She smiled as she heard the kitchen door close. Mrs. Peters was not supposed to leave them alone in the cottage, but she was sneaking over to the carriage house to snatch a nap before Daisy returned from the park to inspect the dinner preparations. A chair creaked upstairs. Andy doubtless was groaning over his Latin because the new tutor was merciless with the rod. This tutor, who had formed a small class to urge half a dozen lackwits into learning enough to return to their usual schools in the fall, had seen no reason to refuse to take on an undesirable if his fees were doubled and he had a whipping boy to frighten the others into diligence. Andy was paying the price of two years' idleness, which made it hard for him to keep up even in such company. Poppy did not sympathize, although sometimes she helped him, just to learn the lessons herself. She had enjoyed every minute of their classes with The Rev, except when she had had nothing to do because Andy was so slow. She had also looked forward to her ballet and music lessons with her mother's friends in the ballet. Now those had stopped, too. Daisy had given many reasons. She was more accomplished than most young ladies. Bookish women were unfeminine, and gentlemen did not like that. But Poppy had heard her mother tell Mr. Hammett that she hoped to find a younger son or a widower who thought beauty and royal blood enough without a dowry, and have the girl married before the winter was over.

Poppy sighed rebelliously. Last year she had been always busy, always had something to do and practice and study. Now she had nothing, and this winter would be worse after the Exhibition closed. Daisy had been mercilessly strict since Gramps had sent them home.

She sighed again and pressed closer against the glass. Down at the end of the lane, there was that old Italian witch, one of the refugees from the revolutions on the Continent in forty-eight, with her cage of fortune-telling birds. Poppy clasped her hand to the chatelaine dangling from her belt and, feeling the shilling tucked into her scissors case, ran out, careless of the door left open behind her.

"A fortune," she gasped. "Your best fortune, please," and held out the shilling.

Grabbing the shilling in one hand, the old crone thrust a stick into the cage. A bird jumped on it and plucked a paper from the box of fortunes.

Poppy tore it open and read. Her eyes darkened almost to purple. "No, no. This isn't right. I don't want this one."

The old woman cackled. "My birds tell all, and it is always right," she gloated, then clumped away to disappear around the corner.

Poppy read again. "Flames will open a path before you, and bars of gold will cage you. Marriage is your fate. Beware. Beware." She shuddered, crumpled the paper, and threw it in the gutter. She had never believed in fortunes anyhow. "Nonsense," she said, and ran back to the house.

Still she could not forget the fortune. "Marriage" and "Beware" it had said. She did beware. She shuddered, thinking of the men Daisy might produce for her to marry if she got desperate enough. But a girl could hardly refuse to marry when no man had offered yet. Neither could she run away. She would not go on the streets. No decent household would have Daisy's daughter, even as a housemaid, let alone a governess. There was nothing to do but to wait and see what happened and, yes, beware, beware.

She idled back to the bow window, sat down at the card table, and took the newest deck of cards from the drawer. Her hands were discouragingly small, so she could not palm cards, but she practiced crimping for the cut, double shuffling, and dealing from the bottom. She had been practicing for three years, ever since the gambling gentleman who had kept Daisy so short a time because he had a run of bad luck and was too fine spirited to ask a lady to accept less than the best, had showed her what he knew, although he swore he never used the tricks. She should learn them well—not to cheat, he had advised piously but with a twinkle in his hooded eyes, but so no one could ever cheat her. She had liked him because he had liked her and Andy, not like this Mr. Hammett, who was acting more permanent every day.

She would not think about Mr. Hammett. He was generous, but he was mean-spirited and dull, never taking Daisy anywhere, not to the Cremore where something was always happening—fireworks, balloon ascents, equestrian performances, not to mention the dancing, promenades, and singing—or even to the ballet or one of the theaters. He just turned up three evenings a week, ate an enormous dinner, and dozed the rest of the evening away in front of the fire while she and Andy crept around their rooms trying not to remind him they were there.

She frowned at a jack that somehow had dropped on the polished table. In the gambling gentleman's hands, the cards had come alive and flown. She could do it, too, if she kept practicing.

As she scooped the deck together, she glanced outside, and her eyes widened. A gentleman was getting out of a hired cab. He was quite young and attractive in a strangely individual way. His coat was beautifully tailored, but the darker collar was a touch flashy, and his skin had a clean, waxy pallor that emphasized his dark eyes. He stood there, glancing up and down the street, turning his head so that she saw the slight curve of his short nose. With his dark, lively glance, he reminded her of something. She had once seen a beautiful, exotic bird in a cage with just that lively look and air of elegance. He sent the cab away, and was coming to the door.

Mrs. Peters was not there to answer it, and Poppy did not hesitate. She ran without even feeling the tight new slippers, opened the door, and smiled up demurely. He stared at her and mumbled. She caught only the word "viscount."

"I'm sorry, but my mother is driving in the park."

"Your mother?" His dark, lively glance saw her completely, and he mumbled again, "Yes. Yes. I did hear something. I thought, a child."

She knew she should not, but she did. "Would you care to come in and wait, sir?"

His quick glance flickered over her again, and he stepped inside. It was only a matter of minutes before he had put away his hat and cane, mumbling something all the while about being newly returned to London from the Continent. He saw the cards on the table and seated himself across from her.

Poppy fluttered her lashes and admitted if he would name his game, she might comprehend the play. She and her brother sometimes held a hand. Then, time after time, the Viscount had more luck than should have been possible for a gentleman trying to stare down the neck of her bodice. She leaned back, pretending to adjust the gold scissors dangling from the chatelaine, and surreptitiously dried her fingers on the red velvet, strawberry-shaped pincushion. They were not playing even for coppers, but she hated to lose, and somehow every time she crimped for him to cut, the cards came back miraculously smooth and cut to his advantage. Feeling reckless and giggling inwardly, she pretended to fumble the shuffle and risked holding a king in her small palm, ready to drop in front of her when she dealt.

The Viscount's white fingers clamped down on hers.

With his other hand, he forced her fingers open and pulled out the king. Throwing back his head, he roared with laughter.

"I thought so, you little vixen," he cried, the mumble gone and his dark eyes glittering. "A lady in Vienna cheated me once when I was fifteen but no one since, I'll swear."

Poppy tugged futilely at the fingers circling her wrist. "It's my hands. They don't grow."

"I'd say you've grown very satisfactorily," the Viscount said, smiling with set teeth as he stood up and jerked her to her feet and into his arms.

Poppy gasped. Daisy's gentlemen callers were genteel and knew better than to treat her like a parlor maid.

The Viscount, still laughing, was kissing her, her face, her neck, the softness where the ruffle on her gown dipped in front. Then he stopped laughing, and a fire flickered far back in his eyes. He was mumbling again and tugging her toward the loveseat.

Poppy dug her heels into the carpet and tore her mouth from his and shrieked, "Andy, Andy!" He lifted her from her feet and swung her toward the loveseat as she thrashed wildly, fingers clawing, elbows punching at his waistcoat, feet kicking at his knees. One foot hit solidly, and he swore and stumbled. They thudded down on the carpet with his weight crushing Poppy beneath him.

"You wildcat," he growled, ripping her bodice open to the waist. "Stop scratching or I'll beat you until you'll be happy to purr for me."

Poppy tore one hand free, snatched out the gold scissors, and thrust upwards. The sharp points caught on his neckcloth, ripping through it, and scratched a long bleeding line across his neck to his ear. He growled like an animal, a guttural sound without words, clenched her wrist, and twisted it until she screamed and dropped the scissors. With a hiss of satisfaction, he wrenched her numbed arm down under his knee and, kneeling above her, deliberately slapped her face, first one way and then the other, until her head thudded back and forth against the floor. Half blinded by tears of pain and rage, she gasped wordlessly, her breath knocked out of her. Then, over his shoulder, she saw Andy beside the fireplace, flourishing a flaming stick of kindling. Sparks flew around the room, and a burning ember lit in the Viscount's hair, but he went on slapping and pounding, apparently too enraged to feel it.

"Andy, no, no," Poppy gasped.

From nowhere, a long arm reached out and snatched the stick and threw it into the fire, brushing Andy away and across the room. The same arm swung around and plucked the Viscount from Poppy as if they were a pair of puppies scuffling on the floor.

"Have you any explanation for this disgraceful scene, sir?"

Poppy had heard the voice before, so deep and vibrant, yet so deadly soft. Struggling to her hands and knees, she looked up and saw a tall dark man, face expressionless, hands now quietly clasped on his gold-headed cane. A sense of power emanated from him, dominating the room. She knew him. She had seen him someplace before.

The Viscount's face was white as he dabbed with his torn neckcloth at his bleeding wound. He looked around the room, first at the curtains and upholstery, where small sparks still glowed, then at Andy, huddled where he had been thrown on the floor, and finally at Daisy, whom he had not seen enter and who was perched tensely on the velvet chair by the fireplace, fanning herself with her lace handkerchief. He tried to speak, but not even a mumble came out.

"Any explanation?" the deep voice insisted.

The Viscount found a thin sound in his throat. "I'm just back from the Continent, and I came to call on" —he permitted the slightest suggestion of a sneer to tint his words—"Mrs. Smith. Or perhaps you know her as Daisy."

"I know Mrs. Smith as a valued client of our bank."

The Viscount's waxen face took on a tinge of yellow. "Of course," he mumbled. "Of course." He dabbed at

41

his neck again, fumbled at his hair, and stared unbelieving at the burned ends that came away in his hand. "I came to call and the"—he wet his lips with a darting tongue—"young lady answered the door. We played at cards while we waited, and she tried to cheat me."

The dark man nodded toward Poppy, who was on her feet and trying to pull the shreds of her torn bodice and chemise together over her bare breasts. "That justifies this?"

The Viscount found a few grains of courage. "I started to shake her, and you won't deny she's a toothsome piece."

"She's a young girl, and I know your reputation as a gambler and libertine," the unemotional voice said. "Be grateful I don't care to dirty my hands on you."

"She tried to cut my throat with her scissors, and that young ruffian attempted to brain me with a burning log," the Viscount sputtered.

"We can hardly hope she murdered you, and your head is notoriously thick."

The Viscount blustered, "Look at this room. Look at it. I was assaulted."

"You intended rape."

"She enticed me."

"You are a helpless innocent, seduced by a young girl and beaten by a boy?" the voice mocked. "That is the story you want me to tell?"

The Viscount edged toward the door. "Not unless you want the girl's reputation ruined."

"Just a minute." Strange cat's eyes looked around the room and went back to the Viscount. "I was not proposing to tell all London. I had in mind a gentleman we both know in Vienna. Our bank had a note from him today discussing limits to be put on your account there. Perhaps it would be best if neither of us mention this in any connection."

The Viscount snatched his hat and cane. "Gentlemen don't kiss and tell."

"Gentlemen, no," the dark man agreed scathingly. "So you will not, either. But you will stop by the bank and make a deposit to cover the damage here to those handsome red overcurtains and other things. I'll inquire not later than noon tomorrow to make sure the deposit is suitably large."

"It will be there," the Viscount mumbled. Then he cried in that thin, odd voice, "You bankers are growing too powerful and arrogant. Someday we'll have the whip hand and you'll come begging."

As he slammed out the door, Poppy sidled toward the stairs. Daisy jumped up, darted across the room, and caught her wrist.

"Just a minute, young lady," Daisy said, pulling off her dark green mantelet and throwing it over Poppy's shoulders. "Just a minute. Andy, pick yourself up and go to your room. We want to talk to your sister."

Andy got up, but he walked straight over to the tall, quiet man and looked up at him confidingly. "Do you go to the Exhibition often? Have you been in the machinery court yet?"

Then Poppy recognized him, too. This was the man who had saved them in the park the day before Daisy sent them to the country. As if she were not already in enough trouble, Andy had brought that up. Once Daisy heard that story, added to what had happened with the Viscount today, her wrath would know no limits. Poppy could not clap her hands over Andy's mouth or thrust him from the room. She could only stand, horrified.

"Often," the man said. "The American reaper is especially interesting. We must discuss it another time," and he pushed Andy gently toward the stairs.

"You know my children?" Daisy cried.

"I had the pleasure of speaking to them one day in the park," the man said suavely, nodded goodbye as Andy went reluctantly through the stair door, and turned to look at Poppy. "Last spring," he added but said no more.

Poppy drew the mantelet close around her and glared back at that cold gaze. He had not told Daisy, but his look said he remembered everything and considered her conduct odious. Rage flared in her. Men looked at her fondly or admiringly. Or sometimes, trying to conceal it, hungrily, but never with cold disapproval. She would not have it. She would not.

With a touch of swagger, she shrugged the mantelet looser around her shoulders and said in her sweetest voice, "I must thank you, sir. My brother goes quite wild when he gets a bit of fire in his hands."

"He's a child. You seem to light fires of another kind. Your mother was telling me about your summer as we drove back from the park. An incident similar to this. Too similar. Your father would be ashamed of you."

Poppy felt her face flame red. "We were in love," she choked.

"Nonsense. You were a couple of children playing at grown-up games. Dangerous games for you. You have everything to lose. Your father meant you to marry respectably. I begin to doubt it will be possible."

"There's no dowry."

"And Daisy rightly believes the rubies were given to her for other purposes."

"What's it to you?" Poppy cried. "How do you know?"

"Knowing is my business."

He looked beyond her. Following his glance, Poppy saw that both Andy and Daisy were gone. From the kitchen came the sound of Daisy hissing like an angry teakettle, interrupted by Mrs. Peters's dripping whine, a duet of accusations and excuses.

"I wonder," he said softly.

He strode over to her, circled her with an arm that seemed as hard and knotted as oak, and pulled her against his chest. Deliberately he prodded her head up with the gold top of his cane and put his mouth to hers. Poppy stiffened and thinned her lips, but he forced her teeth apart, and his tongue explored her mouth while his hand pulled the mantelet and torn bodice aside and teased each breast until Poppy, gasping, could feel the nipples come erect. He pressed her whole body the length of his. As her hair, already loosened from its pins, tumbled down around her shoulders, she felt her knees give way, and she went limp in his arms. She felt

44

her body softening against him and then tensing again, but softly, as she snuggled closer and deeper into his embrace.

He put her from him and straightened his waistcoat. "Yes," he said, as if that had settled something. "You must marry soon, or there'll be no saving you." Then he looked over her head and said, "I have just kissed your daughter, Daisy."

"So I observed." Daisy walked across the room, swaying her full skirt of green rep, and settled in the velvet chair. "I also heard your recommendation."

"Did you see how he kissed me?" Poppy cried, appalled.

"He is a most capable gentleman in all respects," Daisy said coolly and smiled at him. Whatever happened, she never allowed herself to remain in a state of agitation for more than half an hour. It made gentlemen uncomfortable, and besides she felt it was bad for the complexion. "I asked you to come and have a glass of wine with me when we met in the park. Will you have it now?"

He shook his head as the clock struck. "I must postpone the pleasure. His Lordship is expecting me to dinner." He strode across to the door. "Good evening, Daisy. Miss Poppy." And he was gone.

"Who is that man?" Poppy cried.

"Dexter Tremayne Roack." Daisy rolled out the name with satisfaction. "He told you. He's with my bank."

"A banker?" Poppy said dazedly. Bankers were stodgy, dull, and old. He had accused her of playing dangerous games, but he was a dangerous man. She had meant to enchant him. Instead he had kissed her in that outrageous, unforgivable way and casually walked out. "What does he do?"

"Mostly he's heiring."

"Is he a hunting man?" Poppy asked.

Daisy laughed, delighted with the success of her pun. "He only hunts two-legged heirs. That's his position with the bank, and they say nobody in the world knows more about heirs, legit and illegit."

45

Chapter Five

*U*P in her room, Poppy ripped off the ruined bodice and skirt, balled them up into a crumpled bundle, and pushed them back in the farthest corner of her wardrobe. She hurled the bronze slippers after them. Then she put on her blue-sprigged, white-flannel robe, knelt on the rose tiles of the fireplace hearth, and poked the embers into a flame.

"Let me fix it," Andy said from behind her.

Poppy sat back on her heels. "Oh, Andy, what's wrong with you? Everything's fire, fire, fire. You lit this, and you know Daisy said we weren't to have fires up here until October."

"She stopped up my fireplace, and I study better when I can watch a fire, so I came in here."

"You can't watch a fire and study at the same time."

"I can."

"I think we should send you to live on an iceberg out of temptation's way."

"If Daisy would let me go back to live with Gramps and train to be a blacksmith, I could play with fire all day long and be happy and soon be earning besides."

Poppy shook her head in exasperation. With his curly tow head and bright blue eyes and alert expression, he could look like an angel at times. But like most eight-year-olds, he was usually grubby, and his clothes were always missing a button or ripped at the knee or elbow. And he could repeat the same wish a dozen times a day for weeks.

"You know that's impossible," Poppy said patiently,

46

just as if it had not been explained over and over again. "You're a gentleman's son, and Daisy thinks she can get you on a Civil Service list."

"Working at a desk with an old pen," Andy sniffed disdainfully. "Of course a banker like Dexter Roack, traveling all over, finding people, that's different. But then he's one of a kind."

"I hope so," Poppy said emphatically and went over the old arguments. "You're wiry and strong, but you aren't big enough for a smith. And not with Gramps, anyhow. You know he says he's the worst smith in four counties."

"I like making things, and I'd be a good smith. I suppose you're blaming me for going for that man with the burning stick. I suppose you think I should have stood there and said, 'Oh, please, sir, don't hurt my sister, or I'll have to slap your hands.' And he'd have stood up politelike and said he was sorry?"

"You could have yelled for Mrs. Peters. Or hit him with the poker, but that's dangerous, too."

"I might have cracked his head," Andy said indignantly. "Think I want to hang for you? I was just going to scorch him a little."

Poppy sighed. "Anyhow, Daisy's been wanting new overcurtains, cut velvet ones."

Andy's face lit up. "Isn't Dexter Roack the finest gentleman? I recognized him in a minute today. They were selling a picture with him and Toe Dancer, his horse that won the big race last month. Williams has it pasted in his math book."

"A banker with race horses?" Poppy said, shocked.

"Oh, he's a gentleman of gentlemen, I tell you. The boys talk about him all the time. He goes all over the world finding people, and then he tells them they've got millions and millions of pounds coming to them, that he knows about it because his family are the bankers, and he brings them back, and the poor man isn't hungry any more, and the family is happy and—well, he does it all the time."

"Andy, the stories you do make up."

"It's true. It's every word true. True and more. Williams has an uncle that ran away and sailed as a common seaman to China or maybe India or Africa, and he was lost for years. All his brothers died, and Dexter Roack found him and gave him tens and tens of thousands of pounds and a castle. It *did* happen. The uncle came to get Williams one day."

"Andy's talking about that big Irish estate," Daisy said from the doorway and pushed him aside and came in herself. "The uncle has a little friend in the ballet, and she was telling me about it."

Daisy might have come up to scold, but she never could resist a good gossip. She heard most of the town talk through her friends in the ballet and their connections with the gentry. She could not have them at Pallminster Lane because their arrangements usually were of a brief and lively kind, and she had to maintain her reputation for being both fastidious and expensive. But she did find frequent excuses to drop in to visit them discreetly and privately.

"The family was half crazy, with two brothers dying here of the cholera that summer and another killed in the riots in Italy in forty-eight." Daisy shook her head in dismay at the thought and settled down on the end of the narrow bed. "Trust the wild one of the lot to survive, and Dex did find him for them. Now I think he's looking for the Westmorelands. He was walking with Lord Westmoreland in the park when I bowed to him from my carriage, and he joined me to come back here for a glass of wine. Only it wasn't wine he got, thanks to you, young lady, and don't you dare to try to throw that dress away. Where is it? It cost a pretty penny, and we can make a new brown bodice, trimmed with the stripe, and maybe it will remind you to behave when gentlemen come calling on your mother."

Andy never listened to his mother's lectures. "What is Dexter Roack doing for the Westmorelands? Whatever it is, he can do it. He can do anything."

"So you've got a new hero," Daisy said fondly. "That's better than those boxer ruffians."

"I knew he could, the first time I saw him," Andy insisted while Poppy held her breath, but he went on, "The Westmorelands?"

"Sad," Daisy said with a ladylike sigh. "So sad. Everyone's commiserating about it. Westmoreland had four sons, and he placed them as was proper, the oldest for the estate, the next for the army, then one for the church and one for the navy. Didn't the heir marry into the Prowdy clan because their land ran together? Anybody could have told them the Prowdys have been hard put to get one male a generation. They have so many females they can never get them married off, and that's true as far back as you can trace. It's a miracle the name hasn't died out. Oh, how could the Westmorelands not have known? The estate is entailed to the male line, but the heir has five daughters, and they've lost three more, and a boy isn't likely now. The reverend had two sons, but his lady was sickly. The sons and mother have been in Florence coughing their lives away for years now. No, it's worse than that. One boy's gone and the other's not long for this world or the mother, either. And the clergyman's High Church and says he'll convert to Catholic before he'll marry again. The Westmorelands had some Catholic branches once."

"So that leaves two," Poppy said impatiently.

"The army man resigned his commission two years ago and went back to learn to manage the estate, but didn't he break his neck out hunting last winter. And the navy one has no proper family feeling. He says it's the navy or nothing for him, so he's gone on half pay and disappeared. Sent word he'd come back when they settled things so he wouldn't have to be landlocked the rest of his life."

"A missing heir," Andy cried gleefully.

"I don't know what good it's done him to go missing," Daisy sniffed. "He can't sign on as an officer on a merchant ship because the minute he showed his papers Dex would drop on him like a shot. No Westmoreland could sign on as a common seaman. He'd rare up and talk back and be flogged half to death the first week. I guess the silly boy has sense enough to know that. No, he's hiding out in some hole like a rabbit, him that doesn't want to be land bound, and it's up to Dex to find the carrot to coax him out and get him to take his proper place. Why, there are hardly finer estates or an older name in the country, and we can just hope the Westmorelands haven't bred themselves a dunce who can't see his duty and take it up when his poor old father is breaking his heart every day." That reminded Daisy. "You two have given me enough grief for one day, too. Mr. Hammett will be dining, and I haven't started to change. How Mrs. Peters is to get the parlor cleaned and finish the dinner in time, I don't know. I told her to get out a bottle of the best sherry and that will help. She'll bring you two a tray when she gets around to it, and I don't want to hear a squeak out of either of you until morning."

Poppy waited until Daisy was down the hall and the door of her bedroom closed behind her before she looked at Andy. He pulled a long face.

"It was all right when we were babies," he said. "The gentlemen thought we were sweet then."

"It's just Mr. Hammett," Poppy sighed. "He's awfully old, fifty or more, but if he can think of Daisy as a girl, he feels young. With us so big, we spoil it."

"If only they'd let me go to Gramps."

"If only I could marry the Prince of Wales," Poppy mocked, then laughed. "No, he's too young, just a little older than you."

"What if the next gentleman won't have us around at all?" Andy asked, panic in his blue eyes.

That made Poppy's heart ache. "Daisy loves us dearly," she insisted fiercely. "She never even put us out with a wet nurse, and lots of women do that. Do you remember France and how those dreadful Frenchwomen put their children away in places clear out in the country and almost never went to see them, only maybe once or twice a year?"

"I remember. I remember everything."

Poppy poked at the dead ashes of the fire. Andy

was right, but she was not going to wish worries on a child.

"Do you even remember your Latin for tomorrow?" she scoffed.

"I've got my verbs and written out the translation. Do you know, he says he's going to start us on Greek next week? I'll never learn those funny-looking letters."

"I'll help," Poppy promised and felt so sorry for him, she let a secret slip out. "I'm going to the Exhibition tomorrow. What's the use of a season ticket if I don't use it?"

"I'll meet you there," Andy cried. "I might as well. If I don't get beaten for that, I'll be beaten for something else. I want to watch the steam engines again. And the Impulsoria."

What Andy said was true. He might as well have some pleasure for his beating. "I'll be by the Crystal Fountain. Don't let Daisy or Mrs. Peters see you when you get your ticket out of the vase on the mantel."

Andy nodded. He would take his beating without a word. He knew Poppy hoped to slip back into the house before Daisy returned from her drive in the park, and he would not tell on her.

"And the reaping machine," Andy murmured happily to himself as he went back to his room.

Poppy sank down in the sewing chair, put her chin in her hands, and thought. They were an embarrassment to Daisy. This could not go on, and she did not know what could be done about it. No boarding school would take Andy because more proper parents would withdraw their sons instantly from such contamination. Yet a gentleman might tolerate Andy alone here if she could find a place for herself.

There had to be a place. If only she could think hard enough where and what it was, then find it. This was the wonderful modern world with every kind of excitement, opportunity, and discovery breaking out faster than anyone could follow. In California, they said, you could walk up to any stream of water and pull out a fortune in gold, just waiting there to be picked up. But that was half around the world. Still it must be true about the gold.

Then there was France. That silly Louis Napoleon was back there now, elected to something, and the French were welcome to him, and he was having a lottery, the Lottery of the Golden Ingots. The prizes were bars of pure gold, worth millions and millions of francs, just for the price of a little ticket. And the money was to be spent to help worthy people resettle in California, where every kind of skilled worker was needed. But that was in France, and she agreed with Daisy that the French were a sleazy, unreliable people, not only because they had revolutions time after time with blood running in the streets, but they simply were not solid and trustworthy. Still, winning one of those bars of gold would be lovely.

Poppy shook her red-gold head and put her hand to the back of her neck. She was indulging in stupid daydreams about bars of gold in France, but she was in London and her head was aching because she could not think of a single practical thing to do about her future. When no decent woman would have her in her household as a maid or a governess, what else was there for a young woman to do? Still, she knew there must be hundreds of possibilities if she could just think of them.

Let the French keep their Lottery. England had its Great Exhibition, and she was going there tomorrow. She could think about that, and her headache would go away.

Two weeks ago she had been in the Machinery Court looking for Andy to tell him Daisy had said to meet her at the west entrance when she heard the gentlemen talking. They were some of those scientific gentlemen, standing with their noses in the air, looking up at the great spaces above, and they were talking about stresses and all the weight not being on the foundation. She had watched the Palace spring up almost overnight, but she could not believe that.

She burst out, "That's nonsense. Every building rests on its foundations."

The gentlemen smiled at her and then at each other. One of them said softly, "I don't think we should argue with the young lady about how beautiful the proper stresses and proportions can be. She is a lovely example of our Creator's perfect knowledge of all such things."

When Poppy realized what he meant, she felt herself go as red as Daisy's overcurtains. But the gentlemen only tipped their hats politely and turned away. Except for Rupert, Rupert Manning, he introduced himself, who turned back and touched her hand and asked very properly if she had lost her chaperon. Andy had come racing up just then, but Poppy found time to mention she often rested by the fountain late of an afternoon.

When they did meet there the next week, they had hardly begun to talk when somebody saw the Duke of Wellington, and as always, the crowd all started at once for the dear old man. As always, the bobbies surrounded him and got him safely away. Poppy's skirt was torn, and she felt so pushed about she simply gasped that she would meet Rupert there at the same time next week and ran off. She had been silly, because he was a lovely young gentleman, a university man probably. Still they would have time to get acquainted tomorrow. He did look almost too serious, but better that than a young gentleman who ruined himself at the races or chased after every ballet girl.

Her headache was gone because she realized she did have opportunities. Even if Rupert was only after a flirt, and he did not seem the kind for that, something was bound to happen soon. She was living in this wonderful modern world, all of it exploding with possibilities. She did not have to settle for just anything and make the best of it as Daisy had.

Chapter Six

*P*OPPY hesitated in front of her wardrobe for half an hour. Her new costume was ruined, and she had so planned on wearing it because it set off her hair to perfection. She now had a choice between the blue dress that made her look like a schoolgirlish miss or the green-and-white stripe. It was late in the season for the green and white, but it was devastatingly becoming, and she could borrow Daisy's green rep mantelet.

When she had set the green bonnet with its white satin ribbons on her flaming curls, carefully arranged in long ringlets on each side of her face, Poppy made sure the skirt showed just the faintest hint of fine lace edging her outer petticoat and felt satisfied. If Rupert Manning could resist all this, she was not Daisy's daughter. She did not know exactly what she expected, but any young man with his wits about him should be able to invent some way to explain they had met quite properly. And then? She would see what he suggested. Daisy would not question the details closely if his demeanor and behavior impressed her.

Her spirits soared as she showed her pass and hurried to the Crystal Fountain. Just to be in the Palace made her feel like dancing. She adored everything about it, the throngs of people with their faces lifted to stare up at the sunlight streaming through the roof, the mingled sounds from all the organs, the scent of flowers. The carpets were showing wear, and some of the exhibits had vacant spaces, but it was still the most marvelous place in the world.

Rupert Manning was waiting, gloved hands nervously clasping and unclasping around his cane and a small book. He was not too fashionably dressed, not too good-looking with his neatly trimmed brown hair and short mustache, not too much at ease, not too much anything. He was simply an intelligent and prosperous-looking young gentleman, a thoroughly reliable type. No woman would ever come to harm with him. She was glad she had relied only on her own lavender-scented soap and not used any of Daisy's toilet water.

"Mr. Manning," she breathed close to his elbow.

He started and almost dropped first his cane and then the book. "Dear Miss Smith." He looked alarmed at his temerity. "Miss Smith. How kind of you to meet me."

Poppy allowed her long eyelashes to fan modestly against her pink cheeks. "I have looked forward to it."

"And I. And I." He thrust the book into her hands. "Have you read the last version of dear Mr. Wordsworth's *Growth of a Poet's Mind*?"

Poppy looked at it doubtfully, but she knew the correct thing to say. "His death was such a loss," she sighed.

"Indeed, yes," said a hatefully familiar deep voice. The book was plucked from her hand and opened. "Ah, yes, I recall this part. 'Mine was it in the fields both day and night, And by the waters, all the summer long.' "

"No, I don't believe that's there," Poppy shrieked and grabbed the book. The words were there, plain in black print.

"I find the book full of edifying sentiments," Rupert Manning said. "I thought Miss Smith might find it similarly elevating."

"I do not believe I have met this gentleman, Poppy."

"Rupert Manning. Dexter Roack."

Dexter held out his hand. "Of course. I should have seen the family resemblance. I know your father. I had the privilege of being able to help him in a small matter only last spring."

"Oh, yes." Rupert looked both enlightened and relieved. "That Dexter Roack. My father was most grateful. The matter might have dragged on for years without the assistance of your, er, enlightened information. And the money was needed."

"The roof, I believe."

"Yes."

Dex turned to Poppy. "Are you ready to leave?"

"No." That at least she understood. "Andy is in the Machinery Court."

"We'll pick him up before I take you home," Dex said as if it had been arranged. "A pleasure, Mr. Manning, and my regards to your father. Come, Poppy. We mustn't keep Daisy waiting today."

Dexter Roack was no gentleman. She would ignore the emphasized tone in which he said today, meant to remind her of yesterday, and stroll off with Rupert as she had planned. She turned to him, but he was lifting his hat and bowing and turning away quite as if this were all he had expected. Poppy's expectant smile faded in fury. He was a coward, and Dex was beyond all words. She glared at him.

He laughed down into her angry face. "Young Mr. Manning is much too proper to stay and admit he was bent on escorting a lady he had not met formally. As I'm sure he hadn't. Tch, tch, my dear, after all. The Dean's son."

"Dean?"

"A high cleric," he teased, but did not specify which dean. "A grateful lady left a sum for the relief of the cathedral roof, but her heirs were somewhat less pious. Fortunately I was able to point out some peculiarities in their christening records, and the dispute resolved happily for everyone." He laughed again. "Oh, Poppy, Poppy. What an escape you've had. You may thank me that you never had to meet the Dean. I do not wonder his son found you a refreshing breeze in his sanctified

56

enclosure. But really, Mr. Wordsworth's poems. Oh, no, Poppy, you would never have suited each other."

Poppy clasped the book to her breast. "I'll always cherish this."

"You might even try reading it, though I can't believe you have any trouble sleeping. Shall we find Andrew and go home? My carriage is waiting outside."

"How did you know?"

"I have a gift for being in the right place at the right time to find the person I want," he said lightly, and then relented. "I called to leave a message for Daisy, and Mrs. Peters happened to notice your season tickets were missing from the vase on the mantel. Come."

Poppy swore she would not say another word to him. As soon as she got home, she would go upstairs in dignity and silence and shut herself in her room. But nobody noticed her silence. Andy was full of new information he had acquired that day, about the zinc statue and the differences between cast iron and wrought iron. Dex seemed to know an amazing amount about all the sciences. He knew the book to answer some of Andy's questions, and said he would send it to him the next day. That kept Andy pouring out more questions until the carriage stopped at the cottage door.

Daisy must have been uneasy after yesterday, for she had returned early from her drive and was waiting, seated tensely stiff on the red velvet chair by the fire. When Mrs. Peters opened the door for the three of them, she jumped up, and her face brightened.

"You found them?"

"And brought them home," Dex agreed, then handed his hat and stick to Mrs. Peters. "If you would be so kind as to offer me that glass of wine now, I have a matter I would like to put before you."

"Of course. Immediately, please, Mrs. Peters. Children, go upstairs and wash off that grime. Poppy, you know you are not to borrow my mantelet."

Poppy took as much time as she could, washing thoroughly and taking out the ringlets and putting her hair up in an elaborate style that required all her tortoise-shell combs. Then Andy clamored that Daisy had called them twice and that he had more questions to ask. Poppy could do nothing but gather up her skirt and, head high, sweep downstairs and into the parlor. One look told her that Dex and Daisy had had a long heart-to-heart talk and were in perfect harmony.

"Such a wonderful opportunity," Daisy cried.

Poppy was certain she was not going to like this. "What?"

"Not a new school, away to a regular school?" Andy cried in alarm.

Daisy looked disconcerted. "Actually this will mean no school for a short time."

"Yes," Andy said instantly.

"You can make it up later," Dex said with a grin. "For the moment, the important thing is to remove you from the temptation to jump to the defense of your sister quite so hotly. And to keep her from providing the temptation."

Poppy clamped her lips tight.

Dex said, "You had the right idea in rusticating them, Daisy. Your failure was in not burying them deeply enough."

The freckles stood out on Andy's face. "What do you mean?"

"Simply to send you to a quieter, more remote spot. Poppy, you'll find horses to ride, but I believe the sea of Cornwall is too rough for swimming, especially at this season."

"Cornwall?"

"I was conferring with Lord Westmoreland again this morning, and he was saying he had prepared his Cornwall property for his youngest son to manage. He hoped to train him to take over the larger holdings, since the boy has always been fond of that seaside location. But of course, the young man is missing. The household is staffed, with nothing to do. Lord Westmoreland would be happy to have it occupied. It is not wise to leave a place so remote, especially in Cornwall, with only a staff in charge. Even young people, if they are known to have the ear of the owner, have a salutary effect by being in residence."

"No school," Andy smiled.

"But a large library. I'll send you a selection of scientific writings."

"About castings? And furnaces? And chemicals?"

"All of those. You'll have plenty of time to study them. This place is on a point of land quite remote from any of the villages. Separated by some rather treacherous moors, I believe."

"Meant for the youngest son, you say," Daisy mused, and her eyes widened as she looked from Dex to Poppy and back again. "His favorite place? You think he might go there? And a pretty girl to draw him? I said, yes, I did say, you would find a carrot to draw him."

"A carrot?"

"Something to tease him into revealing himself. Is that what you have in mind?"

Dex threw back his dark head and laughed. "Oh, Daisy, what a conniving mind you have. The boy has been at sea for close to ten years, and I believe it's longer than that since His Lordship was in residence. I doubt if most of the staff, though I believe the housekeeper has been there for some time, know the boy, and besides it's remote. Now use your wits and tell me how our young heir is to hear of our Poppy?"

Daisy giggled. "Her father said she was red as a beet, but I won't call her a carrot. I only had the thought."

"A clever one if it would work," Dex said cordially and stood up. "I'll have a word with Westmoreland that you've agreed. You should have a note from him tomorrow morning giving you the arrangements. I regret I cannot attend you myself, but I'm off for France tonight."

"So that's where the young heir is? I should have guessed. Those French demimondaines." Daisy shook her head. "I suppose Westmoreland told you to pay his debts and bring him home."

"My instructions are a little more difficult. I'm to convince him he wants to come home."

Poppy sat silent, quietly seething. Even this spring, the prospect of horses and a wild seacoast to explore would have sent her dancing with delight. She had been much younger and more trusting then. In Cornwall, she knew, they would be even more strictly imprisoned than at Gramps's. She glanced at Andy. He was deftly easing the last piece of cake from the plate. He was still a child and no help in this. The promise of books he wanted and no studies would have sent him happily to the Arctic.

He stuffed the cake in his mouth, swallowed, and gulped. "If there are horses, there has to be a smithy. I almost made a horseshoe all by myself just before we came home."

"You are adept at convincing people to your benefit, Mr. Roack," Poppy said bitterly. "Gullible boys, at least. You bribe cunningly. But I am neither a carrot nor a donkey to chase after one. What have I done? I spoke to a most proper young man in an entirely respectable place, and he offered me an eminently suitable book."

"What is this?" Daisy shrieked. "What happened?"

Dex shook his head, his strange cat's eyes laughing. "I didn't tell. You did."

That only made her more furious. "You advise me to marry and then propose to exile me to a place where I will see no men except stable boys and gardeners. Or do you consider them suitable for me?"

He shook his head. "Poppy, the pinch with you is that you are at once too young and too old. Too young to think before you act. Too old for the consequences of your acts to be childish. In short, you are an *enfant terrible.*"

"Suitable for stable boys and gardeners?" Poppy repeated, nostrils flaring.

"You have too good taste for that," Dex said with a slight bored lift of one shoulder. "I have assured Daisy I will remain alert for some young man who will suit."

Poppy had pictures in her mind that haunted her, pictures straight out of the illustrations for Mr. Dickens's books. "I won't marry a cringing clerk! Or some shop-keeper!" she stormed.

"I wouldn't inflict you on such a man," Dex laughed. "You'd eat him alive in a week. A few months of rusticating, Poppy, and we'll see if I can't come up with someone promising."

Months, he had said, months, not weeks. "And if I don't choose to be promised?"

"We'll climb that hill when we reach it. Which brings me a thought." He dropped on his knees before her and took her nearest foot in his hand, lifted it, looked at the dainty slipper and shook his head. He pulled it off and put it aside, considering the high-arched foot held in his strong hand, then flipped her skirt and petticoats up into her lap and surveyed her slender leg in its fine lisle stocking. Deliberately he drew his other hand down from knee to ankle. Poppy gasped as if his fingers were a fire and tried to jerk away, but he only cupped her foot more firmly in one hand while he removed the other shoe. Then he reached into his jacket pocket and pulled out a pencil and a packet of papers which he spread on the floor. "Stand on these, please, both feet."

Poppy found her voice. "Daisy, did you see what he did?"

"You have very pretty ankles," Daisy said comfortably.

"Nice knees, too, and that's rare," Dex said briskly, still kneeling before the papers. "On your feet, please, Poppy."

"I won't. You can't. Why?"

"Those Cornish rocks and moors are rough. Does she have proper country walking shoes, Daisy?"

"Not for rough country walking, no. Now you stop stamping and glaring, Poppy. You'd have reason to get into a taking if he'd decided your legs were so bad we had to keep you in pantalets until you get your gentleman spoken for and announced. Instead there he is at your feet, so stand on his paper nicely."

Poppy was so shocked at the pair of them she stood up and stayed quietly on the paper while Dex outlined both her feet with his pencil. Then he neatly pulled out the papers, stuffed them in his pocket, and bounced to his feet.

As he picked up his hat and cane, Dex smiled, tawny eyes glinting. "There are no woods pleasantly soft for idling in Cornwall, so I'll make sure these are sturdy. Daisy, you'll hear from Lord Westmoreland."

When the door closed behind him, Poppy stormed. She even managed to squeeze out a few tears. She did not know why Daisy trusted this Dexter Roack an inch. He was devious, cunning, out for something for himself. He was not doing this for them out of a good heart. He wanted something, and somehow they would pay well for all this apparent generosity. He was a banker, a man who made books balance and always in his favor. Somewhere, concealed in this plan to send them to Cornwall, there was treachery and trouble for them.

"He's doing a favor for his rich client, Lord Westmoreland," Daisy said comfortably. "Two at once, Westmoreland and us."

"Why us?" Poppy broke off and stared at Daisy with sudden shock. She stammered, "You haven't—you and he—you weren't—you've never even mentioned him."

"I don't shout out the name of every gentleman I meet," Daisy said tartly. "Now wipe that look off your face. I don't deny we've looked each other up and down, him at me and me at him. But he's an unsettled kind of gentleman and not one to consider for a permanent arrangement."

"You would? If he were? Settled."

Daisy fluffed her curls complacently. "He's pleasant," she admitted. "Besides, I believe he's very rich. It's a family bank, you know, with branches all over the world."

"You would," Poppy gasped. "If he offered."

"We're friendly, but you're the one who's lacking an offer, young lady." Daisy managed a proper, matronly expression. "So don't you go looking gift horses in the mouth. And stop acting so missish."

"You call me missish when he's shipping us off to some desolate place to do his fine Lordship a favor? At our expense? Probably he's using me as a carrot, just as you guessed, and anything could happen to me away off there in a lonely house belonging to a wild young gentleman not even his father can control."

"I'll be there," Andy said.

"Burning it down around our heads."

"Stop screeching like a lunatic banshee," Daisy said. "Lord Westmoreland's boy is in Paris. Dex said so."

"No. He said he was going to France."

"Exactly. And don't muddle your head worrying about his plans. He's always got a dozen irons in the fire, but I don't doubt he has something in mind for you. Maybe he has a rich client who's looking for a pretty young wife and who'll be grateful to the man who helps him. Dex is just keeping you safe. You'll be no good for marriage to anyone if you keep on the way you've been and are spoiled."

"A rich old man. A fat old man. Like Mr. Hammett's friend. With a dozen crying brats. So terrible nobody will have him."

"Now, miss, you stop creating a scene and go upstairs and look over your clothes," Daisy said, impatient at last. "Andy, I'll come up and go over yours. Mrs. Peters will have to wash tonight and iron in the morning."

Poppy grasped at one last small thread of hope. "Maybe Lord Westmoreland won't agree after all. And you don't even know where this place is."

Chapter Seven

$\mathscr{G}$ hate you," Poppy told the sturdy brown walking boots. "I hate you, and I hope you never find Westmoreland's heir and have to come crawling back to England in utter dejection."

Wrapped in her flannel dressing gown against Cornwall's damp and chill, she sat in front of the fire in her room at Sutcliffe Manor and turned the shoes in her hands. They were beautifully made by Dex's own bootmaker, but she would have thrown them straight into the fire except that without them she would have been housebound.

A rocky Elba, that was what this place was. Even while she had packed that evening in London, she had hoped Lord Westmoreland would have second thoughts and be as outraged as she was at Dex's suggestion. They were at breakfast the next morning when the knocker sounded and a man in livery handed Mrs. Peters an envelope. In it were tickets on the night train to Cornwall, but first-class this time, and a cordial note from Lord Westmoreland. Messages had been sent, and they were expected. The tickets were on that night's train so they could be met at the end of the line in the morning to complete the trip by daylight.

Poppy's heart sank. The end of the line. Where was this place? She knew Cornwall was a long, narrow peninsula, a rockbound coast thrust out into the Atlantic, an old place of superstitions and legends. Strange stories were told about ships trading from Crete; Roman soldiers; King Arthur; and even older people than those, who had left great slabs to mark their burial places. She had heard Cornwall was a wild and foggy place at the very end of England, peopled by miners and seamen who were not like other English.

For once, she missed The Rev, who had told her all that and could have told her more. Then the knocker sounded again, and another messenger had a parcel to give Mrs. Peters. He was sputtering so much they could hear only part of what he said. "Mr. Roack and his father before him and 'is Lordship and his father. Never, never, never less than a week for a fitting, not our quality. Impossible. Un'eard of. Bespoke to the gentry, up to the 'ighest, and always delivered as promised."

Poppy's first impulse had been to run to the door and throw the parcel after the messenger. But she opened it and found that the boots were perfect—strong, but as soft as the skin of her hands, boots that should last half a lifetime. She packed them and seethed again when another messenger arrived with books for Andy. He went whooping around the house talking at the top of his lungs about the gentleman of gentlemen who had enclosed a note saying more books would be sent from France to Cornwall.

On the train Poppy was almost speechless with suppressed emotion. Never before had she felt at once so helpless and so angry. She had ten shillings in her purse, and she could not think of a single way she could earn more to support herself, even if she had been willing to abandon Andy. She was being shipped off to Cornwall like a brown paper parcel neatly done up with string, to be held until Daisy or that conscienceless Dex could find some even deeper hole in which to bury her.

For once, she and Andy were not in perfect harmony. He thought the first-class carriage very grand, even though it was cold, and he could only sit and hold the books he could not read in the dark. He was still wild with anticipation when they arrived in the morning. Poppy stumbled out onto the platform and, through a fine mist of salty rain, saw a huddle of houses dropping down to a small harbor. She took a deep breath and clapped her handkerchief over her nose. The place reeked of fish. Then she saw the carriage and knew it was all going to be worse than she had dreamed. That lumbering, springless style was at least thirty years old, and the coachman's livery was creased and faded from being folded away and plainly had been cut for a larger man.

The coach jolted along a road that ran between marshy moors. Only a few stunted trees and tangles of brambles and rocks broke the barren desolation. The few poor cottages were widely scattered. On the last miles of the ride, the rain turned into a heavy fog, and Poppy could only see that they had left the road and were driving on a weed-grown path along a high ledge that dropped off abruptly. She could hear the sea below pounding heavily on the shore. She could not count the miles in this place without landmarks, but she knew they were on a long, isolated point of land thrusting out into the sullen sea. They were indeed exiles.

The house, a massive pile of gray rock, emerged through the drifting streamers of fog and loomed darkly against the colorless sky. No lights showed, except a flickering yellow glow as the heavy front door swung slowly open.

Poppy stumbled from the carriage, thinking only of a warm fire and something hot to drink. Trying to control her chattering teeth, she walked into a dank, cold, enormous hall lit by candles that wavered wildly in the draft. A tall, lank woman with black hair pulled back from her sallow face held a six-branched candlestick. An immaculate white lace apron over her black lace dress proclaimed her the housekeeper.

"One moment," she said as they stood shivering, stiff and sore from the jolting. "I am Mrs. Wilkins, the housekeeper. Before you go to your rooms, I wish to acquaint you with certain rules I have established in accordance with His Lordship's wishes for your comfort and safety."

Poppy listened, numbed past speech by exhaustion and shock. So Andy could work at the manor smithy on such days as the traveling smith was there and otherwise could occupy himself in any pursuits proper to a young gentleman, such as reading in the library or rambling no farther than an hour's stroll away. It was easy to get lost on the moors. He and Poppy might also attend services in the manor chapel when the curate from the nearest town found it possible to hold them. Under no circumstances were they to go out in a boat with any of the fishermen who had cottages along the shore of the estate. They were to avoid all old mine structures or holes in the cliffs, as the abandoned tin workings were crumbling and extremely dangerous. Andy nodded and yawned as Mrs. Wilkins turned her sharp, disapproving gaze on Poppy. She was welcome to ride wherever she liked, and she could have her choice of any suitable horse in the stables. Poppy's shoulders sagged. That could only mean there was nobody interesting, possibly not even a village, within easy riding distance. She also, Mrs. Wilkins went on, was welcome to walk along the shore, although she would see for herself that the rocks and riptides made swimming impossible. Poppy felt colder than ever. Somebody had briefed Mrs. Wilkins well. This woman was an enemy, a jailer, barely disguised in her rustling black silk dress and fine lace apron.

Mrs. Wilkins finished her speech. Both of them were to appear promptly at table for midday dinner and tea and be in their rooms by nine in the evening. For today, a light meal would be served to them upstairs, and hot water would be brought for bathing.

By the time she stumbled up the wide stairway and along the broad upper hall behind a plump, pleasant-faced maid who had appeared out of the darkness, any pleasure Poppy might have felt in her large, luxurious room was smothered under a slowly growing icy resentment. She looked around indifferently. This corner room must have been furnished for a daughter of the house, with its pretty blue curtains, matching bed canopy, and heavy, patterned, blue rug, but they might as well have put bars on the windows and labeled it a nursery or a jail. She was neither an infant nor a criminal.

Dorcas brought pitchers of steaming hot water to fill the hip bath, unpacked hastily, and hurried off to attend Andy. Poppy was so determined not to allow herself to be imprisoned here that she barely listened to Andy's excited chatter when he came in to share their meal. The food, served in front of the blazing fire, was ample and delicious, with hot Cornish pasty and fresh berries accompanied by heavy cream. Poppy ate it as indifferently as if it had been sawdust until she noticed the heavy silver. That would be worth something in London.

She hurried Andy back to his room to read his books. Then ignoring her exhaustion and her soft, turned-down bed, she sat staring into the fire. She must think more and harder about something she could do to make herself independent. Somewhere there must be work she could do.

She wanted decent work. She would not condemn herself to the life-in-death of the streets or a factory. No wife or mother would take her into a respectable household in any capacity. What else was there? Methodically she reviewed the places she had been and the positions in which she had seen women employed. Then she jumped up, eyes blazing with triumph.

That summer by the shore, she had seen dozens of old women, most of them hard-faced and obnoxious, and each of them had had a captive companion at her beck and call. At the time, she had tried not to watch the poor wretched creatures running their legs off on silly errands and listening meekly while they were berated for imaginary faults, for she could picture no more horrible existence. But they at least were free to change one tyrant for another and one town for a new place if the situation grew intolerable.

All at once, she was afire with the idea. She had noticed the old women liked drab, browbeaten companions. They had all looked alike, with sagging shoulders, shabby clothes, downcast eyes, and faces that were only a jumble of the usual features. That could be achieved. The ballet dancers had talked endlessly about tricks of makeup they used in their character roles.

Sagging shoulders were easy. A dress bunched around the middle would conceal her figure. Her brilliantly shining hair was most of the trouble. Hair could be dyed. She caught a bright curl in her fingers and looked at it regretfully, trying to imagine it a dull black. Perhaps dyeing would not be necessary. If she cut it short, a drab brown wig would cover it. The girls had always mentioned how arched brows and color accentuated the eyes. She could shave her brows off and pencil an ugly line low on her brow.

She could do all that and appear the ideal companion. She was sure those old ladies had enough trouble keeping the miserable creatures in their bondage that they did not ask too many questions. Once she had worked as a companion, she would get a written character reference to show as proof she had been respectably employed. If she had one that could be traced, she could add a few more, for she would write them herself and sign them with names she knew could not be verified. With three or four good letters, she might be able to aspire to a position as a governess.

All she needed was money to get away and live on until she could find her old woman. She had ten shillings, and that should pay the fare to some sizable town. For the rest, this house must be full of small valuable items she could load into her portmanteau. She could easily carry twenty or thirty pounds of silver such as they had used this evening. That would bring a nice sum. And let Dexter Tremayne Roack answer the questions and replace it if His Lordship made an uproar.

Poppy giggled, then yawned. Everything was going to be all right, and she was ready for a good night's sleep. Tomorrow and for a week or so, she would pretend to be content and throw them off guard. When she did run for it, they would not suspect anything was wrong until she was hours gone and well away.

In a week of riding as far as a horse could carry her between meals, she discovered what she had suspected and was glad she had allowed herself some time. Sutcliffe Manor was on a large, rockbound point of land jutting out into the turbulent sea. A few fishermen's shacks nestled among the rocks on the long shoreline, and a few more small, isolated cottages housed workers on the estate. In all her riding, she had not reached the limits of the vast Westmoreland holdings or seen any sign of a village.

She had never dreamed such a lonely, unpeopled place existed in all England. A few small fishing boats tossed on the rough waters. Rutted, weedy lanes wandered between the cottages, where she sometimes glimpsed a woman or child working in the garden. Stone fences marked off random fields where sheep and horses grazed on the scanty vegetation. For miles around, little life stirred. When she fled, she could only follow along the shore until she came to a village and hope she could find a public stagecoach there to a larger place where she could disappear before she was missed.

Andy was poor company. When he was not at the smithy, he was absorbed in his scientific books. He read them over and over again. Then, with bits of metal he shaped at the forge, he attempted to reproduce some of the things illustrated. He was so completely happy and busy she knew she could leave him there contented until she herself was settled.

She explored the mansion, but the mantels and tables held none of the fine china and silver decorative pieces she had expected. She spent time in the library with its handsome row of five French windows opening out on a terrace. A fire always burned in the fireplace at the west end, although the one at the east end was never lit. She hoped for something to occupy the long evenings, but the shelves were discouragingly overcrowded, yet empty of anything she wanted to read. They were filled with handsomely bound volumes, many in embossed leathers, but most of the books were in Latin, Greek, or German, and quite beyond her. A few treatises on farming were almost as incomprehensible. She found an old copy of Mrs. Trollope's *Domestic Manners of the Americans* and two books by Mr. Thackeray, but they did not appeal.

70

That evening Poppy was desperate for something to fill the empty hours, so she crept downstairs into the library after she was supposed to be in bed. She looked with surprise at a handsome silver tray, filled with heavy decanters and silver goblets, set out before the fire. As far as she knew, nobody had visited the manor since they had arrived.

The rustle of heavy silk skirts warned her but not in time to move away from the loaded tray. Mrs. Wilkins put down a plate of rich cakes and frowned at her across the tray.

"You are supposed to be in bed, miss."

Rage flared through her veins. She was a guest here, and this woman was only the housekeeper. "I did not know you were entertaining here—and so handsomely." She lifted one goblet and admired it mockingly.

"Since His Lordship is not in residence, we keep no butler." Mrs. Wilkins was almost hissing with anger. "With no one to polish the silver and take care of the valuable china, it is only proper to keep it locked up."

That explained the empty mantels and tables but not this welcoming tray. "You are expecting Lord Westmoreland?"

"I had word his man of business is coming to go over the year's books with our bailiff. Naturally he must be properly entertained."

Possibly the man of business traveled with two clerks, which, with the bailiff, would account for the four goblets on the tray. Except Poppy did not believe a word of it. It was more likely the bailiff would travel up to London to give his accounting to anyone as important as the wealthy Lord Westmoreland's man of business. If the man was to come here, he would be staying at the manor, not just dropping in for a sip of brandy.

She prodded idly, since she dared not accuse Mrs. Wilkins of lying, "I'm surprised you haven't lit both fires for such an important occasion."

"Never, miss, never," Mrs. Wilkins hissed. "It's a superstition, hundreds of years old, but we don't break it in this house. If the east fire is lit, a Westmoreland dies."

Poppy laughed. "Bad flues, no doubt."

"No doubt. Now you get to bed, miss, or I'll have a deal of explaining why you're allowed the run of the house in your night gear."

"I had forgotten," she said honestly and moved to pluck one of Mr. Thackeray's books from the shelf. "I only came down for this."

She knew Mrs. Wilkins was glaring after her, but she did not care. Lord Westmoreland was right. A house should not be left with only the staff in control. Perhaps those strict rules that hedged in every move and hour for herself and Andy had not been completely of Lord Westmoreland's doing.

She wondered if she dared to watch from the head of the stairs and see who did arrive. But she was no sooner in her room than Dorcas followed, exclaiming Mrs. Wilkins was afraid she had caught her death of chill from wandering around the cold house undressed and had ordered a hot bath and a hot drink. Poppy dared not refuse, and by the time she was finished with her bath, she knew the mysterious callers must have come and left again.

Chapter Eight

*P*ERHAPS it was only that Mrs. Wilkins liked to entertain in the grand manner when no family was in residence, but that explanation did not satisfy Poppy. She had seen Mrs. Wilkins's handsomely furnished sitting room, and trays carried in there always held the finest silver and thin, transparent china. Mrs. Wilkins did herself well in her own quarters, though she never seemed to ask anyone in except to give orders or a reprimand.

The next morning Poppy went out to pick a few roses for her room, but the elaborately landscaped grounds had been neglected since none of the family had lived there for so many years, and the few blooms did not seem worth taking inside. This was the smith's day at the manor, and the horse she usually rode was being shod. So she ignored the mist of rain that seemed to fall every day and walked idly toward the shore. She thrust through the rough gorse in a direction she had not ridden because there was no path. Within half an hour, she realized she was in a desolate, lonely place and should turn back.

She heard the sea ahead of her and followed the sound until she looked down on a long beach covered with rough pebbles and sheltered only by a few twisted, stunted trees. The drop was a sheer forty feet, except for a rough path too steep for anything but a sure-footed pony. Small wonder no paths led here. This rough gorse was no place for pleasure riding, and the beach was too rough for walking.

73

She wandered on along the cliff and followed a small stream for a while until it disappeared abruptly underground. It could only flow down into a cave on the face of the cliff and from there into the sea. She walked to the edge again and looked down into a tiny cove. She gave an exclamation of surprise and delight.

This beach was small, of fine white sand, ringed all around by a hollow in the cliff that held it like a cup. The cove had only one small entrance alongside the sheer cliff. From the sea, the entrance would be completely hidden and yet, by sailing parallel to the cliff, access would be easy for a small boat.

The place was charming, but that was not what held Poppy's eyes. Drawn up on the sand beside the stream was a small sailboat tipped on its side. The blue letters painted across its stern read *Corn Dolly*. A man was stretched close beside it on his back, half under it, scraping strongly on the hull to clean it. He worked with long, unhurried strokes. The thin sound of a whistle, in rhythm with the strokes, came from the supine figure.

A whistling man was no threat. "Hello," Poppy called.

His arm stopped with a jerk, and for a moment, his whole body froze. Then he slipped away from the hull and jumped to his feet. For just two breaths, Poppy had the oddest feeling she had seen him before and knew him well and could call his name. Then she laughed at the fancy. He was only a young fisherman, to judge by his rough canvas trousers and heavy blue jersey, with short tow hair and blue eyes. Her call had frightened him, for he was looking around, his fists clenched, his whole body alert for danger.

"It's all right," Poppy called again, laughing. "I won't tell anybody you're trespassing on His Lordship's land to work on your boat. Who wouldn't? It's a lovely spot."

He looked up, brilliant blue eyes squinted. "Who are you? What are you doing here?"

All at once she was aware how lonely and isolated

this place was. She did not want him to know she was alone. "Just walking. Walking with my brother. We're staying at the manor."

He ran, gave a great leap, caught at some projection, and came up the cliff, swarming hand over hand, as fast as a man could have run along level ground. When he jumped up beside her, she stumbled back. He was good looking and clean, not smelling of fish as every cottage and cottager along the shore seemed to, but the expression on his deeply tanned face was dangerous.

"Who are you?" he repeated.

"Poppy. Poppy Smith."

"Smith? Who else is at the manor?"

"Just us."

"Smith." The name seemed to baffle him. "You're visiting there?"

"You could call it that."

His eyes narrowed at her sour tone. "You know Lord Westmoreland?"

"Oh, no, not him. We know Dexter Roack, and that's enough."

Instantly his blue eyes were aglint with laughter. "Indeed it is."

That was not a rough Cornish voice. This man was no fisherman. "You know him, too?"

"Most people know his reputation. Are you a missing heir?"

"No. He knows my mother."

"I'm sure he would," the man said simply and nicely. "Why did he want you here?"

"Because I met the Dean's son at the Exhibition, and we hadn't been properly introduced, and Dex had gotten the Dean a new roof."

He flung back his fair head and laughed. "A terrible sin, requiring dire punishment. And a typical Roack performance."

"Exile," Poppy said. "Elba. Rocky Elba."

"Even Napoleon escaped. What will it take to see you free?"

"Money."

Grimacing, he reached down and pulled out empty pockets. "A universal problem."

Poppy's face flamed. "I wasn't hinting."

"I didn't think you were. Where's your brother?"

"He isn't with me," Poppy confessed.

"That makes it simpler then. I've pulled my boat up here because there's no proper shore at our place, but there's bad feeling between the families. His Lordship wouldn't like it."

"I won't tell."

"Just don't mention it to anybody, not a word about my being here for a couple of days, and I'll be well away. Promise?"

"Of course."

Amazingly, with only a brief smile and a wave of his hand, he turned, went to the cliff, and climbed down it as quickly as he had come up. Incredulous, Poppy stared after him. He might at least have given her his name and told her where he lived. Still, perhaps he thought what she did not know, she could not tell.

Or was that the reason?

She looked out to sea and thought she understood the reason for his haste, if not his secrecy. A scarf of black fog was rolling in, driven by a stinging wind so rough it almost snatched the shawl from her shoulders. A fog like that could turn day into night almost in minutes. He had hurried to get away, and she would have to hurry herself to get back to the manor safely. She had heard stories of people getting lost on these moors and dying of exposure.

By the time she fumbled her way across the garden, she was shaking with fatigue and relief. The black fog had surrounded her. If she had not heard the sound of the smith's hammer and followed it, she might still be wandering, hopelessly lost. But she was going to let no one know of her near mishap. She crept cautiously into the house and up to her room. She changed her clothes before she went down to the midday meal.

For once, Andy only picked at his food, his hastily

washed and still-streaked face disconsolate. "This is the smith's last day here."

"Why?"

"He's sailing for California."

"What?"

"There's two brigs put in at Fowley regular, bringing mine timbers and taking people back to California. They come in half empty and sail out full because everybody's needed in California. Especially smiths, he says. They are using all kinds of ruined things, safes and hinges and stoves and walls, in the foundries, and there aren't enough men for all the ship repair and mine machinery and everything they're making. He says he can name his own wages."

"I don't understand. Why use ruined things?"

"Because they haven't any steelworks. And there's all kinds of ruined stuff. From the fires." Andy's face lit up. "They have lots of fires in San Francisco. Last May the whole town burned down." His face was ecstatic. "The smith said they told him the flames were as high as the hills and you could hear the roar out at sea. Everything there is built of wood, and it burns and burns."

Poppy shuddered. "Then it's a good thing you'll never be there."

"Why? I've never burned anything yet."

"But you frighten people enough, and that must be one town that doesn't need any more frights."

"Silly," Andy said. "I'd like it fine there, from what the smith says, and they wouldn't tell me I'm too small to work, bad as they need men. Poppy, how much would tickets on the brig cost?"

"More than the ten shillings I have." Then she remembered. "When the smith leaves, come to my room. I saw something last night."

Poppy drew the blue curtains against the darkness outside and busied herself with a dozen small tasks. She wrote to Daisy, saying Andy was happy, and that Lord Westmoreland had been right about the staff needing some of the family in residence. She underlined the word family. She mended the lace on a petticoat. She tried pulling her hair straight back, but it still formed ringlets around her face. Decidedly she would need a wig.

Then Andy came in and slumped dejectedly in a chair by the fire. "He's gone, left early because of the fog even if his horse does know the path blindfolded. So what did you see last night?"

"Mrs. Wilkins. She had guests in the library last night. With the best silver, tray and goblets, and brandy and cakes. After we were supposed to be asleep."

"Smuggling," Andy said.

"Of course!"

She should have known. This was the smugglers' coast. That heavy silk and the fine lace cost more guineas than even a housekeeper in a fine position could afford.

"You're sure?"

Andy nodded. "Everybody knows. The first day we were here, the boys in the stables told me to watch out."

"Smuggling," Poppy gloated, seeing her enemy in her hand. "Don't they pay informers?"

Andy looked at her pityingly. "People don't inform. One man did, and nobody spoke to him or his family for hundreds of years. That's the reason nobody is friends with Mrs. Wilkins."

"What?"

"I thought you knew she was a bad 'un. How did you think she got all her silks and laces? Not from any man for her pretty face."

One minute Andy was so mature he took her breath away, and the next he was a child. She only insisted, "Smuggling?"

"No. Informing the excisemen. Nobody'll breathe a hint when she's near, but she's a sneaky one for listening around when a word is passed, and anything she hears goes straight to the excisemen. Everybody knows that. Mrs. Wilkins takes her pay in kind along with them."

"Informing! There were four goblets last night. And today down on the beach." She jumped to her feet, breathless with excitement. "So that's the reason he didn't want anybody to know he had his boat on that hidden beach. Give him a couple of days, he says. That's it. Here I had the silly idea he might be the heir, hiding out on his own land, and all the time he was a smuggler, probably waiting to guide the others in."

"You saw somebody on a hidden beach?"

"Yes."

"Smugglers for sure. And Mrs. Wilkins has told the excisemen."

"They must be coming in tonight!"

Andy was on his feet beside her. "They've got to be warned. If they're warned, they can hide the casks and bales and get away. Tell me where. I'll go."

"No, wait a minute. If you go running off, Mrs. Wilkins will know I guessed."

"They just need warning. They're smart as whips, with tricks that would make you laugh all day. They get the excisemen off their horses and steal the horses to carry their stuff. They pretend there's a funeral and fill up the coffin. They have caves, old mines, barns, holes under their gate posts—all kinds of places for hiding."

"Yes. Yes."

"They're poor and brave, and they sail clear to France and back in their little boats. They bring in wonderful things—silk, lace, rum, brandy, tea, china, and tobacco—and they sell it cheap to people who couldn't afford it at the shops. They use the money to feed their poor hungry families. Anyway, why shouldn't they be allowed to make money their families need to keep from starving? Because the mines are running out and sometimes the fishing's bad. If they paid taxes, the money would just go to pay those stupid excisemen who run around making trouble and never catch them anyhow. Well, almost never."

Andy stopped for breath, and Poppy smiled. He had a new hero, a whole group of them, the smugglers.

She was thinking of money. If the excisemen paid a reward, so would the smugglers for a warning. Andy would never think of that. He would warn them for pure admiration of their daring and for the pleasure of thwarting Mrs. Wilkins. If she went, she could have the pleasure and the means of buying her freedom at the same time. She would go.

"Wait, Andy. Even with this fog, they won't come in until after dark. So we can wait until we have our tea and Mrs. Wilkins thinks we've come up safe to our rooms."

Andy nodded. "She mustn't suspect, or she'll tell the excisemen to hurry."

"I'll have to go. There's no path to this beach. I would never have found it except I was walking today and stumbled on it by accident, watching a stream."

"You could draw me a map."

"For you to follow in the dark? With cliffs that drop straight down forty feet? If you found it, you'd break your neck before you knew you were there."

"But I've got to do something." Andy was agonized. "We can't let them get caught."

"Would it help to tell the stable boys?"

"Yes, yes! They all hate Mrs. Wilkins."

"Then tell them something might happen tonight."

"Yes. They can watch and get hiding places ready in the barns."

"All right. I'll ask for our tea a little early. If she expects to be busy tonight, Mrs. Wilkins will be happy to oblige."

The Rev had been fond of quoting Shakespeare, and Poppy was often surprised at how much she remembered. Lines were always springing into her head. "There is a tide in the affairs of men, Which taken at the flood, leads on to fortune: Omitted, all the voyage of their life is bound in shallows and in miseries." This night was her flood tide. If she missed it, her life indeed would be an endless series of miseries. She would not admit to herself how frightened she was of the very things she had warned Andy about.

Even this afternoon, she had been afraid she might get lost in the moors, and now it was night. The cliff was a good forty feet high, and she could stumble straight over it. She dared not risk trying to find or carry a lantern. Even if she did, it would light little more than the ground immediately under her feet.

But this was her flood tide, the best chance she might ever have. Once tea was over, she changed into the brown boots and her heaviest skirt and blouse and caught up her woolen shawl. She told Andy she thought her best chance was to slip out of one of the long French windows of the library, the ones that opened out on the brick terrace, and leave it unlatched behind her. If somebody was in the library when she returned, or if Mrs. Wilkins had latched the window on her nightly rounds, she would go to the stables and hide until morning when she could try to get back into the house unnoticed. He was to stay in his room. If anybody missed her, he was to say she had been with him until just a minute before. He was to do or say nothing else. Let them search the house. She would worry about an explanation for that in the morning, if she must.

She crept through the house like a shadow, but once outside, she almost panicked as she groped and stumbled her way blindly through the garden. She had barely been able to find her way home this morning. Now the black fog darkened the night. She could see nothing. But the salt-tasting wind, icy cold on her face, was blowing from the sea. If she walked straight into that, she was going toward the cliffs. Beyond the gardens, the coarse, slippery moor grasses caused her to slip and slide. Twice she tripped over rocks and fell to her knees. The second time she stayed down, the wind swirling all around her until she had no more sense of direction.

Then she heard the distant pounding of the sea to her left. As she got up, fighting to hold down her full skirts, she realized the wind had changed and was clearing the fog away. It still hung in patches, but between them she could see dimly as she went forward, gasping for breath, listening for every beat of the surf, terrified she might stumble over the cliff in a black patch of the fog.

Suddenly, she heard sounds that were muffled but

still clear enough to recognize—men's voices, metal jingling, and dull thuds that were not surf. The sounds were straight ahead and, by some freak of the wind, all in one instant, they came up clearly from directly below her. She fell to her knees and screamed as one hand groped forward into nothingness. Below, a man's cursing came back clearly.

"Who's up there? Identify yourself or we'll shoot."

"Poppy. It's Poppy. The excisemen are coming."

Shouting voices answered, and again she heard the hurried clink of harness metal and the slap of hands on animal hides. The wind shifted once more, and for a full minute, she could see the white sand beach below. Four small fishing boats were pulled up on the shore, and a string of pack animals were coming and going along the steep path up to the moor. Men were working frantically, wading ashore with packs and casks on their backs and loading the animals that stood waiting.

One of the men dropped his pack behind a rock and cupped his hands around his mouth. "Where? Land or sea? Boat or horseback?"

Poppy knew that voice so unlike the rough Cornish speech. "I don't know. Mrs. Wilkins warned them last night."

"Then they've had time for anything. Take what you can and run for it, men."

The men ran but only back and forth, carrying the cargo on their backs onto the shore, and to rough hiding places in the rocks. Then from the blackness of the sea, other voices yelled, and the sharp high crackle of gunfire cut across the other muffled sounds. Poppy saw brief yellow flickers in the fog as the guns fired. She gasped as something cracked past her ear and thudded into the ground behind her. From below, men's voices shouted defiance and yelled at the pack animals scrambling up the path.

"Don't fire back," the leader shouted. "Let the cargo go. Get your boats away."

"They'm be too close in," a Cornish voice howled.

"We're four and more than they. They's one boat. Stick with it."

"No. Get your boats away. Away, men, away."

Some men were still unloading. Others ran for the boats, and more yellow flashes lit the night as the fishermen fired back. On one boat a sail creaked up, and on another oars pushed strongly, heaving it out into the deeper water. A heavy ball whipped over Poppy's head and smashed into the ground behind her. Somebody had seen her and was shooting at her. She flattened herself and trembled. She should run for it, but she was frozen with fear. Then a scrambling sound directly below her made her roll away. With a jump, a man pulled himself over the edge and dropped beside her.

"Poppy?" It was the young man. "Poppy?"

"They're shooting at me."

"They think you're our lookout man. You fool. They were close enough to hear you call your name. They'll remember it when they take a minute to think. We'll run for it. Come on."

Poppy started up and then froze again as she heard behind them the pounding of galloping horses. He cursed, jerked her to her feet, and dragged her to the left into a patch of darker fog. Four horses burst out of the night and reined so abruptly on the edge of the cliff that they were thrown back on their haunches. The excisemen jumped down, holding their guns, and began shooting at the rigging of the two fishing boats that had got out into the water.

"Now," he breathed just as the wind shifted again and left them standing in full view, only feet away from the four men and their sweating, heaving horses. "Now. Come."

"There! Two of them. On your horses and after them!"

The young man started off at a run as if he could see in the dark. Behind them, yells, thuds, shouts, and the sharp crack of shots went on, but Poppy was only aware of horses' hoofs thudding close behind them. He pulled her along and suddenly jerked her to the right and threw her down. She hit the ground so heavily the breath was knocked out of her. Dimly she realized they were hidden behind a protruding rock as the horse and rider thudded past.

"Now. Before he knows he's missed us."

He had her up again and running headlong through the thick gorse. It tore at her skirts, and she tripped on sharp rocks, but he never slackened his pace. She gasped, her lungs aching to bursting, her legs shaking, but she dared not fall. She had a feeling he would simply drag her along behind him, relentlessly. He was running for his life and would stop for nothing.

The sounds behind them slackened and faded, but he did not slow his pace. She was staggering from side to side, gasping loudly, whimpering for breath, but still running, dragged by that iron clasp on her wrist. Then he stopped so abruptly she stumbled forward and fell weakly against his shoulder, too exhausted to move, even to sink to her knees.

Incredibly the soft nicker of a horse came through the fog. She looked ahead and saw bands of yellow lights that could only be windows. They were beyond the manor stables, and those lights were shining out through the library windows. How had he brought her straight here?

"Where did you get out?"

"That near window. I left it unlatched."

"We'll look."

He took her hand again, but gently, as he crept up on the terrace. Flattening himself against the wall by the window, he looked inside.

"All safe. She's expecting company, but they're not here yet."

He opened the window and deftly latched it behind him. The tray, silver goblets, and decanters were set out in front of the fire, but the room was empty. He led the way across to the dark fireplace and pressed a panel above the mantel. With a creak, half a tier of bookcases cracked open beside the fireplace. Pulling impatiently, he wrenched the door wide and thrust her inside the low, dark opening. She stumbled against a set of narrow stairs.

"Up. Up. Quickly. Quietly."

She fumbled her way blindly until she felt empty, flat space around her. The dim light below disappeared as he closed the bookcase and climbed up to join her.

"Sutcliffe Manor's priest's hole," he said easily. "This was Catholic country once, you know."

"So that is why this fire is never lit."

"We couldn't have a roasted priest."

"You are the heir!" Poppy cried.

"Of course. I'm Jack Mowbry. Hush. Somebody's coming."

He showed her a long, narrow slit cut into the design of the fireplace overmantel, which gave them a full view of the library.

Chapter Nine

*M*RS. Wilkins bustled in, inspected the tray, and went to the center French window. She turned the handle to make sure it opened easily. Poppy swallowed hard. Only luck had kept Mrs. Wilkins from discovering earlier that another window also had been left unlocked.

The housekeeper put another log on the fire and filled all four goblets before she settled down in a chair with one of them, smiling, prepared to wait. She had hardly put her feet on a small stool before the window burst open and a heavily built man in an exciseman's uniform came through it and walked to the fire. He stood over it, shivering.

Mrs. Wilkins held out a goblet to him. "I didn't expect you for an hour or more."

"It went wrong," the man said and drained the goblet. "A woman warned them. One of the fishermen's wives, maybe. Is that girl who's staying here in her bed?"

"Of course."

"Find out. Miles thought he heard her call out a name like Poppy."

"Impossible. What happened?"

"We had them surrounded. Another five minutes and we'd have taken the lot. But a woman on the cliff saw or heard something. She warned them."

"A fisherman's wife stationed as a lookout."

"They don't take their women on that kind of jaunt."

"You got nothing?"

"Three boats got away, and the fourth staved in and sunk among the rocks. They'll have it up and away, with no identifying it, before we can return in the morning. Our lugger had to return to base. Two men wounded and needing a doctor."

"They must have landed some cargo," Mrs. Wilkins said sharply.

"Most of it, ma'am," he said with a heavy courtesy that held no liking. "Unfortunately the four of us on horseback made the mistake of going after the woman. And missed her, too. So most of the pack animals got clear, and what kegs and bales were left dumped on the beach won't stay there long. I left two men to guard, but our smugglers are old hands at inching a parcel away under our noses. Especially on a night as dark as this."

"Where's your other man?"

"Miles is guarding your stables, for what that's worth. Those and the old mine workings are the nearest hiding spots. I fear, ma'am, you and the smith will get nothing out of this night's work."

Poppy covered her mouth with her hand to suppress a gasp. So the smith Andy thought was so wonderful was also an informer. No wonder he was leaving for California.

"He will be disappointed," Mrs. Wilkins said smoothly. "He was counting on the funds to help him settle in his new country."

"I won't enjoy reporting this at the customhouse myself," the exciseman said bitterly. "I'll check the stables now and let Miles come into the warm here. Would you be kind enough to let me know about your guest when I return?"

"I'll look to it myself."

The room was barely empty before Poppy exploded in an accumulation of sneezes. "I was afraid of that," Jack said. He ripped the dripping shawl from her shoulders and tossed it down the stairs. He felt her soaked hair and ran his hands down the wet bodice to the hem of her skirt dripping on the floor. Then he tore his own soaked jersey off and said, "Is one of your petticoats dry enough to use as a towel? If we stay here soaked and dripping, we'll both sneeze ourselves into the exciseman's arms." Poppy edged into a corner, loosened her skirt belt, and reached inside and let her topmost petticoat drop. She stepped out of it and handed it to him. He tore the soaking wet ruffle off before she could protest the loss of her best lace, then ripped the rest into two parts and handed her one. She dried her hair as best she could and squeezed water from the hem of her skirt. Beside her, she could feel his vigorous movements as he rubbed his head, chest, and arms.

They both went deadly still as the French window opened and a younger exciseman stumbled in and went to the fire, snatching up a goblet and draining it in almost one movement. As he stood rubbing his hands in the warmth, Poppy realized how chilled through she was. She began to shiver uncontrollably and her jaw quivered as she bit down to keep her teeth from chattering.

Jack felt her shivering. Reaching out, he put both his arms around her and pulled her against his warm, bare chest, pressing her head against his shoulder. Though she felt the icy chill biting to the bone, the animal warmth helped. She pressed close against him, and the long quivering shudders of cold gradually subsided.

Mrs. Wilkins came into the room so rapidly her silk skirts rustled with a hissing like a snake. "The redheaded bit of street sweepings is nowhere to be found."

The exciseman stared at her. "You are speaking of His Lordship's guest?"

"The flaunting daughter of a notorious whore."

"I heard she was a pretty young girl and rode very well," the exciseman said slowly.

"She's cost us all a few hundred pounds tonight," Mrs. Wilkins said viciously. "If that's pretty to you. And that scum out of the gutter, her brother, is in it, too. He swears she was with him until just a minute ago. But Dorcas tells me she wasn't to be seen when she went up to turn the beds down, and her room's not been touched since."

The exciseman said with stiff distaste, "What's done is done, and I must be getting back, ma'am," and put down the goblet.

Mrs. Wilkins latched the window behind him with a snap and returned to the tray and refilled her glass and drained it. As she hesitated, eyeing the decanter and plainly debating the wisdom of another drink, Andy burst into the room.

"What have you done with her?" he shouted.

"Done with her? What are you doing up and dressed at this hour?"

"Looking for my sister," Andy said belligerently. "I looked all over, and I can't find her, either. What have you done with her?"

"I wouldn't touch her with my little finger any more'n I'd take poison," Mrs. Wilkins sneered. "Look for her in the bed of one of her smuggler friends."

"I'm staying right here until I see her," Andy said. "I don't trust you or what you'd do. I'll stay here all night if I have to." He went over to the fire, picking up the brass shovel and filling it with coals. Balancing it carefully, he started across the room.

"What are you doing?"

"It's a cold night. I'm lighting the other fireplace."

"Oh, no, you're not," Mrs. Wilkins said. She snatched the shovel and tossed the coals back in the fire.

"You're hiding something, I know it. Something bad," Andy said. "What's happened to my sister?"

"I don't know, but I hope it's as bad as can be," Mrs. Wilkins snapped. "It's none of my doing, and I'm going to bed. You can stay here all night if you like, but you're not burning the place down around us." With malicious satisfaction, she raked the ashes from under the grate until every spark of fire was smothered beyond rekindling. "Now will you go to bed?"

"No. Because you want me out of this room."

"You can freeze in any room in the house for the

rest of the night for all of me," Mrs. Wilkins said. "And believe me, His Lordship is going to hear about this."

Andy waited until the door closed behind her, then ran to the window and tried the latch. His face contorted with fear as he found it locked and struggled to open it.

Jack put Poppy from him and went down the stairs and pressed the bookshelf open. "It's all right. We're here."

Andy turned with a gasp of relief. He ran and hurled himself into Poppy's arms as she stepped into the room. "Oh, Poppy, Poppy, I was so scared for you. All I could think of was to get her out of here so you could get back in. And the only way I could think to do it was to make old Wilkins go looking for you while I waited here. Only she wouldn't."

"But she did leave," Poppy soothed. "And we're all right."

Jack, his bare, strongly muscled torso gleaming bronze in the candlelight, gulped down the brandy in the unused goblet before he went back into the priest's hole and returned with his jersey and Poppy's shawl. "I've got to go."

"Go?"

"I've got to get my boat out of that cove before somebody recognizes her. The excisemen know her. I've sailed the *Corn Dolly* up and down this coast since I was a boy."

"She's on your own land. What's the harm?"

"She's back here for the first time in years. Hidden in that cove. After last night, do you think nobody will make the connection?"

"They can't prove anything."

"True. But they'll suspect. And talk." He grinned wryly. "I can't do that to the Pater and the family name."

"You're the missing heir," Andy cried, delighted.

"Yes. And I'm going to be missing again in about two minutes."

"The missing heir, and a smuggler, too." Andy

beamed. "Do you like being a smuggler better than an heir?"

"Right now I'll trade you both of them for a ha'-penny," Jack said. "I couldn't ship out, and I couldn't live on half pay. So I sailed the *Corn Dolly* to France, invested my little savings in a cargo, and arranged to have a French friend bring it over to meet my Cornish sailors. With the result you saw." He pulled his empty trouser pockets out with an expressive gesture and shrugged. He stuffed them back. "See? So it's back to France again and lie low for a while. You're sure you want to stay here?"

"Let's go with him," Andy begged, dancing with eagerness. "Let's go."

"Why should we?" Poppy asked.

"Maybe they can't prove you gave the warning, but they suspect," Jack said. "Mrs. Wilkins doesn't like you. She'll make the most of it."

"She'll write Daisy and His Lordship," Poppy realized, appalled as she took that in fully for the first time.

"She doesn't want us here, but we don't want to stay anyway, now the smith's gone," Andy pleaded.

"Never mind the smith," Poppy said, absent-mindedly. No use tearing down an idol by telling Andy the truth. "We're in trouble."

"We'll get sent back to London," Andy said.

Worse, after this Daisy would be desperate. She would arrange a marriage, any marriage to almost anyone, to get her troublesome daughter settled and out of the way. That Poppy knew she could not endure. She would rather die first.

"Yes, we'll come with you," she decided suddenly, trying not to think of sailing on the heaving waves of the Channel in that tiny boat. "Just give us time to get our things."

"No." He shook his head. "Mrs. Wilkins won't settle down after a night like this. She'll be napping like a cat with both ears and one eye open. And some of the ex-cisemen may still be on the prowl. We've got to get away while there's still some fog and dark. What's a dress or two?"

"Nothing. If you've money for new."

"I've only a few pounds on the boat," he admitted, frowning. "The few things I brought back in the *Dolly* I gave to my fishermen friends because I didn't want to start an alarm about contraband being around just before we brought in the big cargo."

"Then I need clothes. And Andy a jacket."

"I've a spare jacket on the boat. No. I tell you, no. It's run for it now or we're caught." He went to the window and opened it. "I'm leaving."

"We're coming," Poppy snapped with exasperation. "But I'll need a new dress when we land." She pulled the velvet cover off a table, dumped the four silver goblets in it, and slung it over her arm. She said succinctly, "Worth their weight if you're hard up."

"A most practical lady," he said with a little bow as he ushered them out on the terrace.

She quite agreed with him. Sometimes she despaired of men, they were so impractical. First he destroyed her best petticoat when it would have dried them just as well in one piece. Then, with his pockets empty, he had been ready to walk blindly past a nice piece of cash goods any child could have told him was worth picking up.

Part Two

France
October-November 1851

Chapter Ten

*P*OPPY leaned out the small third-floor window of the rooms they had rented, looking across the beach to the sea beyond Les Sables d'Olonne. She had never seen a place so beautiful or one occupied by people so primitive and menacing. In front of her, the perfect crescent of fine white sand with a black headland at each end encircled the clear blue water. The sun shone brilliantly, but the air was chill. Nothing moved on water or land except at one end of the beach where barefooted men were tramping red dye into a sail spread on the sand. Below her, the sidewalk cafés and shops that looked out on the beach showed no signs of life. The season for tourists from Paris was long over. The fishermen were out in their squat boats with sails of red, blue, and yellow. The children were shut up in school. The women, with their clattering clogs, black dresses, and great white headdresses, had finished their early shopping at the open market. Now they were busy inside their stone houses, which crowded together along the narrow cobbled streets mounting up from the beach.

Poppy shivered and drew her head in and closed the window. It was Dexter Roack's fault they were marooned in this English-hating Vendée province! She had assumed when they fled from Cornwall that they would stay in some spot where the English were known and welcome.

She still would not willingly recall that trip across the Channel in the tiny *Corn Dolly*. She had been wet, cold, terrified, and miserably sick every mile of the way. When Andy called that they were coming into the harbor at Brest, she had staggered to her feet, so weak she could stand only by holding to the rail. She had looked with bleared eyes at the boats anchored closely all around, too exhausted to marvel at the way Jack was slipping between them to get to the wharf.

She could hardly believe they had not capsized or been swamped under those monstrous waves and were not all drowned and dead. She swore she would never again set foot on a small sailboat as long as she lived.

When Jack tied the boat at the end of the wharf, she realized she could not go ashore with the drenched and soggy garments clinging to every curve of her body. She would not parade in the streets like a spectacle to be stared and laughed at. Jack took his pound notes to change at the bank and the bundle of silver goblets to sell. He promised to inquire about lodgings and return with money and a dry shawl to cover her until she could get to a shop. Andy went scampering off with him, calling back they would return with rolls and ham and cheese, too. She nodded numbly. All she wanted was to get ashore to a warm, dry place with a bed that did not rise and fall or threaten to toss her like a shying horse. The meanest inn would seem a palace.

She huddled by the rail, a damp bundle of misery, face raw and hair stiff from salt spray, eyes swollen from the buffeting wind. Then she saw them coming, running as if for their lives, Andy leaping to match Jack's stride. They jumped aboard, and Jack jerked the ropes that tied the boat fore and aft and then leapt to run up the sail. Andy hauled with him. A breeze caught the canvas and began to pull the *Corn Dolly* about.

"What are you doing?" Poppy shrieked.

"We made it," Andy whooped, laughing and dancing as he continued to pull and Jack ran to the helm. "We made it. We got away."

"Away? We just got here."

"He was waiting for us at the bank. There he comes. See? But he'll never catch us now."

She turned dull eyes back to the wharf and could

not believe what she saw. Dexter Roack, impeccably groomed as always, stood at the end where they had been tied up. As they came about and headed back out to sea, he took off his hat, waved it, and bowed an ironic farewell.

"Where did he come from?" Poppy whispered.

Jack did not turn his head as he maneuvered the *Corn Dolly* through the water lanes between the closely packed boats. "Just be glad we sold the goblets and got that much cash before we went to the bank. These two little flies walked straight into the spider's web. Roack was there waiting for us."

"I threw the velvet cloth right over his head," Andy boasted. "Before he got out of that, we were away and running."

"I thought you liked him," Poppy said.

"I do. But we're with Jack now, so I'm on his side."

Jack slipped the *Corn Dolly* between two fishing smacks and slid under the bows of a coastal freighter. "Word of our battle with the excisemen got to Brest ahead of us. The Frenchman who transshipped our cargo to the fishing boats out in the Channel was still close enough to hear the shots and guessed what had happened. Naturally he told the story in Brest when he returned. They know me there and knew I'd made the venture, selected and paid for the cargo."

"That doesn't explain Dexter Roack."

"No? Those merchant bankers have an intelligence system that even our diplomats use. It's faster and surer than their sealed pouches. He probably had word wherever he was the next morning at the latest. He knew I'd run for it and make straight for the nearest French port. So there he was, waiting. He's an extremely clever gentleman, and I'm a simple sailor. Nothing for us to do but run again."

Poppy reached for the rail and shivered as she saw open water ahead. "Where now?"

"Around the coast to the Bay of Biscay to a place no English-speaking person ever goes. He'll never trace us there."

"Is it far? How long?" Poppy asked faintly.

"That depends on the wind. Far enough."

"I'm hungry," Andy wailed.

"We'll find a place to put in for supplies as soon as we've put enough distance behind us that we won't be recognized by anybody from Brest."

"Far." Poppy understood.

"Far enough and safe enough that we'll be able to stay awhile," Jack said, squinting against the sun. "Unless you know a place you want to go."

"No place."

"Then you're my sister, and Andy's our little brother. No one will question that."

He was right. Both he and Andy were the same blue-eyed, fair-haired English type, and her resemblance to Andy, especially around the eyes, was unmistakable. "You really are determined not to be caught," she marveled.

"I'm determined to serve out my time in the Navy because there's no reason for me not to," he said. "The Pater is a fine old gentleman, and we all love and respect him. But he's also a stubborn old tyrant, and he's not taking the best years of my life away from me for a whim."

"But you're the heir," Andy gasped.

"I'm one of the heirs. But when am I going to inherit? The Pater may live another ten or fifteen years. Then my brother takes over for the rest of his life. After that I'll accept with all grace and thanks. Meanwhile, why should I twiddle my thumbs playing the role of heir when I could be happy in the Navy? We're not at war. Nothing's going to happen to me."

"You're right," Poppy said.

"Of course I'm right. If I keep running long enough and far enough, Father will have to admit he'll never catch me and cry 'Pax.' Then I'll go back and resume my commission. With luck, I'll retire a captain. After that, I'll play the heir."

The run around the coast was farther and took longer than crossing the Channel, but it was not as rough. Still, when Poppy staggered ashore, she felt like falling on her knees in gratitude for a solid footing.

Jack had said no English people went to Les Sables d'Olonne. He had not said the people there hated the English. Poppy did not understand it, except that these were an ignorant and isolated people who feared strangers and therefore hated.

If she had realized that, and not been deceived by the great natural beauty of the place, she would have tried to stop Jack before he sold the *Corn Dolly* and left them stranded. Though she knew it had broken his heart to part with the boat, he only had said gruffly they needed the money to live. Even though he knew the buyer would sell it to some Parisian at double the price in the spring, he let it go cheap, in return for the chance to sail with the man's fishing boat and take a share of the profits. Because he was a superb sailor, the fishermen accepted him. Andy was a child, usually busy in some mysterious but surely harmless way at the basin where the squat fishing boats were built and anchored, so he was tolerated.

Only Poppy received the full blast of burning hatred every time she stepped out on the street. A little of it was her lilting English voice and accent. Mostly it was her grace and beauty that made her stand out among the short, squat women with their dark, weather-lined faces like a gaudy cockatoo in a hen yard. She had done her best. She wore a plain, short, black skirt and a high-necked, long-sleeved black blouse such as all the women did, though she could not endure the heavy woolen socks and wooden clogs and wore, instead, her own fine brown boots with thin lisle stockings.

Now she looked around the combination kitchen and living room, with the two small bedrooms opening off it, and tied a black kerchief over her bright hair. Reluctant to leave this shelter, she went again to the window.

Her eyes widened in disbelief. She had loitered until this late morning hour, although it meant little would be left at the market, to avoid the women who shopped early and then disappeared to prepare the midday meal, not to be seen again until late afternoon. Now a woman came out of a shop below and walked along briskly. She soon was joined by two others. That was unusual. Their high, white, elaborately folded headdresses and lace-trimmed aprons were not the same, so this was not a family matter. Each individual fold and shape of the headdresses and each lace pattern were handed down in families for generations and identified the wearer on sight. The three were turning to climb the steep cobbled street that led to the convent and beyond that to the market.

She hesitated. Could they be going to the convent? She had never seen any nuns on the streets or anyone coming or going through the narrow iron gate in the convent walls, except a hobbling, crook-shouldered priest, and had decided it was an enclosed order. Perhaps, though the nuns never left their high-walled home, they did sometimes permit visitors for special occasions, she decided doubtfully.

She had only some carrots and potatoes in the house. She must go to the market and then the bakery. She had never confided to Andy or Jack how much she dreaded this small daily trip because they had never seemed to sense the seething violence she felt barely held in check. She would not be thought a coward for no reason they would credit. She had learned to cook on that tiny primitive stove, and she must do the shopping.

She could not ask anything more of Jack. He had sacrificed his boat. He worked to support them. More, he was the perfect English gentleman, who never by word, gesture, or hint behaved as if they were anything other than the brother and sister he had said they were. Except, Poppy often thought, he probably would not have been so meticulously courteous and careful of her privacy if she truly had been his sister.

She already had delayed far too long. Andy and Jack would be back before she had time to prepare their midday meal. They would be ravenous and must be fed.

She slipped down the dark, narrow stairs and hurried up the steep cobbled street hemmed in by the small stone houses, close-shuttered against passersby. When she reached the high convent walls, she slackened her pace and breathed more easily. She could not imagine what kind of women would choose to spend their lives behind those walls, never leaving them, but she felt no menace here except from the priest. From the darting, fierce glances of his narrowed eyes, she knew this man who spent his life ministering to the self-effacing, praying women considered her a walking personification of evil. That was strange in a priest, but these people of Vendée were strange. For once, he was not by the gate.

As she expected when she reached the small square with the market barrows lined up along two sides, many spaces were vacant and those which remained held only meager scraps, the rejected leavings. She edged along, knowing the market farmers despised her as a stupid foreigner who could not even shop early to get good food for her men. She shook her head at the man with the large dead rabbits dangling by their hind feet on a rope behind him. She had noticed his odd, sneering smile the last time he had sold her one already skinned. After it was cooked and eaten, she had recalled his smile and thought that the hind legs had seemed somehow odd. Perhaps French rabbits were different, but could that man have been malicious enough to sell the ignorant foreigner a skinned cat? She had said nothing to Andy or Jack, but she had determined to buy no more rabbits unless she saw them in their skins.

She found a good head of cabbage and took it. Perhaps Jack would bring home an especially fine fish to grill on the embers of the fireplace, but she must have meat if he did not. The lamb cost too much. She reached the rabbit stall again, searching, and the leering man beckoned to her and held out a skinned carcass enticingly. She smiled as she shook her head, but he said something out of the side of his mouth that made the man beside him laugh. He flourished the carcass again, and involuntarily she shrank away.

"Our good French food is not enough for the Englishwoman," he taunted.

"I have fish," Poppy lied. "I must hurry to the bakery for some of their excellent bread and fine pastries."

"But you don't like our rabbits," the man laughed and thrust it close to her face.

She knew then. That was a cat, and the whole market knew it and had been laughing at the grisly joke for days. "Another time," she said and turned hurriedly. She stumbled straight against a rough black serge shoulder. The priest staggered on the rough cobblestones and braced himself with his cane. He hobbled not only because he was crook-shouldered, she realized, but because he was crippled. She stammered, "My apologies, my apologies."

Eyes blazing in his thin, sallow face, he held out his crucifix in front of him and intoned something. It could only be an exorcism against evil. She saw behind him some thirty women and as many more large boys and girls. She had collided with a procession headed by the priest on its way to some religious ceremony. Frightened, she mumbled meaningless words and tried to turn away, but the rabbit man swung the long, stiff carcass until it nearly brushed her face.

The priest pointed one shaking finger at her and went into a shrill tirade in the local patois she could not follow. But she saw the women's faces, eyes glaring out of their square, muddy countenances and the drab lips contorted to spit. She heard the dull mutter of a mob. Horrified, she thought faces like that must have gloated at the foot of the guillotine, waiting for the dull thud of death. She looked around frantically for a path of escape. Behind her, the man still flourished the stark carcass. The women, their white caps bobbing like the heads of pecking hens closing in to kill a sick member, pressed a half circle on each side. In front of her, the priest elevated his crucifix and began to intone some garbled Latin.

She had to get out of here. The man's voice was rising with each word, hysterically shrill, and she thought she saw a thin line of froth on his lips. The mutter of the women was deepening into an ominous growl as their white caps bobbed closer and closer around her until she could smell the stale odors of their clothes. When they touched her, violence would flare.

Only the priest barred her way to the open space leading to the street. With a rush, she ran toward him and pushed past. As she did, he lurched on his unsure footing, tripped on the rough cobbles, and went down. His head hit the stone with the sound of a ripe melon breaking open. The women howled and closed around him.

Poppy ran. She threw away the cabbage, gathered up her skirts, and raced down the streets to their rooms over the beach. She tumbled up the steep, dark stairs and burst into the sitting room, panting. Andy and Jack were seated on the bench in front of the fire, home early.

"No luck this morning," Jack said. In the poorly lit room, he did not notice her white, terrified face. "The fish moved farther out. We may go out on the evening tide and stay the night."

Andy piped up. "We're hungry, and you haven't even started to cook."

"Please," Poppy gasped and stopped to catch her breath, still rasping from the run. "Please. I went to the market."

Jack stared at her face and asked sharply, "What is it? What happened?"

"I went to the market," Poppy repeated, still too shocked to put the reality into words. She held out her shaking hands. "I went, and they've been selling us cat. For rabbit."

Andy gagged. "They haven't!"

"That wouldn't make you look like this," Jack said. "What happened?"

"They laughed, and the priest came."

"I've seen him. Not at all the usual type of man to be attached to a religious community."

103

"The women were with him and the big boys and girls," Poppy said with difficulty. "A mob, a mob."

"Why?"

"He held up his crucifix, and he was doing something with it."

"Probably an incantation against evil. He had an odd, fanatic look."

"I wanted to get away. They had me surrounded. I pushed him. He fell." Poppy covered her face with her shaking hands and whispered, "His head cracked on the cobblestones. A terrible crack. A horrible sound."

"Then you may have killed him," Jack said calmly. "If you did, we have minutes to get out of here." He suddenly sounded like the Navy officer he was, his voice commanding. "I will leave and appear to be going back to the basin. Andy, you go to the fountain in the lower square as if you were looking for some playmate."

"I don't have any."

"Go to the fountain," Jack ordered. "Not hurrying. But go. Take your jacket and cap. Poppy, you go out on the beach and along it as if you were going to the tide pools directly below the square with the fountain."

"We know," Andy piped.

"Take your shawl. Go up among those high rocks at the end of the beach. I've got the money, and I'll meet you both there as soon as I can, without being seen."

"Are we going to stay up there and throw down rocks on anybody who tries to get Poppy?" Andy cried.

"We're going to meet there and then wade around the headland. It's rocky but shallow. There's more rocky beach on the other side that we can follow until we're well out of sight and can climb up the cliff. I'm sure there are enough shrubs growing on the side so we can make it to the road above the shore. Then we run for our lives."

"Where does the road lead?" Poppy questioned, shocked.

"Don't argue. Let's get that far first. Out. Out. Both of you. As fast as you can without attracting attention."

Chapter Eleven

$\mathcal{T}$HE small roadside inn, perched on a point of rocks high over the sea, was only half a dozen miles from Les Sables d'Olonne, but it seemed a different world. Designed to accommodate travelers along the coastal highway, it was provincial only in its carefully calculated appearance. Alone in the dining room with windows looking out over the water, waiting for Jack and Andy to rejoin her, Poppy stood in front of the fire and tore at her hated, dingy peasant dress. She turned back the long sleeves, making cuffs to show her pretty wrists. She unbuttoned the high, tight neck and tucked it under in a more flattering neckline. Lifting her skirt, she ruthlessly tore off the ruffle of her petticoat and arranged it in the neck to make a dainty white edging. She curled her hair around her finger until it formed long ringlets on each side of her face. She still felt miserably shabby and drab, but she had done what she could.

Then she looked around uneasily. They had not been followed. She was certain of that. Nobody was going to jump out at her and scream, "Murderess." Yet her skin prickled a warning she was being watched.

A board creaked somewhere, and she whirled. There, that inconspicuous door in the corner was open the barest crack. She ran, flung it open, and saw the back of a heavily built man in a handsome traveling coat hurrying down a short hall. As he turned the corner at the end, he glanced back furtively, and she caught a fleeting glimpse of a sallow-skinned face, with dark darting eyes and a short, slightly hooked nose.

She fell back, chilled. It was a birdlike face. For a moment, the remembered fear of those bobbing white hats like pecking hens closing around her started a scream welling in her throat. Then she caught at her courage. The man had the face of an aristocrat, and if it looked familiar, it was probably only a type she recognized. The same thing had happened the first time she saw Jack.

As if the thought had summoned him, he walked into the room, acting completely the English lord for all his salt-stained, shabby clothes. The proprietor followed, gesturing, bowing, and assuring him that he understood how much the English enjoyed these long walking tours *en famille*. Food would be on the table as soon as the young gentleman finished soaking his sprained wrist in hot water. And a picnic basket was being prepared to take with them, though surely they would be in St. Gilles by dinner time.

Jack motioned her to a chair at a table by a window and sat down opposite. "Thank goodness it was his wrist, not an ankle. Madame will bandage it, and we can leave as soon as we eat."

"For St. Gilles?"

"Of course not. I only said that so if they trace us here, they'll look for us there. That's a port, and the coast is too dangerous. As you know, the fishing fraternity communicates swiftly."

"Then where will we go?"

"We're walking straight overland to Nantes. I don't know whether the rails have reached there yet, but if they haven't, we'll have a choice between a river boat or a barge and a public coach."

"How far?"

"Half the distance it would be if we followed the coast."

"How far?"

"I wish we had a map, but I've a fair memory for such things. I'd guess not over fifty miles. It's flat, low country and easy walking. We'll try to stay out of sight, and we may have to sleep in haystacks for a couple of nights. This isn't Cornwall with its daily rains."

"Today, tomorrow, and two nights at least," Poppy estimated. "After Nantes, what?"

"Paris."

"Paris is expensive."

"Paris is our only possible chance of money now. Dexter Roack. Or his bank."

"Oh, no."

"Oh, yes. After all, I'm the one he's chasing, and I'm willing. Shh. Here's Andy, and there's our food. Don't argue in front of the boy. He's too excited now."

Jack was right. First they must get out of this country of primitive, hate-filled people. Then they could argue destinations.

Andy bolted his food, wild to get on with this adventure. They left the inn and told him they were going to walk inconspicuously, not hiding in a way that would cause suspicion but keeping out of sight as much as possible. They would use paths instead of roads, walking at night as long as they could see by moonlight, sleeping out in fields. Andy whooped and danced. This was like playing Robin Hood, but it was real.

Poppy was grateful for her good brown walking boots. Jack had saved the compass from his boat, and he set a sure, straight line across the fertile countryside. At this time of year, the harvest was finished, so only rarely was anyone in the fields to see them pass. Barking dogs ran out at them from farmyards but did not pursue them. The towns were small and easy to avoid. Poppy concentrated on holding the steady pace Jack set, which was to walk an hour and rest, walk another hour and rest; she was lost in the sheer monotony of the movement and the flat land around them. The night was eerily quiet, but they found a haystack in an isolated field and slept soundly. They were on their way again before the first pink streaks of dawn showed in the sky. The next day was cold and gray, but it did not snow as they had feared, and again they found a haystack for shelter.

107

By the time they reached the outskirts of Nantes, Poppy was miserably aware of the bedraggled appearance they presented. The white ruffle on her dress had long since been discarded. Their clothes were soggy and their boots mud-caked. All the better, Jack assured her coolly, as now they could pass for a family of poor English fishing folk come to attend the funeral of a French maternal grandmother in the hopes of an inheritance.

"Sailors have a new story for every port, a different one for each girl," he explained, smiling.

"I do not think our next port should be Paris," Poppy said.

"You're not giving up to Dexter Roack?" Andy guessed. "Oh, you can't, Jack, when you want to be a captain."

"Let me worry about that. The important thing is that this is a Catholic country."

Andy's eyes grew very round and blue. "So a priest is twice as important as a person? And they have the guillotine?"

"You're putting it too high, but Poppy does need the most powerful friends she can find. And the bank is the most powerful one I know. As we are now, I don't even dare inquire how badly the priest was hurt."

Poppy's head drooped. "I suppose a river barge is the cheapest way," she surrendered.

"Especially if Andy and I work." Jack's face lit up. "A long, slow trip but we're in no hurry. And beautiful. First the river and then the canals."

He found a room in a cheap inn by the river and left Poppy there while he and Andy went off to inquire along the wharfs. She ordered pitchers of hot water, though she knew such extravagant madness would be noticed, and scrubbed herself from head to toe. The water was black when she was through, but her hair was still dull and gummy, and her legs were gray streaked. She dared not order more water. She promised herself that when she reached Paris she would have endless baths to scrub and soak in, again and again.

She was smiling at the thought as she opened the door to Andy and Jack. They came tumbling into the room, their faces set and white.

"Poppy, Poppy," Andy cried and flung his arms around her, weeping.

"Stop that," Jack ordered. "Poppy, go downstairs and get in the closed carriage that's waiting. Go wherever the man takes you. Eventually we'll meet you somewhere."

"Eventually? Where? What is this?"

"Oh, Poppy, you killed him, and they know we're in Nantes," Andy wailed.

"No," Jack said in a thunderous whisper. "Be quiet, Andy. It's not that bad. We don't know you killed him, but I think the police are looking for us."

"Oh, no!" she said, covering her face with her hands.

"Fortunately sailors learn to watch out for weather signs in strange ports," Jack said grimly. "I saw a gendarme following us and looking as if he were comparing our faces to a mental description."

"Only you weren't with us, and he must have been looking for three together," Andy said tremulously.

"I went straight to the bank's representative here," Jack said. "I told him I thought the police had orders to arrest you on sight. So nobody must get that sight. I told him you had to be got to Paris secretly and as fast as possible. He's waiting."

"This is the bank's man? In the carriage?"

"Yes. I told you they had an excellent communication service. He'll get you away from here and to wherever he decides is safest. We hadn't time to arrange that, but he'll get word to me."

"How did you arrange this much?"

Jack lifted one eyebrow in an ironic grimace. "I am a Westmoreland. Now will you please hurry, but discreetly? I think you should try to give the appearance of a lady on her way to a rendezvous with the gentleman in the closed carriage. For the benefit of Madame the Proprietress. *À bientôt.*" He kissed her lightly as he opened the door.

Chapter Twelve

ONCE in the carriage, Poppy again began to feel like a parcel in process of shipment, allowing herself to be forwarded docilely from place to place. At first, she did not even know her destination.

When she was told, she did not know why the bank, which she was beginning to think was an all-knowing, all-powerful octopus with tentacles stretching all over the world, decided she should go to Paris instead of being sent back to England. She thought the bank must use every means of communication: carrier pigeons, couriers, telegrams, private and public mails—and pure magic. Anonymous gentlemen, all serious, aloof, and silent, whisked her from one place to another, and she was always expected at each new place. A room would be ready at an inn and a meal prepared and served. On the second morning, a portmanteau of clothes was delivered with her breakfast chocolate and rolls. She unpacked a brush and hairpins, flannel nightgown, stockings, gloves, two scarves, a tight bonnet that almost concealed her bright hair, and a shawl to replace her stained, tattered one. She could have wept with surprise and gratitude. She would still be shabby and in need of a complete change of clothing, but at least she need not cringe every time she caught sight of herself in a mirror. Without time and a dressmaker, she could not have done better for herself. Two days later she was told, by her gentleman escort of the day, she would be put on the train to Paris that night and met when she arrived.

When the train pulled into Paris in the morning, another anonymous gentleman plucked her out of the

crowd and into a carriage. They drove into an area she
remembered vaguely as a discreetly fashionable quarter, although not one where the wealthy and titled lived.
The gentleman escorted her up to a suite of rooms and
left as the door opened.

A small, gray-haired woman in a maid's uniform and
cap took Poppy's shawl and bonnet and said, unsmil-
ing, "I am Delphine. I have a small meal ready. Or
would you prefer to bathe first?"

"A bath, please." During all those weary, jolting,
traveling days and nights, there had never been enough
time or water to wash completely. She had simply
averted her eyes from the gray streaks on her legs and
arms and hastily covered them with clothing. "Then
perhaps I could have a tray in the bedroom?"

"Certainly."

The rugs were thick, and the furniture more delicately elegant, satin and gilt and curved polished wood,
than any she was accustomed to in England. Delphine
quickly filled the hip bath with steaming water. Poppy
pulled off the hated black blouse and skirt, dropped
them on the floor, and tossed her dingy undergarments
on top of them.

Delphine picked them up with two fingers and held
them at arm's length. "I have a night shift, dressing
gown, and slippers for you. You have no further use
for these?"

Poppy stopped, half in and half out of the water. "I
must go shopping," she protested, alarmed.

"Certainly. I believe that is arranged for tomorrow.
Today you rest." Delphine made an irritated sound, as
if dealing with an unreasonable child, removed the
clothes, and returned carrying a plain street costume of
thin blue wool. "I also have this. Will cleaning the shoes
be satisfactory? Your feet are so small."

"Clean them, if there's anything left under the mud."

"They were good boots," Delphine said. "I think
these things will have to do until you can procure something more suitable tomorrow."

Poppy ducked under the water and shivered with

pleasure as she straightened and reached for the soap. She looked at the blue dress doubtfully as she soaped a sponge. "It looks rather large."

Delphine almost smiled as she pinched the material at the shoulder and waist and glanced from the dress to Poppy and back. "I can take a few tucks while you rest. Some gentlemen simply do not have the eye for estimates. Then tomorrow, something more suitable."

"More fitting," Poppy corrected, laughing, and attacked one filthy foot and leg vigorously. "I'll need more water for my hair."

"Rest, and another bath later. One will never remove that dirt," Delphine agreed. "A gentleman will be calling, but not until nine tonight."

The food was light but delicious. Poppy had not tasted any like it since she had been in Paris with Daisy. She slept well in the softest, widest bed she had ever occupied. She got up only to bathe, eat again, then rest on a chaise longue in front of the bedroom fire and leaf through a fashion magazine. She supposed this evening's anonymous gentleman would tell her what she was to do next, but she could not fret over it. She had met too many anonymous gentlemen, all uniformly pleasant, courteous, and dull, and they had conspired only to bring her to this charming and luxurious apartment. The next one could intend her no harm. She had heard of girls enticed into brothels, but she was serenely sure the bank had no such dealings.

When Delphine produced the blue dress and undergarments that also had been discreetly altered, she apologized. "These should be possible, just possible, for tonight and tomorrow. Only that."

The chemise was trimmed with fine lace, and the topmost petticoat was sheer, rustling taffeta. "At least the color is lovely," Poppy yawned as she put on the blue dress.

Clothed, hair smoothed into ringlets from a center part, she went into the small drawing room and walked around, touching the silk panels set into the walls, pausing before the small, delightful paintings of ladies and gentlemen rollicking in a rural playground, and trying the soft satin chairs. She could stay in this place in-definitely and feel no cause for complaint. It made Pall-minster Lane look like a peasant's cottage.

She touched the fruit in a silver bowl, so perfect she had assumed it was wax, and discovered it was real. She looked more closely at the great silver bowls of red roses set around the room, and a petal fell on the polished wood. Incredibly in winter, they, too, were real, the product of some great greenhouse, and they gave off the scent filling the air that she had thought was fine perfume.

She went to a window, drew the dark-rose silk cur-tains aside, and saw the first little flakes of snow begin-ning to sift down outside. Involuntarily she shivered. If winter had come a short time earlier, she would have been walking across those wind-swept, bare fields in the Vendée, protected only by a shawl, wet and chilled and even more miserable than she had been.

All her contentment vanished. Somewhere Andy and Jack were making their way to Paris. If they were work-ing on a barge, toiling up the Loire and then the canals, they would be in for weeks of the hardest kind of work in numbing cold. For the first time she glanced im-patiently at the door, anxious to see this evening's gentleman. If he did not bring her news of Andy and Jack, the all-powerful bank must get it for her.

Delphine, in answer to some signal Poppy did not hear, hurried across the room, her starched skirts rus-tling. Her voice murmured for a moment, and then she crossed the room again, carrying a gentleman's topcoat, hat, and cane, shaking her head at the damp spots on the fine materials.

Poppy fingered her ringlets and made sure the ruffled cuff fell away gracefully from her delicate wrist. Then her mouth rounded, and she said in a small shriek, "Dexter Roack! Not you!"

He laughed back at her from the doorway, elegant in evening dress of a distinctly Parisian cut. "But I have been waiting for you." He strolled into the room and stood in front of the fire.

Poppy lowered her long lashes and told herself she must be tactful. She must be both tactful and diplomatic. He was the all-powerful bank. She wanted news of Andy and Jack. She did not want to be shipped off again. She must pretend to be pleased; she must conceal the rage that filled her at the memory of her last exile.

"You startled me," she said sweetly. She went to sit in a chair beside the fire and gestured toward another. "I, too, have been waiting. For news." He said nothing, and she continued with an effort that made her hands grip together tensely in her lap. "And to thank you. For my most timely and fortunate rescue." She swallowed hard. She was grateful to the bank, but it had cost her something to say it to Dexter Roack.

"The French have guillotined the daughters of kings," he said calmly. "We do not feel it is a practice to be encouraged. Especially of English kings. Even if illegitimate."

"The priest is dead then?" Poppy whispered. Somehow she had hoped Jack had taken alarm too easily and that his terrible assumption had been wrong.

"Yes." He did not sit down but stood with one elbow resting lightly on the fireplace mantel. "Quite dead. Possibly that is not a circumstance to be completely regretted. In our view."

"Your view? Of a priest in a small village? What's that to do with the bank?"

"Nothing. Except the bank believes peace brings prosperity, and he was something of a political agitator. With much local influence. In Les Sables d'Olonne they are screaming for your blood, and they refuse to believe the truth. He was not a priest."

"Oh," Poppy breathed with relief and then stammered, "It is still terrible. But a priest, somehow I could never have forgiven myself for that."

"He was not," Dex assured her in his deep, vital voice. "He studied for the priesthood certainly. But his political interests made the Church decide he did not have a true vocation, and he was never ordained. However, he arrived in Les Sables d'Olonne some two or

114

three years ago, as a priest, and attached himself to the convent. That was a time of turmoil, and nobody will attempt to explain how it could have happened."

"A small place, an obscure priest, perhaps nobody questioned him," Poppy murmured.

"Poor communications," Dex agreed. "Quite possibly. Anyhow, he developed tremendous influence in the community. An odd kind of influence. The people are superstitious, and he specialized in some of the more esoteric rites."

"He was holding up his cross and chanting something," Poppy remembered numbly.

"Driving the devil out of you, no doubt," Dex said factually. "People have been known to die after such ceremonies in such towns. Don't wear a hair shirt over this. He was not a good man."

"I was terrified," Poppy confessed. "Those women, a mob," she said, shuddering.

"You shoved, trying to get away, and he fell?" Dex asked, then nodded. "An accident. Unfortunate. Especially considering the political situation. Everything is politics here today. But that is not for you to worry."

That reminded Poppy. "Andy and Jack?"

"On their way," he assured her, beginning to smile. "When we can do so inconspicuously, without arousing any questions, we'll get them off that barge and bring them to Paris. At the moment, I believe they're rather enjoying the experience."

Poppy felt stupid with relief. "Then we'll be all right and together again. Or?" She stiffened and sat tensely upright. "Where are you sending me next?"

"Aren't you comfortable here?"

"It's beautiful."

"Then let tomorrow take care of itself. I have arranged for the Countess de Bourgemont to call for you in the afternoon and take you shopping. Nobody in Paris knows the shops better."

"That terrible black skirt and blouse," Poppy grimaced.

"Nothing black then," he laughed and touched the

bell pull by the fireplace. "I asked Delphine to cool some wine. I hope you'll like it. It's from our own vineyards."

"The all-powerful bank," Poppy said and giggled a little hysterically from relief.

The wine was delicious—light, not too sweet, and exactly cool enough. Poppy drank two glasses. When she sipped a third, she knew she had had too much. She felt relaxed, warm, giddy, and giggly all at once. She felt wonderful. For the first time since that terrible morning in the open market, she was clean, warm, safe, and more, lapped in luxury. She simply wanted this lovely comfortable feeling to go on and on. She drained the glass, looking a little defiantly at Dex lolling in the chair beside hers and twirling his barely touched glass between his fingers, then held hers out to be filled again.

Instead of taking it, he closed his iron fingers around her hand and the glass. "You know you're getting drunk, don't you?" he asked softly.

The inward giggle bubbled out. "Of course I am. And I'm going to get drunker. And I'll feel better and better, and warmer and warmer. Then I'll sleep and sleep."

"But not alone," he warned. "Pretty Poppy, lovely Poppy, I can leave you now and tell Delphine to put you to bed. Shall I?"

Poppy blinked at him. He was oddly blurred, so oddly he appeared quite the most handsome, attractive man she had ever seen. A small, sharp sweetness jolted through her, and her hand snuggled into his. "Shall you what?" she murmured.

"Leave you? Or stay? That's all I've wanted from the first moment I saw you and have gone on wanting every moment of every time I've seen you since."

That seemed rather complicated when his hand was so warm around hers and his voice so caressing. When she looked at him, she remembered exactly how his lips had felt pressing down on hers, and the sweet pang inside her deepened. That pang was so demanding she could not think why he had to keep on talking about moments and time. There was only this one moment

116

stirring her whole being into a longing turmoil. If she leaned forward just a little, her lips would be quite close to his, and he could claim them again, kissing her deeply, fulfillingly, and then take her into his arms. Surely those strong arms around her would ease this strange, sweet ache that was throbbing all through her.

He muttered something and put the glasses down on the tray. Poppy smiled up at him mistily. He was quite right. They did not want more wine.

He picked her up out of the chair and carried her into the bedroom. Then he put her on the bed, and she smiled up at him, one hand on his arm, lingering, luxuriating in touching him. He smiled and picked up one small foot. His eyebrows lifted as he saw the brown walking boot, cleaned and burnished but worn down at the heel, thin in the sole, and lamentably scuffed.

"Lovely boots," Poppy purred, snuggling into the silken coverlet and soft pillows.

"I can see they've served you well," he said and deftly removed it. "We must write across the Channel and order you some others."

"Pretty others," Poppy said dreamily.

"Many pretty others." The second shoe came off. "Including satin ones such as they make only here in Paris." His fingers were quick and gentle on the buttons of her bodice. "And gowns that fit, too."

Delphine had said something like that, as if this had been planned and discussed between them. Poppy puzzled over that for an instant, but she had already realized the bank knew and arranged all things, so she shrugged the thought aside as he removed her bodice. Really, it was absurd to wear so many clothes when his hands on her flesh left tingles like the most delicate etchings of mingled fire and ice.

When they were naked on the bed together, Poppy wondered why she had not realized how perfectly her body was formed to fit against the length and strength of his. Or that his muscles could be so long and rippling where hers were covered softness. Or that his skin could be a darker, firmer texture. Or that the firelight playing over them would paint such lovely tints of rose fading into dusky shadows where their bodies met and blended. Or that, entwined together, the two of them formed one perfect whole.

Once or twice, she half pulled away from him, startled and shy. She had not expected his lips would be so all-encroaching, touching her neck, her breasts, the little hollow in the delicate swell of her belly. She had not known his strong knee would press her legs apart or that his hands would explore and pry and tease.

His lips, his hands, and the weight of his body against hers sent waves of such tumultuous sweetness through her that she could only moan and pull him back again, closer and closer, as if they could never be close enough. Then when he took her, the shock was lost in such a volcano of emotion, such waves of ecstasy, that she could only moan and cling to him, kissing him madly, begging him to continue, until a final convulsive tidal wave left her limp in his arms. This was a sweeter madness than she ever had dreamed existed, and the only thing in life worth having, she thought.

That night was a long dream in which they slept entwined, woke to make love again, and again slept in each other's arms. When at last he stirred and sat up, starting to throw back the covers, Poppy caught his arm and held up her face for more kisses.

He bent and kissed her, murmuring, even as he slipped out of bed and stood over her, "Until tonight, sweetling. Rest now. The Countess will call this afternoon. Follow her advice. This evening we'll dine here."

Poppy blinked as he picked up his clothes and went through a door she had not noticed. Then she snuggled deeper into the pillows, smiling to herself. Now she knew. Now she knew the only important thing in the world. She knew and understood everything. She understood why Daisy had been so happy in her life even if her gentlemen were sometimes dull. She even understood why the Queen was so content with Albert the Good. Smiling, she slept.

Chapter Thirteen

$\mathcal{P}$OPPY slept late and woke slowly. She stretched luxuriously, testing each arm and leg. A little stiffness, a little soreness, but some of it was still the muscle ache from the constant traveling. She ate a delicious breakfast and demanded another bath. Delphine looked horrified, but she was firm. She was not going to admit that never before in her life had she had so many baths so close together. She knew the hot water would ease her aching muscles and remove any last suspicion of gray on arms and legs. She lingered in the steaming water until Delphine held out her clothes and insisted sharply she must dress before Madame la Comtesse arrived.

The Countess was a vigorous fifty, dark and hard-faced, so elegantly groomed Poppy eyed her with greedy envy. Then she noticed that the Countess's gloves obviously had been cleaned and the velvet ribbons on her bonnet were fresher than the hat, a second or third or fourth refurbishing. She was of the new poor, then, maintaining her position by rendering services to influential people. The waiting carriage was fashionable, but the driver's livery was frayed.

Leading Poppy firmly by the arm, the Countess attacked a series of shops like a one-woman army. Poppy felt like a doll being measured and dressed, a mere object for the profusion of embellishments the Countess looted with a lavish hand. Fine kid gloves in a dozen pastel shades were chosen and sent to the carriage. The thinnest stockings in tones for day and evening were approved. A soft stole, of fur so soft and thick it made Poppy want to purr like a kitten, required a little more time and thought. A few bonnets, not important but possible, came next.

Then the Countess marched her into a lingerie shop. The English miss, she said, dark eyes daring anyone to challenge the story, was the victim of a most unfortunate yacht accident in which all her clothes had been lost. She had been forced to travel, *la pauvre petite,* in what she was wearing when rescued. She required everything. Materials were produced, fabrics so fine they could be drawn through a ring, and samples of delicate laces and ribbons. Madame la Comtesse sniffed and approved but said the garments were required immediately, tomorrow at the latest. Protests and a flurry of conferences blew up around them, but she remained an island of calm implacability. Tomorrow at the latest. A few things, a robe, some nightgowns, some petticoats and undergarments were promised finally. Poppy had a suspicion that some customer of near her size was going to be told an unforeseen emergency had delayed delivery of a promised order. The Countess marched triumphantly out of the shop, barely placated.

A few pairs of slippers were picked up in passing, and street shoes in a variety of materials were ordered. In the next shop, creams, perfumes, oils, and soaps necessitated a serious conference. A single fresh and delicate scent finally was decided on for the moment.

Poppy felt dizzy, and her feet were dragging when they returned once more to the carriage. She could think longingly only of the softness and warmth of her suite. The Countess drew herself even more upright, advanced her chin, and announced that now they would consider the robes.

"Another day," Poppy ventured to protest.

"There will be fittings," the Countess said, unmoved.

Again in a shop so elegant Poppy did not dare open her mouth, the Countess told the story of the yacht. Everyone commiserated politely. Sketches, bolts of materials, and models were shown. A charming walking costume in deepest, most brilliant blue was produced and considered. It had been ordered but not accepted, Poppy gathered through a haze of exhaustion, and possibly it could be altered quickly. At a reduced price, the Countess assented sharply. Preliminary fittings of at least three other dresses, in materials they had selected, should be possible tomorrow. Objections wilted before the Countess's dark look and set jaw. Poppy tried to murmur she would be content to rest tomorrow and the fittings could be postponed, but the Countess's icy stare froze the words before anyone else heard them.

Poppy could barely stumble into her rooms. She wanted only to crawl into bed and drop into unconsciousness until morning. Delphine removed Poppy's shoes and dress, put her in a chair in front of the fire in the bedroom, tucked a silk cover around her, and brought hot chocolate and rolls. Then she began to unpack the parcels the coachman had brought up, exclaiming, approving, or frowning as she put each thing away in the drawers and cupboards of a small adjoining dressing room. That was the door by which Dex had left this morning.

Poppy woke with a start, wondering how long she had dozed there in the chair. The curtains were drawn so it must be evening. Then she saw that Delphine had laid out a delicate but severely styled nightgown and satin robe of ice blue. The Countess must have bullied those out of the lingerie shop sometime during that flurry of conferences. A pair of yellow slippers was set out beside the robe.

"In a few days you will have all that is proper," Delphine apologized soothingly. "For this evening, better these than the blue wool." She did not quite shudder.

Poppy blinked sleepily. "This evening?"

"Monsieur de Roqueville has ordered dinner for nine."

Of course Dex had said they would have dinner here. But de Roqueville? Roqueville? Roack. In Germany and Austria, was he von Roackmann, she wondered?

121

"A small dinner," Delphine promised. "Five courses only and three wines. He has set a kitchen boy to assist me."

Suddenly Poppy felt wonderful. She jumped to her feet. "Water," she said, then laughed at Delphine's shocked face. "No, just enough for the basin."

Delphine looked relieved. "Perhaps if five courses are not enough, I could manage two soups as in England," she said as a peace offering.

"I am sure everything will be perfect." Poppy went into the dressing room and searched through the carved, gilded dressing table until she found the perfumed soap and oils. She explored the cupboards, discovered the stole, and stroked it over and over. She felt completely revived. "A lovely day," she sighed happily as Delphine poured the hot water.

She was dissatisfied with the yellow slippers after she was dressed and in the drawing room, so she went back to debate between a pair of creamy kid and one of dark blue satin with iridescent beading. Thus, she was not waiting when he arrived. She heard his voice speaking to Delphine and completely forgot what slippers she was wearing. She flew.

"Now, now," he laughed as she flung herself into his arms and lifted her face in anticipation. He kissed her long and thoroughly before he held her off at arm's length and looked critically at the ice-blue satin and shook his head. "Too cold a color, too severe tailoring, too old for you." He frowned.

"It's the most beautiful thing I ever owned," Poppy stammered.

"I understand you had to take what you could get today. By next week, you will be a lady I will be proud to show off in my carriage."

Poppy's eyes flashed purple sparks. "I am sorry I do not satisfy."

He threw back his head and guffawed. "I did not say that," he chuckled at last. "I merely suggested the garment is not perfect. A matter that can be remedied."

Poppy turned away with a swish of satin skirts and

went to sit in front of the fire, profile averted. "Won't you be seated? Would you like some wine?"

"So it's compliments you want." Still smiling, he took a chair close to her. "Delphine reports you have a skin like silk and a head like a rock. I fear she measured our wine consumption last night."

Poppy blushed. "I didn't know I was supposed to have a headache."

"You obviously have the magnificent constitution of the English," he said, eyes twinkling. "A valuable asset. I congratulate you."

Poppy was grateful Delphine came in then with a tray holding a bottle of sherry and delicate glasses. He poured, gave her a glass, then sipped appreciatively. Poppy forced herself not to gulp. She felt sick with disappointment and must not let it show. All day without letting the thought rise to the surface of her mind but keeping it comfortably just beneath the talk of silks and colors, like a warm brick hidden under the covers of a bed, she had been counting off each hour as bringing her closer to the time she would be in his arms again. Hugging that hidden anticipation had made every minute of the day brighter, every hour sweeter, even when exhausted from following the Countess from one shop to another. Yet here he was, indolently sipping sherry, obviously looking forward with mild pleasure to a good dinner, and he had been quite satisfied with those few kisses.

He must not know she was quivering inwardly, so disheartened she could have wept. That would be the ultimate humiliation, for him to know she wanted him when he did not want her. She steadied her hand and lips and searched desperately for some impersonal remark.

"Madame la Comtesse knows the shops of Paris extraordinarily well," she said and felt she sounded like a schoolgirl reciting a French exercise.

"She should. She loves them all so well she can meet her bills with them only by rendering services such as she did today."

"But she's almost shabby," Poppy burst out.

"Perhaps she takes her percentage in cash then," he shrugged.

That finished that subject. "Is it snowing again?" Poppy groped desperately.

"In many parts of the country." Amused, his eyes took on a greenish glint. "We must try to get Jack and Andy back here for the eleventh of November."

She had lost track of the date. "The eleventh of November?"

"Almost two weeks. They shouldn't miss the great performance. A would-be august personage is going to stage with great magnificence and impressive flourishes one of the most amusing farces of the century. Some say it will draw a crowd of fifty thousand."

Poppy's lips rounded. She could not imagine what he was talking about. Before she could ask, Delphine opened the doors at the far end of the room and announced dinner was served.

The stiff, shining linen, the glittering glasses, the heavy silver were fine enough to serve royalty. Dex merely nodded, as if the best were only what he expected, and seated her in a slender gilt chair. Delphine had risen to two soups, a thick and a thin, followed by salmon, a game bird, a roast with vegetables, and then an array of small cakes, cheeses, and fruits. Poppy thought of that dubious rabbit cooked over a primitive stove and tried to match his aplomb as if she often ate meals like this. Daisy often dined well in company, but family meals were plain.

They sipped wine in the drawing room, and Dex made idle comments about entertainments she might enjoy. The theater? Ballet? Concerts? He would see if anything worth an evening had escaped the censors and get tickets.

Censors and tickets. As when he had censured her conduct and arranged that railroad ticket to Cornwall. "Did you send me to Sutcliffe Manor as a carrot?" Poppy burst out.

Dex smiled. "Let's say I thought a lovely young girl

124

would not make it less attractive if a young man happened to be tempted to travel that way."

She could not help it. "You threw me at him," Poppy cried bitterly.

"An invitation he did not accept," Dex said, eyes twinkling. "As I discovered last night."

Poppy felt herself blush scarlet. "He is an English gentleman," she said stiffly.

"And I am not," Dex said.

He stood up and pulled her from the chair and into the circle of his arms. Then he took her into the bedroom. When the door closed behind them, he crushed her against him until she felt she could not breathe, kissing her, over and over, without restraint. He ripped the offending ice-blue satin robe from her, lifted her, and carried her over to the bed. Then he threw his clothing on the floor, tumbled on top of her, and removed her delicate nightgown with one savage gesture that left it in tatters.

After those leisurely too-civilized hours together, he took her as if they had been parted for years and he were unable to wait. Poppy gasped, feeling bruised and violated, as he plunged into her without preparation or gentleness. When at last he had finished and lay back on the pillows, she raised herself on one elbow and stared at him with disbelief. One minute he had been discussing the theater with delicate cynicism, and the next he had been an animal thinking only of gratification.

He turned his head lazily and put out an arm, drawing her down against his shoulder and holding her there without pressure. "You are so beautiful I lost control for a moment. Did I frighten you?"

Now again he was the warm and wonderful lover he had been last night. "You surprised me," she said slowly.

He drew one hand down her body from forehead to neck to shoulder to waist to hip. "So lovely, so perfect," he murmured. "So completely beautiful. Kiss me, sweetling, and I will not be so impatient this time."

Held close against his flat, muscular body, she felt again that sweet inward stirring. His slow, deep kisses, his hands lightly caressing her, went on and on until the sweetness deepened to a sharp, imperative demand. She drew him closer to her, pulled his head down for her fiery kisses, parted her legs, and offered herself to him. He prolonged the ecstasy until she felt that she could not endure it, that she would scream and die there in his arms. When at last it was over, she could only fall back, limp and satiated, and yet knowing that ardor still worked in her on a deeper, unsatisfied level.

"We'll sleep a little now," he murmured. "Later, sweetling, later. Again."

When he left her in the morning, she had no thought except to calculate mistily the hours that must pass before he would return to her here.

Chapter Fourteen

SHOPPING was indeed a passion with the Countess. In her still-smart carriage, she arrived every day with a list of places they must go for fittings, new necessities that must be procured, or simply places to explore to see what they offered. She fingered the elaborately decorated garters, exquisite laces, ribbons, and fine veilings, the silk flowers and gossamer fine scarves, and murmured that if one of her tickets won a golden ingot on the eleventh of November, she would have this or that. Poppy remembered then that she had heard of the lottery even in England.

To her, shopping was a pleasure but not a passion, and she insisted they finish each afternoon with a drive when the weather was fine. She had forgotten the islands of Paris, the bridges lacing the city together. She remembered the parks, and they were as charming as she recalled. She searched in vain, her memory of wide avenues and narrow streets confused, for the rooms where they had lived with Daisy. One afternoon they drove to see the building of Les Halles, great markets for the food wholesalers being erected in central Paris, the whole structure with steel girders and glass roofing copied from the Crystal Palace. Louis Napoleon was reported to be so impressed with those features that he would consider no plans for public buildings that did not utilize them.

She lived for the time when she would finally be back in her suite, selecting a dress from her crowded cupboards to wear that evening. The rose satin, the cream brocade, the green silk, or perhaps the blue with the fine embroidery. She chose a different one each evening, and all were admired.

They did not go out. The theater was so heavily censored Dex could find nothing worth an evening. He asked if she liked the pictures in the suite. When she approved enthusiastically, he lifted an eyebrow and said she would hardly enjoy the paintings of Courbet and the other realists who were exhibiting in spite of criticism.

Poppy fluttered her eyelashes at him and did not pout to be taken out. This was not like Mr. Hammett sitting at home evening after evening with Daisy. Daisy would have adored going out. For herself, the evenings and the nights in Dex's arms were all too short. Morning came too soon, for then she had to let him leave, and she could only dream of the night to come.

She arrived at the apartment one afternoon with a delicious new bonnet, row after row of delicate velvet ribbons in rose, blue, and mauve with a haze of blue veiling over it. It would be perfect with her blue walking costume with the rose velvet braid. She dropped the box with a shriek when she saw the two figures sitting one each side of the fireplace.

"Andy. Jack. Where did you come from?"

Andy flung himself across the room and wrapped himself around her. "Oh, Poppy, Poppy, you should have been with us. It was glorious. Only it did get very cold. Then they came one evening when we were tied up for the night and made us leave, with hardly a chance to say goodbye to the cap'n."

"Reportedly a family emergency," Jack drawled. "Our mother's illness was the story, I believe."

Poppy understood perfectly. Some anonymous gentleman had arrived and spirited them swiftly away and into Paris with no excess flurries to arouse comment. "I arrived after a most unfortunate accident to our yacht," she murmured.

"Most capable people," Jack agreed.

"Why are you living here?" Andy demanded. "We're

living in a wonderful hotel. Artists and sculptors and all kinds of people."

"Into which we merge inconspicuously," Jack said. "Perfect, for us. But you know, Andy, not for Poppy."

"She isn't a model or anything," Andy admitted reluctantly. "But this is so—" His forehead wrinkled and he looked around, struggling for words. "Aren't you afraid to walk on these carpets with wet feet?"

"I go out in a carriage with the Countess, and my feet don't get wet," Poppy laughed. "Didn't Delphine offer you wine? Or hot chocolate?"

"We aren't accustomed to such elegance," Jack said. One glance from his blue eyes told her he comprehended the situation perfectly. "We understood Dexter Roack would be here."

Poppy blushed and looked down. Then, looking at the clock on the mantel, she exclaimed in dismay, "Oh, it's late. I didn't know it was so late. Let Delphine give you something, anything, while I change." She scooped up the hatbox, lifted her skirts, and fled to the bedroom.

There she stood, pressing her hands to her hot cheeks. Jack's look of mingled comprehension and reproach still seemed to burn. He realized she was Dexter Roack's mistress, his kept woman, though kept in silken luxury. Then she raised her head defiantly. Did he think Dex had the same English reserve and scruples he had? Or that she would fight to the death to preserve her virtue?

Jack did not understand. She had been frightened and alone, terrified and lost, and Dex had rescued her. Though that was the least part of it. This was not a case of like mother, like daughter. She was not another Daisy, forced into this life through circumstances and making the most advantageous arrangements possible. In all honesty, only one thing mattered. She was mad about the man. She only felt alive when she was with him.

Looking back, it seemed to her this had been inevitable from the moment they met. She had resented Dex, hated him, rebelled against everything he did, was, and suggested. Yet she had been aware of him every instant

—aware as she never had been of any other man. If an extra glass of wine had not torn away the superficial vexations she had counted against him, something else would have, perhaps only a special touch of his hand or a look in his eyes or a tone in his voice. All of those could wrench her heart now and leave her weak with desire.

If Jack had an affection for her, he had let the time in the Vendée slip away without a word or gesture. So now he could hardly quarrel if she had chosen another man. Defiantly Poppy put on a dress she had not worn before, a severely plain green velvet cut so low at the neck, with only three slender bands to mask her shoulders and arms, that she had hesitated to wear it even alone with Dex. Now she put it on, to display that she was a sophisticated adult, and for the first time realized something. The dress was designed as a background and setting for jewels, magnificent jewels, and she had not even a modest string of pearls. Dex had smiled approvingly and indulgently at the boxes of extravagant luxuries that had flooded into the apartment, but he had not given her even one small jewel as a token of his affection and delight in her beauty. She lifted her bright head high and smiled defiance at her image in the mirror. She had never looked more beautiful. She would let Jack assume she chose to appear in this austere simplicity as her own conception of elegance.

Dex was in the drawing room. She had heard his voice while she dressed, but she often thought she would be aware of him by the tingling of her blood, the quickening of her pulse, even if she had no sight or sound to tell her he was near. Her body would sense and know.

When she swept in, Dex and Jack were standing by the fire, deep in conversation, and Andy was contentedly gobbling cakes and hot chocolate. Dex nodded and poured a glass of wine for her and went on talking.

"The lottery will of course put seven million francs in their pockets, above the cost of the bars that are to be the prizes," he was saying. "But Napoleon and his fellow insolvents are not content with that."

"They haven't needed to go to the California gold mines to make a fortune from them," Jack agreed. "Yet the people consider the lottery one of the most magnificent achievements of any government. Let no man call him Napoleon the Little to a hopeful ticket holder."

They were talking about the Lottery of the Golden Ingots. The Countess had explained it in breathless detail to Poppy. A one franc ticket could win one of the 214 bars of solid gold. The first prize was a 400,000 franc bar, with other lesser prizes down to 200 bars valued at 1,000 francs. Of course the government would take millions of francs of profits from the lottery. Proceeds would be used to ship 5,000 poor French citizens with useful skills to California where they were needed and could easily make a new start in a successful life. The money also was understood to be available to help the many poor in France and to replenish the empty treasury that could not even afford to support public schools. But the California feature was the popular one. Many thousands of unemployed had signed up for passage, and the newspapers gave people to understand there were still places available.

"Of course the press prints what it is told," Dex said. "And does not dare print what it knows. Places are not still available, nor are people being selected on the basis of useful skills and need."

"You must admit the idea was brilliant and the execution has been completely successful," Jack said mildly.

"More successful than the public knows. Fifteen and twenty chances on the same number have been sold. And they are not stopping there. Men who could dream up such a scheme would hardly stop short of conceiving every further opportunity to drain the last possible franc out of it. Buying crowns comes high. This will give Napoleon the money. The actual drawing will be interesting to watch. That is in the Circus on the Champs Élysées tomorrow. All Paris will be there. You must be sure to attend."

"You will be there?" Jack asked.

131

"I have arranged a place directly in front of the platform. If we do not see you there, meet us back here afterwards."

Jack nodded. "Come, Andy. We have found an excellent little restaurant near our hotel. Good conversation, too."

"One man draws only muscles, arms, legs, and backs," Andy reported. "Over and over again. With names."

"A medical illustrator," Jack explained. "Andy likes his work better than the painters'."

"There's a sculptor, too," Andy said. Eyes blazing with enthusiasm, he mimicked holding a chisel in one hand and a mallet in the other. "He has this big block of gray marble, and he goes boom, boom, boom."

"We only arrived late yesterday, and he's been in and out of every room in the place already," Jack said, smiling and shaking his head. "It was the same on the barges. He knew everybody."

Andy looked at his sister and saw her drooping mouth. "Never mind," he said and hugged her. "We'll see you again tomorrow."

Poppy only nodded. She was too disappointed to speak. Andy was her little brother, and they had been separated in desperate circumstances. She had thought they would at least have dinner together and a chance to talk of things other than politics.

After he shut the door behind them, Dex said, "The three of you together are rather conspicuous."

"But here?" Poppy protested with a gesture at this private room.

"It's best for them to appear at their meal in a usual place. You'll see them again tomorrow, here after the drawing. And I think the weather will hold fine. Besides being a Sunday. Yes, there will be a large crowd to see who wins the golden ingots."

For once he did not have to rise early the next morning to leave and remain at his business all day. Instead he stayed the night through, and they breakfasted together. Sitting at a small table Delphine had placed by a sunny window, Poppy thought he looked exactly like a large dark tomcat, sunning and grooming himself after a satisfactory night. They got dressed leisurely, and Dex approved the new bonnet to be worn with the blue walking costume and the fur stole.

The day was sunny but cold. They rode in Dex's carriage, and when his carriage could take them no further, they walked with her hand tucked under his elbow. Looking around, Poppy saw dozens of couples like themselves, prosperous top-hatted men with a look of relaxed serenity and pretty, dimpled women clinging demurely to their arms, languidly dependent. So many couples, so many nights of love, here in this teeming crowd of tens of thousands, all determined to see the fabulous drawing of the golden bars.

Dex found his spot close below the platform. "Observe this," he said almost soundlessly. "Watch every move and see if you can tell me where the trickery lies."

"But why do they need trickery?" Poppy whispered back. "You explained they've made extra fortunes anyhow."

He pressed her gloved hand between his arm and side. "Watch closely."

The huge platform held seven wire cages. Six of them contained balls numbered zero to nine. The other, the one indicating millions, had seven balls numbered zero to six. Government officials examined the numbered balls, one by one, then each cage and the connecting rods. Poppy hardly heard the lengthy speeches, puzzling over what could be wrong when everything had been examined so publicly. Then the cages were spun. When they stopped, a young boy stationed behind each cage drew a number. Those together won the first prize. For each new spin, either the boys changed places, or new boys replaced them. With everything so public, nothing could be wrong.

Poppy looked up at Dex, shaking her head as the final numbers were drawn. "The drawing was completely honest."

133

"Of course," Dex smiled. "Shall we try to ease through the crowd and get back to our carriage?"

Poppy nodded, then stiffened, her hand clawing at Dex's coat. She stared, blinked as her stare was met by one that darted from her to Dex and back again, and then stared again and could not be sure.

"What is it?" Dex asked in an almost soundless whisper.

"There on the platform, I thought—no—maybe I'm wrong. But just for a minute, I thought I saw—impossible, of course."

"Don't babble, sweetling. Saw who?"

"The Viscount who attacked me in London. Something about the profile, those darting eyes, that nose, you know. Like a parrot. Or something."

"I know."

"I'm always thinking I see him. Outside Les Sables. Or maybe, the man on the platform was not the Viscount. That's the one from the inn. He was staring at us both. Outside Les Sables—"

Dex's hand on her shoulder stopped the words. "Not here. Don't mention the place. You thought you saw him there? And here? And he saw you?"

"Both. And I thought he recognized you. But maybe it wasn't the same man at all."

"Perhaps. The family is large, and the resemblances are strong. We'll talk of this later in private. Come."

Poppy had no breath to talk. The crush of people around them, trying to leave now the great show was over, literally squeezed the breath out of her and nearly swept her from her feet. Except that she could cling to Dex who forged forward with slow, inevitable strength, she thought she might have fallen and been crushed and trampled. When they reached the carriage, her skirt hem was ripped and dust-spotted, and her bonnet dangled by its strings down her back. Dex helped her into the carriage and when they arrived at the rooms, half carried her to a chair in front of the fireplace and removed her fur.

"Wine," he said, pouring from the tray waiting for

them. "One glass only. Remember we have guests arriving, and you become somewhat impetuous after the third glass."

Poppy sipped and managed to smile up at him. "I didn't think you objected. But what was the trick in the drawing? There was none."

"Not in the drawing. The damage was done before that and with a trick so simple no one would dare to try it at the smallest country fair," Dex chuckled. "I think it was the second wheel. One of the examining officials had a ball in his hand, and when he picked up the balls to look at them, he switched them so there were two of one number and one number was missing completely. That way, the numbers of the false tickets were not included at all. Oh, the mathematical possibilities, the beautiful mathematical possibilities. And they say we bankers can calculate odds. We're purest innocents, not in the same class as our Napoleon and his crowd."

"But why?"

"No bank would finance him. Buying thrones costs money. I've a private wager or two, for amusement only, that it will take less than a month now for him to become Emperor."

"I don't know why I'm surprised," Poppy said, quietly refilling her glass. "He's tried every other trick to get the throne."

Dex quietly removed the bottle. "That one glass and no more until our guests arrive, sweetling. We have too many important things to discuss. You say monsieur, call him Monsieur the Parrot, saw you outside Les Sables d'Olonne. When and where? You alone? Or all three of you?"

Poppy shivered in spite of the bright fire and the wine in her hand. "We went first, to get out of town quickly and quietly, to an inn on the coast highway. I waited in the dining room for Jack and Andy—Andy had twisted his wrist—and I thought I heard something, no, I felt somebody was watching me, so I went and opened a door. He hurried away down a hall, but I saw his profile as he went around a corner."

"Then he was staying there and knew when you arrived and when you left. And knew, very shortly, why you had been there. The family are hangers-on at the Austrian court, a highly political spot, and the priest was a political agitator. Napoleon has just bought himself an emperor's crown and is close to the Austrians. He will wish to please them."

"The Parrot is Austrian?" She had a vague memory the Viscount had mentioned Vienna. "The family?"

"Yes. Our bank, too, has always been close to the Austrian crown, but these days they have too many archdukes, all tremendously royal, and not enough thrones for them. That man has Napoleon's ear, and if he saw you near Les Sables and with me today, this changes everything. We must move quickly."

"What do you mean?"

"As George Sand wrote"—Dex stared into the fire and seemed to quote—" 'In the provinces you have only to be a republican to be branded a communist; and if by chance you are a socialist republican, ha! then you are believed to drink human blood, to be a slayer of little children, a wife-beater, a bankrupt, a drunkard, a thief, and you risk being knocked in the head in the woods by a ploughboy indoctrinated by his master or the parish priest.' "

"But I don't know anything about French politics."

"I speak of the mood of the provinces. Even George Sand was frightened, and she had not killed a so-called priest. Napoleon could gain high favor and support in more than one place by arresting you and throwing you to the wolves. Believe me, they would tear you to pieces. There's only one thing to do. We've got to get all three of you out of the country fast."

Chapter Fifteen

THEY had dined well and then gone into the drawing room where they could talk privately. Jack, for he explained sailors had to know how to calculate, seemed to understand Dex's explanation of the juggling of the lottery balls and spent some time laughing and estimating in wry admiration how tremendous the profits would be.

"Enough to buy a throne," Dex agreed. "Especially when bankers have not been accommodating."

"So you are not in good favor?" Jack asked.

"We are never without influence," Dex said. "Enough for our needs. Not enough to quell an outburst of indignation from the provinces. Poppy tells me she was seen at the inn outside Les Sables d'Olonne and again today with me and recognized. By a person well known to our soon-to-be Emperor. And Napoleon will coddle the provinces until he is on the throne. He would happily gain their good will and votes by throwing them a bone. Or a body."

"Don't frighten Poppy," Jack growled.

"I have already explained this to her, quite bluntly."

Jack leaned forward, white under his deep bronze. "She must leave for England tonight."

"Not necessarily." Dex rolled his wine glass between his fingers and admired the color of the wine reflecting the flames from the fire. "I agree you must all leave soon."

"Jack's an heir," Andy piped up. "He can have a new *Corn Dolly* twenty times as big as the old one."

"Just one of Her Majesty's vessels will make an agreeable fit," Jack drawled.

"Is that what I am to tell your father?" Dex asked.

"Tell him I am making my way home, though not by the most direct route."

Dex nodded. "He'll settle for that. Now for Andy and Poppy."

For the first time Poppy really understood he was sending her away. Still, he was often in London. Perhaps there, too, he had a luxurious suite, though she could not ask in front of Andy and Jack. Since she was not sure how much of this situation Andy comprehended, she murmured, "There's always Pallminster Lane."

"Our man who took over my duties there sent me word of Daisy last week," Dex said.

"Your duties there?" Poppy questioned sharply.

"I expect to be occupied abroad for a considerable time," Dex said.

"Is Mr. Hammett still there?" Andy asked forlornly.

"I understand Daisy got into her high ropes when you two disappeared from Cornwall and was quite inconsolable for days." Dex gave a small chuckle. "Mr. Hammett said he liked a peaceful home, and Daisy said she could not like a man who did not appreciate a wholesome family atmosphere. Without children, a home was a stale and weary desert."

"She *was* in her high ropes," Andy said, awed.

"She blamed Mr. Hammett because we were sent away?" Poppy said. "Not you?"

"Not according to our man in the bank who was present when Mr. Hammett made a settlement to Daisy's account. Of a size to compensate for her great loss. They seem to have stated their differences to him with great frankness. Both speaking at once, I understand. With some warmth."

"Then Daisy is arranged in perfect satisfaction again," Poppy said.

"Daisy is considering a change in her condition in life."

"She's too old to have babies," Andy blurted out and then went a miserable red with embarrassment.

"Not too old to marry," Dex said.

"Marry?" Poppy cried.

"A titled gentleman. Rather a small title, a baronet, but still a title. Accompanied by a small, neat fortune, I believe."

"Daisy married?" Poppy could not picture it. "Married?"

"I'm told he has a small, pleasant place in the country and a smart little town house. Of course at seventy-odd, he is not overset in his emotions."

"He's marrying a nurse," Poppy exploded. "He knows Daisy is sweet and kind and as good as a tonic herself when anyone's sick. He's an old man who wants a nurse."

"Who in return will be his comfortably warm widow."

"Is Daisy going to marry him?" Andy demanded.

"She is wearing a handsome diamond brooch, though not a ring as yet," Dex said. "She seemed somewhat unsettled in her mind."

"Oh, no," Poppy whispered. Daisy unsettled in her mind was a Daisy capable of anything. "Oh, no."

"I understand her only conversation of late concerns the many happinesses for a woman in the blessed state of matrimony." Dex's eyes had a greenish glint of amusement. "I'm sure she would want all the blessings for her daughter."

Enraged, Poppy glared back at him. "She'd marry me off to the first man who offered. A lady of title can't have two illegitimate children at her wedding. Or in her house."

"She'd send me away to school," Andy wailed.

"No." Poppy jumped to her feet. "If we can be traced here, we'll leave. Now. Tonight."

"There is another choice. And nothing need be decided tonight. I am sure more important things are being discussed tonight by Napoleon than a certain red-headed fugitive from the Vendée."

"What is the other choice?" Jack asked.

"I do not recommend it. I mention it." Dex picked up Poppy's glass from the tray, refilled it, and handed it to her. "Jack? Give me your glass. What is your opinion of this commendable effort to send fine craftsmen to California to make a new start, using the proceeds of the lottery?"

Jack looked puzzled. "I thought you'd had reports. At the café, all the talk is that they're taking the sweepings off the streets and scum from the jails. Along with certain people who were not aware they had signed up for the immigration and many who are not even needy but who have been heard to refer too often to Napoleon the Little."

"So no one questions too closely the exact identity of the passengers," Dex said, apparently lost in admiration of the color of his wine. "Many people from many places. Mmm."

"I'm sure you know all this and more," Jack objected.

Dex nodded and sipped thoughtfully. Then Poppy understood. This was his solution to sending her away. No, he *had* to send her away, get her out of France to save her life. He was suggesting nothing. He was giving her a choice.

She could go back to London and Daisy and any hasty marriage that could be arranged with any man willing to take a beauty of dubious heritage. She could go to California, wild, wealthy, and unknown. But she would be herself. She would be free. They said a man or a woman could make his own destiny there. And women were scarce and valued.

Andy? She looked at him. He would hate an English school where his life would be made miserable once his illegitimacy was known, as it would become known. He was a likable young scamp, quick-witted, quick on his feet, and she had a feeling likable scamps did well in California.

As if her heart were not breaking, though she could feel the hard, bursting pain in her middle and had to force her voice to an unnatural high clarity over the lump in her throat, she said, "Then it would be possible for Andy and me to get passage to California?"

"What?" Andy whooped. "California? Gold? Indians?"

"Easily," Dex said. "For you two."

"Not for me, of course," Jack agreed.

That night Poppy did not think she could endure the touch of a man who could so coldbloodedly send her away half around the world. She hardly spoke as Delphine helped her out of her handsome dress while Dex lingered in the drawing room talking to Jack. She dared not speak or say anything of what was raging in her heart. If she did, she would burst out with wild, screaming recriminations that could only make her burn with humiliation later. Of course Dex would not marry her. He had never intended marriage. She was Daisy's daughter. That he *could* marry her, she did not doubt. He had the power and wealth to dare even that. He *would not* marry her.

She was stiff and tense in the bed when he came into the room. She did not speak. He undressed silently, but when he was beside her, his strong arm drawing her against his bare shoulder, his long, demanding leg over her, she turned to him with a half sob and lifted her face. She opened her mouth to his and kissed him wildly and passionately. If she had only this night, she would take it. She would take as much as he could give and only wish for more.

He left while she was still asleep, and she woke to tell herself she might never see him again. The Countess arrived as usual. When Poppy tried to plead a headache, the Countess said emphatically that Monsieur de Roqueville had sent her a message that he was most displeased they had not yet procured a street coat of fine wool when so cold a winter was predicted. It must be ordered immediately. Poppy understood. The sea trip to California would be long, stormy, and cold. She put on a mantelet and bonnet at once, and they went out.

While the Countess fingered materials and haggled,

Poppy quietly selected a severe and simple cut she thought would be proper for an anonymous lady on shipboard. So many people connected with the bank became anonymous, she thought drearily. Her headache had become a reality, and she made a small scene of her own to arrange a fitting for the next day.

But it was not until the fourth evening that Dex said, "The coat is ready?"

"Tomorrow."

"Good. I will see it is delivered in the morning. I will put you and Andy on the train in the afternoon. With a suitable escort."

Poppy could not speak. She simply bowed her head and nodded.

"Delphine is packing your clothes. You will find your tickets, identification, and cash for your trip in your muff."

Words would not come. Until now, like a dazed aristocrat mounting the cart to go to the guillotine, she had not actually believed he would send her away. No, she was not being sent like an aristocrat. More like a heap of old clothes bundled up and shipped off to a needy family, she thought bitterly.

"I have done my best to get you proper accommodations," Dex said. "I hope you and Andy will have a small cabin to yourselves. At least you will not have to travel in the hold with a hundred others."

"Or two or three hundred?" Poppy guessed.

Dex's mouth tightened. "An escort all the way was impossible. Several things were—impossible."

Poppy sat quietly, face averted. She dared not speak. She must not cry out. She must not throw herself into his arms, weeping, or ask if she would ever see him again. If she had any pride and self-respect at all, she must not. She would not even ask if his bank had a branch in California and if she would somehow, someday, hear of him. She might be Daisy's daughter, she might have lived with him and loved him like a wanton, but above all she would not ask if he could send her

142

away to strange and savage shores with nothing but a handsome wardrobe of clothes that could be used to set her up in only one profession.

As if he had read her mind, Dex said, "I understand the ladies of San Francisco order their dresses from the best Paris houses by the fastest possible ships. They are said to be the most expensively dressed women in the world. So your afternoons with the Countess will prove to have been well spent. Take good care of your wardrobe."

The bitter words escaped Poppy's lips before she could stop them. "As if they were my dowry."

"Exactly." Dex was grinning high approval. "You understand that the passengers will be a mixed lot. No matter what your feelings for them, I would advise great caution. With everyone."

"I was not reared in London for nothing," Poppy said scornfully. "I won't present some lady with my fine fur in gratitude for her friendly words."

"Precisely. Not forgetting there will be a variety of gentlemen on board, too. All bound to admire you. It's a long and monotonous trip."

Poppy could have spat that her conduct after she left this apartment was no concern of his, but she only said curtly, "The Countess was much amazed, but I have procured a variety of reading and even some needlework."

"You will be the wonder of all aboard," Dex laughed. "You must thank Delphine prettily when you leave. She has worked very hard."

"I'm sure she packs beautifully," Poppy said stiffly. She had a headache again. "Will the trunks be in our cabin?"

"I hope so. When you arrive, investigate carefully the weights in the hems of your skirts and jackets. I inspected Delphine's work myself and you cannot tell the stitches from the original seamstress's work." Then gently, "Gold napoleons are acceptable anywhere in the world."

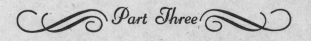

Part Three

On Board the Bonne Irène
November 1851 - March 1852

Chapter Sixteen

$\mathcal{P}$OPPY knew she was dying. The groans and creaks of the straining ship thudded in her pounding head and drowned out her low moans. The sour reek of decay and mold stifled her. Darkness was all around her. She lay in the lower bed of the narrow, heaving bunk, well strapped down so she would not be thrown out against the sharp edges of the trunks that crowded the minute space nor tossed against the upper bunk, and planned her funeral.

She would have a large coffin of dark, polished wood with brass fittings shining like gold. The lining would be a froth of purest white, row after row of delicate lace. In it, she would look tiny and fragile, like a French wax doll. Her lashes would lie like dark fans on her pallid cheeks, and her hair would spread out in gleaming tendrils and curls. She thought she would wear pale blue, a drift of sheer silk, so she would appear to be floating in a pale sky, with more fine white lace at her throat and wrists. Her hands would be folded around a small white satin prayer book with a nosegay of baby pink roses. Or perhaps one perfect half-blown rose, pale on the outer petals but glowing deep ruby at the heart, would be more dramatic. Poppy brushed that detail aside. She would settle it later.

Everybody would gather around, weeping into sodden handkerchiefs and looking absolutely horrid with their faces swollen and reddened with tears. No, they would be veiled. Except when they threw back their veils to bend and give her one last, long kiss. Andy would be gulping, voiceless, throat too swollen for speech, but inwardly he would be vowing to live up to all she had hoped for him and to study his lessons at least three hours every night and never, never to think of threatening anyone with fire. Daisy would be whispering she must never think of marriage or any pleasure again but devote her life as a memorial to her beautiful lost child and keep the cottage in Pallminster Lane as a shrine to the things she had left behind. Dex would be standing with bowed head, a broken man, knowing his real life was ended and, while his gray wisp of body might go on making the gestures of living, all that mattered in his life was finished. Especially women. Never again could he hold any woman in his arms, for the lovely frail ghost of the beautiful young woman there in the coffin would always stand between him and all others.

The whole scene was so beautiful that Poppy sobbed aloud, and two hot tears rolled down her cheeks.

"Poppy, do you want to come to the funeral?"

"What?" Poppy sat up and banged her head against the bunk above. "Ooh. What funeral?"

"The man that fell between decks." Andy peered through the door of the darkened cabin. "They've got him sewed up in canvas with lead at his feet and laid out on a grating. They're going to read something and tip him over any minute now. Come on. Everybody's there."

Poppy fell back and moaned. "Go away. I'm dying."

"Don't worry, you won't," Andy sang out cheerfully and slammed the door.

Her beautiful funeral vanished. If she did die, she would be sewed up in canvas with lead at her feet and tossed overboard, thrown away like garbage, into all that horrible cold, gray, seething water. Probably not a soul would ever know what had happened to her or care if they did hear. Daisy would marry and be a titled lady. Maybe occasionally, between entertaining at the hunt in the country and giving great balls at their town house, she would remember she once had had a child.

Or was it children? So difficult to recall, when one was so pleasantly occupied. Dex was probably right this minute dining elegantly with some beautiful woman, glittering with diamonds and magnificently dressed, in a luxurious palace. Poppy could see it, vivid as life. The room was paneled in red brocade and lit by crystal chandeliers, and the table service was gold. It was not one woman, it was a great dinner with dozens of beautiful women, all vying for his attention. He was only wondering which one he should make love to first.

That did it. She was not going to die. She was going to live and go back and tell everybody, especially other women, exactly what kind of brute beast Dex was. Because she knew. The world was full of whole, solid countries, and they could be reached by roads over land, and she would have been perfectly safe from Louis Napoleon's police in any of them. She could have lived in one of those beautiful, stationary places, a lovely place weighed down by heavy rocks and mountains, with only a few tiny lakes, and close to France. Dex traveled so much, he could have visited her often and stayed for days and weeks even.

Maybe he already had suites in Germany, Spain, and Italy, as he did in London and Paris, places he could have sent her with no trouble. But when she was too frightened to ask questions or make suggestions, did Dex mention that? He did not. Because she was trusting and believed in him, she had let him make all the arrangements, and he had condemned her to this torture in a dark cell that heaved and jolted until it was due to a miracle, and her own brave heart, that it was not going to be the death of her. He had shipped her off, so far away he would never have to see, hear, or be bothered by her again, exiled her to the farthest ends of the earth.

Now she knew. Dex had taken a dislike to her, he despised her because she had been an innocent and foolish child and shown too clearly how much she loved him. She had begun to bore him. That was it. He was tired of her. So he had thrown her away, without a qualm for every mile and minute of this torture he must have known she would suffer, just as that poor body on deck was being thrown into the pitiless sea. He was a beast, a barbaric, torturing beast without a heart, careless of everything except his own desires of the moment and wanting only to be free when the desire passed.

He thought he had got free of her, but he would never be free. This stinking cockroach-ridden floating coffin would reach solid land sometime. Certainly it would. It was going to reach San Francisco if she had to go out on deck herself and keep all sails rigged, or whatever made sails keep pulling the ship along. She was going to live, and Dex was going to regret his cruelty all his life.

She tried to sit up but doubled over, her head whirling and her stomach convulsing. She strained and retched violently but nothing came up. Nothing could. There was nothing left and had not been for days.

The door slammed open again. "Poppy, get up. Jack says you've got to get up."

A taller figure loomed in the doorway, went to the hanging lamp, pulled it down, made it bloom with yellow light, and raised it again. "There. Hook the door open, Andy. I know it's cold and wet, but she'll never recover without fresh air."

"Jack?" Poppy whispered, not believing her eyes and ears. "Jack. How did you get here?"

"Usual way. Walked up the gangplank," Jack grinned. "I couldn't let my little brother and sister sail without me, could I? For once, Dex didn't watch a mouse hole close enough."

Poppy clamped both hands to her reeling head. "How?"

"Once I knew when Andy was leaving, it was easy enough to find out which ship was sailing for California with a load of Ingots and sign on. I made able seaman, and there are three full captains in the forecastle signed on the same."

"They'll all jump ship when they get to San Fran-
150

cisco," Andy explained gleefully. "Going to the gold fields. You never saw anything like it. The crew's all wild to get there, and most of the passengers never wanted to leave France."

"I'm in the best company on the ship down in the forecastle," Jack said. "I've never seen harder cases than this ship's captain and the four mates."

"They need to be, to handle that crowd in steerage," Andy said.

"The scum and scourings of the Paris jails and gutters," Jack admitted. "Except for a few distinguished malcontents Louis Napoleon had picked up and put aboard. For once, it's the passengers, not the crew, that got shanghaied. So our Napoleon the Little was holding a lottery to raise money to send the finest artisans to make a new start in the land of gold? That was as good as most of his promises, good to earn him gold to land him on a throne where he can loot a country."

"You should hear The Prof talk," Andy reported with awe. "He says a man who would live off an English whore—"

"Not now," Jack said hastily. "Pull back that curtain, Andy. I want you to know, dear sister, that you have fine accommodations on the poop deck. Let's see what you've got here in the way of cabin stores."

"Cabin stores?"

"Private food supplies," Jack explained, looking at the stacked trunks and boxes that crowded the tiny cabin. "Everybody brings as much as they can."

Andy hopped from foot to foot. "Let's hope we have some. Gramps wouldn't give his pigs what the steerage passengers are getting. Mostly it's what they call sea pie made out of scraps, salt beef, and vegetables boiled and then boiled some more with a suet crust on top." He clasped both hands around his throat and stuck out his tongue. "Later they say there won't be any potatoes or beans, just hardtack and salt beef." He choked and gagged loudly.

"Stop," Poppy moaned, and then remembered she was going to live. "Maybe a cup of tea."

"Tea and some food," Jack said. "What's in this tin box?"

"You've got to eat," Andy said solemnly. "That's the way seasickness kills, if you keep heaving up after you're empty until you start straining up your innards. The way you're going, next it will be your gizzard. Then your stomach insides and then—"

"Andy," Poppy shrieked.

"Be genteel, horrid boy, and say her heart could get overstrained," Jack murmured, then grunted as he pulled a tin box out from under a trunk. "Now let's see. No. You'll want this for the voyage all right. But it's not food."

"Aren't we cabin passengers?" Poppy whispered. "Aren't we supposed to be well fed?"

"On this old hulk they dragged out of the mud?" Jack scoffed. "What kind of fares do you think Louis Napoleon paid for his Ingots? Convict rate."

"But Dex—" Poppy began, then remembered and snapped her lips tight.

"Dex did the best he could. He had to get you out of the country by the shortest, fastest route, and that meant a ship. And a ship where no questions were being asked. I told you this is on the poop deck." He saw her puzzled look. "On the deck, so you have a window on the deck as well as a door to the corridor. You'll understand when you see the cabins below decks. Half this size and no air or light."

"This isn't so bad," Andy admitted, his blue eyes worried. "Honest, Poppy, it could be worse, even the food. They've got pigs, cows, geese, chickens, and even turkeys, all penned on deck aft."

"A cargo of pigs?" Poppy whispered.

Andy danced with impatience. "For eating, Poppy, for eating. Only they can't carry enough to last. Animals or vegetables or eggs or anything else."

"There's enough food of a sort, and the Captain's putting in at Rio for fresh supplies," Jack said, opening another tin box and pushing it aside, then reaching for a third. He flung up the lid. "Square on the target at last, and high time. Andy, did Chips introduce you to Cook? The Captain's cook?"

"Chips?" Poppy asked.

"The ship's carpenter. He can always use an extra hand, and I've always noticed our midshipmen, boys sometimes no older than Andy, seem to enjoy their lessons with the ship's Chips. I took Andy around to him. He's all right. He's not one of the officers."

"He's teaching me to plait sennit," Andy boasted.

"French style and that's not the same as English," Jack said absently, searching the box. "Here, take this teapot, wash it, and have it filled with boiling water. Ask Cook if he has some arrowroot, and if he has, bring a cupful of that, too."

Andy scampered off, and Jack straightened, just as a bell sounded through the ship. With the door open, Poppy could hear a constant hum, a mingling of many sounds: the hiss of water along the ship's timbers; the creak of the rigging and the whine of the wind through it; the pounding of feet on the deck; the chatter of women's voices nearby, and men's voices calling in the distance; and even more faintly, the sound of a violin playing.

"Next bell, I've got to go on watch," Jack said. "They ring every half hour. You'll get used to it. Now here's a cup and saucer to drink your tea. What's this?" he asked, opening another tin. "Good, very good. Spice nuts. Hard spice cookies, shaped like nuts and just as tough. Good for an upset stomach. Soak them in the tea and see if you can keep a few of them down. The arrowroot should help if Andy gets it. Here's brandy, too. If you keep the other down, try some brandy in half an hour and see if you can get on your feet. Don't try to go on deck, but leave your door open. There now. I've got to go." At the door, he turned. "Don't waste your stores on Andy. He's cadging from the Captain's cook, and that's the best on board."

"Wait," Poppy wailed. "Wait."

"Later. Later."

"How long?" Poppy called after his retreating back. "How long to San Francisco?"

Jack called back over his shoulder, and Poppy collapsed against the hard, lumpy pillow. She could not have heard right. Jack could not have said three or four months. Four days had nearly killed her, and nobody could survive four months of this kind of life.

New darkness against her closed eyes made her look up. A large black body blocked the doorway, and above it a dead-white, square face with a red slash of mouth and two hard black eyes peered from under a black fringe topped by a satin hat. Poppy cringed back instinctively.

"I have looked in to see if you are feeling better," the woman said in surprisingly good English but with a strong provincial French accent.

"A little, thank you."

"Madame misses her girls," a man's voice murmured insinuatingly, and a black broadcloth shoulder edged the woman aside. The man's face was lined and sallow, with a thin auburn mustache lighter than his carefully combed hair. His eyes were as expressionless as silver coins. "We've all hoped to see you on deck soon."

"I am Madame de Ceyenne," the woman said with a sting in her socially sweet tones. "You must come sit with me in the sun when you are better." And she drew away with a swish of heavy satin skirts.

The man leaned against the door in the full light of the lamp. The minute Poppy saw his immaculate grooming and the long slender white fingers lifted to his thin mustache, she recognized what he was. The marks of a professional gambler were international and unmistakable.

"Maurice Santerre," he introduced himself. His English, too, was excellent. "I understand you travel with your two brothers?"

"Yes."

"Good. Madame de Ceyenne saw you come aboard and has inquired about you repeatedly. She is accustomed to the company of pretty girls, and hers are otherwise occupied these days."

Poppy's hands flew to her matted, tangled hair and brushed futilely at her crumpled bed wrap.

"You will look better when you feel better," Maurice said consolingly and eased away from the door. "Au revoir, Mademoiselle."

Poppy stared at the empty doorway. Santerre, without land. That was a made-up name if ever she heard one, the name of a man going to a new place for a fresh start. But he had not been in search of a flirt. Such men found women easily and only cards engrossing.

He had been telling her something, trying to warn her. He had been warning her against Madame de Ceyenne. And those remarks about pretty girls? Madame could be quite literally a madam, on board with some of her girls. But Maurice had reminded her—and she was certain every word of that conversation had been calculated—she was not alone. She had two brothers to protect her.

She always had liked gamblers, Poppy reminded herself, and wondered where her hairbrush was. Andy must look for it and a pretty shawl the minute he returned.

Chapter Seventeen

A westerly breeze held steady, and a pale sun came out. Poppy revived and began to eat.

Andy brought food from the Captain's galley—chicken soup, hard-boiled eggs, hard rolls, cheese. In her own cabin stores, Poppy found hard candies, apples, and dried fruits. The nuts, chocolates, candied ginger, and rich cakes she put back for the future.

She investigated the other tin boxes. One held books she'd bought in Paris, novels by Mr. Dickens, Mr. Trollope, and Mr. Dumas, and two French fashion books. On the bottom were hidden a Spanish grammar, three books of Spanish fairy tales, and lined paper and pencils. Poppy puzzled over the Spanish books. She had thought California was a part of the United States, and Americans spoke English, or almost English, no worse than many Scots.

A wooden box of pastels and sticks of charcoal and a pad of drawing paper filled the top of the next box. Andy might have picked up a fancy for such things in Paris. She put them aside for him. Under them was a pretty little sewing box of gold-embossed white kid, lined with gold satin and fitted with dainty scissors, needles, and thread. She pounced with delight on two decks of cards, and laughed when she saw a bride's book of household hints and cooking instructions. Delphine had selected and packed this box. But did Delphine actually expect her to use that roll of heavy Irish linen and the bright silk threads for embroidery, or the knitting needles and skeins of fine cream wool?

Andy reported the men had rigged up a canvas screen behind which they could freshen themselves with salt water. He brought her a pail of hot, fresh water and warned her Cook would heat no larger amount. When she was clean and dressed for the first time, Poppy looked in her mirror and winced. Her face was pale and drawn, with dark shadows under her eyes, and her hair hung limp. Probably it was for the best, Poppy decided dolefully. Any man on this ship could only be trouble, a fugitive from the law or his own past.

"Dining hall?" Andy snorted when she asked. "Below decks, amidships, there's a long corridor that the inside cabins open onto. For eating, there are rough planks set on saw horses all along that corridor, and it's so narrow the people can barely squeeze in and out of their doors. The second cook—the officers have their own and there's two more for steerage and the crew—slides the plates out of the galley and along the table, and everybody grabs."

"For the cabin passengers?" Poppy gasped.

"You don't think this Captain wasted any space he could sell? I'll fill our plates and bring them up here."

"Isn't there a saloon?"

"That's rigged up as a men's dormitory."

"Could we eat on deck in nice weather?"

"You were sick too long. The deck chairs were grabbed the first day. Maurice took the space aft of the poop deck for the card players. Then everybody started fighting for the other good spots." Andy laughed and capered. "I mean really fighting with fists, knock-down fights. I saw one."

Poppy had been watching out the window. "Then I'll just go out and walk around and around, on days when it isn't so rough."

"Madame Ceyenne found herself a nice spot in the lee of that forward hatchway. It's out of the wind and sunny all during the middle of the day. She's got a couple of boxes, and she said to tell you that you're welcome to join her there when you feel well enough to come on deck."

157

"You must thank her for me," Poppy said stiffly.

But she was disconcerted. She could not spend all her time in the tiny, stifling cabin. Yet peering from behind the window curtain, she had noticed each lady promenaded with a gentleman. She had counted over a dozen ladies, all as elegantly dressed as if for the street. The other gentlemen strolled in twos and threes and looked at the ladies. Alone, she would be intolerably conspicuous.

When Jack dropped in later, Poppy indignantly reported Madame's offer. Jack surprised her.

"You've got to have some fresh air. Madame makes no bones about what she is, but she's turned her girls loose for the trip. Loose and ready, they're acting."

"Naturally," Poppy sniffed.

Jack chuckled. "Cooped up here, you haven't had a good look at our respectable matrons and young ladies. Every day they're rolling their eyes a little wilder and flirting their skirts a little more. They're betting in the forecastle that before we reach the equator, there won't be one that hasn't kicked up her heels and landed in some gentleman's stall."

"Jack," Poppy gasped.

"It's the truth. Long voyages do something to the ladies. The female constitution isn't suited for it."

Poppy stamped her foot. "No human constitution is suited for living in a fish bowl. I suppose the men are patterns of respectability?"

"They take more to drink and fighting," Jack admitted. "Fortunately nobody could bring much liquor aboard, and it's almost gone."

"Then I suppose it will be all right for me to walk around by myself?" Poppy suggested.

"The gentlemen would take it that you're showing you're up and available."

"Like a street girl?" Poppy gasped.

"This is a long voyage," Jack said. "Now Madame's fixed herself up a cozy spot. I don't know a better one. Join her and thank her for it. Her profession's not contagious, and no gentleman's going to try to pluck you out from under her wing."

"I think you're moonstruck."

"Get out of this dark hole, and you'll see what I mean. And don't forget it could be a month yet before we even reach the equator. Meanwhile, all the ladies and gentlemen will be jockeying for places at the starting gate, trying to find partners for the race, so to speak, and alone you'll be, right in the middle of the jostling."

"You are both rude and vulgar," Poppy said crushingly.

"Beneath contempt," Jack agreed laughing, then left.

Poppy spent the next two days watching from behind her curtain. She began to recognize the different faces, and the ladies did seem to change partners from day to day. Skittish was the only word for the way they were acting. The gentlemen had an expression she recognized, too. She had seen it in London, on gentlemen walking along a street and openly looking at the strolling girls, eyeing them up and down, to decide which one they were going to offer an arm to.

She could see that if she walked out there alone, it would be taken as an invitation. Impossible. And Jack had said a month to the equator. Poppy looked around the dark, cramped cabin and groaned.

She was not going to admit she had only the vaguest idea what the equator was and had thought it was somewhere near the Arctic. Geography always had seemed to her the most useless subject, coloring one part of a map blue and another part pink, with a sharp line between them. Anybody with sense knew you could walk right over the spot where that line was supposed to be without seeing a thing. The country on either side was exactly the same, and neither pink nor blue.

Jack came in the next morning limping a little, with a bruise high on his cheek. "Fight down in steerage. The garbage of Paris."

"Was anybody hurt?"

"Two killed. We buried them at sunrise. But I think

we've got most of the knives now. It's hard on the few decent types who got thrown in with the scum. Like the old boy Andy likes so much, even if he did want to teach him Latin. The one he calls The Prof. The poor old guy wanted to swap lessons for some food that isn't pig swill."

"What we get is bad enough."

"It'll get worse," Jack promised, grinning. "So far, we've got some fresh meat and vegetables left. Been on deck yet?"

"No. But I've got to get out of here."

"Right. I put an extra box for you in Madame's corner, and she says to bring your knitting."

"I don't knit."

"Take it anyway," Jack said, digging into a tin box and pulling out needles and wool. "Makes you look respectable, besides being useful for poking the gentlemen if they try to annoy you."

Poppy tied a scarf around her head. She had decided it was less becoming than a bonnet and more practical. Then she put on her dark heavy coat.

Jack approved. "A very model of respectability. Not that Madame's recruiting."

Madame, too, was plainly dressed. Her sensible, well-polished black shoes rested firmly on the deck, her plain black hat was secured by four jet pins. Under her loose black coat, her black satin dress rose in a high collar to her square chin. It was fitted tightly at the wrist and swept the deck with the most modest of circles.

Madame was shocked that Poppy did not knit. She promptly cast on stitches for a plain scarf, put the needles in Poppy's hands, and insisted she work with them.

Madame was frank about her life. She had had a nice house and a good class of trade in Amiens, but a couple of her girls had got in a little trouble, and she had thought it best to make a change. She did not have the money to set up in Paris. The thought of the competition there made Madame click her tongue like castanets. To set up one girl alone in Paris, in a proper apart-

ment with just the barely necessary clothes, cost a
fortune. She wanted to keep five of her best girls—good
girls all, and she understood their little ways and how
to keep them happy—and it had seemed best to make
her change to California, even at the cost of six cabin
fares. She had sent notices on ahead, giving her girls'
names, descriptions, and special talents, for the papers
that were published regularly listing the new arrivals
from Paris. Business would be waiting at the dock for
them. Before she was through, Madame intended to
have the handsomest house in San Francisco.

Then in two years, three at the most, Madame was
certain she would have enough money to retire and return to France. She had it all planned.

"On the edge of the small village where my god-
mother lived," Madame murmured. "I remember it
well, and they recall me as a child at her First Com-
munion. Only that." She sighed with satisfaction. "So
peaceful, so fertile. A little cottage, a small holding. A
few fruit trees, vines for my own wine, a pig, a cow,
some chickens, my little garden, and perhaps, only perhaps if the cottage is large enough, a boarder or two.
For cash for the tax collector, you understand. But
proper, very proper. A teacher, perhaps, or a clerk
from the bank. Meek, no trouble, but a steady salary.
To feed two or even three is little more expense than
one when there is the small garden, the orchard, the
chickens. Ah, yes, and the fish from the river, fine
fish."

"You'd be content with that?"

"It's all I ever wanted. But when one is young, a
man is all one wants. A man that looks like nothing to
other people, not a good man, but he catches the eye,
he appeals for no reason you can explain. Oh, Poppy,
youth is a hard time." She tapped Poppy's wrist. "But
the knitting, once you learn that, you have it always.
For the evenings, the long winter evenings in the cottage,
even if you are not alone."

Poppy looked at the lumpy wool on the needles, already slightly grubby. "But you don't knit now, and you are alone, and the evenings are long," she teased.

"I save it for the cottage," Madame said grandly.

Madame did not pry. If a beautiful young girl and her two brothers chose to go to California, *tout le monde* was gold mad. Still, Madame learned enough, and Poppy discovered she was receiving tactful advice on everything from how to judge the freshness of eggs to the best way to clean and freshen a street dress without tearing it completely apart. Poppy decided that in other circumstances Madame would have made an excellent housekeeper, capable of handling a large staff in any imposing establishment.

Madame's girls had selected their admirers and settled in with them earlier than the more respectable ladies. And perhaps they did change from cabin to cabin rather more often, but they did it with a certain quiet style and social flair. Where the proper ladies floundered and flounced, unwilling to admit intentions that were becoming clearer each day, Madame's girls shifted easily and daintily.

They showed the result of Madame's discipline in every move. The ladies shrieked when spray spattered the decks and drenched them. Madame's girls never raised their voices. The ladies sometimes appeared at breakfast less than perfectly groomed. Madame's girls either came with freshly combed hair and fresh-scrubbed faces, or they did not appear.

They never intruded on Poppy and Madame. Poppy was sure that was on Madame's orders and said nothing, although she had decided at least two of them looked as if they would be good company and the rest were not unlikable. Except for Josie.

Poppy always ducked her head so she would not have to watch Josie and the First Mate when they paraded the deck together. The sight of them sent a shiver down her spine every time she saw them. She knew exactly why, too.

Three or perhaps four years before when Daisy was still letting her take lessons from the ballet dancers,

Poppy had decided little Joan was the prettiest of them all, so it did not matter if she had no talent as a dancer. She had lovely pale silvery hair, soft as silk, and big blue eyes in a small triangular kitten face. She was as dainty and fragile as a small field flower.

One morning, Joan did the thing all the girls understood was not permitted. She came to call on Daisy at Pallminster Lane. Poppy saw her from an upstairs window and ran down the stairs, but had a second thought. If Daisy humiliated Joan by asking her to leave, a witness would make it twice as bad. So she waited, hovering at the foot of the stairs, hidden behind the half-open door.

Joan was almost crying. "Please, Daisy, I know it isn't right for me to come here, but I've got to talk to somebody, somebody wise and sensible. The other girls would either laugh at me or lecture me or tell me I'm a fool. But you'll talk to me sensible."

"I have a few minutes," Daisy admitted. "Unless you've got yourself a fancy man. If you're laying on your back just to give your money to some man who'll only beat you because you don't bring in more, you are a fool, and I've no time for you."

"Oh, no, no. He's a fine gentleman. Young. And educated. And rich. Generous, ever so generous."

"You're not thinking he'll marry you?"

"He's married. An heiress, that his family fixed for him."

"Then sit down and tell me what's wrong."

"I'm half mad for him," Joan said, still sobbing and yet sounding easier. "Only I'm not sure it's right. I don't know what's right and what isn't."

"You haven't been going and getting saved?"

"Oh, no. I like to hear the Bible read. It's real pretty, parts of it. But getting saved isn't for girls like me. I'm not in the gutter and thinking of the river. It's the things Gordon, he, I mean, likes. The special things."

Daisy's voice sharpened. "What does he like?"

"To do, I mean."

"With you?"

"Yes."

"You better tell me and speak plain."

"He doesn't hurt me. He's sweet and gentle as a man can be."

"He's your first regular, as near as to make no difference?" Daisy asked. "Then I'll tell you this, Joan. All men have their little likes and dislikes. And there's no harm in a man being frolicsome. A frolicsome man is usually a happy man. And a vigorous one, not the sickly kind you have to pamper and nurse. A happy man, if a woman keeps him happy, likes his woman to be happy, too. Happy and settled with him and living easy."

Poppy had held her breath. So that was the way it was. Daisy would never talk about herself, straight out like that, to her own daughter, but she would to Joan. Poppy must not miss a word.

"Yes," Joan was saying eagerly. "Yes. That's it. His likes. Frolicsome, maybe you could call it that. He never hurts or bruises me. Just leaves me tingling, like after a massage."

"I suppose that's one way of describing it," Daisy said.

"The ropes are silk. Beautiful. The loveliest pink. And I don't mind the beating with them. Just leaves me tingling like I said. It's the being tied up, even if the knots are loose, that makes my stomach go all queer-like, somehow."

"What?" Daisy shrieked.

"I said he didn't hurt me."

"Oh, no," Daisy said. "No. Just a minute, child. You've knocked the breath out of me."

"Then it is wrong?" Joan whispered.

"No," Daisy said, breathing hard. "Nothing's wrong. No, I don't mean that. Lots of things are wrong. But not lots of things people think are wrong. Oh, girl, you've got my head over a teakettle until I can't talk straight."

"You mean many frolicsome things are all right, even

164

if some people might not think so?" Joan said anxiously.

"But not ropes," Daisy exploded. "Not ropes, girl.
Haven't you any sense in that dandelion top of yours?
He might get so excited he pulls the rope too tight and
hurts you. Or worse. But this won't last all your life.
Then the next one will more than likely be one who
knows this man's tastes, and he'll want the same. Only
more. And not so gentle. Oh, no, girl, oh, no. You take
those pretty pearls I see around your neck, and you get
what you can for them. You tell him you've got to
leave town, you're needed at home, or you've got an
engagement with a solo part somewhere—any story that
fits. But leave, and don't see him again. Ever."

"But I love him, I love him."

"You love life better, don't you?"

"He's gentle. He's kind."

"You ever walk along the Thames of a morning?
You ever see them drag the bodies out?"

"I ain't hungry with a bad disease."

"I mean the ones that died violent."

"Them's poor street girls that went with roughs. Or
boys. Men do that to their boys more often."

"Any man that likes to hurt, even if it's pretend
hurt, has got something wrong with him. And it's like
some with drink. They keep wanting it stronger and
more of it. I'd sooner walk into a cage with a tiger than
into bed with a man like that."

"Oh, Daisy, no. I can't. I can't give him up."

"Hush, girl, hush. My Mrs. Peters is one that will
listen at the door. And tell what she hears. After charging me double, she does, saying she and her mister can't
hold their heads up out in company because they're not
in good service, and there's only the two of them in
service here at that. Hush, now. You don't want this
all over town."

Poppy froze. Daisy might lecture about people who
liked to hurt, but that wouldn't stop her from slapping
her own child until her head rang for the rest of the
day, if she found her here.

"You think this over." Daisy's skirts rustled as she stood up and swept across the room to open the front door herself. "I'll see you, Joan, when I bring Poppy for her lesson next week. Better, I hope I won't see you, and I'll hear you've left town."

Under the sound of the opening door, Poppy had fled up the stairs. But she had never forgotten that talk. Or that when Daisy took her in for her ballet lesson the next week, somebody said her gentleman had taken Joan to the seashore for a week. After that, nobody ever seemed to hear anything about her again, although she had left some of her best dresses and her fur muffs behind.

Every time Poppy saw Josie and the First Mate, she remembered Joan. The First Mate was a big man, with arms that hung almost to his knees. His face was as squared-off and rough-skinned as if he had been blasted out of a gravel pit. Josie was not as pretty as the other girls, thin as a bedpost, with a dark sallow face and eyes and mouth so big that her nose and little chin hardly showed. Still she had a lilting way of moving, so men were apt to touch their tongues to their lips when they looked at her. The looks of the couple were not what bothered Poppy. Despite all Josie's high collars and long sleeves, she could not always conceal the dark marks circling her neck and wrists. Once, her face was so bruised and swollen nobody could believe she had tripped over a coil of ropes and fallen.

She and the First Mate seemed settled together for the voyage. She was not shifting and changing from one cabin to another like Madame's other girls. Marie was usually with the Purser, though not always, and pretty little Amalie always returned to Maurice during his idle hours when he could find nobody to play cards with him. The other two flitted among the men passengers, but they were so good-natured and discreet they caused no bad feeling. Madame merely shrugged and said the girls deserved a little holiday to spend as they pleased. In San Francisco, they would be *très occupé*.

Chapter Eighteen

ON sunny days, the respectable ladies made great pretense that the promenade on deck was the high point of their activities. Their most elegant dresses, decorated with velvet, lace, beads, and braid trimmings, elaborate with stiffened taffeta and overdrapes, were brought out in carefully considered rotation. They wore their feathered, flowered, and ribboned hats, carefully matched to their costumes, exactly as if they had been ashore. Their rings, necklaces, and painted fans were on display.

The pretense grew thinner with each passing day. Nobody was surprised at the former curio dealer and his buxom blond friend sharing a cabin since they had come aboard together. The whole ship soon knew that Mlle. Fanny's violin-playing companion was not her cousin but her lover. Those things were expected on long voyages.

The three women going out to join their husbands, the two girls traveling to marry their fiancés, and two others going to join their newly prosperous families tried to preserve appearances. They did not flit from man to man like Madame's girls, but the ship was too crowded for even the most discreet slipping in and out of cabins not to be observed.

Only the gray-haired, red-faced Madame Dixmer truly shocked Poppy. She had come aboard with her near-albino daughter, who cowered trembling and terrified in her cabin and only stumbled out, looking around her with dilated, bleary eyes, for meals, then immediately fled back to shelter. Madame Dixmer announced loudly that she had married off her other four daughters successfully, but California was this one's only chance. Plainly, she felt her efforts could wait for California, because she had completely abandoned the girl before a week was out. She moved in and spent all her time with a young ex-hussar, a drunkard so unpredictable that gossip said he had accepted his family's offer of a one-way ticket, probably to save himself from something worse than prison, without even the promise of a remittance to follow.

Poppy never joined the daily promenade. She knew she had more and lovelier dresses than any other woman aboard. She opened her trunks, felt the heavy weights in every hem and seam and could not even estimate how many gold napoleons must be sewed into those hundreds of yards of cloth. She locked the trunks again and left them locked. She tied a scarf over her bright hair, removed the stays from two plain blouses so they hung quite limp and, as the weather grew warmer, wore a gray shawl that matched her plain wool skirt. She talked only to Madame and worked at her knitting.

The men were no temptation. She rather liked Maurice, but he and Madame had plainly taken each other in strong dislike, though she did not attempt to interfere with Amalie. The others were a collection of Parisian shopkeepers, journalists, artisans, clerks, and other petty, dull men planning new starts in life in the belief that a geographical change would bring an improvement. When their glances lingered on her, Poppy could look straight through them without a pang of regret.

One day Andy mentioned The Prof again. "He knows eight languages," he reported with awe. "But not much else. He talked too much about Louis Napoleon, so first he lost his job, and then they got him in the middle of the night and put him on this boat."

"He must have talked plain French so people understood him."

"He's used to living alone with his books and his

168

cat. He still worries about his cat," Andy said. "He's down there in steerage sleeping on bare boards, or maybe there's a dirty blanket. There's no fresh air, and he can't eat the food and, oh, Poppy, he's nothing but a shadow."

"He's probably not the only decent man down there."

"But I know The Prof," Andy argued. "Jack and I were talking it over, and we decided Dex put those Spanish books in the box because he wanted you to use them."

"I don't care what Dex wanted."

"The Prof could come up before lunch and give you a lesson on deck," Andy said, as if she had not spoken. "While he's up here, I could find something nice for him from Cook. Oh, Poppy, he's a good old man. He's not going to live even to get around the Horn if we don't do something."

"So you steal for him, and I study?"

"Between us, we can save his life," Andy said, looking his most angelic.

That would be another barrier between her and the promenading gentlemen. It could not be duller than knitting.

So each day before lunch, The Prof gave Poppy a Spanish lesson. Then, because Madame decided it would be most useful in her new house, the three tried to converse in Spanish, with Madame laboring hard to master genteel salutations, remarks about the weather, and, most especially, numbers, which she found amazingly simple. Andy always found a roll and some cheese or a chicken wing for The Prof before he went back to steerage.

With the fine weather, Andy brought their luncheon plates up on deck. Afterwards, Madame instructed in knitting. The scarf, which was almost straight and not too lumpy, was getting quite long. Madame promised Poppy would finish that and knit her first sock before they rounded the Horn. Poppy did wonder what kind of horn it was, that a ship could sail around it, but she refused to display her ignorance to Madame.

Jack guessed, and he explained one day when a squall kept Poppy in the cabin. He selected one of the last of the fine red apples and took his knife in his other hand.

"Andy says you told him Mexico was in South America. Let me show you something. Now this apple is the world, and we left from France, here, sailing across the Atlantic about here." With his knife, he drew a short line around the apple. "That's the coast of the United States. If we landed there, you could walk to California. It's only three thousand miles of plains, mountains, and deserts—an easy little trip, if you don't meet some Indians or a flood or a blizzard or get lost or robbed of your supplies."

"Not everybody walks. I don't believe it."

"I think there is a railroad, there in the east for a ways," Jack admitted. "And there are river boats and horses. But it's still three thousand miles." His knife went back, and he carved down from the cross line. "So we sail this way. Now over here is Mexico, and you'll notice it's in Central America. Then the coast dips clear in here before it widens out again to South America. It isn't far by land across that narrow spot to the Pacific, by water or horse or feet again. Only that's jungle, and if you don't get lost or meet up with a snake or drown in the river, there's the fever, and that's a killer."

"So we stay on the boat."

"Right. Now here's South America, curving around like this, and we're going to put in at Rio for supplies. Then it's down this way and around the Horn. At least, I hope the Captain has the sense to go around the Horn and not to try the Strait of Magellan, even though, with bad weather, it can take a month to round the Horn. Sometimes you can get through the Strait, which you can see is closer and shorter, in days. But if a storm comes up in the Strait, that's the end of you, and if you get calmed in, it can take twice the time of the Horn. One route or the other, we're around and into the Pacific and on our way to California." He drew another swooping line up, in, and up again. "There we are. With a few stops on the way, probably, but those should be rather pleasant. That's all there is to it." He slashed the apple in two and handed half to Poppy.

"I hear all kinds of things about San Francisco," Poppy said miserably. "The ladies dress more extravagantly than in Paris. The place is full of cutthroats and men starving. You can drown in the mud on the streets. The shop counters are covered with gold dust, and you can just scoop up a handful. People live in the street, and it's like a fair. Indians walk the streets. Spanish families live like kings in palaces on thousands of acres, and they ride around with saddles made of pure silver and gold. Only if they're not Spanish palaces, the houses are made of canvas and are always burning up. They have a fine theater. Food is so scarce you can pay a dollar for a potato or starve. All those things can't be true."

"Are you sure?" Jack asked. "We have a nice Yankee kid in the forecastle. He's been there, and he says there's never been anything like it. He jumped ship in China to go to the gold fields. Only he got on a whaler instead, and by the time he jumped that one, he got to California at the wrong season, so he signed on a coaster up to Oregon. From there he went to France, and now he's hoping to pick up a clipper with a Yankee skipper when we reach San Francisco so he can get back to Maine."

"I thought you said he wanted to go to the gold fields?"

"He does seem easily distracted," Jack admitted. "I think he plans to try to make his fortune while he waits to sign on with a skipper he likes."

"So he's not an adventurer, he's a sailor."

"A good one and a good man. He's had some hard experiences. Like this ship. He says on some of those clippers the captains have their wives with them, with all the comforts of home, down to pianos and prayer meetings every night. And make themselves rich in the China trade while they're at it. Even if they never touch

171

the opium. You know I'd like to make one trip on a ship like that."

"Do clippers take passengers? To take us home?"

"Let's arrive before we leave again."

Poppy finished the scarf, and Madame started her on a sock. She insisted it was more useful than a mitten. The Prof admitted his lisping Spanish pronunciation was Castilian, which was not spoken in all parts of Spain, but he thought it was what the aristocrats in Mexico spoke.

Then on a warm, sunny day when the wool clung and tangled in her damp hands, Poppy started to avert her eyes from Josie and the First Mate swaggering past, seeming to flaunt themselves more than usual, and suddenly she froze. Her hands jerked, and all the stitches went.

Madame clicked her tongue and took it from Poppy's hands. "Now you'll only have to start all over again." Ripping, she glanced up and said idly, "That's a handsome stole on Josie. The Mate must start each voyage prepared with presents for a lady."

"Yes," Poppy said numbly.

"Cost him a pretty penny," Madame said and shook her head. "Oh, this is a tangle, and I don't want to waste the wool."

Poppy was beyond answering that. Passing them again, preening her head and looking out of the corners of her eyes, daring Poppy to say anything, Josie tossed one end of the stole over her shoulder. She started with surprise as it struck her back a small blow.

Poppy felt herself turn dead white and ducked her head. The heavy, blue-satin stole, of a material that took on subtle peacock tones of green and purple in the light, with the heavy, knotted silk fringe eighteen inches long on each end, was *hers!* She had worn it only once.

Josie had been in her trunks. And she was so sure of the First Mate's protection, she was daring Poppy to say anything. That was bad.

It was not the worst. The drape of a stole like that

depended on the rich material and the heavy fringe. The hems were never weighted. But Delphine had sewed gold napoleons into that one.

Had Josie ever possessed a garment that fine? Would she know it should not be weighted? If she discovered it was, and with what, would she guess all Poppy's clothes were literally worth their weight in gold?

"I don't feel well, Madame," Poppy whispered. "I had better go to my cabin."

Chapter Nineteen

$\mathcal{I}$N half an hour, Poppy knew Josie had stolen only one of the fashion books and the stole. The lock of the topmost trunk had been forced open, but it held mainly shoes, bonnets, and shawls. Only the handsome stole had appealed to Josie's greedy vanity.

The fashion book Josie could keep. The stole she had to get back somehow. And she had to make sure Josie helped herself to nothing else from the trunks.

She must talk to Jack, but she never could remember when he would be free. Those silly bells counted off the half hours, but the watches were divided into four hours or eight hours, and they seemed to change every day. Jack told her that was so each man could get eight unbroken hours of sleep every other night, which sounded like the only sensible thing about the arrangement. Men did so enjoy making simple things complicated.

When he loomed in the cabin door late that afternoon, Poppy flung herself at him. "Josie opened one of my trunks and took a stole. We've got to get it back."

Jack examined the broken lock. "Only a stole?"

"And a fashion book. That doesn't matter."

"There's no space below decks to stow luggage, and there's no way to lock this cabin," Jack said, examining the locks and straps on the other trunks. "These will never hold, either. I'll have to get some cordage and net them shut so it will take time even to cut into them."

174

"Yes, yes," Poppy said. "That, too. She mustn't get anything else. But we've got to get the stole back."

Jack straightened. "Josie? Isn't she the First Mate's girl?"

"Yes."

"Then I can't help you. I'm a seaman, and he's an officer. If I ever disobeyed a direct command or raised a hand to him, even in self-defense, I could be hung from the yardarm. And this Captain's the man who might do it."

"That can't be true."

"It is. And you're not to tackle Josie, either. She and the First Mate are a pair, and they're poison. Let her keep the stole."

"I can't. I can't. I've got to get it back."

Jack's mouth tightened. "Don't be a greedy soft top. You've got more beautiful clothes in these trunks than any other woman on board. Don't begrudge Josie a stole."

"It's not the stole."

"Then what is it?"

"The gold napoleons."

"What gold napoleons?"

"The gold napoleons Delphine sewed in all my clothes."

"There are some in that stole?"

"Loaded in the hems."

"Heaven protect and preserve us," Jack said and collapsed on Poppy's bunk.

"So you see we've got to get it back before she discovers why it is so heavy," Poppy said, frightened by the expression on Jack's face. "Oh, why did Dex do it this way? He's a banker, and there must be banks in San Francisco. Why couldn't he give me a draft I could cash there?"

"Yes, wherever there's business, the international bankers have connections," Jack admitted. "I don't know about banks. My Yankee friend was warning me to have a good money belt when I went ashore there and said if he hit it rich, he'd have to find a businessman with a safe to hold the gold until he sailed. Maybe the banks are small and local."

"Bankers still deal together," Poppy said fiercely. "Dex could have done this some other way. Unless he's ashamed, ashamed of me, and didn't want anybody in San Francisco to know of our connection. That must be it. Oh, I hate him, I hate him. I despise him."

"Poppy, stop raving and yelling. Do you want everybody to hear? Dex saved your life when he got you on this boat. Remember that and quiet down and let me think."

"The Captain," Poppy said, her mind darting back to what Jack had said. "The Captain can do anything. He can get back my stole. He can keep my trunks safe."

"Poppy, quiet down. Don't say anything to the Captain or even look at him. I've been at sea since I was a boy, and I've sailed under some hard men, but this is the only one who ever frightened me. He wouldn't be Captain of a shipload of passengers like this unless he had the reputation of being able to handle anything and stop at nothing. The First's a mincing dandy by comparison."

"Then what are we going to do?"

"Exactly what I suggested at first. Net the trunks so nothing else can be taken. And pray Josie values that stole so she guards it against the smallest snag."

"If either Andy or I stay right here every single minute?"

"On guard? So everybody wonders what you're guarding, and the whole ship's buzzing? And trying to get in to see what you've got in here? No. I'll bring the cordage in under my jacket. Nobody wonders to see me go in and out. You and Andy go on exactly as you've been doing every day."

On deck, people could talk of nothing but Rio. The ship would stay at least two days and two nights for minor repairs and to load fresh supplies. Not only that, the Captain would make special arrangements to permit everybody to spend some time ashore. For the first time, the unapproachable and scowling Captain was popular.

Jack laughed when Poppy told him that. The ship was not supposed to carry cargo, but the Captain had French wines, laces, porcelains, and other luxuries to trade for his own account. Doubtless a few cases of wine given into the right hands would get him any special privileges he wanted. They certainly would stay in port long enough to allow him to make his price on his wares.

Passengers with money in their pockets planned to spend the nights ashore. The others would land for a day. Even the steerage passengers, Jack contributed with a small smile, were to be allowed to land. The crew was muttering because having to row everybody back and forth meant little shore leave.

"You wait until the second day to go ashore with Andy," Jack said. "Take plenty of money and bring back all the fresh fruit and cabin stores you can carry. I'll row extra hours the first day for time off the second. Let them think I want a long roll with the girls ashore."

"Jack!"

He grinned. "Then while you're ashore, I'll hide out in the cabin. We don't want anybody to land carrying one of your trunks and saying it's their shore-going gear."

Counting coins into her reticule made Poppy think of The Prof. She slipped a napoleon in her pocket when she went on deck for her lesson.

When the lesson was over and The Prof had finished his roll and cheese, Poppy held out the coin. "While you're ashore, get yourself a decent meal or two."

The Prof shook his head with its scanty gray hair. "Dear Miss Poppy, I want no pay. Teaching you has been my pleasure. And probably saved my life."

"Please." Poppy dropped the coin in his coat pocket. "If you don't, I'll only have to give you more of the stores I buy for myself."

"You won't have to do that."

"You're insulting me if you refuse."

The Prof picked up her hand and bent his head over it, but Poppy saw the glint of tears in his eyes. "You know you have my lifelong gratitude."

Poppy wanted to pat his poor balding head, but she only swore to herself that The Prof would live to reach California if she had to go scant on food herself. Then voices from the rail called, "Land!" and she jumped up, grateful the too emotional moment had been broken, and ran to see for herself.

Seen from the ship, the mountains along the shore formed the contours of an immense man lying on his back. They passed two islands, and the bay opened before them. Sailing through a narrow passage with the guns of a fort on the right and a high conical peak on the left, they reached a bright, sparkling bay, dotted with beautiful islands, which extended before them for miles inland.

As they sailed through the entrance of Botafogo Bay, back of the conical mountain, Poppy saw beautiful houses on the shore, and beyond them, she could see ranges of hills and mountains covered with luxurious tropical foliage. They anchored among many other ships off the city below Cobras Island, and a boat brought the doctor and other officials out from shore.

Poppy yearned to be among the first ashore, but she knew Jack's plan was wise. Still, she felt doubly cheated later when she could not find Madame and The Prof at their usual spot on deck. They must have gone on one of the early boats.

By the time she and Andy stepped into a boat the next morning, Poppy had heard enough from the excited, exhausted people who had been ashore the first day to know exactly what she wanted to do. She found an open carriage that looked clean, with a well-groomed horse and a driver who spoke a little English, gave him a gold napoleon, and carefully explained what she wanted. Miraculously he seemed to understand completely.

He drove them through the district of luxury shops where each street was devoted to a different kind of merchandise—jewelry, millinery, shoes, or dry goods. Everybody had insisted the botanical gardens were unparalleled, and the driver nodded vigorously when she repeated the words over and over.

The road to the gardens was like a garden itself, planted with every variety of tropical fruit and strange, vivid flowers that drenched the air with fragrance. In the gardens, the great display was a fine collection of tea plants. A mountain towered high above the park, and they saw an aqueduct many miles long that crossed a deep valley on two tiers of arches, carrying water to the city.

When they left the gardens, Poppy thought they were returning to the city. Dreaming over the scenery, so beautiful it seemed to be a dream landscape in an endless painting, she sat up with a start when she realized they had driven around the conical mountain to the area of beautiful homes she had seen from the ship. This must be a resort for the wealthy, she realized, with its luxurious dwellings set among towering palms and surrounded by a wealth of flowers. They passed magnificent hotels and faintly heard the music of harps and guitars. They drove along a smooth, broad road that ran around a crescent-shaped bay of crystal clear water, edged with yellow sands. Soon they began to meet elegant carriages filled with ladies in rich dresses of bright colors, accompanied by gentlemen in conventional black.

A wave of temptation swept over Poppy. If she had her trunks, if she had her gold napoleons, she and Andy could stay in this beautiful place and never go near that horrible, dangerous ship again. They would not have to endure more weeks and months of bad food, fear, and the ceaseless pitching and rocking of the ship that would only end by landing them on a savage shore where anything could happen.

Except she did not have the gold. Except she could not abandon Jack, who had abandoned everything himself to be with them and protect them. Poppy frowned, puzzling. Sailors talked endlessly about the ports they had seen. Jack might even have been in Rio before on one of Her Majesty's ships. He must have known what a magnificent place it was. When they were talking of the dangers of the ship, he could have suggested they all come ashore. He had gold fever, but he was not so gold-mad he would insist they must go on to California unless he had good reason to distrust a landing here even more.

The sun was slanting well past midday, and they had not done the one important thing ashore. Poppy called to the driver, "The native market. The native market," and pointed back toward the city. He nodded and turned his carriage. Poppy leaned back, shading her eyes with her hand. The sun was so hot even the sparkling brilliance of the clear air seemed painful.

Pulling up at a city street corner, the driver pointed down a long street jammed with open stalls and teeming with people, who were shouting and talking at the tops of their voices, laughing and gesturing, moving constantly, elbowing their way up and down and through the crowd.

Poppy pulled out another napoleon. "You will wait for us?"

"I wait. One hour. Two hour."

She poured a handful of silver into Andy's palms. "Find a nice present for Chips and another for Cook. I'm going to get a basket and buy fresh fruit and bread. Look for me at those stalls. And don't you dare get lost."

"It's all one street," Andy said reasonably. "And you're the only lady wearing a proper hat. I won't lose you."

Poppy found a large basket with a brilliant geometric design woven into it and two sturdy handles. When she looked at the fruit stalls, she felt dizzy. The fruit came in so many sizes and shapes that even the familiar ones began to look strange and exotic. She decided the ones with the toughest rinds would last the best and heaped them in her basket. She was even tempted by the vegetables, but everybody knew to eat those raw would

180

send the stomach into strong convulsions. Still it reminded her how horrid the ship's food was, so she hurried to find the bake stalls. She bought large, heavy loaves of dark bread. At least it did not smell sour, and it did not seem lumpy. Some of the lumps in the ship's bread had a very suspicious aspect. She found sticky rolls and added those by the dozen and some strange flat ovals that looked tasty. When all those were heaped in her basket, she found she could not lift it.

"Andy," she shrieked. "Andy."

He popped out of the crowd. "I've watched you, Poppy. Honest I have."

He too had found a small basket and loaded it, but Poppy saw only one thing. Tilted jauntily over his shoulder like a gun, Andy had a broad bladed knife, heavy as an ax, with a glittering sharp edge. He held it by its massive handle.

"What is that thing?"

"It's a machete, for cutting sugarcane," Andy boasted and tightened his grip as the heavy blade threatened to slip from his slender shoulder. "Or through jungles. I can use it in the jungles of California. See?" He grasped the handle in both hands and tried to swing it. It slipped from his wet palms and slashed down across Poppy's basket, cutting through the corded handles as if they were paper.

Poppy jumped back, white-faced. "I could have lost a leg. Or you could. Get rid of that thing. Drop it. Right now. Oh, how on earth are we going to get this basket to the carriage without any handles?"

"Please, I know, please," Andy cried, jumping up and down. "There was something else the cowboys use that I wanted, too. Only I couldn't afford both. But this cost lots more so if I take it back, maybe they'll let me swap."

"No. No. Drop it."

"But the other is a leather rope thing, Poppy. That we can use to tie up the basket. Just what you need. Please."

She did not see how they could carry the basket

without some kind of rope. Her knees felt weak with exhaustion, and her head ached from the brilliance of the sun. She could not think.

"All right," she said weakly. "All right. Only hurry."

Andy cradled the machete in both arms and ran away through the stalls, as Poppy waited. They had stopped once to buy a glass of lemonade from a street vendor, but they had eaten nothing all day. The strange smells, the jostling people, the loud voices, the uneasy feeling of land under her feet after all these weeks. worry about being away from the ship and what might be happening there, all were making her feel giddy and sick. She only wanted to get back to the cabin and stretch out in the quiet dark.

Andy raced back and showed her a long, thin line of leather with a hard ball at each end. "A bola," he panted. "See, it's long enough to tie around your basket twice and still leave handles for us to hold."

Poppy barely glanced at it. She certainly did not care what Andy intended to do with it. "Tie it on and let's go."

Chapter Twenty

THEY were under way again by the time Jack brought hot water for her morning tea. He was intent on looting the basket of fruit, for he had been at the oars of a boat rowing back and forth to shore half the night.

"The Captain only called us a gang of one-legged, blind, misbegotten landlubbers, or to be truthful something a little stronger than that, when we rowed him back. He was in a fine humor, as his humors go. His private venture must have gone well. But the steerage cooks caught it this morning."

"The steerage cooks?"

"They counted heads when they served breakfast, and we only lost about twenty passengers. The Captain was hoping for fifty. Think of the saving in food."

"Lost?"

"He certainly didn't hold the ship past the tide, but I doubt any were left on the dock. Our Captain simply hadn't counted on gold fever."

"Gold fever? I'm surprised they didn't all stay there. I was tempted. For all of us."

Finishing off a piece of fruit, Jack wiped his dripping mouth. "A beautiful blond alone in a Latin country? Without family or introductions? Maybe you'd enjoy being captured by a tribe of wild Indians, too."

"I wouldn't have been alone. With you and Andy. And we have money."

"We wouldn't have lasted three months. We don't speak the language, and we couldn't have earned our livings. At best, we'd have been picked up by the police and dumped on the first ship back to France. Speaking of languages, The Prof stayed."

"Then he'll get sent back to France? Maybe to prison?"

"Not The Prof. The beggars and pickpockets and petty thieves, yes. The police will clean them out fast, and it doesn't make much difference whether they're in jail in Rio or in Paris. The Prof's different."

"Oh, I'll miss him," Poppy cried.

"He may be better off there than he ever was at home," Jack said, hovering over the basket, trying to make another selection, and finally taking a sticky roll. "As the Captain knew with his little private venture, Rio is a wealthy city, and price doesn't matter on luxuries. The Prof is a very fancy luxury for people who dote on their children. He'll probably end up as somebody's pet tutor in the lap of luxury."

"They'll love him," Poppy said dolefully.

"He was fond of you, too. He ran into my Yankee friend Bill on shore and sent a note back to you. Bill says he seemed terribly worried. Maybe you can understand it. I can't."

The stained and greasy paper looked as if it had wrapped food The Prof had bought from a street vendor. The penciled scrawl was agitated, not his usual scholarly hand, and the large grease splotches made parts of it illegible.

She read, " 'My dear and valued friend Poppy, I left you in sorry and—' no, in something—something 'distress because'—oh, that's a big grease spot, but I think one word is 'passenger,' and 'street of the goldsellers' is quite clear."

"That's where they sell jewelry."

Poppy started and looked at the roped trunks. "And buy it?"

"That's one of the luxury streets. Strictly selling, not buying."

"Who on this ship has the money to buy luxuries?"

"Women do enjoy shopping," Jack grinned. "From

184

what I've observed, shopping doesn't necessarily mean buying."

"All right, a woman passenger shopping for jewelry," Poppy agreed and puzzled over the stained paper again. "I think one word is 'exemplary' and 'life' and something about 'paying for the past.'"

"If it were not exemplary, it would seem more suitable to our ladies."

"Here at the end the part about his 'esteem and undying gratitude and prayers' is quite clear," Poppy said, annoyed enough to cry. "He only wrote the important part so I can't read it."

"The Prof is a scholar," Jack said with resignation. He wiped his hands, took the paper, and held it up against the light from the hanging lamp. He muttered, "I think I can make out a few words. Necklace? Yes. The lady could have been shopping for necklaces. Maybe a shoplifter? Now what's this? Hmm. Looks like 'Pearls of the Guillotine.' Is that possible?"

"That could be the name of a famous necklace," Poppy cried. "Part of a *crime célèbre*. A necklace somebody was guillotined for stealing."

"The Prof recognized the necklace in a shop? That's hard to believe."

"Unless the stones are especially famous. Big pear-shaped ones. Or a certain color. Like some of the crown jewels. You know?"

"I do not know," Jack said, handing her back the paper. "Don't get yourself into a taking, but The Prof did think this was important."

"I will not get into a taking," Poppy assured him with hauteur. "I will notice what necklaces the ladies are wearing."

As each day passed, she realized even more how much they did miss The Prof. Madame did not share her interest in the birds that followed the ship or the strange fish they saw. Poppy admired the carving Andy was doing with Chips but sensed his disappointment that she did not understand, as The Prof had, the importance of Chips's scrimshaw. She finished one sock, so lumpy she was sure it would leave Andy a cripple, and had no study as an excuse not to start another.

In desperation, the next day she took one of her pretty new decks of cards to her seat beside Madame and tried to practice a double shuffle. She was sadly out of practice, and the cards fell and scattered on her lap. Poppy snatched at them before they could blow away.

"You have not the hands for that, Miss Poppy," Maurice said.

Poppy glanced up with surprise. He always avoided Madame, but now he was looking at the cards.

"That is a handsome deck."

"A bon voyage gift."

"Then you enjoy cards?"

"Very much."

"Perhaps you would give us the pleasure of your company then, in our quiet corner," Maurice said with a small bow. "Not for stakes, merely for our amusement?"

Madame looked shocked, but Poppy did not care. She jumped to her feet. If Jack was shocked, too, she would tell him that endless knitting was driving her into the low dismals.

Maurice found two other players. The large man, with an Italian look about his outdoor-red face, was a winegrower going to California for reasons he did not disclose. The dried-out, withered man was a journalist and told everybody why he was fleeing France. His bitterness against Louis Napoleon exuded from every crusty pore.

"Have you found many people with interesting stories on board?" Poppy asked courteously.

"None with stories they wish to carry with them where they are going," he said pointedly.

He was a nasty little man. She fluttered her long lashes to hide the angry sparkle in her eyes. "Or perhaps there is no story," she shrugged. "My brother has the gold fever, and we are a family. You will also write for a paper in San Francisco?"

"I start again," he said sourly. "In Paris, I hear a name, an event is mentioned, and I remember this or that, and then I am informed, and I can write my story. Now it is to begin over again."

Poppy caught her breath as she remembered The Prof's letter. "Have you ever heard of the Pearls of the Guillotine?"

He folded his cards and stared at her. "That is an old story. I would not have thought even your mother would remember it."

"I only heard an argument," Poppy hazarded. "About the size."

"Size? Small, quite small."

Maurice folded his hand. "I refuse to both talk and play cards. Since we are talking, let's hear the story."

"A sordid story, ugly."

"I am not a missy person," Poppy said, raising her chin. "Tell it."

"The only unusual thing about it was the phrase you remember," the man said with a grimace. "A sordid story, as I said, but common. A young girl, seduced, was brought to Paris, and the man attempted to turn her on the streets to earn for him. She rebelled. She had spirit, that one. He beat her, brutally, for refusing to work, and she killed him. It was a crime of passion, so she escaped the guillotine. That was all, Miss Poppy."

"Had he given her the pearls?"

"He gave her only a ruined life. Dishonor. Notoriety so she was forever marked."

"But she could disappear, change her name, start over."

"But she was marked by the Pearls of the Guillotine. People made much of the mark, in talk, in the papers. You see, she had a row of moles around her neck, like a necklace of black pearls, high, tight, like a line for the guillotine to cut, not unpleasant on a pretty young skin but, under the circumstances, unfortunate. Because it was always with her and unusual enough that anyone who saw it would remember."

"How horrible," Poppy said faintly.

The Prof had not seen a real necklace in a jewelry shop then. He had seen a woman with that unusual mark in a jewelry shop and most probably, for him to remark it, she had been trying on necklaces. And surely he would not have written in such distress unless he had recognized the woman as one of the passengers and most likely, a cabin passenger.

Still, a woman who killed in a passion to protect herself seldom killed again. The Prof would not understand that. He was a man of books. To him, any killer was a wild animal and mortally dangerous. If the woman with the necklace of moles was a cabin passenger, she might well be one of the matrons capable now of nothing more reckless than drifting from one man's cabin to another until she reached San Francisco and settled once more into her proper staidness.

Poppy told herself she would remember and watch but she need not walk in fear. Then she reached for her cards. She might as well enjoy this game. She would not make ship's talk of herself by sitting too often with the gambling men.

As they sailed down toward the Horn, brief squalls with rain, lightning, and sudden winds hit almost every day. On a bright morning, Poppy went up to sit with Madame in the sun while the ship sailed briskly before a strong westerly wind. She meekly took her knitting, and Madame cast on another sock, but then they sat, enjoying the spell of fine weather, and watched people stroll up and down the deck.

Andy, the long leather bola he had bought in Rio in his hand, came to lean against Poppy's knee. He was as tired of carving as she was of knitting. He held one of the balls in his hand and whipped the other out across the deck with a snakelike lash and hiss.

"What is that horrid object?" Madame demanded.

"A bola," Andy said. "Like the South American cowboys use. Instead of lariats. I've been practicing. See?" He lashed it out again, and the ball at the far end whipped back to form a loop. Andy exulted, "Right around his leg. Caught. Pull it in and down he goes. Bring on the branding irons."

"Just a child, playing games," Madame sniffed.

"Pull it in, Andy," Poppy said. "Somebody might trip over it."

Beside her, Madame stiffened. "I thought so. I thought so." She nudged Poppy's ribs with her elbow. "The necklace Josie is wearing. When I saw her come back with it in Rio, I knew he'd never bought it for her on the goldsellers' street. Though I did see her peering in the window when I was in a shop there."

Josie was promenading up and down the deck on the First Mate's arm. She had the stole looped back across her elbows, fringes dangling from her hands, to show the heavy gold chain set with blue stones around her neck.

"See the tarnish on her neck?" Madame cackled gleefully. "If she must wear cheap trash, she should at least wash thoroughly."

"It's a pretty thing and matches the stripes in her dress," Poppy made herself murmur indifferently.

Madame preened in her high lace collar with the heavy trim of white around the edge. "Some girls, they will not learn. Now, me, this lace, it must come off and be washed every second day. But clean." She pulled it out to display the immaculate inner side. "A little trouble, a little ripping and stitching, but clean. The gentlemen notice and pay for such things. Still, some will not learn. The jabot, also." She lifted and held out the ruffle that fanned from the top of her collar down the front of her black dress, then leaned back complacently. "Immaculate, immaculate."

Poppy blinked her eyes. She could not believe what she had seen.

"Yes, today everybody promenades in their best," Madame observed, nodding. "Amalie looks well. A sweet girl. Not always practical, but modest, sweetly modest. Not like that Josie. Look at her now. The way she flips the fringe on that stole is as dangerous as our young man here with his bola. It is a handsome thing, too handsome for a ship like this."

Josie had stopped directly opposite them and was making a great play with the stole, moving her arms so the magnificent material rippled and shone, twirling the fringe under the noses of other passengers. She tilted her mocking face and slanted her eyes toward Poppy, preening and challenging.

Poppy set her lips. She could do nothing but endure the taunting.

Close at her elbow, Andy drew in a gulping breath. "That stole, I saw stuff like that in your trunk. Is that why Jack netted them shut? Because somebody's been in them? Is that why she's prancing in front of you like that? Because she thinks you won't try to tear it off her thieving back?"

"Andy, shut up," Poppy hissed.

"Of course a lady can't mix with one like that," Andy said grandly. "But I can. I'll get it back for you. I'll lift it right off her arms."

Andy lifted his hand, one ball swinging, raised his arm, and whirled. Poppy jumped to her feet, reaching, but it was too late. He had let the leather fly. The ball flew through the air and thudded against Josie's shoulder, tangling in the heavy material, and knocked her staggering. With a whoop, Andy pulled in the leather, dragging the stole with it. As it ripped from her arms and snapped through the air, it hit a protruding hatchway and caught on the brass latch. Josie shrieked and dived for it. Andy jerked, and Josie snatched at the fringe. Both tugged furiously. The satin ripped, and a heap of gold poured out on the deck. Josie's hands clamped down instantly, and she crouched, covering it.

Poppy turned pale and swayed. Madame's strong hand caught and whirled her around. With her other hand, Madame was grappling with Andy, swinging him behind her, holding him back as he fought to pull free. Neither of them had seen the gold. Neither had the First Mate, striding toward them, eyes blazing and fists clenched.

He caught Andy by the collar, tore him from Madame, and shook him until his head snapped back and forth helplessly. Then he lifted the boy with both hands and dashed him to the deck. Andy lay stunned as Poppy jumped between them.

"Shame on you. Shame. He's only a boy."

"He's big enough that if that thing had hit Josie higher or harder, he'd have brained her or swept her overboard." The pitted, heavy-jawed face was purple with congestion. "If he was a man, I'd call it attempted murder."

Poppy swallowed sickness. "He's a child. He was only playing, and he's sorry."

"He's as old as our apprentices, and they obey the book. We'll call it assault on a passenger."

"But he's not an apprentice, he's a passenger," Poppy said shrilly. "A child."

"Just a child," the man said in a viciously mincing voice. "Just a sweet dainty child who likes to carve pretty things with Chips and help Cook pass the nice little cakes. I think the child needs a lesson."

"I'll see he's punished."

"This is ship's business. He could have killed Josie. I think he'd better learn what killing means. They're slaughtering a beef for dinner tonight. He can go aft and clean up after the men."

Andy shrank back against Poppy, and she could feel the shudders shaking him. She opened her mouth to scream a refusal. Then she saw that the First Mate's cold, pebble-hard eyes held a glint of light, a glint of anticipation, and his tongue snaked out and touched his lips. He wanted her to refuse. He was holding back something horrible, some worse punishment to inflict.

Then she saw Madame was flicking her fingers in a small gesture, prodding Andy aft. If anybody understood what this man was capable of, it was Madame.

"If you think that's a proper lesson," Poppy forced herself to say through stiff lips.

Disappointment flickered in the pebble eyes. "It'll do for a starter."

That was too much. "It will do for the punishment," Poppy said definitely. "Andy, go and apologize to Josie. Do it, I say. Then you go aft immediately and tell the men you're to help with the cleaning up."

Andy gave Poppy one shocked, disbelieving look. She looked back, stony faced. Shoulders sagging as he read her expression, Andy went slowly over to Josie, muttered something, and went dragging back along the deck.

Poppy faced the First Mate. "That will be the whole punishment."

"Until I catch the imp at something next time."

"There'll be no next time."

Poppy stood rigid as the First Mate stopped to speak to Josie. She had thrown the stole around her shoulders again, her hands clenched around the bunched, torn material. She only nodded sullenly when he spoke and turned away to leave the deck.

Poppy crumpled weakly on her box. Josie was not going to share her secret or the gold with the First Mate. That was one small good in this disaster.

Chapter Twenty-one

$\mathscr{P}$OPPY leaned on the rail, watching the first streaks of sunset. The days and nights were long, and she was lonely.

An arm went around her shoulders. "You have not been back to play cards with us."

"No."

Maurice did not attempt to hold her. He put his elbows on the rail and leaned beside her. "We would enjoy having you."

"I enjoyed playing." Poppy hesitated. After his punishment, Andy had staggered back to the cabin, white faced, gagging and glassy eyed, and lain prostrate on his bunk, hating her with his eyes. He would not believe she could not have saved him. Jack explained that the First Mate could have had him confined to his cabin for the duration of the voyage or even put him in irons for a second offense, but Andy turned his back on them both and refused to talk. When Chips and then Cook had told him they had orders he was not to mix with the crew, he had burrowed into a lonely spot under a lifeboat. He came out only to eat and sleep. She said awkwardly, "There's Andy."

"I myself would have given him this." Maurice slapped her sharply on the bottom and said instantly, eyes twinkling, "Not you. I'd never lay a finger on you."

"Am I to believe that, sir?" Poppy laughed, feeling better.

"No." Maurice laughed back at her. "Have you friends in San Francisco?"

Remembering the Cornish smith, Poppy felt quite virtuous as she said, "We know a person or two."

"And your plan?"

"Jack's for the gold fields."

"We'll arrive at the right season, as I understand it. When the winter thaws and rains have freshened the streams that carry down the gold. And you?"

"I hear so many different things. I don't know yet."

"If you wish employment, do not forget me," Maurice said and then with deliberate comic dismay, "Not as a player. But a gambler meets many people and hears many things."

"I won't forget."

Maurice looked deep into her eyes. "Your company would give me great pleasure. Do not forget that, either." And he was gone with a jaunty wave of his hand.

Poppy drew her coat closer against the chilling breeze. Maurice might like and admire her; he might spend some of his nights with Amalie; but he had only one true love, Lady Luck. Still, she had always liked gamblers. She understood their code. Win or lose, do it with style.

Andy was not in the cabin. He must be eating at the crowded cabin table and leaving her to fend for herself. But she was not hungry for the salt pork and moldy bread.

She trimmed and lit the lamp, then tried to fluff the one hard pillow. Then she stared at the bits of fiber on her hands and caught her breath sharply. She jumped into the bunk and pressed against the bulkhead, peering down to see the backs of the netted trunks stacked beside it. When she straightened, her face was white.

Jack did not come to the cabin until the next morning, bringing hot water for tea. She pointed wordlessly, and he shifted the trunks while she made the tea.

"Neat work," Jack said. "The netting's cut in the

back and on the top, too, so that it doesn't show, but it would only take a minute to get them down and open."

"Not neat enough. I found bits of cuttings on my bunk."

"Somebody limber, with small hands to reach back in that space."

"Josie, of course."

"Maybe she thought we were putting in at Buenos Aires so she could claim somebody came aboard and robbed you."

"Aren't we?"

"No. It's far up a river, and the Captain's taken a freak to get to California as fast as possible. In this hulk. Let's hope he doesn't try the Strait." He held out a cup so she could pour the tea. "That settles it. I'll get some canvas and make money belts. The weather's worsening, so you'll be spending whole days in the cabin, and nobody will question it."

"Question what?"

"What you're doing in here. I'll open the trunks one by one so it won't be noticed. You're going to pick out the stitches so you can remove the gold from those clothes and transfer it to the belts. Then you can sew your clothes together again." He grinned. "Happy sewing, sweet."

"Buffoon," Poppy said without spirit.

The weather worsened rapidly as they sailed down the coast of South America. Even when Poppy ventured on deck to sit with Madame, as often as not a flying squall would send all hands racing aloft to take in the sails and send the passengers scurrying to their cabins.

So she got out the fine gilt embroidery scissors and ripped recklessly through Delphine's fine stitches. She sewed back, though not so finely, because she felt there might be little time once they landed. The two top trunks filled Jack's money belt so heavily she wondered he could wear it and still climb and cling to the tall masts. He only grinned and produced a small belt for

Andy. She filled that, but in the brief times Andy spent in the cabin, except to sleep, he was in such a fractious mood she did not feel like confiding in him. She hid that belt in the bottom of a trunk and went on working.

Finally she made a knitting bag out of the roll of linen. She embroidered it with bright pink and red thread and lined it with red silk she took from the end of a sash. Then she gathered it with a pink ribbon she drew from the neck of a morning robe. She took it to show Madame.

"I would not have expected you to do such neat handwork," Madame complimented. She picked it up and stared with surprise as it slipped through her fingers and thudded on the deck. She cried, "What do you have in there?"

Poppy ducked her head. "I made a little space in the bottom for a necklace and a couple of rings."

"So? Perhaps that is wise, if you always carry it with you," Madame approved dubiously with a glance at the promenading passengers watching them. She said loudly, "Yes, the scissors and the darning hoops, they are heavy."

"Clever Madame," Poppy murmured, and then jumped to her feet, eyes wide with fear.

That sound, like the distant roar of a thousand locomotives approaching. "A squall," someone shrieked. "Run. Run." Poppy ran. Before she could reach the cabin, the storm hit. The ship trembled from stem to stern, the massive masts shaking like young saplings. Hurled against the rail, Poppy clung on desperately as the ship tilted again to the other side, leaving her dangling in the spray-drenched air. Then it fell back with a thud that knocked the breath out of her. Gasping and choking, she saw the crew swarming up the rigging like a gang of monkeys, fighting the wind to reef the heavy, soaked canvas on the whirling heights.

She drew in a breath, filled her lungs with air, and realized she could move. She dived into the cabin, drenched to the skin, hair ripped from its pins, and skin stung raw from the salt spray. She was bruised, but nothing worse.

The next day, while they were sailing close-reefed under only the topsail, the Captain tacked to speak to another ship. The report flew among the passengers that the ship had just rounded the Horn. Its captain reported the weather the worst he had known in a dozen voyages and warned against trying the Strait.

After that, all the days were violent, squalls of rain and hail, fog and snow. The passengers who were not too ill to leave their cabins huddled in the dining corridor and bickered, complained of the food, and grew quarrelsome as they dragged out hoarded bottles of wine and brandy.

Those first terrible days of seasickness had cured Poppy. She read all her books. She even worked on her Spanish lessons. Five days in a row she tried to go out on deck, but found she could barely stand and, with all the rain, hail, and snow, could not look windward. She glimpsed a cold, cheerless, barbarous coast beyond the mountainous seas of white, foaming water. No small boats could survive in that, and if they could, the coast offered no shelter for survival. She could only hope their hulk was less old and fragile than Jack feared.

Then after fifteen days, the word went out that they were around the Horn, although the weather continued dark and squally for another week. But then the weather moderated, and a light, fresh breeze sprang up. The Cape pigeons that had deserted the ship returned. Sharks started following them, and schools of elusive dolphins came and went. One day the sea was alive with a school of cowfish, thousands of them, larger than dolphins. The Yankee, Bill, took up a position in a bobstay and harpooned one, eight feet six inches long, weighing four hundred pounds. That was fresh food for all.

The word they were to have a day ashore at Valparaiso sent all the passengers a little crazy. Like prisoners anticipating freedom, they freshened their clothes, counted their money, and babbled endlessly of their plans.

Poppy stood beside Madame at the rail. They sailed past the long spur of the Andes with the lighthouse on the tip and houses crowded on the long, narrow strip of ground, until they reached the anchorage. Madame drummed her fingers on the railing, poised to run for the first boat ashore.

Poppy wondered. Such eagerness was not like Madame, but she only said, "Jack tells me those three hills there at the south end of town are called Fore, Main, and Mizzen Top. That big handsome house there with the American flag on the pole belongs to their consul."

Madame nodded without interest.

"Jack warned me all those places that seem to be tumbling down the sides of the hills are gambling halls and the retreats of criminals and desperadoes."

"All of them?" Madame sniffed.

"And sailors' boarding houses. The homes of the respectable people are up on the hills."

"I do not concern myself," Madame said grandly. "I wish to see the shops, the public streets. They seem wide and straight. And you?"

"Jack says prices are triple what they should be and to wait. We'll be making another stop."

"You are not going ashore?"

"Andy and I will try to find a respectable hotel to have lunch."

Andy was still sullen, hardly speaking, and the price of the lunch made Poppy gasp. Still, she could not resist hiring a carriage to drive around the public squares. She watched the Chilean women strolling there or driving past in their carriages and felt intolerably crumpled and travel worn. They all seemed so beautiful, with pure complexions and fine black eyes flashing under the thin gauze headdresses thrown over their shining black hair. They behaved more freely than the women in Rio, walking with superb bearing and grace, allowing glimpses of fine ankles in silk stockings as they lifted their skirts to cross a street. If the Spanish women in San Francisco were that handsome, she would need all her fine clothes not to appear the merest drab.

The next day, Madame made clear she also had observed the women closely. "Handsome," Madame admitted as they sat in their corner in the sun. "And very free in their manners. But with these tropical women, the looks do not last. And they have not the éclat."

"No?" Poppy puzzled.

"I am told there are many Chilean women in San Francisco," Madame said. "They come by the hundreds. But they do not command the prices. They do not have the experience, the skills, the discipline. They find some useless man. Their looks fade. They do not have the éclat as those from France."

Poppy flung back her head and laughed. "Oh, Madame, you are the complete woman of business."

"Of course. What else? Yes, I was a little anxious, the reports of these Chileans. Now I have informed myself, it is of no importance."

"None at all," Poppy agreed, eyes sparkling. "And we have only four hundred miles to our last stop, and it's Robinson Crusoe's island."

That news worked a miracle in Andy. Grudge forgotten, he was wild with excitement. He would not listen when Poppy tried to tell him Crusoe was only a character in a book. A man had been marooned on the island, and one of the sailors who had stopped there before said they could take a boat and sail around and see the cave where he had lived. They were stopping for two days, perhaps three. He must see the cave, he must.

"Take him the first day," Jack agreed, watching Andy prancing up and down instead of huddling in the shade of the lifeboat. "And do take a boat. By land, it means a whole day of scrambling over a mountain and back again in this heat."

"You take him," Poppy said. "You won't want to get the reputation of being the sailor who never goes ashore."

"We have to man the water rafts, and there's a woodcutting detail. I'll see."

"I'd as soon wait and go ashore the second day."

Jack gave her a sharp look. "Is Andy wearing his belt?"

"He's been in such a fractious mood, I didn't think it was any time to confide in him," Poppy admitted. "It's in the bottom of a trunk."

"You've ripped out every bit of that gold?"

"Every napoleon," Poppy said virtuously.

She saw Jack and Andy off the next morning and settled down to watch the ship take on water. The sailors swore it was the best water in the world. From a spring high on the mountainside, a wooden flume ran out into the deep water, so casks placed on rafts could be towed close to the beaches and filled. Some of the crew went into the woods to cut wood for the galley stoves. Almost all the passengers went ashore and returned sunburned and laden with fruit.

Jack reported, with a twinkle in his blue eyes, that the cave was exactly as represented, high on a hill with a full view of the ocean. It was remarkably preserved considering the many years that had passed. Andy said hotly, whether it had been Crusoe or a real man named Alexander Selkirk, he hoped someday he could live in a cave like that.

The next day, Poppy took Andy ashore, and again he was in a lively, prancing state. He must see the other caves, the ones that had sheltered Chile's criminals in the days when the island had been a penal colony. He scampered through them and then helped fill their baskets from the overgrown orchards, also abandoned by the penal colony, but still heavy with fruits. Poppy had never seen anything like these, even in the finest shops in London and Paris. They staggered back on board with their wealth of fruits.

They sailed on the early tide the next day. This was not a pleasure cruise, the Captain barked at the passengers who begged another day ashore. His orders were for San Francisco with all speed. He knew these treacherous Pacific winds, and they did not.

The days grew oppressively warm. As they sailed off the coast of Peru, Poppy saw a thick yellow mist rising perpendicularly from three rocky islands. Then the ship was blanketed with a fine dust, strong with the odor of ammonia, and she choked, sneezing and coughing, her eyes watering until her face was wet.

"What?" Poppy gasped.

Jack ran to her side, whipped out his kerchief, and tied it over her nose and mouth. "Fertilizer. From birds. They've got gangs of prisoners and Chinese coolies over there using picks to dislodge the stuff. Then they put it in wheelbarrows and dump it in a canvas tunnel that leads to launches that take it out to the ships you see anchored off there, waiting to be loaded."

"You mean people breathe this for days?"

"Weeks. Months. These are the Galapolas. One of our seamen says he signed on once for the extra pay. That yellow stuff is wealth for the owners, but he'll starve before he ever does it again."

"I'd die."

"Don't complain yet. Have you unpacked your cool frocks? I don't think we're going to make any quick and easy landfall."

Jack was a sailor. He knew his latitudes and weather signs. But even he had not expected them to be becalmed for a week. The sails hung limp, the unmoving ship was mirrored in a glassy, unbroken surface bounded only by a horizon. A slight undulating swell rolled the vessel lazily from side to side. The sun hung over them like a ball of fire, and the pitch and tar bubbled out of the seams of the vessel until the deck was like a furnace. Even to sit under an awning spread over the deck was torture.

Light breezes finally carried them into the North Pacific, but they were running counter to the prevailing winds. They sailed great distances, but made little progress. Sudden, violent winds threw them back to lose in a few hours the distance they had taken days to gain.

Poppy sat on the deck day after day beside Madame. Madame had grown rather thin and silent, but she sat as straight as ever.

"In this California," Madame said suddenly, "I wonder if there are perhaps small villages where one could have a few fruit trees and a little garden?"

"I've heard of San Francisco and great ranchos and gold towns. I don't know about villages."

"Perhaps not," Madame said and sighed heavily. "It is a long trip. But I must have my little village."

"Maybe none of us will ever go back," Poppy whispered, awed by the realization. Never see Dex again? Or Daisy? Never walk known streets or open familiar doors? Live always in a wild, foreign place among strangers? "For all our lives."

"But we will arrive," Madame said with determination.

Poppy stirred uneasily. She and Jack had traveled and lived together, had faced danger and hardship for months in perfect amity. Not once had he behaved as less than the great English gentleman he had been born. Not once had he failed in courage, honor, or respect. He had left comfort and position, dear friends and family, behind him. She had brought him jeopardy and trouble, but he had not once reproached her. In return, he had a right to her perfect honesty and confidence, and she had failed him.

The next morning when they were alone in the cabin, Poppy said, "Everybody's saying we'll be sighting land soon, and Andy's so much more himself, I'll show him how to wear the money belt tonight."

"Good. We'll all be glad to get ashore."

"Yes." Poppy hesitated. "You remember the Pearls of the Guillotine? I know who it is."

"You know?" Jack asked sharply.

"I've known for weeks," Poppy confessed. "But everything was happening at once. And she did only kill one man and that in a passion."

"You've known and didn't tell me? Then it's fortunate you've associated with nobody except Madame."

"It is Madame."

"What?"

"She killed only to keep from being forced into a life

202

on the streets," Poppy cried passionately. "Then when it was over, that was the only life open to her, and she's been in it ever since. All she wants or ever wanted is her little holding in a village with her cow and chickens, garden and orchard."

"You are too innocent and trusting," Jack said heavily. "This has been a terrible voyage, but once we're ashore, you won't ever need to see her again. I'll be happy when we're all ashore in San Francisco and safe."

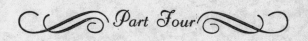

Part Four

San Francisco
Spring 1852

Chapter Twenty-two

$\mathcal{J}$ACK and Andy had been gone for hours. They had walked off the wharf, leaving her alone, and simply disappeared. That was terrifying, but everything here felt wrong, silent and menacing. This was the waterfront. Waterfronts were always abustle with life and movement. Yet now the gray afternoon light was beginning to darken, only a few yellow beams showed behind iron-barred windows, and only an occasional furtive figure hurried along the sandy street. Even the stray dogs had stopped their prowling and sniffing.

Poppy perched on her trunks stacked between the prow of a stranded ship and the wall of a closed shop. She could hear, faint as echoes, the voices, shouts, music, and rumble from San Francisco spreading out beyond the wharf. But around her was only silence, except for the faint lapping of water against the pilings at the end of the wharf.

Jack and Andy had hurried up the street from the wharf to find a place to stay and a wagon to carry her trunks. Even if they could not find a wagon, surely in all this time they should have been able to hire a couple of porters with wheelbarrows.

She slipped to her feet and ventured out on the wharf, standing on tiptoe so she could look up the street and still keep her trunks in sight. Now she could see a glowing halo of lights from the town. Out in the bay, she could see the heavy gray fog hanging like a canvas curtain over the derelict ships, stranded there when their crews deserted years before to run for the gold fields. Nothing moved in the ghost fleet, but around its edges the dozen ships that had sailed in that day swung at their anchors. As she watched, the chill breeze that had been sweeping down over the inland hills sharpened and moistened. The cold cut through the heavy, padded basque and wool coat she was wearing. Streamers of fog floated away from the solid curtain and began to drift toward her.

She took an impetuous step forward and then shrank back. This strange, dead waterfront street, oddly composed of stranded ships with shops and warehouses crowded in between, was intimidating, but nobody had bothered her. If she went stumbling around, in this heavy basque and coat with all those weighty skirts underneath, and stepped off into deep water, she would drown before she could even call for help.

She went back and perched on the trunks again, settling her reticule and knitting bag in her lap but not loosing the strings from her wrist. She was going to ask the next person who passed to get her a sheriff. Yes, that was what they were called here. She wanted a sheriff urgently. Because something was terribly wrong. The fog was worsening, not as dark as a London pea-souper but as thick, wrapping her in gray tendrils until she could see nothing.

"Ashore and safe in San Francisco," Jack had said. He could not foresee all the little mischances of the landing and this day.

The week before had been bad enough, when her very fingers and toes were tingling with longing to get ashore, to feel solid land under her feet, to see the town some people said had streets paved with gold and others said with drowning-deep mud. She wanted to be in San Francisco.

The ship had sailed far and long in search of the trade winds. Jack had tried to explain the long distances of this coast and that they would be lucky if they found the hidden entrance to the bay at the first pass. That brought impatient shrugs. They were in sight of land and other ships. There was the goal. There was California.

All the passengers were sure each day would be their last on board. They plunged into a scramble of packing. Jack and some of the other sailors produced their gold-mining equipment. The tin pans, the pickaxes and shovels, the belts and bags to hold gold, some hastily fashioned out of the tops of worn boots, were put in carryalls. The chemical retorts and crucibles for gold tests, the goods for trade, the city clothes, were already in trunks, many with false bottoms and special locks. Guns and pistols, knives and powder flasks, were stowed in pockets and holsters. The women put away their bright, worn gowns and appeared in severe street costumes. Friends, bosom-close for months, parting cabin mates, inseparable companions, barely smiled and nodded to each other as they hung on the rail, peering shoreward. The voyage was past. Eyes strained toward the future.

They jostled at the rail as the ship sailed along the shore, past uninviting stretches of wasteland with straw-colored hills, austere and forbidding. They muttered in dismay over the stunted shrubs and few trees, wondered at the sight of the hundreds of horses and cattle feeding on those brown hills, and were reassured when they glimpsed deep green valleys with tall oaks. The rains came only in winter, knowing passengers reported, and then for a brief time the hills were green and bright with wild flowers. But even though the hills were brown and sterile-looking, the livestock could live on them. Beyond, in the faraway Sierra, the talk ran, spring warmth was melting the snow and ice on the mountainsides. The streams and rivers were surging into life, watering the fertile inland valleys, brightening the land. And most important, the rushing water was un-earthing the wealth of gold from rocks and ledges, and carrying it down from the heights.

If the Captain did not find the trade winds, if he missed the bay entrance, they would be too late, too late, and others would have scooped up that wealth glinting in the water, dazzling in the sunlight. Knuckles were white on the railing as eyes searched for the break in the brown hills, the magic entrance to the golden land.

The greed in those eyes, so naked and all-consuming, shook Poppy. Repeatedly she fled from it to the disorder of the cabin only to look around her in baffled despondency. She could not get everything back in those trunks. She could only roll and stuff, cram and pound, and still the trunks brimmed. Her bunk was covered with Andy's dirty clothes and her own crumpled petticoats and sleeping robes. Dirty clothes must be larger than clean clothes. At least they did not fold as neatly. In desperation, she pulled out a heavy padded basque, cut like a skating jacket, and crowded Andy's clothes into its place. She grabbed all the books from the tin box, tied them in netting, crammed her things in, and managed to close it. Now if Jack sat on the trunks, she could wear the basque ashore, though it would be a struggle to pull her heavy coat over it.

The ship tacked sharply, and she reeled against the bunk.

"Land! Land!"

Poppy sniffed. They had been in sight of land and of other ships also sailing parallel to it for days, and much good that did them.

"The bay! The bay!"

That was different. She ran out on deck.

They were sailing up a narrow channel, running among floating streamers of fog, beating against strong currents. Ahead of them she glimpsed another ship and, turning, saw still another behind them. After months of seeing only an endless horizon, distant ships, and land miles away, this boxed-in closeness was terrifying. Even as she shivered, they broke through into a spacious landlocked bay, broken here and there by small islands. Ahead she saw a bluff with two or three small cannons and a tall flagstaff. That was San Francisco.

In the middle of the bay, she saw a solid thicket of ships, a forest of ships with broken masts, moored so close together she was sure anyone could step from one to another almost as easily as walking across a creek-broken moor. Those were the abandoned ships, left in the early gold rush days when the crews broke and ran for the gold fields without waiting to unload.

As they drew in closer, she saw other ships stranded on land with shops built around them. Or perhaps the land had grown out around the ships, it almost looked like that. Extending past them were great wharves, one shaped like a T at which three ships were unloading at once. None of the wharves was vacant.

Talk rippled along the rail again. "Wait our turn." "Going to land us over there." "Cheaper fees at that one if I know our Captain." "No, not any more. That was last year, when the Vigilantes were meeting the ships and turning people back." "Afternoon before we get ashore."

Poppy almost jigged with impatience. Jack, closing the trunks, was reassuring. The crew had been paid off, and everybody was packed. The Captain, the First Mate, and a few seamen who were being paid double would stay on board to take the ship back to her anchorage. Once the passengers had landed, everybody else was free. So Poppy was to let the other passengers go ahead until he and Yankee Bill could unload the trunks between them. They would be only minutes behind the others. They would be ashore and settled in time for dinner.

They drew in to the wharf, and the Captain gave the ceremonial order to drop anchor. The crew jumped briefly to the riggings and cheered, then they tied up. The gangplank went down. All order vanished in a struggling, shouting melee. The cabin passengers went first, pouring like milk from a broken pitcher, kicking, elbowing, shoving. The men headed up the wharf and to the street at a dead run. The women, kicking and pushing their trunks ahead of them—for none of the crew would help—were only a little behind. Then the steerage passengers flooded up over the deck. Poppy moved back. Their faces were pale from long confinement, for they had been allowed up on the afterdeck only for brief periods. The stench from their unaired, unwashed clothes and bodies was almost palpable.

Silence fell on the ship, and Poppy realized she was the last passenger and alone, waiting there by the cabin. Even Andy had vanished.

Then he ran up to her. "Jack and I have to carry everything down to the wharf."

"What happened to Bill?"

"Some old steerage passenger claims Bill stole those pans and that shovel from him, but Bill says he's got a list from where he bought them in his duffle bag. The Captain says he's got to produce it or pay up."

"Not many of those steerage people had mining gear. They were brought straight here out of jail."

"Of course it's a crook game," Jack said, coming and bending to hoist a trunk on his shoulder. "That man knows the crew's been paid off and thought he could collect some cash to take him ashore. He just picked on the wrong person. Lend a hand here, Andy. The Captain wants to cast off before these wharf charges mount up."

"Bill will fix it in time to help us get these things to town," Andy said.

Poppy had no sooner carried the last of the tin boxes ashore than the gangplank was drawn up behind her, and the lines were cast off. The ship began to move away from the wharf. They all stared incredulously.

"Bill must have had trouble finding that paper," Jack said uneasily. "He'll have to row ashore and find us later."

"What do we do with all this?" Poppy cried with a gesture to the trunks and boxes stacked all around her.

"I'll find a porter with a wheelbarrow or a wagon or something," Andy offered. "There were plenty here when we landed."

Jack and Poppy looked at each other uneasily. The afternoon was wearing away, and they were in a strange and foreign city. They had depended on Bill because he had been here before and at least knew the names of a few streets and hotels.

Andy came running back. "One man told me everybody was his own porter here, and it looked like I was a strong boy. Another man said all the wagons are over at the big wharf where two ships are still unloading. A man with a big wagon full of whiskey barrels asked where we were going and told me we'd better find out because nobody's going to tie up his wagon and horses and lose three other fares while we drive around trying to make up our minds."

"He's right," Jack said. "We'd better move all this off the wharf and find a quiet spot where Poppy can stay with it and wait. And we'd better find rooms and engage them before we come back with our wagon."

So they moved everything into a spot between a store and a stranded ship, in the shadow of the curving hull, and went off together, leaving her to guard all their possessions. Now hours had passed, and the fog had closed in around her.

She dared not move from her perch. Yet she knew Jack and Andy would not willingly have left her here alone in this isolated spot for so long. What could have happened to a grown man and a strong boy? She must find help, give an alarm, and start a search for them.

Then she sensed movement, saw darker shadows in the fog.

"Jack, Andy," she cried with a sob of relief. "Here. Here I am." She put out her hands, groping.

A slender beam of light from a partially covered lantern struck the knitting bag and reticule dangling from her wrist. A knife flashed, slashing the strings, cutting her wrist as the two bags were snatched away. The light vanished. She stumbled back, but a heavy body followed, towering over her, pressing her against the trunks while the knife slashed again and again, tearing the thick wool of her coat and the padding of the basque beneath.

Poppy threw back her head and screamed. Above her, in the hull under which she was sheltering, an un-

213

seen door opened, and a broad beam of yellow light
flooded down on Poppy staggering back against the
trunks, her wrist streaming blood, and on a dark figure
ducking to scoop up something from the ground and
then turning and disappearing, feet pounding away, into
the all-encompassing grayness.

"Help," Poppy screamed. "Help. I'm murdered."

"You sound pretty lively to me," a man's voice
grunted.

A tangle of wood and ropes rattled through the door,
unwinding into a rope ladder with wooden steps. A tall
man slipped down the ladder, lantern in hand, and
flashed it full on Poppy, studying her, and then circled
the light around the trunks.

He decided, "Doesn't look like he got away with anything."

"Just my knitting bag and reticule."

"I saw you sitting down here. Why'd those men of
yours go off and leave you?"

"To find a place to stay and a wagon for the trunks."

"No sense," the man growled. "No plain common
horse sense. All right. You're hurt but not killed. Get
yourself up the ladder, and I'll fix that cut."

"But Jack, Andy—something's happened to them.
We've got to find them."

"First things first. You're dripping like a stuck steer.
Now these trunks. Usual story, I suppose. Everything
you've got in the world?"

"Yes, but Jack, Andy—something's happened to
them."

"Probably has." He drew in a deep breath and yelled,
"Efram. Efram. Open the shop door and haul these
trunks inside and lock up again. I'm taking the lady upstairs. Efram, get out here."

Another unseen door in the hull cracked open, level
with the street, and a tall, lanky, tow-headed boy with
long, powerful arms loped out. He bent and gathered a
box under each arm.

"I'm getting them, Father, I'm getting them. You
mind the lady."

Chapter Twenty-three

$\mathcal{P}$OPPY stood in the center of the bright bare room, keeping her dripping wrist over an enamel basin on the scrubbed board table. With her other hand, she held her chemise up around her breasts while the man bent to examine the cuts across her ribs. He grunted, straightened, then went over to the steaming teakettle on the iron stove, and poured water into an enamel pitcher. He put that, a bar of yellow soap, and a cotton towel on the table.

"You've got lively blood, but except for that wrist, you're no worse'n if a cat scratched you. Lucky you were dressed so heavy, or I'd be trying to explain how we got a deader here. Wash, and I'll get you some brandy to put on those cuts so they won't go putrid on you, and we'll tie up that wrist. You'll be as good as new in a week."

"Don't you think we should get a doctor?"

"Miss, if there's any doctors in this town, they ain't doctoring. If they're doctoring, they probably ain't doctors. Wash like I told you, and I'll find that brandy bottle."

Poppy watched, fascinated, while he went to the neat plank shelves beyond the stove. This room, walled in from space between decks, was as scrubbed and sparse as any place she had ever seen, and yet it lacked nothing. The shelves, stove, and a wide ledge holding wash basins and water buckets were arranged along the wall beside the door. The table with four straight wooden chairs set around it was placed squarely in the center.

At the back, two bunks were neatly made up with bright blankets. A trunk was set at the foot of each, and clothes hung from pegs over them.

The man returned with a large brown bottle and a thin cotton towel he tore into strips. Before she could take them, she jumped at the sound of a thudding and bellowing from down below.

"Stop, thief. Stop, thief. Where are you taking those trunks?"

She knew that voice. Poppy rushed to the door, flung it open, and looked down. Beside the few small trunks still outside, Efram and a smaller figure were wrapped together, swaying back and forth, panting and grunting.

"Bill," Poppy called. "Bill, stop that."

"I know Jack's gear when I see it. Where is he? This man's stashing it in his place."

"I know. I know. He's putting it inside for me."

Bill pulled back, looked up and let out a yell. Rapidly he started climbing up the ladder. Poppy glanced down at herself, bare shoulders shining in the bright light, chemise crumpled and ripped. She whirled and tossed the padded basque around herself as Bill burst into the room. She threw herself at him.

"Stop it, Bill. Stop it. It's all right. He saved me. We're just washing out these cuts."

Bill flung a protecting arm around her, pulled her close against him, and glared over her shoulder, fists still clenched. "How'd you get those cuts? What happened? Who are these men?"

"What happened to you?" Poppy flung back.

"I found my paper all right, but then I asked that dirty, lying thief how he knew what I had packed in my shoregoing trunk. How'd he get in the crew's quarters?"

"The First Mate," Poppy muttered.

"I thought he was supposed to stay on the ship, but I didn't see him," Bill brushed that aside. "Anvhow, that started a big hullabaloo, and before I ever got an answer out of him, the ship had left the wharf, and I got carried out to the anchorage. The captain said to forget it, and a sailor rowed us back to an anchorage clear around the bay. I booted that Ingot into the water, and then I had to walk for miles to get back here. Now—where's Jack? Andy?"

"They're gone," Poppy wailed. "They went to find a place to stay and get a wagon and they didn't come back. Bill, something's happened. You've got to go find them."

"First you tell me what happened to you."

"They left me to guard the trunks. It was hours, and the fog came in. Then somebody, a man—maybe two but I think it was only one—came at me with a knife. And these people opened up and came out and rescued me."

"Where were they before?"

"It's the Sabbath, and we're closed. We saw the lady out there but in this town, we don't accost a respectable-appearing female who's waiting for a gentleman, even if the gentleman is delayed."

Behind Bill, Efram came up the ladder and stood quietly beside the door, a heavy wooden cudgel in his hand.

"The trunks are inside, and I've locked up below."

Bill released Poppy, swung around, and looked from one to the other and then all around the bare room. Unexpectedly he said, "Maine."

"Vermont," the man said.

They stepped up and shook hands while Poppy stared. So this place was like England in one way, people could recognize one another's birthplace by the way they spoke, for all they did not speak regular English.

"Bill Mainwaring."

"Sea cap'n?"

"My uncle."

"Josh Wiggins. Josh Wiggins and Son, Efram. General Merchandise and Findings. Came out two years back, but Ma and the girls didn't make it even to the mountains. Took the cholera."

"Lost a young brother from it, cabin boy, took it in New Orleans. Likely young 'un."

They stood silent for a moment.

Then Bill turned to Poppy. "Jack and Andy started for town from here? Right after you landed?"

"We were about the last ashore. Even the crew had landed, and they pulled up the gangplank right after us."

"I'd better start looking and asking questions."

"Efram can go with you, he knows the town," Josh said and looked at Poppy. "I don't hold with asking other people's business, but is everything you own in those trunks?"

"They had money belts, both of them," Poppy whispered. "With gold."

Josh's mouth thinned. "I didn't like the Vigilantes, but they did some good," he said obscurely. "All right, Efram. Don't come back until you find them. I'll be down in the shop."

Poppy washed, then poured the brandy on her wrist, wincing at the sting of it. Then she bandaged her wrist and put on her blouse. She poured the blood-tinted water into the slop pail under the ledge, rinsed the basin, and put the used towel beside it. All at once she was saggingly weary and yet tense. She was parched and longed for a cup of tea, but it did not seem right to help herself from a kind stranger's supplies. She sat staring at the door, willing it to open, and heard only the faint creakings as the old ship moved on its bed of mud and sand.

Then she heard men's voices outside, one oddly familiar and yet unexpected, and sprang to open the door. Josh came in and behind him, a tall, elegant figure.

"Maurice!"

"I ran into that Yankee sailor Bill acting like a dealer trying to locate the fifth ace. I had to tell him I didn't think Jack and Andy ever got up into town."

"He didn't find them?"

"I hadn't seen them. We asked, and neither had anybody else. So we had to bet they never left the waterfront here. That's a big area, and the boy didn't know them by sight, so I came along."

"That was kind of you."

"I did not wish our acquaintance to end with the ship, so I had been watching for you."

Then Poppy noticed what Josh was doing. He was folding the blankets from the beds and putting them on the trunks. Then he turned back the coarse sheets and settled the pillows. He went to the stove, hefted the tea-kettle, and carried it over to fill from the bucket on the ledge.

"They're hurt," Poppy breathed.

"Bill got Jack on his feet," Maurice said. "Efram is carrying Andy. That Efram's a good boy, and he knows this part of town. Once we were sure they had to be down here, he worked up and down and across every lot like a bloodhound on the scent. He found them back of a shop across the way and in the next block above the wharf."

"Somebody was waiting for them." Poppy understood bleakly.

Jack came first, staggering, his face a mask of mud, his clothes filthy and ripped and dripping with blood, with Bill lifting and supporting him from behind. Efram carried Andy cradled in one long arm. He put him down on a bunk and went to get a lamp to hold close as Josh bent over the boy.

Andy was unconscious and limp, eyes closed, a trickle of blood running from one nostril. One side of his forehead was scraped and raw, surrounded by a deep bruise already turned purple. His breathing was so slow Poppy held her own breath waiting for each one. Josh felt the whole head with gentle fingers and then put a second pillow under it.

"Boot with nails," Josh said. "Missed his eye, and I can't feel any mushy spots or hear any bones grating. If nothing's hurt underneath, he'll come out of it. Only he's not to be touched or moved. No fussing. No nursing. His only chance is to heal himself." He drew a blanket up over Andy and scowled around him. "Leave him alone. Got it? Now let's look at you, mister."

"My—right—collarbone's—gone." Jack said haltingly and with great effort. "And some ribs on that side."

"Dumped him to drown in a muddy ditch," Maurice said. "He's tough, this one."

"They were trying to kick us to death."

"French gutter fighting," Maurice said. "Steerage scum."

"Like the one who fixed me up so I got held behind on the ship," Bill said.

"No steerage scum arranged to have you dropped so far around the bay it took you hours to find us," Poppy raged. "They were only tools, and I know whose hand pointed the way."

"You don't think it was just bad luck we were delayed and got left behind alone?" Jack asked.

"I know it wasn't," Poppy cried. "I had my warning, a shiver down my spine every time I saw them."

"If there's one thing I can't abide, it's a hysterical female," Josh said.

Jack put in quickly, "If you'll cut my coat and shirt off, I'll show you how to set this collarbone and strap up these ribs. I've broken bones before when I've taken a toss riding."

Jack was hurt worse than he was admitting, or he would not have made that slip. Simple sailors did not refer to riding. But he had given Poppy time to quiet herself.

Efram and Josh set to work with scissors, hot water, and towels. They, too, seemed to know about broken bones.

After Jack's ribs were bound up and his arm in a sling, he sat leaning back in a chair, white faced. Maurice picked up his shirt and jacket. "These are ripped. The boy's, too. Money belts? Who knew you were wearing them?"

"Josie knew we had gold in our trunks," Poppy said, careful to keep her voice low and even. "She must have guessed we'd try to find a safer place. I deliberately put a little in that knitting bag and flaunted it. I wanted Josie to notice it. I thought it would draw attention away from the belts. And I didn't think she'd tell the

First Mate because I didn't think she'd want to share with him."

"Women usually do tell the men they sleep with everything," Maurice said. "No woman could have arranged this. The First Mate could have very easily, even to letting everybody think he was staying aboard and then slipping ashore for a few hours."

"You must never risk yourself like that again," Jack ordered.

"So they got all three of you," Maurice said. "They cleaned the board, and you'll never be able to prove a thing."

"Yes, they've cleaned us out," Jack said and then slowly, "Is there a British consul here?"

"No," Poppy cried. "No, you're not going to—" she stopped. She had started to say "give yourself up to Dex" and stopped just in time. She finished instead, "We're not going to ask for help when we can manage."

"How?" Jack asked.

Poppy hesitated before she smiled and shrugged. If anybody here was going to think the less of her for this, well, let them. She pulled up her street skirt, untied the short wool apronlike one underneath, and let it drop heavily to the scrubbed floor. She tried not to remember the moment when she had started across the wharf and thought how those tens of pounds of weight could pull her under the water if she stumbled or lost her way.

"I don't know how much this is in American money, but this was in my furs. The linings of the fur stole and the two muffs had been packed solid." Poppy explained, "Your belts were full when I got to the furs in the bottom of the last trunk, so I made myself a kind of belt, too."

"So you are not without means to pay for a lodging," Josh said.

Poppy understood. Josh would succor and shelter them, but he was a businessman, not a charity. He would assist if he could, but they must stand on their own feet.

"I'm paying twenty-five a week for a bed, in a room with others," Maurice said. "Forty-five with meals."

Bill and Poppy looked at each other in dismay. She was sure he would stay with them until Jack and Andy recovered a little, but those prices were impossible.

"When I was here before, plenty of men were pitching their tents up on the hillsides," Bill said.

"Not for Andy," Poppy said as Josh objected. "Not any more."

"Carl Syler was in buying that outfit yesterday," Efram said in his self-effacing way.

"Yes." Josh nodded. "Always remember they say advice is worth exactly what it costs you, and this is free. I'd say that might be your answer."

"I'll listen and thank you," Poppy said.

"Carl's worked hard for a couple of years and done well, running a livery stable with a feed store on the side. But he's had a falling out with his partner, and he's taking off for the gold fields. They shared things out. The partner's keeping the business. Carl took the two houses, pretty far out, but the lots are good, nice and high and dry."

"How far out?" Poppy asked.

"A good twenty-minute walk."

Poppy laughed. A man who had walked a continent was balking at a pleasant stroll, but the others seemed to think that it was a fair statement of distance.

"I thought Carl would rent, even if he had trouble collecting, but keep the properties. I know a man did that last year with a lot he swapped for a barrel of whiskey. He came back from the gold fields broke and sold that lot for close to twenty thousand. Fact. Carl wouldn't listen. He wants to clear out lock, stock, and barrel."

"He's anxious to sell?" Jack asked.

"Set on it. But he wants cash on the barrelhead. That's not so easy. Now I don't know how much you've got, but he wants to leave town, and nobody else has offered. They're all figuring to beat him down on Monday."

"You want me to get Carl and bring him here now?" Efram asked.

"Take Bill and Maurice with you. They'll know whether Miss Poppy would consider the places fitting. We'll get Jack in the other bunk before he falls out of that chair, and we'll weigh out this gold and see what's what before you get back."

By the time the three returned with a tall, thin man, his dour face shadowed under a broad hat, Jack was asleep, and Poppy was shaking her head over the long row of figures Josh had added up so deftly. So much money, yet she was sure it would not be enough.

Josh held out the paper. "Here's all they've got, Carl. They was assaulted and robbed when they landed, as you can see." He jerked his head toward the two limp figures in the bunks.

Carl clumped across the room and looked at the paper. "T'ain't enough."

Poppy flared. "Anyhow we'll need something left for furniture and to live on."

"They're furnished except for a few things I sold or gave away."

"We have to eat."

"Your roofs are all right, but aren't the partitions canvas?" Josh asked.

Carl ignored the question. "Glass windows, four in each house."

"Just steps up from the street, no proper stoops," Efram said.

Carl looked at the paper again. "Cash on the barrelhead?"

"Gold napoleons. Weighed them myself."

"You keep them in your safe until I come back in the fall." Carl turned to leave and halted. "I mean I'll take it, ma'am."

"Just a minute," Poppy gulped.

"You want a bill of sale," Bill said.

Josh put out a clean sheet of paper and picked up his pen. "You got the legal description with you, Carl? We want to do this fair, square, and legal. Are you the purchaser, Miss Poppy?"

"I seem to be," Poppy said and waited. Josh did not suggest they could stay here for a couple of days while she looked around to see if she could find just one house and cheaper. Maurice and Bill did not say renting might be better until she learned the town. In despair, she muttered, "Miss Poppy Smith, formerly of Pallminster Lane, London, England."

She wanted to cry and stamp her feet. Those men were going right ahead and writing up that paper, nodding at each other, serious but pleased. There was not one thing she could do to stop them, so she might as well act like a lady about it. She would act like a lady if it killed her. And it might. Because nobody seemed to realize she would not have one penny piece left after this, just a scrap of paper, and that was not going to feed two sick people or buy wood to keep them warm and comfortable.

Carl signed and turned to leave again. Bill joined him.

"It's not wise to leave houses vacant overnight. I'll go with you."

"I won't leave until sunup," Carl said.

"Better for me to be there. I need a bed. I'll get a wagon, Poppy, and come for you and the trunks in the morning." He looked at Josh. "You carry groceries? I've still got my pay packet."

"Keep ten dollars for the wagon and give the rest to Efram. He'll have supplies and stove wood waiting when you get here."

Maurice lingered. He ignored Josh and Efram bustling up and down the ladder, settling the shop and room to rights for the night, bringing up a thin pallet and blankets Poppy knew would be her bed, banking down the fire in the stove and filling the teakettle.

"Both houses are vacant. You'll rent the second one?"

Poppy pushed the heavy hair from her forehead. She

had not eaten since noon, and she was achingly weary.
"Yes. I'll need the money."

"She'll want to be careful," Efram said, picking up
the pail of dirty water to carry out. "She'll want to
know who she's neighboring with."

"Exactly," Maurice said. "There's not six inches between the two places, I observed. Now my present
quarters are expensive, and I suspect somewhat overly
inhabited." He pinched his hand between two fingers to
illustrate a bite. "I also suspect several of my confreres
at the card room are similarly situated. I could speak to
them tonight. Say, three or four of us together, all quiet,
hard-working gentlemen, seldom home except to sleep
and change our clothes. For superior quarters, I'm sure
we would agree not to entertain any ladies, and we gamblers do pay our debts the day they're due."

"I know that," Poppy said, remembering Daisy's
friend.

"They'd have to find their own cleaning and any extra
furnishings that's needed," Josh said. "I'd say a married
couple, Miss Poppy, but they're few in this town, and
two ladies living close don't always agree."

Josh was a plain man, but he was not simpleminded.
He had seen she was young, pretty, richly dressed, and
had carried a large amount of money. She was traveling *en famille* with two brothers, but she had neither a
maid nor a lady companion. He knew she could not be
a housewife or a schoolgirl. A respectable woman might
object to her as a neighbor and landlady.

She said tiredly, "Speak to your friends, Maurice,
and I'll see you tomorrow."

"Also I have observed something else. I will be playing monte at one of the tables in the Palace."

"That's our best," Josh said.

"Several young ladies, well-dressed but appearing of
complete respectability, are employed there."

"Window dressing," Josh said. "An ounce a day and
found."

"Merely to be pleasant to the customers." Then with

pretended horror, "No, no. Not to touch the cards. That is not permitted. Ever. Fortunately."

"Bar and card tables," Josh said. "They bring in food for the customers but no private dining rooms. Respectable trade only."

"This is for the afternoon and evening. Your free time, that is as you please." Maurice shrugged.

"They would have to understand I have my household responsibilities," Poppy said sharply.

"That would be as you wished, I'm certain."

Chapter Twenty-four

$\mathcal{P}$OPPY sat at the kitchen table, stared at the blank sheet of paper, and chewed thoughtfully on her pen. She must write to Daisy. Every day for the last month, she had told herself she must write to Daisy. But what?

Daisy must have been notified when she and Andy disappeared from Cornwall. She might have been told there had been trouble with smugglers that night. Possibly Dex had seen Daisy in London and told her that he had seen them in Paris and knew they had sailed for San Francisco. Or he might not have.

She simply could not explain everything that had happened. She could tell how things were now, and if that left Daisy in utter confusion, it could not be helped.

She drew a deep breath, dipped her pen and wrote.

Dear Daisy,
Andy and I are safe and well in San Francisco.
We can collect our mail at the post office here.

And a pretty penny that would cost. She had seen men just come to town walk into the post office, shell out every dollar in their pockets, fifteen or twenty, grab their letters, and not seem to grudge that they had nothing left to pay for a meal. Still, no answer could possibly arrive for five or six months, or twice that if the ships were slow or delayed by storms, so she would not worry about that today.

Our thoughts often turn to our dear Mother and our happy home in Pallminster Lane. We miss London.

Poppy blinked rapidly. She would not allow herself to think she might never see London again.

Even now in late summer, the weather here is delightfully cool with bright sun and brisk breezes. We have a comfortable house.

She thought about that and nodded agreement with herself. Daisy would say horses were stabled better than this, but Daisy had never lived in San Francisco. In these few months, houses had been built up all around them, proper two- and three-story houses with railed porches, some prettily painted in two different colors, and with small trees planted in front.

We own it and the house next door.

Daisy would not question that. Everybody all around the world knew hatfuls of gold dust and fistfuls of nuggets were to be found in California for the mere scooping up.

That house is rented to three respectable gentlemen from the same emporium where I am employed.

Poppy beamed self-approval. The use of the word emporium was masterly. It could mean anything Daisy chose to think it meant.

Andy is employed at an iron manufactory under the tutelage of a smith we knew in England. He likes his work.

Truly she had a gift for writing. That word tutelage was very nice with Daisy so dead set on education. Andy did like his work, and she had seen no reason to spoil his pleasure by telling him the smith had been an informer on the smugglers. The poor man doubtless had been driven to it, frantic to get money for his fare to California.

She chewed her pen again. Daisy had never heard of Yankee Bill, so she would not be interested to know he had been so disgusted after one week in the gold fields that he had come back to town, sold his outfit for fantastic prices—fifty dollars for his boots alone—and shipped out on a Maine clipper, swearing never to leave the sea again. Daisy might be seeing Dex in London— no, she would not let herself feel jealous—so it was best not to mention Jack, either. Despite all Bill could say about the hard conditions out in the gold fields, Jack had been wild to get there, and he had left before he was really healed. He wrote, swearing he was quite recovered and everything was going well, but he had moved on twice now to places where he heard talk of rich new strikes. She did not like it that he wrote he always panned enough to have money to pay for his food when he went to town for supplies. Surely it was not possible for a man to pan those streams running with gold and find so little he starved. She knew nuggets as big as fists were not found every day, but gold was everywhere.

She frowned and sighed. What else could she tell Daisy?

There are not many married ladies and almost no respectable unmarried females here. Most gentlemen would like to be joined in matrimony, but life is hard on the ladies even with a kind gentleman who provides well. They must do their own cooking, washing, and scrubbing and are held at it all day long.

She glanced around her with approval. Andy was good about carrying wood and water, and since she had ruled that outdoor boots must be removed at the door, one floor scrubbing a week did very well. Her house was not a burden.

One gentleman highly regarded in the community spends much time trying to persuade me to that state. He was a Vigilante and is a member of a Volunteer Fire Department.

Daisy would not understand how important such things were, especially to a man with political ambitions. But she would not cross the paragraph out or Daisy would vow she had lost all trace of gentility.

He promises he will hire a cook—though one stepped off the boat here last week and was instantly offered six hundred dollars a month, as I understand she has a notable hand with pastry—or take rooms in the best boardinghouse. He also offers a carriage and to make a settlement.

Poppy shook her head. She had not meant to run on like that, but it was always a shadow on her day knowing Jeremiah Dunbar would be waiting for her at the Palace, patient and respectful, but always there. She had not taken him in aversion, but she could not imagine kissing him any more than she could Josh. Except she could imagine kissing and hugging Josh like a brother or a father, because he was a sweet, dear man. He had left his shop the day after they moved in here, and that was like a mother leaving a month-old baby, for all he admitted Efram was the best of sons, to tell her about the two dead Ingots. They obviously had been newly arrived steerage passengers from the *Bonne Irène,* by their filthy French clothes and half-starved, pallid appearance, and they had been found stabbed, in back of a cheap sailors' lodging. Josh had gone to look at the bodies because he had heard one of them had gold napoleons hidden in his shoes. He had noticed the shoes were covered with the kind of sand and mud found in the shop yard where Andy and Jack had been attacked. Somebody had made sure they would never tell about that attack or who had planned it. Later, Maurice had visited Amalie and reported Josie was still working for

Madame. The First Mate seemed to have sailed with the *Bonne Irène*.

Poppy shivered and shook her head. Her mind was wandering, and she must finish this letter so she could take it with her to the Palace.

> I am content with the condition in life in which I find myself and do not contemplate any change at this time.
>
> With all expressions of esteem to our dear Mother and kindest wishes for your continued health and happiness, we remain your dutiful children,
>
> Poppy and Andy

Captain Stowe had said he would stop by the Palace tonight to take the letter when he sailed for England in the morning. She folded it and hesitated over the address. She did not know whether Daisy was married and a titled lady, or still living in Pallminster Lane. Frowning, she sealed it and writing large and clear put down the name and street of Dex's bank. Daisy still would have her business affairs there. That would not have changed.

The blue satin dress, with the cream ruffles at the breast to match the ruffled underskirt, was laid out on her bed. She held it up and shook it. No doubt about it, the dress was shabby with that cigar burn in the skirt and the rubbed places at the waist. She would wear it just this once, for all the gentlemen said it made her look as if she had just stepped out of a stained-glass window.

She tied a lace scarf over her smooth curls. The wind sweeping down over the hills would tangle them into a mop of hoydenish tendrils. The letter went with her cream satin slippers—those were sadly shabby too —into the small marketing basket. Then she put on her shawl and boots. The planked sidewalks and streets were spreading everywhere, but with all the new building there were always mud holes.

The walk to work was as good as a fair every day. With the houses so small and crowded, people lived on the streets. Even the crowds at the Crystal Palace had not been as mixed as these. Chinese and islanders, Spanish men in serapes and pretty Chilean girls in scarves, Indians and odd-speaking Australians, blacks and frock-coated city men, peddlers and sailors with their sea gaits, all overflowed the sidewalks and jostled in a slow-moving stream on the street along with the burros driven by the miners, the loaded horse-drawn wagons, and the fine carriages. Poppy always looked for new arrivals with their trays of trade goods, often things that had been scarce for weeks. One man was having luck with his shoestrings. While she watched, the price went from fifty to seventy-five cents. Another, with an open red face, was selling eastern newspapers at a dollar apiece and saying frankly he had used them to pad his packing but, yes, they were the newest, only came ashore yesterday.

She longed to buy a *Pacific Daily* but that was Nicholas Amberson's paper, and she did not quite dare, for Jeremiah might see it in her basket. She did not understand why the two men hated each other so much, but then she did not understand politics. Instead, she bought the new *Golden Era.* She had not seen this week's issue, and if it did not compare with dear Mr. Dickens's *Household Words,* still it was very good.

Then she saw the fine black carriage and stepped forward and bowed. She laughed when the two ladies looked over and straight through her. Madame Dixmer had been quite right about her near-albino daughter. Within a month, she had her married to a gold millionaire, at least he was called that, who had set them up with that fine carriage and was building them a handsome mansion on the edge of town. Now neither of them seemed to have the faintest memory of the *Bonne Irène* or a certain ex-hussar.

What had become of the ex-hussar? Probably he was another one who had ended up knifed in some dark alley. If lucky, he had been quietly buried when nobody claimed him, instead of being tossed out on the sand at the water's edge with dozens of others who had come to similar ends. Poppy shivered.

She stopped to watch the antics of a sailor's monkey and listen to a street fiddler. The steam paddy passed, carrying sand from the hills to fill in still more of the waterfront. It was followed by a wagonload of whiskey barrels, but the oxcart behind that was something she did not see every day. The whole world was swarming the streets on this fine sunny day.

She bought a string of dried chilis from a peddler. Andy had got so he liked his beans Mexican style. Then she again stepped to the edge of the sidewalk and bowed. This time her bow was returned. More, Madame waved and beamed. She had done well, renting a fine three-story house Poppy had seen but never entered. Now she had a carriage—though perhaps it was hired—and was showing off some of her girls. She had a new redhead, a touch carroty but pretty in the face, and a slender dark girl who looked like Josie at first glance but was only the same type. Poppy frowned, then shrugged. She was not going to think about that.

She should turn off toward the handsome red brick structures with music blaring from them that housed the gambling establishments. But the motley rows of shops and peddlers lining the long wharf were enticing. At the corner she hesitated over a bargain in men and boys' socks in an iron store that had not exploded in the last big fire. Last winter every merchant in town had decided men's socks would be in short supply and had ordered them by the gross. Now they were selling below their factory cost. Andy wore out a pair of socks a week.

A pale blue flash on the street caused her to swing around. That carriage, with the smart chestnut horses, was the only one of its kind in town. She glared at the pale, elegant girl riding in it, chaperoned only by her black maid. Félicité Pannet did not usually appear in public without her mama, and yet she was obviously driving out on the Long Wharf to meet an arriving ship.

Gossip said the international banker's daughter was more strictly chaperoned than even the daughters of the wealthy Spanish rancheros. So somebody important and very special must be arriving. Félicité's pale blue dress, exactly matching the carriage, and the faint blush and smile on her delicate face hinted at more.

Poppy twisted the handle of her basket until the fibers crushed under her fingers. Who could be that important? Perhaps she was driven, obsessed by bitterness, but she thought she knew.

Before she had been three days in San Francisco, the minute she felt she could leave Jack and Andy alone, she had gone out ostensibly to talk to the owner of the Palace about a job but actually to inquire about banking arrangements in the town. That gold nearly had got them all killed, and she had to know if Dex had been helpless to provide for her in any other way.

Pete, the head bartender, had a genial face, and she questioned him. "Girl, if you expect to be saving money you've got all the banks you could want in this town. There's even an English bank if you want to stick to your own nationality. International? There's Guy Pannet. He's not connected with any bank that I know. He's more a representative, you could almost call him an ambassador, for important people all over Europe. Like the titled gentry that come over here with their own servants and horses and cases of liquor and dozens of guns to look at the wild westerners in the auriferous districts. Don't widen your eyes at me—that's exactly what I've heard them call the gold diggings. And they like to take a look at the aborigines and do a little huntin'. As for regular banks, go over to Montgomery Street and see for yourself."

Poppy did. She looked at the long row of red brick buildings and went into the English bank on the corner. Through the clouds of tobacco smoke, she watched the men go up to the counters and thump down large leather bags of gold dust. The clerks extracted the black sand, weighed the gold and packed it in boxes. The customers were unwashed men with long beards and jack boots, come straight from the diggings to deposit their wealth, but she did not doubt that in a few hours they would be washed, shaved, and changed so they could hardly be distinguished from the frock-coated bank officials. She looked at the huge lumps of quartz on exhibit, listened to talk about the fireproof cellars that had proved safe even in the last big fire when the brick buidings did burn, and went out with rage at Dex burning as hot as that fire inside her.

With a few scribbles of his pen, Dex could have arranged a draft or a credit for her here. Any bank or banker would know who he was and his banking connections and honor his request. Instead he had put them in a position to be terrorized during that long, terrible voyage, and in danger of their lives once ashore, with actual scars they would carry for the rest of their days.

He had done that, deliberately made the choice, because something was more important to him than her safety. That was close to unforgivable, though she might have been willing to listen to a reasonable excuse.

Then after she caught a glimpse of Félicité Pannet and listened to the talk about her, she knew it was beyond any forgiving. The girl was wealthy and a beauty, and everybody knew the only suitor her family favored was that handsome young fellow, scion of another of the great banking houses, who turned up in San Francisco every now and again inquiring about some titled heir who had disappeared into the wilds and was rumored lost. So because of that pale-faced, yellow-haired girl, that daughter of a member of the great aristocrats of international banking from whom no secrets of fund transfers, however handled, could be kept concealed, he had risked Andy and Poppy's lives rather than let it be guessed he had paid off a lovely young mistress. She had meant that little to him, and the girl was that important. She could only hate Dex, futilely.

But what if it was Dex, arriving in San Francisco, setting foot on the wharf in minutes now, that Félicité had gone to meet? Would he continue to try to pretend that a girl named Poppy did not exist?

Chapter Twenty-five

POPPY longed to run down to the wharf, to be there to watch the passengers step ashore. And what would she do if Dex did walk down the gangplank with eyes only for Félicité waiting to meet him? Fling herself at him to his horror and embarrassment? Or stand aside like some gutter waif while he brushed past her without a glance?

Félicité could be meeting any of a hundred other people, Poppy told herself and knew she lied. All San Francisco knew that that arrogant beauty could not be bothered to bestir herself to as much as a smile for anybody less than the heir to a great title. Or a great bank.

To go running down to the wharf with her little marketing basket, to hover in the shadow of that fine matched pair, could only bring hurt and humiliation. She had a job, a job that milk-faced ladylike chit could never fill in a hundred years, and she had better get there.

As she stepped into the Palace, she twitched her skirts so they made a rich rustling sound on the red carpeting. Perhaps nobody could hear that sound over the six-piece band playing full blast, but when sailors and miners had not seen a woman for six months, it was amazing how sharp all their senses were. She tilted her head this way and that so the blaze of light from the crystal chandeliers, reflecting back from the gilded ceiling, would catch the glint of gold in her curls. A drunken miner had thrown a whole handful of gold dust over her head last night, and while she had brushed her

hair carefully over a sheet when she got home, she
knew enough remained to sparkle beautifully. Strolling
across the room, she paused under one of the large oil
paintings. She was not nude, but anyone could observe
that her wrist was more finely turned and her bosom
and waist neater than the painted beauty's.

From the end of the bar, Pete murmured, "You're
late."

She slipped around to him and smiled. They were
firm friends. She was the most beautiful and popular
girl at the Palace, and he was the best bartender in San
Francisco.

His handlebar mustache was always groomed to a
hair, his white shirt immaculate and his red velvet waistcoat impeccable, but it was his art that fascinated
Poppy. He could serve a party of thirty and never write
down an order or mistake one. Men swore he could
remember their drink if he had served them only once,
even if that was six months before. He kept the long
mahogany bar, the great ceiling-high mirrors in their
ornate carved frames, and every bottle and glass sparkling. There were no fights at Pete's bar. He never had
to do more than lean forward, his great fists resting on
the gleaming mahogany, and speak quietly. Loud voices
dropped, and angry men turned away. Only last week
when a new assistant, who simply did not understand
the proper Palace tone, had thought he saw a man
starting to draw a gun and jumped over the bar, everyone had been so horrified there was hardly a sound in
the great room for a full thirty seconds. Then Pete had
moved quietly around the bar, picked up the new assistant by his pants and shirt collar, carried him to the
door, and kicked him into the street. Everybody drew a
vast sigh of relief. This was still the best-run bar in
town. The band started playing louder, the gamblers
slapped down their cards with élan, and every customer
bellied up and ordered a double.

Poppy stepped out of her boots and shawl, into her
slippers, and handed the filled basket to Pete to put
under the bar. "Has he been waiting long?"

"Got here early to read the papers."

Poppy glanced toward the corner where easy chairs were set around tables covered with newspapers and periodicals. "Did you get a *Punch* or *Illustrated News?*"

"No, but somebody brought in a *London Times* an hour ago."

That was good. In Pallminster Lane, they naturally had never read the *Times,* but the gentlemen sometimes discussed what it had said, and Daisy repeated their remarks. Now Poppy had come to feel the *Times* was a great comfort because once you knew what it said, you knew exactly how you should stand on any issue. It settled what was right and proper. The San Francisco papers were most confusing. Each paper reflected its editor's attitudes, and no two editors agreed on anything.

"Perhaps later," Pete said. "There's an English ship unloading today."

"Is there?" Poppy said, moving toward the back.

Jeremiah was waiting beside the table where Maurice was playing. It was not only his great height, his prematurely white hair framing a clean-shaven face, and his impeccably tailored black broadcloth suit that made him conspicuous; it was that he was not gambling, smoking, or drinking. In a town where two men could not meet without a quick drink, he never touched a drop of anything. He was only there waiting for Poppy, as he did every day.

Poppy smiled, tilted her head, and drifted gracefully toward an upholstered chair set against the wall. Jeremiah drew another up beside her. A waiter appeared instantly with a small table and a bucket of ice holding a bottle of champagne. Another brought a silver tray set with a glass, a bottle of whiskey, two cups of coffee, and an oyster roll in a heavy linen napkin.

The waiter opened the champagne, and Poppy took a dutiful sip from the glass while he slipped the bottle back in the bucket, then whipped it away again. Pete could make champagne cocktails from that for the miners to buy for the other girls. Jeremiah put the bottle of whiskey in the deep pocket of his coat. He would take that to the clubhouse of his Volunteer Fire Company. Poppy drank coffee and nibbled on the oyster roll. This was a daily ceremony, the price Jeremiah paid for fifteen minutes of her company.

"You look tired," Jeremiah said jealously.

Until then Poppy had felt in the bloom, though the flush on her face rose from rage at the thought of Dex and Félicité.

"You should let me send a carriage for you."

That walk was the most pleasant part of her day and her freedom. "It's enough that you send one to take me home at night." At least she had stopped his accompanying her, but she was certain it would be reported to him if she ever went any place other than home and alone.

"I have to go to Sacramento next week. You've never been on a steamer. It's a pleasant trip there. We could stay the night and return the next day. You need a little rest and a holiday."

"Andy and I must make the trip sometime. You are settled on running for this senatorship?"

"Running for the Senate," Jeremiah corrected, smiling fondly.

"You are?"

"We are holding discussions. Policy. How best to maintain law and order. We brought back respect for law once, but the disorders are growing again. Rowdies still infest the town. The Sydney Ducks are still with us. A whole shipload of Chinese prostitutes landed lately. We have thefts on the wharfs, cases of arson, robberies, and violent deaths every night."

Poppy put down the crust of her oyster roll. She knew Jeremiah was proud of his service with the Vigilantes, but she thought San Francisco was doing very well for a town that was growing like a balloon inflating. What Jeremiah said was true. Yet he made it sound like a forest fire of lawlessness running out of control, and she thought of it as more like a constant series of little bonfires that only needed watching so they did not spread. She knew she would not like to live in a place where plain citizens took it on themselves to act as judges and hang other men. In England, they sometimes had hanging judges, but at least they were judges.

"I think this is a fine city, Jeremiah," she said gently.

"You've told me what happened the day you landed —robbery, assault, close to murder. Lawlessness, violence, rampant, rampant."

She had told him, and she heartily regretted it. "Now we find living here very pleasant."

"Women do not understand the broader aspects," Jeremiah pronounced, patting her hand. "You need a man to think and act and care for you."

Poppy was startled at how warmly she disagreed. She enjoyed reading the *Times* and being informed, and once she was informed, depending on the respect she felt for the source, and she did respect the *Times,* she felt she could make up her own mind, decide what she thought was right. She did not think she respected Jeremiah, and she was far from sure he was right. She certainly did not want him to decide and control her life.

She fluttered her lashes, only grateful he could not dream how she resented his remark, while she groped for words. In the little silence between them, she was aware of a stir rippling around the room, indrawn breaths and a murmuring. She glanced toward the door and felt a chill run through her. The tawny-haired man standing there, wearing a pale, elegant gray suit, was handsome and distinguished looking. He was poised like a man looking for trouble. Conversation stopped. Every man and woman in the room knew Jeremiah Dunbar had only been stopped from drawing on Amberson, not once but at least twice, because the editor had announced he was not armed. He said he believed in settling political disputes by intelligent debate, not gunpowder. But everybody believed that one day Jeremiah's taunts would bring him out armed and ready to fight.

Now Amberson strolled across the room as Jeremiah got to his feet. He bowed to Poppy and held out a copy of his newspaper to Jeremiah.

"I considered my editorial today might be of interest to you, so I brought you this. I didn't want you to miss it."

Jeremiah did not move or take the paper. "The subject?"

"In honor, if you can call it that, of the first anniversary of the Vigilante-type hanging of a woman. You remember Juanita?"

"She was a killer."

"She was protecting her man. Maybe he wasn't much, but he was hers."

"You'd have turned her loose to kill again?"

"Such people don't kill twice. She was a simple soul, a woman, a very young woman. She was murdered by a mob. There are mob murders going on again around the mining camps, lawless hangings, brutal hangings, slow strangling deaths."

"Because for too long such snakes were turned loose with only a warning to leave town and allowed to carry their venom to the next diggings. Now the lawless are being hung. As they should be."

"We have provisions in this state for due process of law and proper procedures of trying and sentencing." Amberson's voice was soft, but clear and carrying. "I believe in our state constitution. I believe in law and order. I don't want to see a return of so-called law enforcement outside the law."

"I am proud of my record with the Vigilantes."

"At the time you probably rendered a necessary service," Amberson admitted. "It is no longer necessary. I don't want to see it return."

"I think you *will* see it return."

"I may. I hope not. But I don't want to see it return because of trumped-up, false charges of the failure of proper procedures when there is no failure. I don't want to see it return simply to feed the vanity and greed of power-hungry men."

"Sir, I think we should continue this discussion outside. There are ladies here."

"I am saying nothing improper for a lady to hear. I want everybody to know and hear how I feel about this."

"Use your filthy newspaper for that purpose. I won't dirty my hands with it."

"I'll spread my ink thinner. But not my convictions, Dunbar. This is a fine town, a lusty town with growing pains, but it's going to be a great city. I won't have your warped views from another day distorting the present situation."

Jeremiah's face was white. "Do you care to make that clearer?"

"We'll soon have fifty thousand people here. We have fine homes, churches, schools, theaters. We have a busy port, many manufactories, prosperous trade. Your warped view chooses to see none of this. You see, 'Here malice, rapine, accident conspire, And now a rabble rages, now a fire. . . .' "

"You phrase it well."

"I?" Amberson laughed, turned on his heel, and went toward the doors.

"What was he laughing at?" Jeremiah demanded and started after him. "He's going to explain that to me."

"Please, please." Poppy caught his arm. "It was—I just remembered. I heard The Rev say that."

Jeremiah glared at her. "What are you babbling about?"

"That's from a quotation. I mean it is a quotation. About London. By Dr. Johnson, I think."

"A sawbones." Jeremiah relaxed. "Those university fellas have their heads stuffed full of books and their mouths full of words, but sometimes they do manage to hit the nail on the head. I'm surprised Amberson would quote him." He paused. "Just trying to show off his own fancy education," he decided.

Poppy let go of her long-held breath. Amberson had come in here looking for trouble, and it was a mercy she had managed to distract Jeremiah to herself.

"I'm going over to the Firehouse," Jeremiah said. "I want the Company to know Amberson's up to something. He's going to fight us on every issue straight down the line, and he must have strong backing."

"He just doesn't want to see the Vigilantes back again."

"Sweet child, stay that way," Jeremiah said absently and then roared, "He was trying to trap me. He was trying to get me to make a statement that would defeat me in this election. It's going to be an all-out fight."

"Then you won. You didn't say anything."

"I will. I will. I have a civic conscience. I'll make a statement. I'm not going to stand still until he manages to convince people they're living in paradise and can relax so they end up with their throats cut and playing their harps in a heavenly paradise before they figured on it. I'll have a statement in our papers before I see you tomorrow, sweetheart."

Shaking her head, Poppy watched him go and then drifted over to watch Maurice play. He had been tight-lipped and tense ever since he had had to draw on a player last week. The man had backed down without shooting, but Maurice's eyes still seemed to glitter as brilliantly as the diamond in his stickpin while his fingers dealt the thin Spanish cards. Today he smiled briefly and looked more natural.

She sat for a time with a weeping miner who repeated over and over, "Finest partner a man ever had," until she realized the partner was dead and the mourning man was the sole owner of a rich claim. Then she strolled over to the entrance. The tone of the Palace did not permit the display of a table heaped with gold, or girls waiting just inside the doors, but a glimpse of a smiling face and a fluttering skirt never hurt business.

She fluffed her ruffles, catching a breath of fresh air and laughing at a small boy being pulled along by a large dog on a rope. She stiffened as she caught a glimpse of the pale blue carriage rolling down the street toward her. A man was sitting beside Félicité, a tall man with his tall hat tilted jauntily over one eye and the gold head of his cane glinting between his knees. Félicité was leaning forward, her pale face animated, gesturing and laughing, making a pretty play of a delightfully flustered lady showing some dubious sights to a visitor.

She pointed her ivory fan straight at the Palace and at Poppy standing in the doorway. Dex's head turned, and their eyes met, but his face did not change, and he made no sign. He did not smile, bow, or acknowledge Poppy in any way. Instead he turned to Félicité, his head tilting attentively, and made some small comment that made her shake her head and laugh again.

Poppy clutched the door frame and watched the carriage drive away down the street.

Chapter Twenty-six

$\mathcal{S}$HE was fainting inside, sinking away into nothingness, while outwardly she still stood by the door, smiling in the sunshine. Then with a surge of rage the blood rushed through her, and she turned with a graceful swing of her skirts, to stroll back across the red carpet. She was blind and deaf and shaking inwardly with fury while she stood and seemed to listen admiringly to the musicians and move slightly, enticingly, to the beat.

He had not even given her a private smile or glance. He had looked straight through her, cut her dead. She had been right. Félicité was the only woman he valued. For Félicité, he had risked *her* life. When he was with Félicité, she, Poppy, was merely one of the sights of a gaudy part of town, a cause for shared secret smiles, made sweeter by a slight maidenly confusion.

Poppy did not know what she was doing or saying. Once or twice she had a fleeting impression Pete or Maurice had been staring at her. From somewhere outside herself, she heard laughter and a high shrill voice chattering and knew they were her own.

Yet she could not have appeared too strange. A nice young miner who had hit it rich bought a bottle of champagne to sit with her and made a small jest about anything so light costing so heavy. He told her about his girl back in Connecticut and asked if she thought the girl's parents would consider a necklace of gold nuggets improper. They were betrothed. Poppy had no idea what she answered, but the young man seemed happy.

She knew she talked and laughed with others, but finally she was only sure it was midnight, and she could leave.

The carriage Jeremiah hired for her was waiting.

"Big doings up on the hill tonight," the driver chatted. "The banker's got some important man visiting from France. Or maybe it's England. With those follows, you never can tell."

"A dinner? Important men?"

The driver hooted. "Important everybody. A reception. All the big men and their ladies, and I honest-to-God think they was all wives there tonight, and everybody in their best bib and tucker and stepping high. They even had the old Mexican government officials and their ladies in those fancy mantillas. Real polite spoken, those always are. Didn't really fight us when we came in here and raised our flag, and I know because I was here."

Her head was bursting, but she did not need to answer. The driver was a man who liked to talk.

"I think maybe it was for the girl. The girl and him, the visitor. Yes, siree, that's it. I heard she met him at the boat, and they both got bags of gold, and they like somebody of their own kind, no matter where they're from, to sit with them, don't they? Didn't your Queen marry a German?"

"A queen and a banker are a little different."

"Anyhow, I'll bet this was to let people know they're getting hitched." The driver cackled. "I'd like to see a big wedding in this town. We got the churches, and they could put on a show for us."

"We can stand in the mud and watch."

"Sure. I'll be hanging out the highest window, not to miss a thing. Here we are. I see your brother left a lamp in the living room, but I'll wait until you're inside the door."

She thought she would toss and turn all night, picturing Dex and Félicité together. She thought she would cry herself to sleep. Instead she dropped her clothing on a chair and, exhausted by emotional turmoil, fell on

the bed, barely pulling the covers over herself before
she dropped down into unconsciousness.

Andy shook her awake, wanting his breakfast, demanding sandwiches for his lunch. Poppy stumbled
numbly into the kitchen where Andy had the stove blazing and water boiling, and she began to fry cold mush.
She had the coffee made before she woke enough to
remember fully.

"Andy, Dex is here."

"When's he coming to see us? Shall I ask to get off
work? How long is he going to stay?"

"I don't think we'll see him. He's staying at the
Pannets'. They gave a big party for him last night. I
heard it was for him and Félicité."

"Félicité Pannet? But, Poppy, you were his girl in
Paris."

"In Paris."

Andy heard her tone and faltered, "Oh, Poppy, I'm
sorry. Are you sure?"

"He saw me, and he didn't even bow. Here's your
mush. I'll give you rolls and cheese for lunch."

"What are we going to do?"

"Nothing. Just nothing. I know you won't go running
after him. Any more than I will. It's just as well. He
doesn't know Jack came with us, and if Dex was around
here and Maurice happened to mention our brother out
in the diggings—no, we wouldn't want to risk it, anyway."

"If I see him, I'll run, that's what I'll do, I'll run the
other way," Andy said as he left.

"He won't bother to come looking."

Her head told her that, every bit of common sense,
and she could not believe it. She looked around the
house, the house she cherished and lived in with pride,
and saw it was flimsy and makeshift. All the white paint
she and Andy had spread on the walls and the brown
on the floors could not conceal the rough wood beneath.
The inner partitions were still of canvas, and the curtains were red calico. The red carpets were worn ones

the Palace had thrown out and replaced. She had begged for them, scrubbed, sunned, and put them down. They cut the drafts from underneath, but they were streaked and faded.

Her comb, brush, and mirror were fine silver, Dex's gift, but they were spread out on a dressing table made of boxes covered with more red calico. The mirror showed her fine English skin darkened to cream by the California sun and a sprinkling of freckles across her nose. Gold dust, the gaudiness of a dance hall girl, still sparkled in her hair.

Dex would never come here. He would not want to betray himself by inquiring where that redhead from the Palace lived. So it was quite logical to bathe and scent herself with a Paris perfume and put on the chemise and petticoat covered with dozens of rows of dainty half-inch lace and step into blue satin slippers. Then she washed her hair and toweled and brushed it into shining, curling tendrils frothing halfway to her waist.

When she heard the knock on the door, her blue satin robe was ready. She tied the wide white ribbons at the waist and, head high, opened the door. She stood in silence. She knew she had changed, but she also knew she looked her loveliest.

Dex only said, "May I come in?" He stepped inside, looked around, and raised an eyebrow. "I would have thought you could do better than this."

"Better?" Tall with shock, her eyes flashing blue fire, Poppy said, "We were extremely lucky. I own this and the house next door."

"I know prices are high, but I intended you to settle in a suitable place, with conveniences." He looked at the canvas partitions. "A comfortable place."

"We were lucky to settle with a roof. And our lives."

"You had trouble?"

"Gold is not as safe as an order on a bank."

"Not for a young girl and a boy alone," Dex agreed. He leaned on his cane, hat in hand. His black hair was crisped from the sea sun, his face darkly bronzed and his narrowed eyes brilliant. "But I understood you arrived accompanied by a young man."

He had not come to see her. He had not even asked what trouble or danger the gold had caused. He was still the heir hunter, interested only in finding Jack, and he knew Jack had disappeared from Paris the day they sailed.

She snatched at a half truth. "Yes. Yankee Bill. A nice young man crazy for the gold fields. He did come ashore with us."

"I heard you had a brother in the gold fields."

So he had inquired, and not even the Pannets could object to his heir hunting, but had got only her address and some vague talk. "Bill tried it for a week and went back to sailoring."

"Andy?"

All at once, she wanted to confide in him. She wanted to tell him that Andy was working with the smith and happy with it, but that she had uneasy moments about his doing it. The smith had informed once, betrayed for money, and what a man did once, he could do again. Dex would tell her whether he thought Andy should be left with the smith.

But he was not interested in their perplexities and dangers. His inquiry was merest courtesy.

"Andy has never been so happy. He's working in an iron manufactory."

"I hear a prominent and well-regarded gentleman is seriously interested in you."

"I am content here for the present." That reminded her of the letter to Daisy. She had to know. "Is Daisy married?"

"Most happily." A corner of Dex's mouth twitched up. "Her husband is not a young man, but he is reasonable, most reasonable. They do a reasonable amount of entertaining both in the country and in town. I understand he has no objection that she has taken a reasonable, reasonably small, interest in the betterment of fallen women."

Poppy felt a pang of pity. Poor Daisy, married to a

reasonable man. Still, she had no doubt that Daisy loved being a lady and saw to it her husband was a contented man.

"You say you own the identical house next door? Who are the men I saw there?"

Poppy snatched again at yesterday's inspiration. "They are employed at the same emporium."

"Gamblers, then. At the Palace. I had hoped for better for you, Poppy."

Poppy hunched up like a spitting kitten. "They have never intruded here, never set foot here except by invitation or in company. Maurice helped me when I was alone and hurt and didn't know where to turn." The bitterness spilled out. "I could have died from that gold you seem to think should have done so much for me. A lot of the thanks that I'm here today, safe and well, and have everything I do, are owing to Maurice, in spite of the gold."

"Then your fancy is fixed on this gambler?"

"My fancy is fixed—?" Poppy gasped to a halt.

"Yes?"

Poppy blazed, "I have a good life. I have everything —home, friends, family, work, everything, all my own. You walk in here asking questions about things that have nothing to do with you, criticizing, condescending, knowing nothing. I tell you I have everything I want."

"Poor Poppy," Dex said gently.

"I can be anything I want, and I will."

"That's why I am afraid for you."

"I don't want anything you can give me," Poppy said, and burst into tears.

He threw his hat and cane on a chair and caught her in his arms. Poppy flung herself against him and clung, raising her hot, wet face for his kisses, and then kissing him back wildly like a child seeking comfort after great fear.

She had no pride. She had no anger. Later, there would be time for those. Now was the only moment. The only reality was Dex, the sensations that were Dex, the deep, quiet sound of his murmuring voice in her ears, the remembered scent of soap and some dry-wine fragrance that seemed peculiarly his own, the rippling strength of his shoulders under her clutching fingers— all were life warmth after long, chilling near-death. His kisses sent deep throbbing waves surging all through her, until her whole being yearned toward the moment when it would become a part of his being.

Dex lifted her and carried her into her bedroom. He tumbled her on the bed and tore off his clothing. Poppy waited for him, eyes shining and lips softly smiling. They had this time of sharing, this mingled tumult and peace, this hunger and fulfillment, this remembered ecstasy and a new tearing of emotions.

They did not talk, only murmured and whispered broken phrases. Poppy could not have spoken. She had no words to bridge the long, echoing emptiness that had been the time without him. She had not been in his arms for so many months, had known no love. No man had kissed her, and she had not wanted any other man to kiss her. Now she could only tell him that with her kisses and embraces.

She could not get enough of kissing, his kissing her, her kissing him. She had thought he would never be with her, never love her again, and yet he was, and she could not bear for it to end. She held him, clung, enticed. Twice he started to leave, and twice he returned.

When she knew she could not hold him any longer, Poppy turned her face to the wall and refused to watch him leave. Her eyes refused, but her ears heard the door close behind him. Naked and alone, she stretched out on the bed that no longer held him. When she finally raised her head and looked around, something young and tender was gone from her eyes. Her mouth had a deeper, stronger curve, a woman's acceptance.

She had feared she might never see him again. She had tortured herself they would never make love again. Yet, they had, though that had not been his wish or intention when he came here. She knew that. But he had loved her, and for him, too, it had been complete while it lasted.

He had left, thinking only that they had had this one last time. He did not intend to return. To him, it was finished, there would be no more. His silence had told her that more clearly than words.

But he had betrayed himself. Away from her, he could be completely devoted to the beautiful Félicité, the woman who was the perfect wife for him by breeding and station. With Poppy, with her kisses warm on his lips and her body close to his, Félicité faded to a distant image, a pretty picture of a woman, not vital flesh and blood. His banker's mind planned to marry Félicité. His man's body responded to red-gold hair, scarlet lips, and deeply violet eyes.

Poppy sprang out of bed. She did not regret what she had done or what had happened. At worst, she had had the only thing in life she had ever really wanted, had had it this one last time. She would not despise either herself or Dex for the way it had happened. She would hold it close to her, alive in her memory, knowing she was revitalized and brought to life again by the miraculous burning flame of Dex's love.

She would go out and behave as usual. But she would go armored with a new weapon he had put into her hands today. In her presence, Dex could not resist her. His body answered hers as a magnet drew steel. She would give him cause to remember that. He was not married to Félicité yet.

Chapter Twenty-seven

*T*ODAY she had remembered she had not always lived in a board and canvas shack. Today she had held the living memory of a rich, elegant life close to her. So she put on the gray dress of stiff satin embroidered with an elaborate design in tiny iridescent beads so that when she moved, she seemed to be the center of a thousand multi-hued sparkling, flickering lights. Her shoes were beaded to match and so were the gray shoulder-length gloves. She smoothed them on tenderly. She would never be able to afford gloves like these again after they were soiled, and even if she could find them in the same gray, they would not be beaded. But she looked and felt as elegant as if she were setting out for the opera in Paris.

For the street, she covered herself with her largest shawl, but when she stood beside the bar in the Palace and removed it, she could hear the hiss of admiration run all along the mahogany length. Then a young miner, as tow-headed and blue-eyed as Andy, was standing before her, mouth rounded in admiration and holding out his hand.

"A lovely day," Poppy said graciously and then saw what was cupped in his palm. The earrings were almost the same color as her eyes, elaborately carved, of some strange smooth stone she had not seen before. She stared at them. "How beautiful."

Behind her, Pete whispered, "I think it's amethyst jade, Miss Poppy. I've heard of it but never seen any. Very valuable."

"I was in a sailors' place, looking for a game," the boy said simply. "I'd seen you here yesterday, and when I spotted these on the table, I sat in."

"That's Imperial stuff, treasure, probably stolen," Pete murmured.

"And I've still got my poke," the boy said, patting the bulge on his chest under his shirt. "These, please, miss, I won them for you. Because they match your eyes."

"I never saw anything so beautiful."

"If I"—the man's face reddened—"could just put them on for you and see you wearing them."

"Of course," Poppy said and tilted her head.

Breathing heavily, he fumbled and finally managed to fasten them on her ears. Then he stood back. "It's just the way I pictured you," he whispered. "Like a picture, only better, because you're perfect and alive."

"Dazzling," Pete supplied

Poppy stood absolutely still. The earrings did not feel firmly fastened, and she was afraid if she moved, they would fall.

"Miss, if I—" His face went even redder.

"Yes?"

"—if I could just kiss you. Once."

Every head at the bar nodded. Even Pete beamed paternally.

Poppy laughed. This would be like kissing Andy, kisses that did not count. She smiled and tilted up her face.

The young man took a deep breath, held out both arms, then grabbed her in a bear hug and kissed her soundly. Then he jumped back, stared at her adoringly and said in a low, awed voice, "Hey, now!" He jumped in the air and clicked his heels before he whirled and started for the door at a run. Just inside, he turned, laughing, and yelled, "Hey, now!" and jumped and clicked his heels again, then ran outside and disappeared in the crowd.

At the bar, every man whooped and banged his glass in an order for a full one. Pete grinned and turned, reaching for a bottle, while Poppy hesitated. The earrings still held. The least she could do was walk across the room and let everybody see them.

Jeremiah was waiting, and he was scowling blackly. "Take those off."

Poppy looked back at him, level-eyed. "He was a nice young man. He reminded me of Andy."

"Do you think I want people saying my wife was mauled by any dirty miner who happened into the Palace? That man wasn't any Andy. I can see the look on your face. I never saw your eyes shining like that before."

Poppy caught her breath. Jeremiah was too involved in anything that touched her, too observant. He was reading this morning's lovemaking still glowing on her face. He had only mistaken the person.

"I never wore Imperial jade before," she said quietly.

"And you won't again." Jeremiah's voice rose. "Take those off and give them to me."

"No. I think you should take yourself off and find another kind of woman for a wife."

His face collapsed. "I'm sorry, Poppy. I went crazy for a minute. I can't stand the thought of any man touching you. And I had to watch." His voice threatened to rise again.

"Then you needn't come in here to watch ever again."

"No, Poppy, no. I said I'm sorry. I am. Come have something to eat. There's fresh brook trout. Or maybe a quail?"

She was starving. If she refused to sit with Jeremiah, she might go all afternoon and evening without anyone else offering to buy her a bite to eat. Besides, she remembered Daisy saying only a stupid woman parted on bad terms with a man unless his behavior had been so freaky and fractious as to reduce her to humiliation and despondency. Jeremiah had not behaved that badly. He was only jealous.

Poppy condescended to a brook trout and tried to

appear to be only toying with the rolls while she ate every bite.

"Work like this when you could live in every comfort and luxury," Jeremiah was mourning. "That dress, it's fit for a governor's ball."

"I'm happy you like it."

"I'm not happy. How do you think I feel? Knowing any man can come in here and look at you and touch you. And the rest of the time, not knowing where you are or what you're doing."

"You know I'm home with Andy."

"And the mornings, after he leaves for the manufactory?"

Jeremiah could not know. What had happened was not written on her face. "Are you implying I compete with the Chileans in my free hours?"

"I know you don't, I know you don't," Jeremiah groaned. "But if we were married, I could protect you. What did you do this morning?"

That was a simple query. Jeremiah had asked it before but not in quite the same tone. No, it was only her lively awareness of what had happened that was making her uneasy. "I was at home."

"Just at home, just as usual?"

Jeremiah could not have a spy on her at home. He would not dare. But this town was as full of gossip as a dog of barks. Dex had mentioned the men living next door, so he had seen somebody entering or leaving. If they also had had a caller, who had seen Dex at her door, that might have been mentioned later at the Palace.

"Were you?" Jeremiah insisted.

That gloating sharpness. Jeremiah was trying to trap her into a lie. Daisy had a saying about that, too. When you were caught, tell as much of the truth as you dared.

"I had a message this morning," Poppy said and stretched the truth not at all as she admitted virtuously, "I have written my mother, but I have not heard from her."

"Your mother's alive? You've never said anything about your family."

Poppy felt a little giddy with success. "You didn't ask, but of course asking questions about a person's past is not *à la mode* here. Of course my mother's alive. And my grandparents. You should ask Andy about them. He adores them."

"Then why did you arrive here with that batch of misbegotten Ingots?"

"When you have questions, you should ask me, sir, not brood about the matter in silence. It was a matter of time, an English boat we missed." They certainly had missed Jack's boat, sold in the Vendée, for if they had had that, they would not have needed to walk those wet and muddy miles on miles. If that was another time and place, Jeremiah did not need to be informed of every small detail. "So the first available boat." She shrugged delicately.

Jeremiah still was not entirely content. "You had news of your mother?"

"Yes. Important news."

"What?"

Jeremiah was too insistent. He knew something, so as much of the truth as she dared. Poppy dabbed daintily at her lips with the heavy linen napkin, put it down, and looked at Jeremiah with wide, innocent eyes.

"Of her marriage. When we left, she was still unsettled in her mind. But we could not wait." Poppy sighed gently. "I am so happy she decided on the gentleman, for he is a most reasonable man."

"I still don't understand why you are here if you have such happy family ties at home."

"Jack and Andy."

"I know your brother had the gold fever bad, but most young men don't drag their sisters with them when they come here."

Never, Poppy thought, had a trout been paid for so dearly. "Andy," she sighed, scrambling through her mind for a likely story.

"Andy?"

"A sea voyage, his health." Nobody could deny sea air was healthy. "But he could not accompany Jack to the gold fields once they arrived here or be left alone in San Francisco."

Jeremiah looked at her from under knotted brows. Plainly he doubted her, but he could not find a flaw in the story. "So somebody brought you a message about your mother's wedding?"

"Yes." So Dex had been seen and probably recognized. Poppy complied with more truths, though not that she still had no idea of Daisy's name and address. "Since her husband has a country place and a town house and she could be at either, I wrote to her at her bank. And the bank returned her message."

"So that was it." Jeremiah relaxed.

That was proof he had known of Dex's visit. Poppy did not know whether she was more frightened or furious. If every word she said, every step she took, every person she saw, went straight back to Jeremiah, all the simple pleasures of her life were over. She might as well be in prison.

"I've kept you too long," Jeremiah said, courteous again.

Too long for your own good, Poppy seethed. She would never again sit quietly and let him question her like a prisoner before a judge. She should not have done it now. Except the memory of Dex's kisses, his strong body close to hers, all the miracle of their love alive again for that brief time, had been so overwhelmingly fresh in her mind, she had been weak and off guard. She would not be caught twice.

She could only be thankful Jeremiah was less astute than Josh, the merchant. Josh had seen at once that her rich clothing did not fit the manner in which she had traveled and arrived. Jeremiah was himself too much the product of a raw new society to perceive the great difference between her fine Parisian creations and the gaudy, locally made gowns the other girls wore. He did not appreciate the incongruity that a girl who claimed to be of good family had arrived without funds or introductions.

Poppy gave the earrings to Pete to put in the Palace

safe. She drifted over and saw that Maurice had steadied down and was himself again. She spoke to Polly, who was putting on weight but was so reliable the Palace kept her. Polly touched the satin dress enviously and whispered that two of the girls had not appeared, so they were supposed to keep moving to give an impression there were girls at every table. Sue was there, but she had been out all night and to make it worse, she was drinking straight brandy. Poppy did not ask about Elsa. Elsa had a crippled husband to support and was always there. Phillipa was reliable, too, but she was as lack-brained as she was pretty and, if nobody asked for her company, might settle in just one spot and smile bemusedly for hours.

Poppy kept moving with a flutter of her skirts and a smile and a word to every man she recognized. The day had been too full, too loaded wtih joy and pain and happiness and outrage, but she acted the beauty, amusing and amused. That was her job, and the hours dragged endlessly.

Her head and feet were aching by the time the carriage called for her that night. The city never really slept, but most of the businesses were closed, their doors and windows barred, and every doorway held a sleeping body. The steam paddy had stopped for the night, no big whiskey wagons rolled and rumbled, no miners drove their loaded donkeys out of town, and no fine carriage sped along. An occasional serape-wrapped Mexican galloped past, a few men walked briskly as if on some urgent concern, a couple of tired Chilean girls paraded late, a discreet closed carriage carried some man on his private business.

Once they left the blare of light and music from the gambling halls behind, the only sounds were the squalling of cats in back yards and the occasional faint twanging of a Mexican guitar. Only the madams' houses were brightly lit, though their curtains were drawn. Later the produce wagons would roll in to feed the city, and at first light, loading would begin on the wharves, but now the town dozed.

Poppy leaned back with closed eyes. For some reason tonight the driver was not full of his usual gossip, and she was grateful for the silence because she was too tired to listen or answer. She heard the rush of feet, the driver's shout of dismay and was thrown forward and half out of the seat as the carriage stopped with a jolt.

They were surrounded by masked figures, one holding the rearing horse, one dragging at the driver, trying to pull him from his seat, and another trying to climb up beside him. Others were tearing at the door beside her. Poppy tumbled back in the seat and reached in her basket. She had not put on her boots for the drive home, and their heels were hard. She slashed at the hands pulling at the door and saw the driver was lashing out with his whip, slashing away at both sides until the sharp leather snapped and hissed. Poppy pounded harder at the blur of faces at the door, and the men yelped and fell back as the driver's attackers jumped away from his lashing. With a shout, the driver slashed out at the rearing horse and the man holding its head until he dropped the head strap and jumped clear.

Poppy held the door closed as the driver whipped the horse and they raced up the road. Behind them, the men raised a futile yell, and then they were lost in the darkness. The driver half stood, whip rising and falling, and the horse laid out at a dead run.

"Pull up," Poppy ordered. "Pull up. Do you want a runaway?"

The driver sawed at the reins, and the tired horse seemed content to slow to a trot. "Them Sydney Ducks, miss, it was them Sydney Ducks. They're busting out again. We'll never clean out that nest of murderers until we turn the Vigilantes loose on them again."

"Hey, now," Poppy said softly. "Hey, now."

"You weren't here in the old days, miss, so you don't know how bad it was and what a difference the Vigilantes made and how grateful we can be to live here now when things like tonight don't happen very often. You can't imagine how bad it was and how quick they changed it. But maybe it could go bad again, looks like."

"I'm listening," Poppy said. "I'm listening to every word you say." They sounded remarkably like Jeremiah's words.

The driver pulled up in front of her house. "We were just mighty lucky, miss, to get away as easy as we did."

"We fought them off," Poppy said. "Didn't we?"

Chapter Twenty-eight

$\mathcal{T}$HE next morning Poppy did not care if the whole town was watching her. She waited until she heard voices and smelled coffee next door. Then, in the plain blue wool she wore around the house, she marched over and knocked on the tenants' door.

Maurice, shaved and dressed but still in his shirt sleeves, opened the door, smiled, and raised an eyebrow. "Miss Landlady, my dear, surely we're not behind in our rent. So how may I help you?"

"I want to talk to you. If it's not convenient to talk inside, I'll talk here."

"There's a foggy chill in the air this morning," Maurice said and stepped back. "My friends are still in their rooms dressing, but we're always delighted to see you. May I offer you a cup of coffee?"

"Offer and deliver. Black, please."

Poppy always was amazed at how neat and clean the men kept their house. They had no rugs, curtains, pictures, or pretty pillows, but everything was scrubbed and every piece of furniture in place to an exact inch. She took a chair at the round table in the middle.

"Maurice, you always wear a gun."

He put a cup of coffee at her elbow and seated himself opposite with another. "It is one of the necessary ornaments for a gambling gentleman's attire."

"Do you have more than one of those little ornaments?"

Maurice's eyes narrowed. "What has happened?"

"Nothing. That's the reason I want a gun."

"I'm offering no reward for riddles."

"My carriage was attacked last night."

"That's nothing. You had those earrings that miner gave you, worth a small fortune."

"They're in Pete's safe. And, yes, it was nothing. We would never have got away if it had been a real attack. It was supposed to scare me and make me see the error of my ways."

"I think instead it made you very angry."

"Yes again. Jeremiah." Her hands clenched into fists. "He questioned me yesterday as if I were a criminal in the dock."

"He was very jealous, and you—" Maurice chuckled, "—you looked exactly like a little girl swearing she has not been in Mama's box of sweets, and all the time her face is smeared with chocolate."

Poppy stared at him. "I'm glad you're not in love with me. You know entirely too much about women."

"I had six sisters and no brothers."

"No wonder you're a gambler." Poppy shook her head and then said intensely, "Jeremiah is determined to marry me. Now. Today. Immediately. And he'd be a tyrant. I couldn't draw a breath without his spying on me."

"I think so, yes."

"Those men attacked us, at least six of them. We couldn't have got away. But we did, and nobody was hurt. The driver will report my every move to Jeremiah." Poppy shuddered. "I'm sure he arranged it, and he'll be waiting for me at the Palace as usual, and it'll be questions, questions, questions."

"The song is called 'Marry Me and You'll Be Safe.'"

"Exactly. The driver is Jeremiah's man. I've always thought he reported straight back everything he saw or I said. Then last night he betrayed himself completely after it was all over. He began parroting everything Jeremiah says, about the Vigilantes and how great they were and how we're going to need them again."

"But the drive home is a great convenience."

"I'd have to hire somebody, and I wouldn't feel easy with a different driver every night."

"So you think if you have a gun you can show it to Jeremiah and say you can take care of yourself? Have you thought of telling him you know the attack last night was a piece of playacting?"

"With anybody else, yes. With Jeremiah, I don't know what kind of a storm it might blow up. He's not reasonable. He tried to get those earrings away from me, not that he wanted the earrings but because another man gave them to me. I don't think he could stand having a bluff called."

"He is not a man for you to marry," Maurice agreed and drummed his fingers on the table. "I do not like this always carrying a gun. I think it is a bad habit. I do it only because a gambler is obliged." He shrugged.

"Why is it a bad habit?"

"Because if you have a gun, you can be tempted to use it. Just once. That once can be too often."

"I wouldn't use it," Poppy said. "I'd just have it to show."

"That is even more dangerous. What if the other person also has a gun and that person shoots? You should not carry a gun unless you know, *complètement,* how to use it."

"Then what am I supposed to do?"

"You go to the Palace and see what kind of a storm Jeremiah blows up today. I will watch. Perhaps you might give me the pleasure of having coffee here again tomorrow morning?"

Poppy's eyes sparkled. "I'll give you the pleasure of listening to what he has to say about my being in here this morning. I have ten dollars that says he will know about it."

"I do not bet to lose."

Poppy put on a pink, candy-striped dress that she usually considered too missish for the Palace. Today it seemed right, making her look like a sweetly lovely woman, not a professional beauty. She did not expect Dex. His mind was set on Félicité, and he was not a schoolboy to rush back to a flame that fascinated him when he knew its dangers. Still, she put on a dress he would admire.

For the first time Poppy dreaded walking into the Palace. Until now she had thought she had the most desirable job in the world. She liked almost everybody she worked with, she worked in a place designed for amusement. Everything was conducive to pleasure. She wore her beautiful clothes and was extravagantly admired. She listened to music all day long. She walked on the softest carpets, ate the best food, drank the finest wines. She knew everybody who mattered, met all the strangers who came to town, and heard immediately everything that happened. She listened to all the stories of defeats and triumphs, adventures and delights, until each day was like reading a new fortnightly book full of fresh stories.

Now the Palace seemed like a gaudy dream in a long twilight, contrasted to the vividness of her only real life, the life that included Dex. Still, she could have strolled into the Palace today and felt she was only playing a part in an amusing charade, if the dread of the obligatory half hour she must spend with Jeremiah had not hung over her like a dark cloud, smudging everything.

She must have been lack-witted ever to have listened to Jeremiah's proposals. Or else she had been drifting half awake in that twilight dream. That she had not realized what kind of man he was did not excuse her. She had been bitterly angry with Dex, but she should have known she should never marry anyone else when the mere sight of Dex or the sound of his voice could arouse her.

Now she must try to make Jeremiah understand, and she hoped she could do it sweetly and kindly, that he would be happier if he stopped seeing her since she could not consider marriage, now or ever. That was simple and reasonable. But she knew Jeremiah's response would be neither simple nor reasonable.

Poppy felt so nervous as she walked beside him to

the handsomely upholstered chairs beside the wall, she did not see how she could eat a bite. She murmured she had a fancy for only a small cake with her coffee.

"You had a frightening experience last night," Jeremiah said understandingly.

"Where did you hear that?"

"The same driver calls for me in the morning. A convenient arrangement. A single man has no need of a private carriage."

Jeremiah was growing sure of himself to admit that much. "Not too frightening," Poppy murmured. "Nobody was hurt."

"I rewarded the driver well."

"I am sure you did."

Jeremiah's eyes narrowed. "Something has happened. You've changed."

"*Au contraire.* I am content with my condition in life. Well content. I have no wish to change it."

"A young and beautiful woman should not be alone in this town."

"I have a brother."

"A mischievous young chap. Worse than nothing."

Caution slowed her tongue. Jeremiah knew she had a brother out in the diggings, but if he was forgetting him, this was no time to call attention to Jack. Dex was adroit at picking up the smallest breath of rumor. She had told him her brother had left California.

"It would be better if you did not come here every day. You only distress yourself."

"It can't be that flashy gambler. You wouldn't stoop that low."

"Maurice? He has been a good friend."

"As long as you don't gamble with him," Jeremiah sneered. "An Ingot."

"Don't call him that to his face."

"Exactly. This is a dangerous town. No woman is safe alone."

"I am content." Anger made her voice shrill. "Well content."

266

"When you could have so much more? I could give you everything."

"I have everything I want."

"Beautiful child, this next election is only the beginning. The first step. Once I'm in Sacramento, I'll stay there a while. Build a name, a reputation. A strong man is needed, wanted. The right people know what I stand for, the public will learn. The voting public, the sheep that know they need someone to lead and protect them. Your position as my wife, you can't dream how great it will be."

Something in his eyes, a fanatic gleam, frightened Poppy. She sprang to her feet. "I don't want to be your wife. I don't want you to come here any more. I don't want to see you."

"I know what you want and should have. I'll see you as usual in the morning."

Poppy stood, fists clenched, her bodice straining with her heaving breath. Then she turned and ran to the bar. She stood beside it until Pete worked his way down the gleaming mahogany and stood beside her.

"I should have slapped his face," she whispered, not knowing whether she was more furious or frightened. "I should have jammed those stupid words right down his throat."

"What did he do? Or say?"

Poppy's glance wavered. Jeremiah had simply promised, quite honestly and sincerely, that she would have a fine position if she married him. She knew he would persist in seeking her out, pursue her with unwanted attentions, and set spies on her, but those were causes for anger, not fear. He could not force her to stand in front of a minister and say the words that would make her his wife. He was not a threat, only an embarrassment.

That she had taken him in strong aversion did not matter to the owner of the Palace. She was here to be pleasant to the customers. If Jeremiah had behaved offensively, said something obnoxious, done anything people could see would make him distasteful, she could have complained, and he would have been warned that only gentlemanly behavior was tolerated here. His demeanor had been perfect and his spending generous. He was a prominent man and a good customer who would be valuable to the Palace five years from now and ten. She was only another pretty girl, and some girls lasted five months at the Palace, and few stayed more than ten.

The owner would not lift a finger to help her. If she wished to be free of Jeremiah's attention, she must handle it herself and so pleasantly the Palace did not lose his good will. If she did anything else, she could lose her job, become known as a troublemaker, and have difficulty finding any other place.

She felt wild as an animal in a trap. Once she was with Dex again, had made him realize he must have her, that no other woman could be to him what she was, she would not need this job or anything else. She would have Dex. Until then she must stay steady, be available.

She said quietly, "I don't like him, Pete. I have a feeling he could cause me trouble."

"He has his enemies. And powerful friends."

"I'd better move around and make a few friends myself."

As she circled gracefully around the tables, smiling, laughing, and making murmuring answers to whatever was said to her, her determination solidified. With so much at stake, now when every thought, move, and emotion must be concentrated on Dex, she would not risk having Jeremiah do something that would put her in a false position in Dex's eyes.

She did not doubt Jeremiah would try to do something. He did not know about Dex, but he did know she did not intend to let this situation continue. He would be thinking, scheming. He would have no scruples about trying to force her into a situation from which she could not retreat, could do nothing but marry him. She could only try to act before he did.

Everybody in the Palace had seen her rush away from Jeremiah, skirts flouncing, eyes flashing, fists clenched. Maurice's eyes never seemed to leave the cards in his hand, but he missed little that went on around him. When he rose to turn his table over to another dealer while he went out to dinner, he glanced at Poppy and nodded toward the doors. She met him there. To stand just outside, in the full glare of the lamps, so people could see them and be enticed to the pleasures inside, was permissible if they did not do it too often or for too long.

"I'm not going to give you a gun," he announced immediately. "Shooting is one way of discouraging a man permanently, but I won't encourage it."

"Would you believe me if I promise the gun is not for Jeremiah?"

"I'd believe you mean it now, when you're not in a temper."

"He's going to try something worse than that attack on the carriage. If I won't marry him for love, and he knows I won't, he'll try to force me to marry him for protection."

"I think so," Maurice agreed and tried to joke. "He's a very fine gentleman according to his lights, but his lights are a little dim."

"I can't walk straight into a trap with no way to protect myself."

"They hanged one woman in this state. If you shot somebody, he would be the only person who could protect you."

"Do you think I'd put myself in that position? That's what I'm trying to prevent. You do have another gun?"

Maurice nodded reluctantly. "A lady's gun, yes. Tiny but it could be lethal."

"Where did you get that?"

"Madame gave it to me. I go to see Amalie now and again. By the way, Madame is shocked at what it costs to outfit her girls. She might as well have gone to Paris, she says."

Poppy was instantly sympathetic. "You mean she won't get her little place in the country?"

"If she can last a few more years, it should be a large

place. She serves only champagne. At a five-hundred-percent profit, I believe she said. Just lately she has expanded and installed a fine chef. Nice little dinners do not run over a hundred a plate, I'm sure."

"The Palace doesn't do that well."

"The Palace has eight gambling tables. No, the girls are a heavy expense but necessary. The first necessity. Madame is a businesswoman. She has already bought one house and is considering building an addition."

"So why did she give you a gun?"

Maurice grimaced. Plainly he had hoped to distract her so she would forget that. "One of her girls had it and made an ugly scene. Madame is a wise woman. She distrusts guns in the hands of females. She did not even want it in her house. So she gave it to me."

"Why did any girl have it in the first place?"

"Perhaps it is as well you know," Maurice decided. "She took it from Josie. Before she finally had to tell her she must leave."

"What happened? Where is Josie?"

"I have never understood fully what happened when you landed, and you need not explain. I observed several oddities on the ship and more about that disaster on the waterfront. From those, I assume Josie and the First Mate were involved. I know he sailed with his ship. Before he left, he and Josie had some trouble. He left her broke, took even her little trinkets, and he marked her. Permanently. Madame tells me that that has a certain appeal, rare, but it pays well, and Josie has special talents. After the First Mate left her, however, she was no longer pleasant to have in the house. Not at all pleasant."

Maurice was only hinting but at something so dark and morbid Poppy was glad he did not inflict the telling on her. "So she left, too?"

"Madame tried to be patient, but after she was forced to take the gun, she placed Josie in a house in Sacramento. For old times' sake, since they came out from France together. From Sacramento, if she continues to be not pleasant, it will be the gold fields. A hard life."

"I intend to have a good life, and I don't intend to hang. But I need a gun, Maurice. If you don't give it to me, I'll find one elsewhere."

"I make the bargain," Maurice said with a gesture that admitted defeat. "If you have the gun, you must know how to use it. Without that, it is worse than nothing. I show you how to use it, some morning when no one is observing, out in the back yard. But I do not give it to you unless I think you really need it."

"I'll have my first lesson tomorrow, please," Poppy said.

Chapter Twenty-nine

THE next morning Poppy could not look without pain at the round table in the living room where Andy always left a lamp burning. Last night she had hurried inside, certain she would find something there beside the lamp, and the table had been bare. A gentleman always sent some small token, if only a note, after he called on a lady, even if he had stopped for nothing more than a cup of tea. Dex had sent nothing. He could not hold her in contempt, so he must have another thought in his mind. He must be planning to see her.

She had her first shooting lesson with Maurice, using only a small practice load, and found it as fussy as the elaborate ritual of a ballet dancer's makeup. The girls had shown her every little nicety, and now she paid as strict attention to this new ritual with brushes and oils and cleaning cloths as she had then.

Afterwards, she selected a gown she had never worn and never even considered for the Palace before. When she had ordered this pale green with the tiny lavender and white sprigs, banded in lavender velvet, she had dreamed of strolling through a Paris park on a summer evening to listen to a concert, with her white-gloved hand on Dex's arm. She vowed the dress was exactly to his taste, and when he saw her in it, he surely must think of Paris and spring. Paris, spring, youth, and love—every line and flutter of the dress fairly sang of those things. He had never seen her in anything quite so sweet or with a bunch of silk violets tucked in her bright curls. He would see her thus and remember and regret. He would not hesitate one moment longer in deciding to take her back where she belonged with him.

That terrible accident in the Vendée was long ago and far away. It would be forgotten by now. When he landed here, Dex might have thought he, too, had forgotten her. Now he knew he had not forgotten and could not.

Deliberately, she did not reach the Palace until mid-afternoon. She would not risk his walking in while she was with Jeremiah. She shuddered as she pictured his fastidious recoil if Jeremiah made a jealous scene.

By the time she strolled in, she was certain Jeremiah would be gone, and he was. She knew the pattern of his days. He lived in an elite boardinghouse that catered to prosperous single men. He had breakfast there before he came to the Palace. He spent his afternoons at the Firehouse clubroom with his close cronies, and he was never seen in the evenings. She assumed those were spent in business and political conferences.

Yesterday Dex could not have had a free minute even to write the note she had expected. By today, he could reasonably be expected to want to stroll around and see the local sights. He could drop in at the Palace, and nobody would raise an eyebrow.

Pete said nothing about her being late. He only slipped a small box into her hand and whispered, "Mr. Dunbar was sorry he couldn't wait, but he left this for you."

Poppy cupped the box unobtrusively in her palm and slipped off the lid. Then she gulped and barely bit back a shriek. Each diamond earring dangled two inches long, from the round diamond at the lobe through a string of small stones to a large pear-shaped one at the end. She had never seen anything so shockingly tawdry. A woman who wore them might as well hang out a sign she had been bought and paid for.

"Sparkle, don't they?" Pete said.

He knew they were in atrocious taste. Perhaps he did not know what she had learned from the ballet girls, who were shrewd judges of the value of the gifts they received, that diamonds of the first water did not

273

have that yellow tinge or a certain dinginess in the depths that meant flawed stones.

"I cannot accept them, of course," Poppy said instantly and then added demurely, "They are much too valuable."

"That's between you and him."

Poppy hurried over to the chest-high table-desk where paper and pens were kept so gentlemen could write bank drafts or other business papers without wasting time to sit down. She wrote quickly, then went back to Pete and showed him the note. "These are too beautiful and valuable. You must keep them for your wife. Poppy."

"You always know the right word," Pete said.

Poppy nodded. She thought she did, too. Jeremiah could understand he was to keep the earrings until they were married if he chose to take it that way. "Keep them in your safe to give to him the minute you see him next," Poppy begged. "I can't draw an easy breath with them on me." Because she was suspicious. If she wore those and was robbed, would Jeremiah claim she was indebted and must marry him? If he chose to misread her note, that was better than making him angry.

Pete took them. "Four boats unloaded yesterday, and three more are unloading today."

Poppy understood. She had been hours late, and now that she was here, there was work to do. She looked around and recognized the Australian who had landed yesterday. He had come straight to the Palace and immediately bought her a champagne cocktail. He had expounded so long on the tens of thousands of acres in his station, by which she assumed he meant his ranch, and the thousands of sheep he ran, and she thought that meant fed, that she had wondered if women were as scarce in Australia as in California and as valued. But he had seemed shy too, as well as unwilling to go on buying cocktails at Palace prices, so she had not had a chance to ask him.

Now he was standing with a group of others who must have come over on the same boat. They had been joined by more, who, judging by their heavy shirts, boots, and unshaved faces, had been out in the gold fields. They were all clumped together at the far end of the bar, filling the whole corner, and were talking only to each other, apparently interested only in themselves, as if they had never left Australia and come to explore a new land full of different and interesting people.

Nobody needed to tell Poppy these men were of a different breed than the notorious Sydney Ducks. Those were the convicts who originally had been sent to populate Australia, had come from there to San Francisco, and now infested the gutters of the town like a creeping pestilence, robbing, killing, and burning.

From their manner and dress, these were men of good family. They were handsome men, and even the ones from the diggings were wearing rough clothes of good quality. All had a vigorous outdoor look about them. Their accents were only a little stranger than most. One of them was drawling, with a smile, that he had ridden over his station just before he left and realized that, with the new settlers coming in, from his highest hill he now could see land that did not belong to him. While it was friendly for a man to know he had neighbors, the country was getting crowded. Another said the better class of new arrivals, as was also true here, was turning away from the diggings to trade or set up their own stations. A third pointed out he had always told them there was more gold at home than here, the same kind of country but more of it, and they knew how to keep their mining communities decent and law-abiding, but the real gains to both countries would be in the miners who turned to other pursuits.

Poppy stiffened indignantly. Those men were claiming they had gold fields and a gold rush, too. And bigger than California's. And bigger ranches. Did they know how big some of the old Spanish ranchos were? And people thought Americans bragged!

Now they were talking about the Sydney Ducks. One older man was saying he wished Americans would remember there was at least one Australian state where no convict or ex-convict had ever been allowed to settle. Another started talking again about the lack of law officers here, the terrible living conditions in the diggings, and comparing them with conditions at home.

One of the men noticed her hovering and smiled. "Another all around here, young lady," he said genially.

Poppy's mouth rounded with shock. He thought she was here to serve him. That was what these Australians thought of women. They thought women did not belong in a place like this except as servants. They did not realize that the hostesses were one of the reasons the Palace was so successful. Now she noticed the nice young man who had bought her a cocktail was acting as if he had never seen her before, looking half frightened she would speak to him, as if he had done something shameful.

These Australians were certainly different, talking and looking around so superior to everything, when they did not have the least idea how to behave in a place like the Palace. She had noticed they were not playing at the tables at all, except to toss on a dollar or two in passing. Men most certainly did not come to the Palace to stand and talk to other men they could see at any time and any other place, as these were doing. They came to get drunk, gamble, or look at the girls. Of course they could also eat or glance at the papers. If they did want a word with some man, they met, had a quick drink, and went on. Men streamed through here all day doing exactly that.

Then she realized that almost all of them were drinking beer. The Palace only stocked beer for the drinkers who liked it as a mix. Nobody ever walked in here and just ordered a beer. But these Australians had.

"Beers and three whiskeys," the man said as if she were lack-witted and had not understood.

Now that she had considered it carefully, she decided she did not like these men at all. "I'll speak to the bartender and see you're served," Poppy said icily.

She flounced over to Pete. "Those men. Those Australians. They say they have a gold rush too, and it's bigger than ours. And better behaved."

"I've lost a few good customers to them," Pete said calmly. "I hear a lot of European ships are going there instead of here. Good thing. Leaves all the more for us."

"Then what are they doing here?"

"Some of them probably are on their way to Washington. Government business. And others could want to see our processes in the deep mining."

Poppy sniffed. "You mean they'd admit we have something they don't? Oh, they want three whiskeys. All the rest beer. Beer!"

"They drink a lot of it. I'll send it down, our best local."

She did not go near that corner again. Those Australians were happy together, and they could stay together, alone together. Plenty of men were happy to buy her champagne cocktails or slip a part of their winnings into her hand if she just stood beside them at a table while they played. Nobody else would even think she should carry great slopping mugs of beer to them. Americans knew how to treat a lady.

No tall English figure appeared. Poppy began to make excuses. Dex had social obligations, business appointments, all doubtless arranged before he ever sailed. He had been able to find only that one short space of time since he arrived, no matter how much he longed to hold her in his arms again, even if he had resolved not to see her again. She thought he had. She did not think now he would be able to hold to that resolve. Her whole being was set now on the belief he could not. So she made excuses: He dealt with large sums, estates, governments, and he probably had to go to Sacramento for a day or two. He might even have to go to look at one of the great ranchos. Some were as large as whole kingdoms. He was not able to call his time his own. That was all. He was the prisoner of the great wealth he handled.

Then she had another idea. Dex would not enjoy

coming here and buying her a drink as if he were any casual stranger. How much better if they could meet and see each other in a pleasant social atmosphere. How much better, too, if she did not have to see Jeremiah at all.

She strolled over to Pete and asked if she could see The Boss. If that was not convenient, would he please say she would like a few days' holiday. She was in need of a change and a rest. The word came back promptly. The Boss appreciated that a change would bring her back to them refreshed. Pete beamed. Plainly word of her impasse with Jeremiah was known to everybody, and what was taken as an effort on her part to avoid an ugly scene at the Palace was appreciated.

She felt tired and bedraggled by the time the carriage arrived to take her home. She told the driver she was taking a few days off to rest and that he need not call for her again. He looked at her sharply as he let her out at her door and said she did look a little down at the mouth and no wonder because working with all them drunks at the Palace was no life for a young lady. He was indeed Jeremiah's echo.

Chapter Thirty

THE day dawned clear, so she planned a day outside. She turned the possibilities over in her mind as she fixed Andy's breakfast. Where would the social and business aristocrats of San Francisco take Dex if they wished to combine business and pleasure? She could think of a number of places, places where she could appear quite naturally.

Andy shook his head when she told him she was taking a short holiday from the Palace. In many ways he was still a scamp. He got in tussles and romps that tore the knees and elbows out of his clothes faster than she could mend them. He would disappear before dawn on a Sunday and return after dark, soaked to the skin, hands raw, face sun- and salt-blistered, smelling of fish and beer, and blandly swear he had only watched the men unloading fish at the dock when she knew perfectly well he had sneaked aboard a boat and spent the day baiting and hauling nets on one of the small, tossing, dangerous craft. Sometimes he would seem shockingly adult and even prim. Now he asked, alarmed, if she could be sure they were holding a place for her at the Palace.

"I've a little dust put away in our poke," Poppy said.

"You'd better," Andy said, gobbling mush. "We haven't had a shipment of iron in a month, and we're getting low. Mighty low."

"So six ships will come in loaded with iron all at once," Poppy shrugged.

"Sure, and they'll make whole buildings out of them instead of selling us the iron to work." Andy was determinedly grim. "Those old iron buildings either explode or bake the people in them when there's a fire. Everything should be brick."

"Most of the new places are. Why are you so worried?"

"We have orders for fancy railings, fences, posts, and bars, and we're running out of iron. If the manufactory doesn't have any iron, we don't have any work."

"I'm only taking a few days, Andy. And we have our rent."

"Gamblers can go broke in one night."

"Young man, you've got an upset stomach," Poppy said. "I'm going to see if I can find some rhubarb and boil it up for you."

"Just give me a couple of rolls for lunch. We've got to be careful."

"I've already fixed fish rolls, and you'd better take them before they go to waste."

Poppy was laughing when she joined Maurice out in back of the house for the shooting lesson. He brightened immediately.

"Today we do not wish to shoot anybody?"

"Today we wish to learn to hit the target."

"We will use this ammunition I have fixed. Very light, not to hurt, only to show if you hit where you aim."

The day was almost windless with only a few fluffy clouds in the pale blue sky. This was a day nobody would choose to spend shut in four walls.

After the shooting lesson, she put on a pretty blue suit, trimmed with white braid, a blue- and white-checked blouse with wide ruffled collar and cuffs, and a hat with blue- and white-checked streamers fluttering below her waist. She sent a boy to call a carriage and remembered she had a little blue and white parasol, too, meant to twirl and flirt.

"The races," she said and settled back to enjoy the drive out the planked road past the Mission Dolores to the track.

She hurried to the rail to see the horses parading to the post. She did like the gray, but some man whispered to her that grays never won. Then she saw a bay with such a mean flat head and rolling eyes, she was sure no other horse would dare to pass him. She would bet on him, and if she won she would have a sausage roll, perhaps two sausage rolls.

Then she looked over to where the horses were being saddled before their jockeys mounted. The sunlight faded, and the day turned chill. Dex was there, as elegantly dressed as if he were at a Paris track, and Félicité was clinging to his arm. She was all in creamy white with a broad-brimmed straw hat and a fine wool stole. Her father was beside them, nodding and pointing out a frisky dancing black with a white blaze and feet.

Poppy forgot the bay. She could not have swallowed a bite of sausage roll. Because she knew she was overdressed, fussy and frumpy, looking just what she was, a girl from a gambling club. Plain-tailored cream was the only dress for a lady. Plain cream to accentuate a pale, fragile beauty. That gloved hand on Dex's sleeve was impossibly long and slender. Like a skeleton, skeleton bones, Poppy told herself, but she still felt sick.

Then she reminded herself why she was here. She was here to see Dex, to remind him of everything between them. She forced herself to stroll around the track, slowly, twirling the parasol slanted over her shoulder, until she stood quite close, with only a railing separating them. As she reached it, the last horses were led out on the track, and the crowd in the enclosure hurried to the rail.

Turning, Dex looked straight at Poppy. His eyes narrowed slightly, but his expression did not change as he looked away, saying to Félicité, "The sun is too warm here. Let me find you a place in the shade," and strolled off unhurriedly with Félicité on his arm and Mr. Pannet marching beside them.

Poppy gasped with shock. Face to face, he had cut her cold. He could not do that to her. She would go after him, she would say—what should she say? Of course. "Aren't you the man from the bank, my mother's bank?" He could not refuse to answer that, to

281

greet her, introduce her, and include her in their party. She might be overdressed, but once he saw her beside Félicité, he would have to see that she was strong red wine beside the other's thin skim milk.

They were gone, lost in the crowd. She had missed her chance. She should have come prepared, with the words on the tip of her tongue. Now it was too late. She could not elbow through the crowd, openly searching.

She turned and walked blindly out toward the road. She did not think she would have cried in public, but her eyes felt so blurred she could not have seen a race. At least she had told her driver to wait, and he was sensible enough to have found a place where he could see the track and she could see him.

She went home and worked out her fury in scrubbing the house. She was not going to let Dex get away with that, not a second time. There were a limited number of places for the Pannets to take him, and where they could go, she could. Next time she would have her words ready, say she had thought she recognized him at the track but had not been sure at first. He was not going to be allowed to pretend she did not exist and forget her that way. She refused to be out of mind because she was out of sight.

Andy came home, starving as always and delighted to have a hot meal waiting for once. He was quite happy with his gloomy announcement they had only a two-week supply of iron at the manufactory unless a shipment arrived.

"So stretch the work out and make it last," Poppy said. "Take tomorrow off, and we'll pack a picnic lunch and drive out to watch the sea lions on the rocks."

Andy looked shocked. "I've got to work while there is work."

Poppy slammed a baked apple down in front of him. She would not have the boy feckless, but the Pannets were sure to take Dex to see the sea lions and that was one place she could not go alone without looking a freak. Still she could not force Andy. She would have to think of other places.

They would take him to the theater. That was certain. She did not even need to know their taste. She had only to dress, stroll outside the theaters until she recognized their carriage, then follow them inside, and wait her opportunity between the acts.

She dressed in her handsome gray satin, and the second night she saw the Pannet carriage drive up to see the drama. But they were not alone. They were part of a procession of carriages, obviously a party for dinner and the theater, the men in evening black, the ladies in light furs that did not completely conceal the sparkle of gems. If she did go inside, she would not be able to work her way into that close, chattering circle.

By Sunday she felt grim but not yet quite defeated. She told Andy he could spend a civilized day for once away from the fishing boats. So they went strolling in Portsmouth Square. Later there would be a concert. She knew everybody would be there, so she only nodded when Andy nudged her.

"There's Dex. Is that the Pannets in the carriage with him?"

"Yes."

"We'd better get out of here."

"Why?" Poppy widened her eyes innocently. "Maybe we should go up and speak to him."

"No. Come on." Andy tugged at her arm. "We don't want to see him."

"Why not?"

"Dex is clever. He's still looking for Jack, and he might trick us into telling him something."

"We wouldn't."

"We shouldn't take a chance. Jack'll go back and be an heir when he's good and ready and not before, and we mustn't give him away. Come on. He's with that other girl anyways."

"So he is," Poppy said flatly. "All right. Let's go."

She wrote Jack that night to tell him Dex was in San Francisco and had questioned her. He had not mentioned Jack's family, so she judged all was well with them. She did not know what business had brought Dex to California, but he was seen almost daily with the banker Pannet's daughter.

When she was through, she discovered her hands and wrists were bruised where she had pounded them, unknowing and unfeeling, on the table as she wrote. She looked drearily at the marks. She could wear long gloves until those bruises faded. The bruises inside might last a lifetime.

She was through trying to force Dex to recognize a passion he could not deny but did not want or value. He had made love to her, yes. She had been waiting for him, seductive and eager. He had responded physically as any man would to an attractive woman who offered herself. If she had not offered, possibly he would not have lifted a finger to possess her. Now, if he truly loved Félicité, he might even resent that she had played on his masculine weakness and made him betray the woman he loved.

No, that was drawing it too strong. Dex was not a man to have regrets after pleasure. But neither would he value what came too cheaply.

Their lovemaking had meant nothing to him beyond the moment. He had glimpsed her more than once, and his failure to give her the slightest nod or look of recognition had been deliberate and not because he feared a break in his perfect friendship with Félicité. He had been saying, in all but words, in every way short of a brutal demand to leave him alone, that he was through with her. He had finished when he had shipped her out of Paris.

She went back to work at the Palace the next day. Jeremiah was there the following morning, but he made no attempt to resume their old ritual. He simply ordered a bottle of whiskey to take to the firehouse and sent drinks over to the band.

To Poppy he said only, "You don't need to run away and hide from me. Someday you're going to marry me, and I'll be here when you're ready."

Then he bowed, an impressive-looking man with his white hair and dark face, and walked out. Poppy watched him with a shiver running through her. Jeremiah was only waiting for a chance. She would have to watch every step and every word. Each day she would be uneasy, for she could not even imagine to what lengths his scheming might go.

She found a carriage and arranged for the driver to call for her regularly. Jeremiah might watch and question him, but she was helpless to stop that.

A week passed, and she saw Jeremiah only once when he stopped in to glance at some eastern newspapers. She had a letter from Jack. He had moved on again and sounded low in his mind. The season was passing. The best claims were taken or worked out. Still it was all luck, and his luck might turn.

That night started badly. A drunken miner, collapsed in a chair, caught at her skirt as she passed and tore it at the waist. She had to pin it up as best she could and felt a sloven. Phillipa, lack-witted as always, stood too long behind a man who was losing at the poker table until he jumped up and claimed she had been signaling his cards. Everybody knew Phillipa had only been staring into space, big blue eyes in her china doll's face seeing little, but it was an ugly scene, the kind the Palace abhorred. The man's money was restored with the request that he never return, but it broke up the game for the night.

Poppy did not know when the rumor began to stir through the Palace. She saw men starting to slip away, but a fight or word of a big game at one of the other places could cause that. Then she heard the first clanging of the fire engine bells and minutes later heard the pounding of galloping hoofs as the first engine raced past and down toward the wharves. The band struck up "The Moon on the Lake Was Beaming" which usually had a soothing effect on a crowd.

Pete beckoned to her. "Keep moving. Don't lose the crowd. Last fire I might as well have been tending bar at a camp meeting. Only I've seen livelier camp meetings. Didn't have six customers until afterwards, and then they dragged in so much mud and soot on their shoes we had to put new carpet under the foot rail, and it took us two hours to get that brass shining right again."

"What if it's a bad one?" Poppy whispered.

Pete made a great rattle with ice and glasses. "Won't be a bad one. We got all the Volunteer Companies now. If the idiots don't get to fighting each other. And this ain't a wood and canvas town any more. Go on. Sweeten up the customers."

Poppy swirled her skirts, walking slowly, smiling, and men relaxed and gestured to ask if she would like a drink. She smiled and nodded; she played with a glass and murmured. All the time her heart was pounding until she could hardly breathe. A sense of impending doom had been hanging over her ever since she returned to work. She did not know how Jeremiah could turn a fire to his advantage, but she knew he must be at this one, standing high on the engine of his company, and bawling orders.

This town had had dozens of fires. It had burned to the ground more than once, three times in a single year, all before they ever arrived. It was just she always had a nagging worry about Andy, who loved to watch any little fire that started. And this terrible fear of what Jeremiah might contrive.

Abruptly her nerve broke. She turned and went to the end of the bar where Pete kept her basket and shawl.

"I've got to go, Pete, I've got to."

"That fire ain't anywhere near your house. It's way up above the wharves someplace, where all those manufactories are."

"I'm going, Pete, I'm going. Give me my basket."

"If you start a stampede out of here, The Boss ain't going to forget it. He won't want you back."

Poppy bent, snatched the basket, and broke for the doors. The minute she was outside, she could smell the smoke and see it rising in three black columns high above the roofs. As she watched, a flickering red tongue of flame burst in the center of one of the columns.

She moaned and started running. She stayed close to the building fronts, away from the galloping horses in the street, fighting clear of the men running all around her. She tripped over one of a pack of mongrel dogs, nearly went down, but caught herself on a doorjamb and kicked her way clear. The smoke was thicker now, making it hard to breathe, and waves of unnatural heat beat on her skin. A strong, steady wind blew down over the hills, but it was blowing toward the water, away from the town. If it shifted, the whole town could go up in flames once more.

She panted and ran, stopped and caught her breath and ran again. She was being foolish, foolish, foolish, her pounding feet thudded in her ear. Yet that terrible gnawing fear drove her on.

She knew where the fire was even before she reached it. While she was still pushing her way through the crowd, dodging the fire engines jostling each other on the narrow streets, their members shoving and shouldering each other aside for the places of privilege so they could throw their streams of water on the flames, she knew. She did not even try to scream a question over the roar of the fire and the yells of the crowd. When she finally stood in the forefront, the flames licking hot enough to blister her face, the smoke choking her until the breath whistled in her lungs, and her eyes half blind, she saw what she had guessed already.

The fire was in the iron manufactory, Andy's place. Already it was gutted to the collapsing brick walls, and the roofs of the two nearest buildings had caught, so the firefighters were concentrating the water there to try to save them.

Her frenzy of anxiety about Andy had been no freak. Her mind had added up a dozen hints and arrived at this total, instantly, completely. Andy had said the manufactory was running out of iron and therefore work. The smith had said, long ago and far away in another country, that the manufactory used iron from burned buildings. The smith was capable of any treachery that profited him and kept him in work. This fire would make work rebuilding the manufactory besides producing enough burned iron to stay open.

Still she need not have run, unreasoning, half mad. Her emotions had connected Andy and fire, but he had nothing to do with this. He had left the manufactory hours ago, and she did not see him among the spectators. He was safe at home, long asleep. If she could fight her way back through the mob to the street, she might be able to find a carriage to take her home, too.

She struggled and wiggled through to the fringes of the crowd. Her bodice was burned in a dozen spots from falling soot, and the odor of her singed hair made her sneeze. Her shoes and skirts were drenched with flowing mud.

She worked her way around one Volunteer engine and tried to force her way between two others beyond that. She found herself hemmed in and submerged by a barricade of men's shoulders. She prodded and pushed and said, "Please, please let me through," but nobody seemed to hear or even feel her thrusts. Finally one man lifted an arm, and she wedged her head past his shoulder. Then she stopped moving and even breathing.

In the flickering, reddish glare of the fire, Jeremiah and the smith confronted each other. Jeremiah, ax in his hand and great fireman's hat pushed back on his white hair, towered over the square, belligerent figure of the smith.

"I'm here because I want to know what's happening to my place of employment," the smith said. "Would you want me to be sleeping easy in my bed while perhaps I won't have a job tomorrow?"

"What if somebody says they saw you sneaking around here earlier tonight?"

"Then they're lying." The smith's voice rang with indignation. "I was at my boardinghouse for the evening, and my mates there can tell you that."

"You haven't been talking about the lack of iron so the place might be closing down?"

"So's the whole shop been talking, and now it is closed. Please, mister, use your noggin."

"I am. One of my mates in the Fire Company carries the insurance on this manufactory, and he tells me it's underinsured. If there's too much damage, it won't re-open. Even if this has been a big fire that left plenty of scrap iron."

"That's not so," the smith screamed. Then he whined again, "Now any way you look at it, I wouldn't be doing myself out of a job. I don't know anything about fires and scrap iron. The big fires were over before I landed here."

But he knew, he knew, Poppy wanted to scream.

"Manufactories are apt to have fires," the smith blustered.

"It started in three different places at once," Jeremiah said. "That's proof enough it was set."

"Well, then," the smith said, "I know one person here who has a fancy for fires, likes them real good and has been caught trying to set them." He sighed dramatically. "I thought it was just a boyish prank. Treated him like my own son, I have."

"Who's this?" Jeremiah demanded.

"That English kid, Andy Smith. Sent down to Cornwall where I lived, he was, for fire trouble they had with him in London."

Jeremiah stared at the smith, face suddenly vulturine and avid. "You're sure of this?"

"Positive sure."

"Poppy Smith's brother."

"That's the boy."

Jeremiah licked his lips, and his eyes shone red in the light of the flames. "London, huh?"

"Sure. They've had big fires there, too. This ain't the only town that's burned to the ground."

But that was years ago, centuries ago, Poppy wanted to scream. And Andy never set any fires, much as he liked to watch them.

"So a certain newspaper editor was telling me only the other day," Jeremiah said thoughtfully. "Perhaps he was trying to tell me more than I realized. You are sure of your information?"

"Well, now, I don't know that I could find you witnesses clear from Cornwall. You've got to be reasonable, mister."

"It certainly would be reasonable to question the boy," Jeremiah said. "Thank you, mister. We always appreciate honest information. This fire setting has got to stop. Nobody who's guilty, and I don't care if he is under age, can be allowed to commit this crime and escape punishment." He nodded and licked his lips.

Poppy never knew how she battered her way through the crowd and back to the street where she found a carriage with a driver who decided the best part of the fire was over and he could leave for a double fare. She sat tensely forward in the seat, fists clenched, and listened to her labored breathing rasping in her ears.

She could not believe the smith actually knew the truth about Andy and his two impulsive graspings at fire. Dex would not have confided anything that trivial and yet intimate when he arranged to send them to Cornwall. More likely Andy, scolded by the smith for some playful gesture at the forge, had blurted out a boyish half-confidence that he had gotten in trouble that way before, possibly even that it had got them sent to Cornwall.

To her, the truth about this fire and who set it was as clear as if she had seen it happen. She knew Andy. He was impulsive but not warped or criminal. He was not capable of such an act. The smith was a sneak, an opportunist, and an informant. For him to be out of employment was serious, important enough that Andy had childishly echoed his fears, which did not at all apply to a boy with a sister and a home. The smith had set the fire to provide iron to keep the manufactory working. He had mates, equally angry about their pay packets, who would back up his lies about where he was when the fire was set. Even better, knowing what he did about Andy, he must have planned from the first to divert suspicion from himself to Andy, telling a story that could not be disproved at this distance. The small truth in his big lie lent it credence. Besides people were always more prone to think a boy guilty of some mischief than to blame a mature and skilled workingman.

The smith could not have known his great luck in telling his story to a man so eager to believe it he would make no effort to discover whether or not the accusation were true. Unwittingly, thinking only of his own protection, the smith had put a terrible weapon in Jeremiah's hands.

This town was fanatic in its hatred of arsonists, and no wonder when it had burned so many times. The law of England would consider a boy Andy's age enough of a man to hang. And if not by order of the American courts, then he might hang by the Vigilante-type justice Jeremiah wanted. With his power in the Vigilantes, Jeremiah could dictate a verdict. And Poppy knew what his fee would be if he saved Andy. Anything was better than the kind of justice and mercy Jeremiah dispensed.

Long shudders were shaking her whole body as the carriage stopped in front of the house. Except for the small light in the parlor, both houses were dark and silent. Andy was undoubtedly inside and asleep, but nobody would have seen him since he came home from work. Nobody could prove he had been there all this time.

Poppy knew what she must do and say. Jeremiah was adroit at getting information from drivers.

"Good night," she said. "I don't know why I ever go to fires. They're so exhausting. I'm tired enough to drop."

"Sleep well, miss."

Poppy yawned and walked slowly, as if unutterably tired, up to the door. Once inside, she ran. Jeremiah would not be far behind her.

She shook Andy awake and said, "Get into your clothes. Fast. We've got to run. No, don't make another light. Dress and meet me at the back door."

She snatched up her dark coat, fished their poke of gold dust out from under the loose boards beneath her bed, and stopped for nothing else. She met Andy in the kitchen and said, "We'll go through the back yards. Quick now."

Chapter Thirty-one

IN the morning Poppy found it steadying that in this world some things and some people did not change. Madame was as discreet and as forthright as always.

When Poppy had stumbled in on her the night before and, once in Madame's private sitting room, had blurted out the whole story, Madame had only nodded and pushed them into her bedroom. She herself brought hot water and fresh sheets and told them to take her big, canopied bed. She had a most comfortable padded chaise longue in the sitting room.

When Poppy, wrapped in a large silk robe, poked her head out in the morning, Madame gestured her back and, a few minutes later, knocked on the door. Three breakfast trays were waiting on Madame's large businesslike desk.

"I've told Bella, that's my black girl, not to talk, and she'll keep her mouth shut. But usually I eat at the long table in the kitchen with my girls, so everybody knows I have somebody in here. And with me, it won't be any fancy man."

"I didn't know where else to go."

"You did right. If I could, I'd keep you, and welcome, until this affair straightens out. Luckily nobody was in the parlor when you two walked in, but my girls will be talking and trying to put two and two together. Sometimes they come up with two dozen right on the nose. So I can't."

"You can't hide suspected criminals," Andy said in one of his odd, grown-up moments.

"You didn't set any fire, boy, but you do have a talent for being in the wrong place at the wrong time."

"And doing the wrong thing," Andy said with a quiver of his lower lip.

"You did nothing except work as hard as a man," Poppy said fiercely. "I understand, Madame. Jeremiah is a powerful man in this town."

"I can't offend any politician, whatever his party and whatever I think of him."

"We'll leave," Poppy said and hoped the despair was not reflected in her face and voice. The thought of walking through the streets with Andy, when the whole town must be looking for the brother of that redhead from the Palace, was a horror. Somebody would shout and point them out within ten minutes. She touched the voluminous wrap. "I do need a plain dark dress."

"Yours and the shoes too, ruined, and I myself put them in the kitchen stove," Madame said. Then, hearing sounds in the hallway, she tilted her head and rose. "No. No customers at this hour. Bella knows that."

The voices in the hall outside continued and drew closer. Then the door burst open. From behind him, Bella gasped, "I could not stop him, Madame." Maurice, smiling, a portmanteau in each hand, strode into the room.

Delighted with himself, he bowed and put them at Poppy's feet. "I hope I have packed to your satisfaction." He drew the tiny derringer from his pocket. "I also have decided you have earned this."

"Maurice, I could kiss you," Poppy said, almost in tears.

"I commend the idea."

Madame was on her feet and frowning. "Who directed you here?"

"I myself have decided it," Maurice smiled. "When I arrived home last night, I found Miss Poppy's doors all open but nobody inside."

"I didn't leave them open."

293

"I closed them again. Then one of my friends who had played late at the tables came home with a great story. We watched from our windows and discovered other watchers in the shadows across the street."

"I knew it," Poppy cried. "They must have been right behind me."

"So you were out before they arrived and searched the house," Maurice shrugged with a wave of his hand. "My friend and I conferred, and we decided that ourselves. Also that you had not delayed to pack. The rooms alone told us that, one bed untouched, everything in perfect order for the morning. So just before first light, when everybody dozes, I let myself in the back door and packed the small necessities a young lady and a boy need when traveling."

"Who directed you here?" Madame repeated grimly.

"I myself. Who else does Miss Poppy know in this town? If I make the mistake, I still can leave the portmanteaus here to be recovered later, more easily from here. But I make no mistake."

Madame shook her head, still frowning, and put a finger to her lips. Outside, Bella was protesting again, her voice unusually loud, "No. Not at this hour. Madame forbids. No guests. You saw nobody enter. No, gentlemen, no."

"I have been followed," Maurice said.

Distantly, they heard the slam of a heavy door and almost relaxed. Then they heard a scuffling, Bella's voice protesting again, and the thud of men's feet on muffling carpets. Madame reached the door in two quick steps and shot the bolt.

"I can only protest and delay them a little time," she said. "Behind you—beside my wardrobe on the inner wall. There. The door to my new wine cellar. I would not trust it any place else. Down. All of you. Down quickly."

Maurice pulled the door open and threw down the portmanteaus, and Andy tumbled after them. Poppy half fell down the wooden steps, and Maurice pushed close behind her. They huddled in the center of the roughly bricked room, lit only by two small barred gratings.

Above, they heard a pounding on Madame's door and her protesting voice, followed by Jeremiah's deep tones in short words of command. Madame did not prolong the argument. They heard her door slam open, and her angry invitation to enter if they must and search a lady's solitary chambers, an indignity beyond words, past description, completely outside all law and all rules of gentlemanly behavior. Therefore she was saying nothing, Madame proclaimed, and for two full minutes proceeded to voice her outrage at five gentlemen invading a lady's privacy at this hour.

Jeremiah's deep tones rumbled in answer, but Poppy was too horrified to hear what he said. She was staring up at a thin oblong of light. The latch of the door at the head of the stairs had not caught. It was ajar.

She poked Maurice, and he saw it. He looked around the room at the racks for holding bottles, the casks of wine and beer, and the cases of wine stacked along the back wall. He peered closer there and beckoned, pointing to a space between the cases and the wall. Andy and then Poppy scrambled over and squeezed themselves down, huddling low so their heads would not show.

"Do you have mice in your walls, Madame?" Jeremiah asked. "I hear rustlings and squeakings. Where does this door lead?"

The oblong of light broadened as the door opened. Maurice kicked the portmanteaus back of the steps, strode forward, and looked up.

"Good morning, sir. Madame is not prepared for visitors so early, but I am an old friend, and I am bringing up my own supplies."

He pulled several bottles from a rack and climbed the stairs. The oblong of light started to narrow behind him, and then stopped.

"Just a minute," Jeremiah said. "What's down there?"

"My wine cellar, m'sieur. Do you wish to inspect it?"

295

"I think I'll have a look." He went half down the stairs, stood looking around for a long minute while Poppy and Andy held their breaths, and then climbed back up. But the door stayed open. "So you two are old friends? You must have arrived on the same boat. With the Smith boy and his sister. Of course. Maurice even rents from her."

"Naturally," Maurice said.

"So this would be a natural place for them to come for protection."

Madame laughed magnificently. "Here, m'sieur? Here? Miss Poppy is a most discreet young lady. She would not come to a house like this."

"I know all the young lady's virtues," Jeremiah said curtly. "If you had her good at heart as I do, you would give me any assistance you can to find her. As long as she is alone with that boy and people are as angry as they are over this arson, she is in danger. I too want to protect her."

Poppy held her breath. Maurice would not believe that. But would Madame?

"We all wish only her good, may Heaven help the poor child," Madame said piously.

"What's this?" Jeremiah snapped, and his voice rose triumphantly. "I see three plates. You had three breakfasts in here. Now do you still claim that pair isn't in this house?"

"Three breakfasts certainly," Maurice said. "You do not understand lives less—shall we say—less well regulated than yours. I have a little friend here. We were friends on the boat. Unfortunately for me, she is very lovely and very popular. So by the time I leave the Palace, she is seldom free. But Madame understands. I am permitted, I only, to call in the mornings when I am free and also Amalie is free. We three old friends breakfast together, and then I take up the champagne, and Amalie and I have our little comfort together. If you will excuse me, Madame, I will take this to the kitchen to be iced. Amalie and I will be in her room."

"You're a gambler, a bluffer by trade," Jeremiah snapped.

"My game is monte, seldom poker. *À bientôt.*"

Madame waited until the door closed and then said coldly, "I assure you gentlemen I have nothing here in my private rooms that could interest any of you. However, if you would be interested in seeing the rest of the house, I would be glad to have you inspect. Everything is of the finest, the best to be found in town, of an elegance, a convenience unmatched. The piano, rosewood no less with painted panels, so dainty, so genteel. The stemware, the linens, the china of the finest. The champagne buckets, silver naturally, and the candlesticks of an exquisite silver gilt. In the parlors, the spittoons of brass because that is expected. But in the bedrooms, *au contraire,* the finest porcelain to match the other accommodations. The curtains, the best imported lace, with the embroidery—no, you should see for yourselves."

Feet shuffled on the floor. Somebody muttered, "Ah, the girls are jest crawling out of bed, and in the kitchen, they're washing up. I looked when we came through the hall. There's nothing to see."

"Poppy and the boy went somewhere, and to a place they could walk," Jeremiah growled. "Not a carriage or a stagecoach carried them out of town. We're still checking the hotels, but I'm sure I'd have heard. They dived into some rathole they knew."

"I would not presume to offer you refreshment in a rathole," Madame said.

"A walk around, including your attics, will be quite sufficient."

Poppy and Andy did not dare stir. The chill and damp of the cellar seemed to seep into their very bones. Time dragged in ominous silence. Someone entered the room above and removed the dishes. They could hear the footsteps and the rattle. Someone else came in and stamped around the bed, making it, and then swept both rooms, brought in wood for the fireplace, and opened the windows wide. The morning moved through

its daily routine as if they did not exist or had been forgotten.

Then men's heavy footsteps shuffled overhead again,
and Madame said, "If you gentlemen are satisfied, I
have business matters waiting here. The butcher is in
the kitchen. I want only the best for my customers, but
so far only his bills are of the best. His chops, an
abomination. The steaks, for soling shoes. The roast
beef—perhaps I could forgive him that."

"Have you put a watch on the steamers?" a man
asked.

"Of course. At least I know she's still in town and
can't get out." With a heavy attempt at courtesy, Jeremiah added, "My apologies for this intrusion, Madame.
As you promised, your appointments are of the handsomest."

"Not to mention the girls," someone said, sounding
loud with relief. "That's a pretty little brunette you
have there. I'll remember her."

"Florette. She's only lately arrived, a pretty child and
talented. Bella, the gentlemen are ready to leave. I will
be in the kitchen with the butcher."

Poppy and Andy pressed close together, numbed with
chill, not daring to speak or move, but tense with dismay. Madame and Maurice could not have forgotten
them. For some good reason, they were continuing to
ignore the cellar. They had a reason, Poppy argued with
herself. No matter how their teeth chattered, how their
legs cramped, and the darkness threatened them, they
must stay where they were. If they went bursting upstairs, they could run into a trap. Time dragged, while
creakings and gratings that promised crawling things
surrounded them. People had fingers and ears eaten off
by rats, Poppy recalled with horror. She only hoped
Andy did not know that. There were live things in the
cellar all around them, and her flesh crawled in fear of
an attack.

Distantly in the quiet, she could hear a clock striking
upstairs. The quarter chimed. Then an hour passed.
Another quarter chimed. Could Jeremiah have left a

guard with orders to stay literally around the clock? Could they be trapped here until night? Or longer?

Then the door slammed wide open, and light flooded down on them. At the head of the steps, Madame swore. "Pigs, animals from a swill pen, diseased rat-tailed skunks, misbegotten mongrels born in a sewer, filth of scab-ridden fleas," and she got better as her imagination took hold.

Poppy stumbled up the stairs, dragging Andy behind her. She stumbled over to the fire and huddled down in front of it, teeth chattering uncontrollably. Andy crouched close beside her, and though he had not made a sound all that long time, his dirty face showed betraying streaks of tears.

Madame threw a log on the small flickering flames and poked them into a blaze before she slammed down the windows and caught her breath to fume again. "So cold, so damp, so abandoned, but I could do nothing. One of those—those animals had to stay. With poor little Lorene, so busy last night, so tired, so deserving of a little rest, but that animal stayed. He would not leave. I must remain in the kitchen, berate the butcher, make the complaint with the bread. I dared not even send Bella to you."

"We thought somebody must have stayed behind," Poppy said. "To guard, I thought."

Madame snorted dramatically and demanded, "Then what? When he came to leave, the great gentleman? With thanks. Oh, no. I charged him, which he did not expect, he thought the powerful man was his free ticket. I charged him well, but it was no satisfaction. If I could have emptied the chamber pot—but, no, I am a businesswoman. I only charged him double."

Someone knocked briskly on the door, and Maurice stuck his head in. "May I?"

"Why not?" Madame threw up her hands. "A terrible morning. Terrible. In this business, the people I must permit in a house of the most elegant! The people—" she was beginning to warm up again.

"And I had to drink so much champagne I do not

know how I will be able to sit in my game," Maurice interrupted gloomily. "Add to this I do not like champagne, but Amalie adores it. I thought I had my hand on the good dry wine you keep for yourself, but it was champagne and when Amalie saw the bottles!" He shook his head.

Madame made a wide, generous gesture. "I will bill only for what you have actually drunk."

"I'm sorry to have caused so much trouble," Poppy said miserably. "If you have one idea of where we dare go, we'll be out of here in two minutes."

"I must go to the Palace because I must not in any way act as if this is not the usual day," Maurice said. "I am almost late now."

"Thank you for everything, Maurice," Poppy said unsteadily.

"You did not hear," Madame said. "You were upstairs when we discovered the stagecoaches, the carriages, the steamers, the hotels, everything is watched. Now as you know how to make the spot disappear from the cards, do you know how to make Poppy and Andy disappear?"

"I am an honest gambler, Madame," Maurice said. "The table percentages give me all the advantage I need. And other men's stupidities."

"You think Jeremiah stupid?" Poppy gasped.

"Very," Maurice said absently, frowning. "Where do you want to go, Poppy?"

She had thought of that in the long, cold time in the cellar. "To Jack. He's kept moving so nobody here has any idea where he is, if anybody ever knew, and he's just moved on again, to the Injun Creek diggings."

"He is well located?"

"No. He sounds discouraged and half sick. But we won't be a burden to him."

"He probably needs you," Maurice said. "You want a stagecoach then."

"Madame told you. They're watched."

"Watched leaving town. Not watched for passengers

300

who get on later, outside town." Maurice frowned, debating. "Now which coach, where, when?"

"I have the schedules of all the coaches." Madame nodded approval of herself. "Some men, they think it enough if they bring to town once a week their vegetables, their fruits. No, no, no. For my customers, the freshest, the most delicate, the fruit still with the bloom, straight from the tree, the little peas so dainty, so fragrant, the oysters just from the water, all the specialties my house offers, I arrange for the stagecoaches to bring daily." She sighed ecstatically. "Yes, for my customers, the best."

"All you have to do is get to the first or second stop outside town," Maurice said. "Do you know the schedules out of town, Madame?"

"Of course, again my customers." Madame made her eyes very wide. "Sometimes gentlemen like to entertain in private. I do not approve. I do not like it when gentlemen come here, and I have in my parlor only three or four girls to entertain. I will not take the scuffings from the streets, but the best girls, so demanding, so expensive to dress. So I select, select, discard, select. But still sometimes when I must send five or six for some private entertainment and we are busy upstairs also, I have in my parlor only two or three." Madame wagged her head sadly.

"How do the gentlemen entertain privately?" Maurice probed.

"In the small lodges, for the hunting, the fishing, they say, outside town. Sometimes they ask for the girls to come in the stagecoach, and they meet with their carriage. Sometimes I send my girls, four, five, six in my own carriage. And I charge—oh, how I charge."

"In your own carriage," Maurice said thoughtfully. "Then people are used to seeing your girls drive out of town."

"I have just told you that."

"What would your driver think if you changed the program around a little, if he drove two girls out of town and then they got on a stagecoach?"

"He thinks only that some man has a reason to pay well for that special arrangement. He knows I plan, arrange everything always of the best, so he is not surprised when I tell him to leave in time to meet the stagecoach. Yes, I must consult the schedule, yes, to meet the stagecoach at the second stop." Madame nodded vigorous approval of herself. "Poppy and Andy, yes, Andy he will be a very small girl but, yes, in large capes with hoods, two of my girls leave in my carriage for an evening out of town. Under the capes, they can be quite presentable for the stagecoach."

"Jeremiah is suspicious," Poppy said. "He's not apt to forget you have a carriage and to have a lookout to see if it leaves town."

"I have good horses."

"Let's hope they're good enough," Maurice said.

Part Five

The Diggings
Fall 1852

Chapter Thirty-two

SOMETIMES, up on the small hill under the old oak, languid in the sun-speckled shade while Jack and Andy worked knee-deep in the water of Injun Creek, when she had finished reading the newspapers the miners brought back from town each week, Poppy put away thoughts of the world she had left so completely and made lists of things she would never understand. She mused while she mended their ragged clothes or tried to brush the scent of wood smoke from her hair or worked a bit of bacon fat into her water-reddened hands to keep them from cracking.

Gold fever was the first thing she could not understand. Sometimes, though she never would hint so to any man here at the diggings, she thought it was literally a fever, a kind of sickness and a madness, too. She strove to think and feel as they did, to understand. She could not. Her mind could comprehend only the facts she had learned, so she turned those over and over in her mind.

Though now the season was edging into autumn and Injun Creek ran slow and shallow, she pictured how it would look next spring. On the horizon, the mountains loomed like an intimidating presence, cupping this long, narrow valley and all the others on each side in a circle of dark and towering strength. Up there, the snows would soon begin to fall and pack. The snow would mount all winter until men who had seen it said the whole range glinted blindingly bright in the sunlight. Sometimes, under a brilliant sunset, the peaks reflected

pink, blue, green, and purple like scooped-up heaps of
party ices on a giant's table. Then in the spring, the sun
would melt the snow, and the little creeks and wider
rivers would run fast and full as the icy water came
surging down, leaping and springing, bounding from
rock to rock with a spray like rainbow-tinted lace filling
the air. The gentle tinkle of the little falls would
deepen to thunder. As the water roared down, it would
tear at the earth and the rocks, loosening gold that had
been waiting there for centuries, carrying it down to
the streams running through the valleys. The streams,
too, running fast and full, would give up their deep-
buried hoards of gold left there in the soil by former
spring runoffs, and bring it to the surface for the taking.

Then all the men working up and down the streams
like Injun Creek, sifting their pans and cradles from
sunup to sundown, standing patiently in the water, who
now this late in the season were lucky if they made a
dollar a day, might become rich with a dozen lucky
pans. They might find even greater wealth. Probing and
digging in the valleys that had been flooded over in
centuries past, they might find soil so deeply permeated
with gold that hands and shovels could not bring up all
the deep-buried veins of metal. With such a great strike,
mere surface scraping might bring a man enough in a
day to live like a king, but machines were needed to
bring the tons of gold-drenched earth to the surface. A
man who made a find like that and got his claim recognized was as rich as a king for life.

That was the stuff of fairy tales, the dream of fools
or madmen, yet it was true. Hundreds of sober, decent
men, alive now in this California, had found their gold
and lived like kings to prove it true. Anyone could see
and talk to them and know it could happen. So every
man here at Injun Creek and all the places like it believed that dream and was betting his life on it.

Poppy, too, knew it was true, as she knew night followed day, but she could not believe it in her heart. An
orange was round and gold, and she could hold it in her
hand. That she believed. Great fortune by chance, she

could not believe. Men claimed such a failure to comprehend was the proof of the weakness of a woman's
mind.

If ever she saw a man bring up a king's wealth in a
day, and she did not think she would, she still would
feel she was seeing some fanciful tale acted out on a
theater stage. She would believe it when it brought her
an orange to eat every day. That was wealth she understood and yearned to have.

She did not understand and knew she never would.
She wished she could. The men here sustained their
hard life cheerfully because they had their fever, their
dreams. She was too sane and had no dream to soften
the hard reality of the days and nights for her.

Her second musing was a mere trinket to dangle before her curiosity. When her mind was escaping the
dreary monotonous present by picking up and looking
at pictures of the past, she remembered and wondered
about something that had happened on the stagecoach
ride. She accepted she would never know the answer.

Madame, ever practical, had produced two confiscated hooded capes she had highhandedly told their
owners were shabby past public wearing and had
wrapped Poppy and Andy in them. With them well
wrapped and installed in the carriage, portmanteaus at
their feet, the driver had set off with strict orders about
where and when he was to meet the stagecoach and put
them on it. The Concords ran to smooth and exact
schedules, and Madame had schemed so there was barely time to make connections. They set off at a brisk
pace to meet the midday coach, twenty miles out of
town.

Just inside the city limits, Poppy saw three mounted
men waiting under a clump of trees on a side lane. As
the carriage drew abreast, she saw that they were wearing the black broadcloth of businessmen and were
mounted on good horses. They were watching every
vehicle that rolled along the highway. At the sight of
their carriage, the men kicked their horses into a rearing start to race out and intercept them. Poppy gasped,

caught Andy's hand in hers, and huddled down into the seat. The three men reached and circled them, one on each side and one reaching toward their horses' heads. Suddenly, five *vaqueros* on their quick, rough little horses galloped up from nowhere, whooping and shouting, jostling the men away from the carriage into the streams of traffic on each side. Drivers cursed and pulled up or lashed their horses away from the scene of the trouble. By the time the tangle unsnarled, their carriage was rolling ahead of the disruption, while the three men were left fighting their horses to get them off the crowded road. Their driver whipped up his horses, and they swept past the market carts ahead. Poppy kept looking back, peering through the cloud of dust rolling behind them, but no mounted men came pounding up from the rear. They were barely in time to make their stagecoach, and as they tumbled from their carriage into it, Poppy thought she saw one of the *vaqueros* riding like a guard on the edge of the road behind.

Had that been lucky chance, men in town from a distant rancho, rollicking and happening to break the line of carriages at just that point, accidentally, to halt the men who seemed to be watching for Madame's carriage? Or had Madame spoken with some rancher who sold her produce and valued her business and asked him to set his men on guard? Poppy realized she would never know, but she did wonder.

Sometimes in the long, sultry afternoons, she mused about men. She decided every nationality was different.

Maurice was a typical Frenchman, she decided, gallant to all women and faithful to none. She thought a Frenchman would make a good husband if a woman realized the marriage was only one of life's set conditions, like an income of five hundred pounds a year, and a man was expected to have his other little amusements.

Englishmen were her own people, and yet she had her reservations. Jack was the best type of English gentleman. To him, women were either good or bad. Bad women could be enchanting baubles in their prime.

Or, as they aged, sad examples of what happened once a woman fell, and they could be aged at twenty. Good women were potential wives and mothers and must be treated as treasures, guarded, protected, and respected. To Jack, in spite of everything, she was a good woman. The other men on Injun Creek knew Jack would use his fists on any man who as much as uttered a profane word in front of the woman he called his sister. Poppy marveled but accepted the situation. It made it easy for her to love Jack. As she loved Andy.

American men she simply did not understand. They had their own code, and she had learned it, like some foreign language, but she still thought it strange and sometimes outrageous. They had something of the Englishman's attitude of reverence toward women as wives and mothers, and yet they treated them as equals, too, and expected more of them. In other ways, and she still did not understand all its intricacies, they had a strange code of conduct. Some things were men's work, and some were women's. A man would not touch women's work, through he might cook, wash, and mend for himself if he was alone, and brag about how well he did. But while he might treat women with a respect and even awe that seemed more sincere than an Englishman's ritual politenesses, he still left women's work to them when they were there. That was what Poppy, looking at her rough, reddened hands and feeling the new muscles in her arms and back, found outrageous. Washing shirts was physically brutal labor, yet American men would watch dotingly while she strained and heaved. Though it was profitable, she admitted, and they needed the money for food, it did not endear the Injun Creek miners to her, though otherwise she found them likable enough.

Her thoughts always ended with Dex, in mingled sorrow and anger. She did not even know whether he was English or French. Perhaps that was why his attitude was so incomprehensible to her. Either a Frenchman or an Englishman could have kept her as he had done in Paris. Either could have discarded and paid her off as

ruthlessly when he decided to marry. But what kind of
man could send a girl and a boy on board a ship like
the *Bonne Irène* with an invitation to murder in their
luggage?

That, more than the memory of Félicité, was the hurt
that stabbed Poppy every time she thought of Dex. His
memory was a seeping wound that refused to heal. She
could keep busy all day, her mind occupied with a
dozen trivialities and practicalities, and swear his name
had never crossed her mind. At night, asleep and off
guard, the wound broke open again and again.

Alone in the lean-to beside the tent where Jack and
Andy slept, curled up on the straw mattress to get the
most warmth from her one blanket, she would doze and
drift in restless sleep. Then she would be once more in
the big bed in Paris, everything around her soft and
silken, and she would be held close against his strong,
warm body, enraptured, glowing with tingling response
as his hands caressed her and his lips found hers and
moved on down her body. She would reach for him
with a murmuring whisper, to draw him closer, to feel
his strength entering her—and then she would begin to
wake, chilled, empty-armed, and alone. The murmur
would sink to a whimper in her throat, and her face
would be wet with tears. Desolate, angry, hating Dex,
despising herself, she would swallow the sore rawness
in her throat and dry her face on the blanket. She would
not cry and whimper and long for the man. She would
not admit the hurt that left her heart withered and
crippled. Awake she did not. Asleep her dreaming body
betrayed her again and again.

Chapter Thirty-three

SABBATH peace encompassed Injun Creek. Along the whole curve to the bend and beyond, nobody waded or worked in the fall-shallowed water. In the clearings along the banks, the smoke of cookfires rose straight up in the still air. This early in the day, no sounds broke the silence. The men were reading their Bibles or the newspapers they had got in town yesterday, writing letters home or penning long pages in their voluminous diaries, doing their week's cooking, scrubbing out a washing, or, for some of those who had spent yesterday in town, still nursing aching heads.

From her shelter under the oak, Poppy looked down at the camp sprawled along the banks of the creek and relished her solitude. Her excuse for getting away, three handfuls of greens brought out by the unseasonably early rain last week, wilted in the red calico kerchief at her side. She wiggled her toes in her crudely mended boots and smoothed out her green rep skirt. The heavy silk was wearing well, though the gloss was long since gone, but she must not have rinsed out the cast-iron kettle well enough before she washed it this last time because it had streaked badly. The green boy's work shirt was holding up just fine, except she had no way to iron it.

She glanced at the sun and settled back against the oak. Andy and Jack could warm up their own beans for lunch. They would not worry. No Indians ever came up this part of the creek, and anyhow the Digger Indians only wanted to be left alone to weave their baskets, fish, and gather acorns. Privately Poppy thought they seemed a little lacking.

No miner would do anything but fight to the death to protect her. That was the trouble. That was what she had felt she could not face today. Every Sunday the same thing happened. One by one, or in twos and threes, the men would all wander over to their clearing, hang around a while, shifting from one foot to the other, talking a little of the latest news they had heard in town or read in the papers. And all the time their eyes would never leave her. She knew, and they knew she knew, they came only to look at her, to see a woman moving around and working at homely, familiar tasks, to hear her voice and wait for her to smile. At first she had been touched and a little awed. She was the only woman this side of Injun Gulch, the only woman for fifteen miles around, the only woman some of these men had seen for weeks if their claims were far up the creek and they had not happened to go into Injun Gulch. Just to see and hear her was a wonderful, refreshing thing to them, something they looked forward to all week.

She disliked none of those men, but that ritual Sunday staring had been getting on her nerves for weeks. She began to feel like a battered but cherished Christmas ornament that was dragged out once a year to be seen but not touched and then put away in cotton again to be preserved for the next ceremonial viewing. So today she had announced she must gather these first new greens to cook before their teeth began to loosen with the scurvy, and she had come up the hill where she could be alone for a few hours.

She must have dozed. The sun was heating up, though it was getting so chill at nights now that her one blanket, no matter how tightly she curled herself into a ball, left her cold and stiff in the morning. She moved out from under the shadow of the oak and let the sun beat down on her as if she could store the warmth against the night. Down below, the men were beginning to stir in their clearings. Each was a little separate from the others, some with tents, some with board shacks and a few like theirs with a combination of tent and rough timbered lean-to thatched with small branches.

She could see Dutch's red shirt moving toward their clearing. Below the bend, she could hear faint, sweet tones. Frenchy was playing his violin. Those distant deeper sounds were Little Joe and Ted Miller having one of their religious arguments, yelling Bible texts back and forth at the top of their lungs. The quartet should have worked off their headaches and should start singing over on Tunner's claim soon. She always enjoyed that.

As usual they started out with "Oh, Susannah." Then they went on to "Hangtown Gals." That ha, ha, ha, in the last line always made her smile, the way the men roared it out. Now they were starting Tunner's favorite. He had come overland to California.

> Oh, don't you remember sweet Betsy from Pike,
> Who crossed the big mountains with her lover, Ike,
> With two yoke of cattle, a large yellow dog,
> A tall Shanghai rooster and one spotted hog?

Little Joe and Ted Miller must have gone over for a visit because they were singing hymns now. No, they were mixing them, first a hymn, then something else, and then another hymn. People said Little Joe had been a preacher and Ted Miller had been a doctor, but nobody asked, and they never said. If they ever wondered how an English sailor like Jack had found the money to bring his sister and brother to the States, they never asked that, either. It was not considered polite. Anything people wanted you to know, they would tell. Sometimes men hinted that asking questions was not only impolite but unhealthy.

Poppy sat up abruptly. What was that they were singing? That was a new tune but what were the words? Had she been hearing that, without really listening, because it was certainly related to what she had been thinking. The quartet was singing it again, trying out the harmonies.

Oh, what was your name in the States?
Was it Thompson or Johnson or Bates?
Did you murder your wife?
Did you fly for your life?
Oh, what was your name in the States?

Now that was different. Here people sang what they thought and felt. If they were beginning to ask, "What was your name in the States?" maybe California was changing, getting settled and civilized.

The mere thought was invigorating. A new song, as small a thing as that, was a bright shining spot in the endless, monotonous chain of days. For weeks, she had been feeling she was on an endless treadmill, plodding on and on, each day like the last, and none of it getting anywhere. She had felt bogged down, completely mired in a hopeless situation that only got a little worse all the time. She had been wrong. She and Jack should have a talk. She must tell him she understood now that sometimes to move on to a new place was for the best.

She picked up her kerchief of greens and started down the hill, bending and nipping the few tender young shoots she had missed on the walk up. She would boil these and drench them with vinegar. She had baked bread in both the skillet and the cook pot yesterday, so there was plenty left. She had put their last onion in with the chilis for the beans, and that would make a fine Sunday dinner. She had saved back only the dried apples, and no argument was going to get her to touch them because the apples must stretch through all of next week when they would not have a single vegetable until Jack walked in to Injun Gulch next Saturday.

She went quickly across the narrow valley bordering the stream, avoiding the other camps. She circled around ropes strung between trees to form corrals for the horses. A burro tied to a tree to graze on the scanty underbrush brayed at her, and a dog or two barked, halfheartedly. She passed close enough behind Red Luke's shack to hear the slap of cards and the low-voiced mutters of the weekly card game within.

When she reached their clearing, she stood looking at it as if she had never seen it before. Jack had made it shipshape, and she kept it clean. The tent and lean-to stood close to the big elm, and their straw mattresses and blankets were hung neatly on the line between the lean-to and the tree. Poppy believed firmly that only daily airing kept them free of vermin, and since she did the hanging and took everything back inside in the evening, nobody argued with her. The fire was out under the big washing kettle and would not be lit until next Wednesday, but embers glowed in the cooking fire with its log backing. Poppy put the greens on the crude wooden chest Jack had hammered together to hold their food supplies and nodded approvingly when she noticed somebody had scrubbed out their tin plates and the wooden platters Andy had carved. She kicked her shoes into the lean-to. They must be saved. She kept the ground around the camp swept clean with a broom she had made of twigs, and it was safe enough to go barefoot. Her house was in order.

Jack and Andy must have gone visiting to hear all the news from town. Without a horse, the long walk of fifteen miles to Injun Gulch and fifteen back meant a whole day's work lost. Jack tried to go only every two weeks or even three if he had enough gold to buy supplies to last that long. The walk was too much for Andy. He had only been out of the diggings once when Dutch let him ride with him on his horse, weeks and weeks ago.

Poppy nodded decisively. They had been drifting, dulled into numb acceptance because they had shelter and food, but winter was coming. She would talk to Jack at dinner. She would not complain. They had come to him desperate for protection, and he was giving them everything he had. He was a proud man and a decent man. She would be the worst of ingrates if she let him feel his best was not good enough. But he was a practical man, too. Perhaps he also had been wondering what they could do through the winter and had hesitated to worry her by mentioning it.

She had the coffee brewed and the beans heating when Jack came striding back into the clearing. His shoulders were back and his blue eyes shining as they had not in weeks.

"I've been hearing about the deep mining in that big strike in Grass Valley," he called.

Poppy's heart sank. This was not news to open a reasonable talk about the winter. People were right when they called this gold fever.

"Originally two men just stumbled on the stuff, glittering down among the grass roots," he said, flinging himself down on the two logs he had flattened to make a seat. "Filled two sacks with nuggets as fast as they could pick them up, as much as their burro could carry, and took it in to an assayer. Thirty-six thousand dollars just like that."

Andy came rushing up to the cookfire and stood hopping from one foot to the other. "Little Jim's packing and pulling out in the morning."

"Do you want to go?" Poppy asked flatly.

Jack's whole face changed and set. "How?"

"How far is Grass Valley?"

"Too far."

Poppy knew to a dollar how much gold they had, enough perhaps for one person to travel some distance but not three. "Could you make it alone?"

"No," Jack said. "No. Never suggest that again. I've fallen pretty low here, but not so low I have to abandon women and children."

"Then let's eat," Poppy said quietly. "Andy, you take a towel and have a good wash in the creek. I'll have dinner dished up by the time you're back."

She dished up the beans and the greens and put a big slice of bread on each plate. She filled tin mugs with coffee for all three of them. She was out of the cocoa she usually mixed with water for Andy.

Jack took his place on the sawed-off stump, and she and Andy sat side by side on the logs. Jack looked at his plate without touching it.

"Try the greens," Poppy urged.

"Hey, this is a fine Sunday dinner," Andy cried.

Jack's face flushed brick red. "Fine for paupers."

"Are we paupers?" Andy piped up through a mouthful of beans.

"What else?" Jack growled. "I don't even have a gun to shoot meat for our meals. There's quail, rabbit, deer, duck, everything, but we eat beans."

"Then eat them," Poppy said shortly. "Andy, what other news did the men have?"

"Aw, just politics," Andy said. "They'll bring you over a paper, and you can read it for yourself. A lot of men are speeching at each other as usual. Including ol' Jeremiah. That's all."

That night an icy chill clamped down on the valley. First snow in the Sierra, the men said, and told tales of other winters and drifts twenty and thirty feet deep. The sun burned warmly by mid-morning, but that chill had bitten deep into Poppy. They could not stay in this camp through the winter.

She must talk to Jack. She was willing to do whatever he wanted, but they must do something. She turned secret schemes in her mind, always remembering she must not let Jack feel he had failed them. Then too, geography was betraying her again. She had only the vaguest, most general idea where she was.

Guided by the address on Jack's last letter, Injun Gulch, she and Andy had left the stagecoach at what the driver assured them was the nearest stop with a decent hotel where a lady could stay. She had found a man riding to Injun Gulch and sent a message. Jack had turned up two days later with borrowed horses. She had barely glimpsed the town as they rode past on their way to the diggings, and she had had no reason to go there since.

She only knew it was a town. In a town, she could somehow support herself and Andy. She had no doubts about that. Or if Jack did not have his heart set on Grass Valley and wanted to return to these diggings in the spring, his remark about game had given her an idea. She had the little derringer Maurice had given her.

317

It was a beautiful little object, the butt elaborately inlaid with silver. Surely it could be sold for the value of a shotgun. If Jack shot the meat and she had a place to cook and serve meals, they might do very well in Injun Gulch through the winter. If Jack had his heart set on Grass Valley, wherever that place was, would he be satisfied to see them settled in Injun Gulch and go off alone? A man on his own could travel on almost nothing if he must.

As if he sensed what she had on her mind and did not want to discuss it, Jack avoided her. He worked down in the creek all day, ate hastily, and then either drifted off to another camp until she was asleep or went to bed immediately himself. The days passed, and Poppy did not see him alone for five minutes.

That only made her more determined. The nights were icy, and the days were growing short. They ate breakfast and dinner now by firelight.

One afternoon, Poppy went up the hill to a spot where she could see all up and down the creek. The men stood knee-deep in the stream patiently shifting the gravel and water to separate out the few grains of bright gold. Some used a pan, slowly working it back and forth, and if they washed twenty pans a day, that meant hard, steady work. Far to the left she could see the spot where Jack and Andy had built themselves a wooden cradle. Andy carried the buckets of water and gravel and poured them into the cradle. Jack, because he had the greater strength, judgment, and patience, carefully turned the handle of the cradle, swishing the water back and forth until the water and sands floated off leaving the heavier gold behind. At the other end of the valley where the stream made a sharp bend, the three men who had merged their claims into one long stretch were still working on the sluice. They had dug a narrow ditch to divert the water down it and were carefully riffling the bottom so it would catch the gold as the water flowed over and through the sluice to rejoin the stream farther down.

Those three would stay here through the winter,

Poppy knew, and when the spring floods carried the gold down from the heights above, they would reap their reward. She wondered about the others. Whether they were using cradles or pans, they were lucky if they brought in a dollar a day now. Jack would have had trouble paying for supplies the last time he went to town if he had not, idly digging with his knife at the base of a rock on the edge of the stream, dug out a thirty-dollar nugget. But there were no more, and that was the only sizable nugget he had ever found.

Evenings now, Andy came in with his lips and nails blue with cold and shivered over the fire for an hour before he was warm. Poppy put on a jacket and wrapped up in the hooded cape under her blanket and still woke whimpering with the cold. They could not stay the winter here.

Thinking of winter made Poppy feel old and grim. The men admitted a few had died here last year of the scurvy but said it would not happen again now that they knew to eat raw potatoes and drink spruce tea. Nobody mentioned pneumonia, and she thought that spoke louder than anything they could have said. That was last winter. Whoever suffered and died here this winter, it was not going to be one of hers. Before the weekend, she was going to talk to Jack.

Meanwhile they needed every penny, and she must earn her share. Every man along Injun Creek knew if he wanted his other shirt washed by Poppy, he must get it to her by Wednesday morning so she could wash it on Wednesday to let it dry on Thursday. Then, on Friday, he could pick it up, giving her a dollar or a pinch of dust, whichever was handy. It was ready to wear to town on Saturday.

When she first arrived, found the big kettle on an abandoned claim downstream, and saw it could be used for washing, every man up and down Injun Creek whooped with delight and offered to help. They hauled the kettle up for her. They dug the fire hole and settled the stones. They told her how to make soap by boiling grease and lye together, and faithfully saved and brought her their bacon drippings. Someone gave her a bag of lye, too. They stood around and watched admiringly while she cooked up the foul mixture, gagging at the stink, and poured it into pans to cool. They found a part of the creek nobody was working and pointed it out to her. Then they watched while she carried their dirty shirts down there, weighted them with rocks and left them for the running water to wash away the lice and fleas and the heaviest part of the dirt. They watched while she carried bucket after bucket from the shallow well they had dug ten feet back from the stream and filled the big washing kettle. If they were around, they would build the fire under the kettle with the wood Andy and Jack kept stacked by the lean-to. Apparently that was men's work. But carrying the heavy, wet shirts from the stream was women's work again and so was stirring them with a long pole while they boiled.

That was the part Poppy hated the worst. The last laundress over at Injun Gulch, everybody told her, had coughed something terrible for months and finally died of a congestion of the lungs last winter. Poppy believed them. The big kettle gurgled and steamed with a sour, nauseating odor. Using both hands on the pole, Poppy thrust her whole body back and forth to stir the heavy mass of shirts. The rising steam filled with fatty vapor stung her eyes and made her choke. Then when the water cooled and she managed to tilt the heavy iron kettle enough to pour it out, the splashing water drenched her feet and skirts.

By the time she carried the wet shirts down to the stream to rinse them and then carried them back to hang on tree limbs to dry, she was soaked to the skin and perspiring as well. She was just lucky she had a complete change of dry clothes and could get into them quickly, though she usually was so tired on wash nights that she only pretended to eat.

Still that brought in fifteen dollars every week. Fifteen dollars bought flour, coffee, and beans, with sometimes a little left to put by in the poke.

On this Thursday afternoon, it started to rain. Poppy

ran, grabbed the still-damp shirts off the trees, got the long pole, and draped them somehow inside the tent. When Jack and Andy came up from the stream, she was in the lean-to, protected from the steady, pounding downpour.

"Come in here," she called. "The shirts are drying in the tent. And we'll eat cold beans unless somebody wants to try to build a fire and cook in the rain."

Andy huddled against her, shivering. "The men say once this starts it can go on for weeks and months."

"Not quite that bad," Poppy soothed, handing him a towel. "But this is the end of our regular wash money."

"I shouldn't have let you do it anyhow," Jack muttered.

"So it's over." Poppy was cool now that she had him at last. "Jack, could we all go in to Injun Gulch this Saturday?"

"Fifteen miles there. Fifteen miles back."

"Just fifteen miles there," Poppy said.

Jack made a long, shuddering sound, half sigh, half groan. "You're right. We can't spend the winter here. I didn't realize until now, this rain. It's like being underwater."

"What kind of a town is Injun Gulch?"

"Growing. Seems to be at least one new building every time I go there. Why?"

"Do they have a place that serves good meals?"

"There's a hotel. Two stories. I haven't eaten there."

"If I cooked and you hunted—" Poppy began.

"With bows and arrows?"

Poppy did not know what Jack would say if he knew she had the derringer. A lady might handle a sporting gun at an English shoot, but a pocket gun was different. He might be shocked, and she would not risk losing it. "If you had a gun?"

"I might get a few dollars for the kettle and the chest and the things we can't carry," Jack admitted.

"You mean we're leaving, going to live in Injun Gulch?" Andy demanded.

Jack hesitated. "I didn't say that."

"Can I ride with Dutch again? Who will Poppy ride with?"

"If wishes were horses, beggars would ride," Jack said harshly.

Poppy winced inwardly. Jack was hating himself, feeling a failure again. "Jack enjoys a walk," she said with forced cheerfulness. "I'll do some hinting when the men get their shirts. Tanner's old plow horse could carry two easily."

Chapter Thirty-four

$\mathcal{P}$OPPY sat on one of the two wooden rockers on the porch of the hotel in Injun Gulch and appreciated she had been given the best the town had to offer. She concentrated on behaving with all the decorum that honor merited.

Maurice had chosen well when he packed the portmanteau, and she had kept the black and white suit untouched while everything else was worn to rags. So she sat demurely, skirt well spread to hide her torn, roughly cobbled shoes. Mitts hid her reddened hands, and the green satin bonnet, too elaborate but the only one Maurice had managed to cram in, was tied closely to hide the sun streaks in her bright hair.

Injun Gulch was bigger than she had guessed from her one glimpse of it. Injun Creek cut deep in a horseshoe curve on three sides, and the town was built on the enclosed flat pancake of land with a small range of hills at the back. A high, narrow bridge with only cords for railings crossed the creek. Poppy had been relieved when the men from the diggings had not tried to force their horses across that bridge but had ridden through the shallow water to the livery stable and stockyard at the water's edge beside the bridge. From there, they had pointed out the hotel.

Since it was so early in the day, the serious gambling and heavy drinking would not start yet, so she told Andy he might stay with Dutch if Dutch did not mind. Then she had walked across the square with its one old straggly oak and two spindly pines to the hotel, and asked if she might wait there for her brother, and had been given this place of honor.

Now again she felt like a Christmas tree ornament. Or perhaps like the tree itself, on the night before Christmas, with all the children tiptoeing down the stairs to try to get a secret look before they were discovered and hurried back to bed. Muffled footsteps sounded at the hotel windows behind her, and she knew men, and probably women too, were coming in the back door and peering out at her. All around the square she could see men walking slowly from one building to the next, and their faces were always turned toward her. The yards of every one of the few houses required the mistress's attention too this morning, to hang something on a line or inspect individually each of the few straggling flowers around the doorstep.

Poppy forced herself to sit quietly, as if unaware. Inwardly trepidation gnawed at her. Jack was late, hours late. He had started long before them and should have been here when they arrived. He was not, and none of the men riding into town for Saturday necessities had brought her a message.

She told herself any of a dozen things could have happened. Jack could have come across a camp with sickness and stopped to help. He could have found a likely place to run a few pans and been unable to resist. At worst, he might have twisted an ankle and be able to walk only slowly. Lateness did not spell tragedy. No.

Meanwhile if Injun Gulch could look at her, she would look at Injun Gulch. The church stood centered with its back to the hills, the cemetery on one side and the parsonage on the other. Another small cottage, a pretty place with a small porch and a peaked roof, stood beyond that. The hotel with half a dozen houses straggling out behind it stood alone on this side of the square. Opposite it, at the foot of the bridge, was the row of stores and businesses.

She counted them over carefully. The one with the sign Groceries and Provisions was only one story, so the owners must live in the rear, but the bakery was two stories with living quarters above. The general store looked as if it had offices above it. The unpainted shack next to it had two front windows with Assayer on one and City Hall on the other. The sprawling, rickety building with the sign Theater painted across its false front was plainly a combination fandango parlor and bar with rooms above. She looked again and saw there was another bar, the kind that would have gambling tables, there at the foot of the bridge.

The hotel served meals. Somebody in one of those houses must take in laundry. Probably at least one of the women did sewing and mending.

The town seemed complete, and it was a sizable place. Poppy tilted her chin. She would like to see what kind of meal the hotel served. She thought she could do better, especially if Jack hunted for the meat. She wondered if anybody kept chickens. Or raised vegetables—the ground looked as if it could grow some things if they were well watered. Surely she could make a place for herself here.

A couple of dozen horses were tied to the railing on the business side of town. By noon, there could be fifty. Those men, after they bought their supplies and before they started drinking and gambling their money away, surely would enjoy a home-cooked lunch served by a pretty woman. If she could hold the price at less than the hotel cost—Poppy nodded approval, yes. And if only Jack could see it.

She looked around uneasily again and saw Andy running across the square toward her. Jack must have arrived, and she had missed seeing him.

Andy clung to the arm of the rocker and said, "Dutch wanted to make sure he got a girl while he still had the money, and they don't let boys upstairs. So he sent me back to you. He says he won't be long."

Poppy swallowed hard. She could add another national type to her list. Germans were direct and plainspoken. "Has anybody seen Jack?"

"Dutch thinks he walked around to have a word with that man who had a letter from Grass Valley."

"That sounds probable."

"I'm hungry," Andy said and promptly looked guilty.

"I can spare a dollar," Poppy assured him. "In fact, you can help. I don't want to go in and order a whole meal here, that might cost five dollars, but I would like to know what kind of food they serve and what it costs."

Andy's eyes sparkled with understanding. "The men are eating cheese and crackers in the general store, and they'd sure like it if they could have a cup of coffee with it. They said the hotel's expensive."

"That's what I wanted to know."

"I'll find out and come back and tell you," Andy promised and scurried inside.

Grass Valley. Where was Grass Valley? How could they get there, with no horse, no money for stagecoach fare, nothing? Fifty miles they might walk. But what was this Grass Valley? Was it just camps and diggings, like theirs up the creek, or a town like Injun Gulch?

Gold fever was madness, madness. So she must stay calm. If she got herself in a frenzy before she even knew what Jack had on his mind or what he was planning, she could do nothing. She would stay calm.

She could hear Andy's piping tones and men's deeper voices inside the hotel. Youngsters were rare enough here that it was likely the men were buying him everything in sight and he was stuffing it down as only a growing boy could do.

She listened again and frowned. Andy's voice was too shrill. He was getting overexcited.

He had been up long before his usual hour, stirring up the cookfire, calling them to wake and get dressed so the men would not leave them behind, then hopping from one foot to the other, unable to eat, half sick with excitement. Poppy thought it was pitiful. They had sold a few things and packed a few to take with them. They were breaking camp, but Andy had taken leave of places before with scarcely a lift of the eyebrow. He had traveled half around the world, lived in great cities, London, Paris, San Francisco, but here at the diggings he had been so isolated and alone that a trip to Injun Gulch had him almost hysterical. This life was hard and unsettling on men; Andy needed a normal boyhood. But she had said nothing, and the ride had quieted him.

Now his voice was again loud and shrill, working up to a shriek, followed by whoops of laughter, high and cracking, above the deeper rumble of men's mirth.

"Andy," Poppy called sharply. "Andy. Come here. This minute."

He came running, face purple with laughter, puffing out uncontrollable whoop after whoop.

"Tell me what you find so comical," Poppy commanded.

"It's—" Andy began, whooped and held his sides and fought for breath, "—it's on the bridge there."

"What happened on the bridge?" Poppy asked, voice flat.

"Do you know that Chinese are white men?" Andy asked and whooped again until he collapsed in the other rocker holding his sides, whooping and writhing helplessly.

"Is he all right, ma'am?" a deep voice asked anxiously from the doorway.

"Just leave him alone, and he'll quiet down."

"Is he often taken like this?"

Poppy stiffened indignantly. "He's not taken," she said. "Didn't you ever get the giggles, say in church, when you were a child?"

"So that's it." The deep voice was relieved.

He sidled out and stood in front of her, a tall man with a bushy beard, dressed in his clean best with his boots shined. Four other men followed him sheepishly and lined up to stare down at her.

"We're sorry, ma'am, but he was enjoying the gingerbread, and there was some real cow's milk, and we just got to teasing him, I guess."

327

"About Chinese being white men?"

A younger man with a thin, intellectual face under his fair beard colored a little. His voice was that of an educated man. "It didn't really happen on this bridge, ma'am. We were just stretching a good story."

"I'd like to hear it." Then sharply, "Since it's a story you felt you could tell a young boy."

"It's not that." The young man realized the explanation was being left to him. "These Digger Indians around here, well, they're not as sharp as the Indians back over the mountains."

"I've heard that."

"So they got to arguing whether Chinese were white men, and they know white men can't swim. So they saw a couple of Chinese crossing a bridge like that over there, and they went up to them, and I guess they found out Chinese can't swim."

"So the Indians decided they were white," Poppy concluded crisply.

"It's not really funny, ma'am. We were just telling it."

Andy straightened up, looking unnaturally white. "It sounded funny in there."

"We're sorry, ma'am," the older man repeated.

"You were simply trying to amuse the boy." Poppy remembered a line from a newspaper that had brought chuckles all over California. "You did your best according to your lights, but your lights were a little dim." She remembered Maurice using that quotation, too.

They understood they were forgiven and gathered closer in a circle around her. Poppy knew exactly what was on their minds. Curiosity was eating into every one of them. Andy probably had confided they had been living with their older brother on a claim up Injun Creek, but the big questions remained. Where did they come from, where were they going, what were their plans and the most important of all, the question they could not ask, was it possible a girl as pretty as Poppy could also be good? That was agitating every one of these men, and, whatever the answer, each had some idea in his mind.

Andy sensed he was no longer the center of attention. "Do you suppose Dutch is finished?"

"You stay with me. I won't have you hanging around that fandango parlor."

The bushy-bearded man smiled and leaned forward to prove he also could quote. "The place has a bad reputation, as has its owner."

"There's Jack on the bridge," Andy whooped.

Relief flooded through Poppy. "Run and meet him and tell him I'm here."

"Will you be staying around these parts through the winter?" the young man asked.

The whole circle waited for the answer.

Andy had indeed talked, but there was no harm in that. "I don't know. It's up to my brother. This seems to be a nice town."

"Growing every day," the bushy-bearded man said. "There's every opportunity here. Every opportunity."

"There's six decent women in town already," somebody back of her said, his voice hoarse with shyness. "And we're putting together to buy a piano for the church for the use of any of the ladies that play."

Poppy sighed. "Jack was always sea crazy until he got this gold fever. He's never been one for towns."

"We'll have a word with him about that," the bushy-bearded man said heartily. "Perhaps we'll see you here at lunch, ma'am. We can recommend it."

Poppy nodded and smiled. She would not have them guess her pretty little bag, for all its elaborate decoration of tasseled drawstrings, held only the derringer and her pitifully light poke, and she would part with those only for something she considered vital. Lunch was not that.

A half hour passed before Jack came wearily across the square to join her. He sank down in the other rocker and did not speak for a few minutes.

"Took a little extra walk," he said at last. "Five miles or so."

"For news of Grass Valley?"

"It's big. Maybe the biggest."

"You want to go?"

Jack looked past her, at the square. "How do you like Injun Gulch?"

"It's a nice little town."

"You'd like to stay here?"

"We can't stay at the diggings."

"This Grass Valley strike is different," Jack said.

"How?"

"I admit I haven't talked to anybody who's been there. But I've got the same story secondhand from three or four people. The ore is rich, and it runs deep. Needs big machinery, there's more than one mine, and the gold will last for years. That means a town, permanent."

"How far?"

"You always ask how far."

"And it's always far. Jack, Andy and I would be safe here. You could go ahead, and we could follow in the spring when you're settled a little."

"San Francisco was one thing. You had a house, friends. I wouldn't leave you alone in a place like this."

"In the spring?"

"Too late. The cream is being skimmed off right now. This minute." He forced his voice down. "There's still a good chance. Some men can't see the winter through, and they walk off without leaving even a shovel for markers. But it's rich, rich. People are pouring in there every day."

Poppy wavered. Jack had moved on again and again, running after his dream, and each place seemed to have been a little more desolate than the last. Any place more desolate than Injun Creek would be death for them all. But a man never forgave the person who cost him his dream, however futile it was. And without it, he died another death, though not of the body.

"I don't see how we could get there," she said.

"They've got a couple of broken-down old nags over at the livery stable. Taken in for bad debts and look it, but they'd get us there if we ride them easy. One could carry you and Andy together. Fifty dollars if I take them both."

"I have thirty."

"So do I. I got a fair price for our gear. That leaves ten for food."

He had it planned, though she had dreamed of living here at Injun Gulch. They could not both have their dreams.

Suddenly from the square she heard a strange sound, but with something familiar about it. She jumped to her feet and stared. Andy, oddly bent over as if on four feet, was running around and around the straggling oak. He would bend over until his face almost touched the ground and then rear back and let out a strange baying sound, mingled with half-hysterical laughter. And then he would stoop over again and go galloping around the tree before he repeated the whole performance.

Men were lined along the rail where the horses were tied, howling with laughter and yelling encouragement between gasps of hilarity. With every one of their yells, Andy bayed louder.

Poppy jumped off the porch and crossed the square at a dead run. She reached Andy, grabbed him by the hair, and jerked him upright.

"What do you think you're doing, young man?"

Andy's face was purple, and his eyes were glassy. "I'm a bloodhound," he howled, then threw back his head and bayed. "I'm a bloodhound, smelling the blood. See?" And he pointed to the hard-trodden dirt around the tree.

Poppy looked at the men lining the rail. "What story have you told him now?"

"He looked all right," the bearded man muttered. "We didn't know he was apt to be taken strange, that way."

"He wasn't taken any way," Poppy snapped, but her

heart sank. The men had concluded Andy was simple, a lack-wit, and he would be the butt of practical jokes as long as they stayed in this town. "He's excited by his first trip to town in weeks, and you've been feeding him wild yarns to see what he'd do. So what was it this time?"

The young man with the educated accent stepped forward. "We're sorry, miss. We were just making a little fun. You know how it is when men come to town on a Saturday. Everybody's ready for fun, frolic, or a footrace."

"I'd like to hear about your fun."

"We had a little trouble here last week, and we took care of it as we usually do, public hearing and trial by the alcalde," the young man admitted and glanced toward the bearded leader.

Poppy nodded. The men at the diggings had talked about such trials, where an informally elected alcalde and a committee held immediate trials and gave immediate verdicts on local crimes. The men thought the justice was usually both quick and fair. Poppy shuddered away from the thought of such Vigilante-type proceedings.

"What kind of trouble?"

"A little thieving," the young man said reluctantly and added with pride, "After he was punished, we found out the poor fellow was broke and hungry. We outfitted him and gave him money and supplies before we sent him on his way. Please, miss, we're decent men at Injun Gulch."

"You're the best judges of that. What was the punishment?"

The bearded man spat. "Thirty-eight lashes. I decided it, and I'll stick to it. Thirty-eight good ones."

Poppy closed her eyes and pressed Andy close to her side. She could feel his heart beating wildly. They had seen a sailor get six lashes on shipboard, and the sight of the blood had left Andy sick and white for days. That was before his shattering experience with the slaughtering of the beef, and the two experiences had left him with a horror of bloody punishment. These men could not know that or that Andy had fled in fear of his life from a Vigilante-type punishment. Their cruelty in calling up those memories was unwitting but it was nonetheless cruel. They were not bad men, but Andy could not live in the same town with them.

At her elbow, Jack said quietly, "I think Andy's going to be sick."

She looked down at the white face and twisting lips. "I'll take him down to the water where it's cool. You buy the supplies, and we'll meet you at the livery stable."

Chapter Thirty-five

*A*FTER the torrential downpour that had driven them from Injun Creek, the weather turned hot. Poppy thought she had never known summer to be as hot as this country's autumn. The sun beat down out of a cloudless sky, and there was no breeze. Even the nights were warm. They held their horses to a walk and tried to ride in any shade they could find, but they still were uncomfortable, hot, sticky, and plagued by flying bugs.

The third afternoon they rode past a series of camps along a deep canyon that had every sign of being prosperous diggings. The shacks had a settled look. Many had chimneys and even small porches. A few had rough garden patches scratched out beside them, and a couple even had chickens penned in the back. The horses looked well fed, and the dogs barked saucily. Still something about the place seemed strange.

They rode at a slow walk because they were climbing a steep incline and their horses were damp and were tiring in the hot afternoon. Then Poppy realized what the strangeness was. The place was deserted. It was settled but not inhabited.

Jack looked back at Andy and Poppy. "I don't see a single deserted claim, but I haven't seen a living soul, either."

"Right you are, brother, right as rain from heaven," intoned a deep voice. A long-legged man on a small, rough horse came riding across the stream and scrambled up the bank to join them on the trail. "Not a living soul, as you say, not a living soul."

Jack touched his hat. "I didn't see you, Reverend Doctor."

"Reverend's good enough, young man, just Reverend. Christened a Christian, living a Christian, and preaching of Christ out of the living spirit and His own book, and never touched by the dead hand of a diploma or doctrine. As you say, never a living soul to be seen. Because they're all waiting around the bend with the lamented and departed to be seen into his grave with fitting words."

"Which you have come to provide," Jack said.

"Ridden twenty miles, young man, twenty miles. I get many calls from roundabouts when a man's the kind that's properly honored and his friends want to see him off in fitting style. Some men can read a service, and some can preach one, but I tell you it's power that's wanted when we lay our lamented in the ground and know we'll look upon his face no more. Yes, it's a powerful thought, and it's powerful praying that's needed."

"I'm sure that's so," Jack said hastily. "A sad errand, Reverend. But I'm sure you'll be a consolation to the survivors." He started to rein his horse off the road so the Reverend could pass.

"Follow me—young man and young lady and young fellow too. Because there's only bush and disaster once you're off this trail. So follow me and listen to the words of the Lord and know afresh that it pays to stay on the right trail, the Lord's trail, and then be on your way rejoicing."

Jack looked back at Poppy with a raised eyebrow and a shrug. She shrugged back. She had heard a few such preachers on San Francisco street corners and she knew that once they started that intoning talk, they could keep up for hours without seeming to stop to draw a breath. But if, as the man said, this was the only trail they could follow safely, they must go with him.

The trail twisted up abruptly, and they rode out on a small, flat plateau looking over the water. Some twenty miners were waiting there, grouped around a rough wood coffin standing beside the already-dug grave. The dead man must have been respected and loved by his fellows for them to have selected so impressive and beautiful a site for his grave and gone to the trouble to send for a preacher. Besides, she could see nobody had staked a claim this high above the water.

Touched, Poppy dismounted and walked over to stand beside the group around the grave, intending only to join them for a ceremonial minute. Then as she saw Jack's disapproving face, she realized she had made a mistake. Now they could not leave without giving deep offense. They would have to stay for the funeral.

The preacher tied his horse under some trees to one side and strode over to stand at the head of the grave. Poppy gestured Andy to her side as Jack took the horses to tie them in the scanty shade. A half hour's rest would do none of them any harm.

The miners circled around the grave and coffin, leaving room for them on one side. Poppy composed herself, clasped her hands, and bent her head.

As the man had promised, he was a powerful speaker. He only knew the dead man had come overland from the east and had been honest and generous, but that was all he needed. A half hour passed, and Poppy was swaying on her feet. Andy was slumped against her, and Jack was closely hemmed in by miners on the other side of the grave.

"Let us kneel in prayer."

Poppy dropped gratefully to her knees and almost yelped as she felt sharp stones dig into her legs even through her heavy skirts. She wiggled and put her hands down, trying to brush the stones away, and was aware of similar wiggles and movements all around the grave. Cautiously she eased forward and rested part of her weight on her hands. Looking from under lowered lashes, she saw many of the miners were doing the same thing, their hands, unused to idleness, working at the stony soil, pulverizing it and straining it through their fingers. Twisting a little, hands working to try to ease the discomfort, they all knelt with bent heads. Andy was digging a little hole in front of him, but she nudged him once with her elbow and let it go. She could not blame him.

"Let us pray for him on the first step, an innocent baby in his mother's arms."

Poppy wondered if the preacher was going to take the man up every one of those golden steps to the gates of heaven. At least she could try to scratch a soft spot to rest her hands. Then she might be able to take more weight off her knees.

"Let us pray for him on the next step, a fine young boy but now not so innocent."

Scratch, scratch. Beside her, she could hear Andy digging at his hole.

"He mounts the next step, not yet quite a young man."

The preacher was taking him up every step of that long flight, Poppy mused as she scratched away. Would he stop long at the gate? But he had a way to go yet.

"Now a young man, a good man, and a joy to those who knew him, but no longer innocent. Let us pray for him now on this step."

The sun was hot, and her knees had burning holes in them. Those stones did gouge. Maybe she could clear enough space to move forward. She brushed and scratched energetically, making a little pile of dirt to one side close to Andy.

"A fine young man, but young manhood is filled with temptations. Let us pray for him now in the temptations of the flesh that assail him."

Poppy's flesh was stinging as if those stones had cut holes. Could they be deep enough to bleed? She had to do something. Scratch, scratch. There, she had those pebbles strained out and could push them to one side and move forward to the cleared spots.

"Then again let us pray for him as he feels the temptations of the other senses. The temptations, the greeds, the indulgences of lusty young manhood, ah, yes, all the dire temptations of young manhood. Let us pause a little longer on this step."

Poppy had a terrible feeling the prayer before the

heavenly gate was going to be even longer. Perhaps she could make smooth spots for both her knees and her hands. Scratch, scratch.

"Now he has mounted another step and reached his full strength and powers, and he is indeed in need of our prayers."

Poppy peeped up from under her lashes and felt better. Every one of those miners hunched around the empty grave looked as uncomfortable as she felt, and every one of them was trying to scratch a smooth spot in front of him. Every pair of work-knotted hands was busy. Only Jack was kneeling properly, head bowed, hands folded.

"Each of you know your own weaknesses. I lay it upon you now to make a special prayer for this our brother, to send up your prayer in the field in which you know what it is to suffer, and indeed we are all sinners and sufferers in this world. So now let us pray and invoke the special indulgence for our beloved sinner. To each his own now, in silent prayer."

Not being a man, Poppy felt a general prayer was better in her case. Scratch, scratch. What had she done? Where she had intended to smooth small resting places for her hands and knees, she had leveled a large patch of earth. Had anybody noticed? She glanced around. Not a single person was watching her. They were all much too busy doing exactly what she had been doing, scratching at the dirt in front of them, sifting it through their fingers. But they seemed watchfully aware of what they were doing. One man was even bending far over into the grave, pulling away at the dirt on the inner side.

"Now he is at life's turning point, the years that point his destiny. Let us hold strongly to our faith as we pray for him now."

She should fill in that hole. Pat, pat.

Andy's elbow dug into her ribs. "Stop that. Look."

She followed the direction of his pointing finger and gulped. The heap of dirt and pebbles she had separated out shone with gold. She saw two nuggets the size of her thumbnail.

Even as she stared, the man who had been pawing so frantically into the side of the grave jumped to his feet, both hands flung over his head. "Strike!" he howled. "Gold! Strike! Big strike!" An enormous nugget glittered in his fist.

They were all on their feet, howling and capering. Only Jack rose quietly and stood looking at the preacher.

"This doesn't seem a suitable burial spot, sir. I suggest we find another and dig a new grave. I'll get my shovel."

The preacher looked around and licked his lips. Then he said firmly, "The good Lord put this here for us to find when He made the earth. Now it can wait another thirty minutes while we bury our brother as is proper."

The men looked at each other. Then one said, "Everybody get his shovel and start working under those trees. They don't look likely. And nobody stakes until the Reverend has said amen."

"Amen," the men howled and ran for their shovels.

"Come, Poppy," Jack said, every inch the officer in charge of a work crew.

"I'm with you," Poppy said and scrambled up.

She was careful not to look at Andy as she pulled out her kerchief and dropped it beside him. Perhaps Jack did not notice, but he made no comment when Andy did not follow them to the spot under the trees.

The men carried the coffin and dug with a will. Shovels in hand, they stood with bowed heads while the Reverend said a short, crisp service. Then they lowered the coffin and stood quiveringly alert, awaiting the final words.

"I'll be happy to stay and fill the grave," Jack murmured.

"You are a true English gentleman," the Reverend said. He bent, grasped his shovel in one hand, and raised the other hand in benediction. "We now commit our brother to the mercies of the earth and the good Lord. Amen."

In two breaths, the clearing under the trees was

deserted except for Jack and Poppy. Then Andy ran
up, holding his short-handled shovel. "I'll help," he said
breathlessly and, hand behind his back, wiggled his
fingers for Poppy to take the bulging kerchief.

Jack filled the grave, patted it smooth, and laid two
crossed branches on it. Then without a look at the
furious activity on the plateau or any comment, he led
the way to their horses and tightened the girths. When
they were well away from the plateau, he began to angle
off from the stream.

"Full moon tonight," he called over his shoulder.
"Should be bright as day. I saw some flat grazing land
over this way, maybe five or six miles across. Easy riding. We can keep going until we hit water."

Poppy did not protest. If half the weight in that kerchief was gold, their money worries were over for weeks
to come. She dared not pull it out to look, but she could
feel its heavy weight in the pocket against her thigh as
a promise of food, shelter, and comfort. As long as she
had that, she did not mind how late they rode.

Andy whispered the question that had been in her
own mind. "Why didn't Jack stay and stake us a claim
there?"

"A couple of those men were wearing guns."

"I saw."

"I think Jack decided they felt that was their plateau,
and they couldn't like a stranger coming in."

"Anybody can stake, that's the law," Andy said im-
portantly.

"The law about claims is what the miners on the spot
decide," Poppy said. "They decide, and they're good
about abiding by it, but I think Jack was right. Besides,
he's got his heart set on Grass Valley."

"He thinks it's richer than that?" Andy asked with
awe.

"He must."

Andy whistled and drooped tiredly against her shoulder. The sun went down, and the blue twilight was
brief. Then the moonlight was brilliant, turning the yellow tableland to silver across which their horses moved

accompanied by their black shadows. Jack led the way steadily but slowly, for their horses were tired and beginning to stumble, toward a long, dark line of shadows showing against the sky.

Poppy was nodding by the time they reached them. When she realized her horse had stopped, she jolted fully awake and looked around. For a moment she thought she was in a dream. A silver stream rippled between rows of willow, widening into deep pools and then narrowing to curve on to the next pool. In the grassy spot beside the narrowed part of the stream was a squat, dark structure. All silver and black, it was like an illustration in one of those romantic books the ballet girls used to give her when Daisy was not looking, the solitary, romantic crypt beside the murmuring stream where the beautiful girl had died for love.

Jack dismounted and went up to the structure, found a door and peered in. "Some kind of shelter. The *vaqueros* must use it when they're out herding. Needs airing. Indeed, it needs airing. Here's their fireplace. They've left some wood, too."

Poppy slipped off her horse and steadied Andy to his feet. "You go wash. I'll start water boiling and heat the beans while Jack gets the tent up."

Jack kept sniffing the shed all the time she was cooking dinner. Finally he decided, since the night could turn cold, to pitch Poppy's tent close beside it for a windbreak while he and Andy rolled up in their blankets in the shelter between the outside wall and the open door. The odor could not bother them too badly as long as they slept in the open. Poppy and Andy did not care. They had ridden hours longer than usual, and all they wanted was to eat, then stretch out and sleep.

Poppy dropped down into sleep. In her sleep she kept dreaming, twisting and muttering protests as she dreamed. She was in a deep black well, a cool well lined with silver, cool water, cold silver, and yet fiery sparks kept stabbing at her. She moaned and half woke. She must have been dreaming of that fire in San Francisco when the sparks showered down and stung and burned her. That was strange. Then she started convulsively, sat upright, pulled her bare arms out of the blanket, and stared at them.

Pink bumps. Her arms, even her hands, were swollen with pink bumps all over them. Measles, but she had had the measles. Smallpox, then, and that was deadly. Then she pulled her blanket away and looked down at her white camisole. Not pink bumps, black bugs, and they were jumping and hopping all over her. Her hair, she could feel them moving in her hair.

With a howl, she jumped up hopping and kicking, slapped at the jumping, biting tormentors, trying to brush them off, shaking her arms, swinging her legs. And still she was covered. Her hair, each separate hair, felt as if it had its own moving creature. That was the complete horror.

She ran for the deep pool and jumped in. She pulled off her clothes, threw them on the bank, and ducked her head under water, pulling her hair out of its pins, swishing it through the running stream. She raised each leg in turn, washed it free, and then worked on her arms. Even her waist and back were bitten and itched intolerably. She stretched out in the water and let its soothing coolness flow over her. That helped, as long as she stayed exactly where she was.

Then she heard a deep, muttering exclamation from the shed and the thud of feet hitting the ground. Quickly she paddled to the far end of the pool, crouching and sheltering in the shadows of the willows, as Jack ran down and jumped into the middle of the pool, tearing off his clothes and throwing them up on the bank beside hers.

"What is it?" Poppy called. "What are these things?"

"Fleas," Jack yelled in a terrible voice. "Thousands of fleas. That smell. Why didn't I recognize it? They store their uncured hides in that shed. And those cattle are alive with fleas!"

"I'm alive with fleas," Poppy almost sobbed. "What can I do? They're still on me. In my hair. Oh."

"Stay where you are. I'll get the soap. Work up a

good lather all over. Stay where the stream runs fastest, and they'll wash away."

He splashed out and back again and threw the soap to her. Poppy bent forward, modestly spattering water in front of her, and managed to catch it. She soaped herself all over, ducked and splashed, then washed again. Then kneeling, she soaped her hair thoroughly, scrubbing until she worked up a lather even with the miserable homemade soap, and floated on her back and let her hair stream free around her. She could almost feel the horrible little creatures struggling to hold on in the mass of suds and surging water, before floating helplessly away. They were gone. She was pink bumps from ankles to forehead, but she was free of them and clean.

Then she thought of Jack and peered up the pool to where he stood waist-deep in the water. He had their clothes and was beating and whipping them vigorously against the water, stretching them out to let them float and then beating them again. Finally he looked at each piece, nodded with satisfaction, twisted it as dry as he could, and tossed it up into the branches of the willows to dry. Then he ducked, pulling at his hair, scratching and tugging, and ducked again.

"Jack, poor Jack, you need the soap. There isn't much left, but here it is. Catch?"

He jumped and caught it, then began to lather himself with cracking slaps. Poppy lay back in the water and let the coolness flow over her. She knew the minute she left the water, every separate bite would sting and itch like fire. For now, the water felt like cool silk against her skin.

Then a wave of suds hit her face. Jack's suds. Of course, the water was running this way. She clamped her eyes against the blinding sting and fumbled forward, groping, trying to feel clean water. Finding some, she splashed handfuls against her face. She tried to open her eyes, but they closed again involuntarily, tears streaming down her cheeks. That horrible homemade soap, literally as strong as lye. She fumbled around again, and her foot slipped on a rounded rock. She went under the water. Rolling helplessly, she flung out her arms to try to balance herself, and felt herself caught and pressed close against Jack's bare, wet body.

"Poppy," Jack said hoarsely, pulling her face up out of the water. "Poppy, did you swallow any? Can you breathe? Are you all right?"

"All right," Poppy gasped, gulping and coughing. "All right. I can swim."

They stood, arms around each other, molded together, close in the bright running water. His skin under her hands was smooth as wet satin and yet muscular and strong, the long muscles of his shoulders rippling as cleanly as the running water around them. His body was a long, lean pillar of strength, from narrow hips to broad shoulders. Her smaller, softer curves fitted against him, her head tucked into the hollow of his shoulder, as he bent his head and kissed her. When his lips claimed hers, hotly, demandingly, she learned in one burning instant that Jack never had felt toward her as a brother to a sister. This was a man's demand on a woman.

His body was sweet, young, strong, and clean, with all the power of manhood still in its first youth. This was a young lover for her young girlhood, found here in a primitive Eden. She could feel his whole length pressed against her and his masculine response to her. Her own body crept closer and glowed in answer to his desire.

His arms shifted to lift and carry her, when a voice shrieked through the silver-flooded night.

"I'm on fire. I'm on fire. Where are you?" Andy yelled.

They fell apart and looked at each other. The moment was over, shattered beyond mending.

"In the water," Poppy called. "Bring us our saddle blankets."

"Why?"

"Because everything else is full of fleas. And so are you. So come and jump in and wash them off."

Chapter Thirty-six

AS soon as it was daylight, and they had gulped some coffee, they fled from the beautiful, flea-infested meadow. They were aware they had not left all the pests behind, but they could do individual combat with those that were left. They were tired and uncomfortable with their rough outer clothes rasping their bitten skins. Their still wet underclothes, in which they had been sleeping, were rolled in an untidy bundle with the blankets.

As they rode, the land changed to gentle, soft hills and placid, small ponds. By midmorning they were riding through a pleasant valley divided into small farms. Poppy looked wistfully at the little frame homes. But even if the people were hospitable, those two rooms housed whole families. Then she realized that Jack, aided by some navigator's sense he seemed to have even on dry land, was leading them with some definite goal in mind.

Unreasoning hope sprang into her mind. "How far to Grass Valley?"

"Too far." After a moment, Jack relented. "I've heard of a place that should be just what we need. The men who passed through it at different times used to talk about it evenings, when they were trying to remember they hadn't always been cold, broke, hungry, and lonely."

Poppy raised an eyebrow. "Are you sure it's the kind of place you want to take Andy and me?"

"Exactly the kind. Now we can pay."

"Oh." Poppy blushed and patted the lump in her pocket. "I don't know how much there is. I haven't looked."

"I was careful," Andy cried. "You were in such a taking over the funeral, Jack, and I had to hurry, and I couldn't wash it, but there are six big nuggets and the rest are grains, not dust. With some dirt, but I did my best."

"A good best, I'm sure, and now we'll all enjoy the profits," Jack said and reined his horse. "There. Those trees. Look to the west. That should be it."

They reached a well-traveled road and followed it into a small town. A long rambling building, with stables and other small structures grouped around it, sprawled beneath huge, dusty oaks. There was a neatly raked gravel entrance, with geraniums in tin pails marking out the half circle of drive. But it was the green painted sign above the broad veranda that set Poppy gasping. It was the Hot Springs Hotel. She read the sign: Rooms and Meals. Hot Mineral Baths. Stagecoach Stop.

Poppy rode up to the veranda steps, jumped from her horse, and handed Jack the kerchief. He weighed it in his palm. Then loosening the knot, he stirred the contents with one finger. He nodded.

"I think you can tell the hotel keeper we'd like a suite."

"They won't have that."

"Then two adjoining bedrooms."

"Those aren't diamonds," Poppy said.

"They'll do. You and Andy arrange the accommodations while I take care of the horses and find an assayer. Don't wait for me. I'll join you as soon as I've had a look around." He pulled out a nugget and handed it to her. "In case the owner doesn't have a trusting nature."

Poppy waited only for Jack to untie the portmanteaus from behind the saddles. Then she and Andy made an effort to walk sedately as they went into the hotel. She had almost forgotten such places existed. Carpets on the painted floors, pretty colored-glass chandeliers, up-holstered chairs, and a glimpse of a dining room with red and white tablecloths. She thought she caught a whiff of an odd odor, but it was a clean one.

Even the bedroom had small rag rugs and brightly painted furniture. The bed pillows were of real feathers. Everything was immaculate. She looked around and could have wept with happiness and relief.

When the plump, pretty girl who had showed them upstairs said they had robes for those who wished to use the baths, Poppy did not hesitate. She said they wanted three wraps, immediately, please. She also wanted every stitch she and her brothers were wearing taken away, also immediately, and boiled.

"We had an unfortunate experience in our last accommodations," Poppy said truthfully.

"The beds some people rent as clean should be against the law."

Poppy stuck to the truth. "We did not examine the place with sufficient care." Then she remembered. "Could we also purchase soap? Three large bars of soap. Your best."

"There's some with a lovely violet perfume you'd like, miss."

The hot springs were surrounded by whitewashed fences and separated into two sides, one for men and the other for women. For once, Andy did not protest. He grabbed a bar of soap and ran. Poppy sat on the wooden steps above the bubbling water, not even minding the sulfurous smell, soaped luxuriously and plunged in, gasping from the heat. She went up and down, up and down, soaping and rinsing, until she realized she was not only bright pink all over but beginning to develop tiny blisters where she had rubbed the bites the hardest. She dried and wrapped herself up, weak-kneed from the long immersion, and stumbled back to her room.

Laid out on the bed was a short-sleeved, low-necked white blouse, the sheer material heavy with bright embroidery, and a brilliant, full, blue satin skirt with two rows of ruffles around the bottom. On the floor, a small pair of black slippers held white stockings. The Mexican señoritas wore such clothes for their festivals.

Poppy cracked open the door between the two bedrooms. "Jack, where did you find these?"

"He's down in the baths," Andy said sleepily. "He said there's a general store that has quite a lot of things for gentlemen who bring their lady friends here and want to buy them something pretty. And he says dinner's at six." He yawned loudly, and the bed creaked, then was silent.

Poppy closed the door. Andy was exhausted, but she was too excited to stay in her room. This was civilization again at last, and she was not going to lose one minute of it. Tomorrow Grass Valley, but today she was going to enjoy.

She got only as far as the lobby. The plump girl was watching for her.

"Your brother said you missed lunch. I took the boy something on a plate, but I've got the tea ready to serve you two as soon as he comes down."

Jack knew how a gentleman should take care of his traveling party. He would hate it if she went running alone up and down the street, peering in at shops, looking at the people. Resignedly, she settled down in one of the rocking chairs on the deep veranda to wait for him.

Jack had found only work pants for himself, but his white Mexican shirt had elaborate ruffles at chest and wrist. Poppy had the odd thought that some of the ancestral portraits hanging on the Westmoreland castle walls must look much as Jack did at this moment. They were famous for being a handsome family. Royal regard for their looks had added greatly to their fortune at times.

The tea was served in crockery on a painted tin tray. Though the sandwiches were hearty rather than dainty, and the slices of cake over-large. Poppy thought they might almost be back at some seaside resort in England. Jack was silent, sipping his tea and gazing idly at the quiet scene around them. Poppy kept glancing at him, trying to decide if only the shirt made him seem so different.

He was different. Something had changed. Always before, from the moment she met him in Cornwall, he had had a mischievous glint in his blue eyes, the sparkle of youth overflowing with sheer joy of living, the ebullience of healthy young manhood in its full flood of physical vitality. Later when the gold fever caught him, the brightness had sharpened, like the glittering spark of an actual fever, but now it was gone. His eyes were only thoughtful.

Suddenly Poppy realized when Jack had changed and why. She had not seen that glitter in his eyes since the funeral service. He had been thoroughly shocked. To him, committing a body to the grave was a matter deserving of the greatest solemnity, a rite performed with all possible decorum. That shrieking greed erupting out of the very grave had blasted him out of his own fever. He had seen it as an evil thing and foresworn it forever. He had grown up, become an adult, in those few minutes when he had assumed responsibility for a proper procedure.

Poppy nodded agreement with herself and remembered an odd note in his voice this morning. "You said Grass Valley was too far?"

"Much too far."

"You're planning to go home and behave as an heir should?"

A hint of the old mischievous smile touched Jack's lips. "It's not quite that simple."

"But you are going home," Poppy said and tried not to sound sad. It was the right thing for him to do, but it meant she must say goodbye to her good friend, companion, and almost brother. "When?"

"That depends. I've always said I'd go but I'd choose my own route, and it wouldn't necessarily be the most direct."

"Oh, Jack, what now?"

"I said, that depends. Once I'm home, my family will have to make me a suitable allowance."

Poppy stared. "Of course. Suitable to an heir's station in life. I never heard your family was mean."

"Generous to a fault, as the saying goes."

"Then you can buy anything you want. Just think, anything."

"Everything I want if you were there and my wife."

"Your wife? Jack, I've never—you know—I—it isn't suitable."

"I have always considered it completely suitable. I said nothing before because I didn't want to embarrass you in a situation where you felt at a disadvantage, I didn't want you to feel you owed it to me."

"I never thought that." All at once, Poppy giggled. "I must be turning American. I've always thought of us as almost partners."

"A capable partner." Jack smiled and then said seriously, "Also I wanted to be sure I could offer you what you should have. I can now."

"I told you, it isn't suitable."

"Why not?"

"You know why not."

Jack scowled blackly. "Dex took advantage of you when you were frightened and helpless. You can't be blamed."

"I stayed with him."

"Where could you go?"

Poppy bent her head over her clasped hands. "I had only to protest. Believe me, Jack, he would have let me go in an instant."

"He took advantage, and you had no one to advise and help you," Jack insisted.

Poppy sighed. "I can't marry you, Jack. I don't love you."

"That comes later."

"Maybe if you were the first man. You wouldn't be."

"You can't love Dex." Jack's face was stiff with indignation. "He was in San Francisco and ignored you. Andy told me."

"Yes."

350

Jack cut her off. "If you won't marry me here, will you at least come back to England with me?"

Poppy sat quite still and thought seriously. She did not think she could ever marry Jack. She did love him, and not quite like a brother, not quite like Andy. She had learned that in the water last night. But she did not love him as a woman should love her husband. Desire for him was not a flame that drew and consumed her. Affection held her to him, but that was too flimsy a bond to hold a lifetime.

England pulled at her. London was her home. But what was there for her in England? Daisy, married, would be more determined than ever to have her daughter married. Daisy's new position might mean she could make a favorable bargain, probably even provide a modest dowry, but it still would be an arranged marriage for a girl of dubious parentage. More, perhaps Daisy could try to make people believe she had been rusticating in Cornwall all these months, but the world was becoming a small place. She had been seen in Paris and in San Francisco. Sooner or later, somebody would see her again and remember.

No, a return to the role of Daisy's young daughter was impossible. An arranged marriage was more impossible. Better to marry Jack than that. It could mean marrying Jack. Once Daisy learned of the possibility, and Andy would babble about it if nobody else did, nothing could keep Daisy from forcing a marriage so prestigious. That would bring no happiness to anybody.

She would be all right in San Francisco. She had her little properties. She could always find work. There she was her own independent person. Independence did not frighten her. She enjoyed the challenge.

But would it be safe to take Andy back to San Francisco? Trying to decide, her face clouded.

Jack seemed to have followed her thoughts. "Andy must have a proper education."

"Yes." Poppy nodded emphatically. "I won't have him back in any place like that manufactory. Or brought up around men like those at Injun Gulch—not bad men, but not for Andy."

"Never. He needs a good education, with perhaps some tutoring in special subjects, a solid education."

"That means England," Poppy said unhappily.

"I think it must. Do you so dislike the idea of returning there?"

"I can't. I can't."

"I see." Jack sighed sharply and turned his head away. When he looked at her again, his face was composed. "Then I have a suggestion for your consideration."

"Of course, Jack."

"I'll need some information. I know the year of Andy's birth, but what is the exact date?"

"January the sixteenth."

Jack nodded as if that confirmed something. "Did his father provide for him?"

"Why, no," Poppy admitted.

"Why not?"

"Daisy was unsettled in her mind right then," Poppy said delicately.

"Meaning what?"

"I think perhaps she fell in love," Poppy admitted.

"With a London business gentleman who rode a beautiful chestnut with four white feet?"

"Who told you that?"

"Andy. I didn't question him. He was chattering one day."

Poppy believed that. Andy did get talking spells and when he did, words flew out of him like a tight spring unwinding. "Then that's what he told you."

"Few London business gentlemen ride the finest chestnuts in the park."

"No," Poppy admitted and groaned inwardly.

Daisy knew a nag from a fine horse, but she was no connoisseur of horseflesh. But whenever she started thinking of her handsome young officer, she went on and on describing his chestnut with the four white feet. Poppy had heard it described fifty times until she won-

Poppy

dered if Daisy went into such a frenzy of description of
the horse because she would not describe the lover who
had not even given her his right name. It was respectable to remember a horse with admiration.

"Owned by a London gentleman?" Jack probed mercilessly. "That rich and yet he didn't provide for his
son?"

Poppy closed her eyes. She would not have Jack
think Daisy less than she was, and perhaps the truth
was not so bad. "He never knew."

"Why not?"

Poppy sat upright, eyes open and flashing. "Because
she wasn't sure, that's why. She and the London gentleman were not in perfect amity, and it was spring, and
Daisy was in love. She was unsettled in her mind."

"So who owned the horse?"

"A young officer on leave. And you mustn't think
Daisy ever did anything like that before or since. Then
he disappeared, and Daisy wasn't sure."

"Now that I understand the situation, this is my suggestion. I'd like to supervise Andy's education, possibly
arrange for him to go to my old school, though that
would depend somewhat on the recommendations of a
good tutor, and have him spend some of his holidays
with me. If it proves necessary, I could assume his expenses without it being a burden on me."

"You'll take him back to England with you?" Poppy
asked with a pang in her heart. She and Andy had
never been separated. But there was nothing for him
here and everything in England. "Immediately?"

"If I'm returning to England without you, I see no
reason for hurrying. I would like one more trip before
the mast. I've never sailed on a clipper. I'd like to sign
on one to China and go home the long way 'round.
Even clippers run short of men in San Francisco, so
I'm sure I could find a place easily and probably sign
Andy on as a cabin boy apprentice on the same ship."

"He enjoyed that before, the taste of it he got."

"Signed on with proper articles, I could see he behaved himself."

"What if he doesn't want to go? We can plan, but what if he hates the idea?"

"He hates California, and the very idea of San Francisco throws him into a panic."

"You two did talk all those hours you were working on Injun Creek," Poppy cried. "I didn't know."

"He would never have complained to you. And I don't believe he'll realize how much he's going to miss you until after we're gone. He'll be too excited at the idea of sailing on a clipper. Then he'll be too busy."

"I'll behave myself. I won't suggest he might be sorry to leave me," Poppy promised.

"Good. Then we can catch a stage out of here at midday tomorrow. I think we'll be safe enough in your house for a couple of days while I find a ship."

Poppy began to practice her perfect, strict behavior. "Oh, to ride in the comfort of a stage again."

Talk of that and the ride would keep Andy occupied tomorrow. When they had fled from San Francisco, he had been terrified, and they had huddled inside, faces hidden in their capes. This time he could examine the Concord coach in all its glory, the six horses, the egg-shaped crimson body with the golden scrolls for decoration, perhaps even look at the underside, slung on the leather thoroughbraces that made it ride so smoothly and comfortably. She would prefer to be one of the nine inside passengers, but perhaps Jack would let Andy join him on the top, which carried ten.

"We'll tell him he's going from land clipper to sea clipper," Poppy planned.

"The owner says this driver can make sixty miles in six hours. We'll be in San Francisco before you know it."

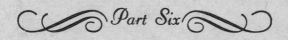

Part Six

San Francisco
Late Autumn 1852

Chapter Thirty-seven

WHEN she went in to see Pete at the Palace, Poppy wore gloves to hide her reddened hands and contrived a scarf around her hair to shadow her tanned face. She knew she would have wear a lace stole for weeks so nobody would remark the difference between her brown face and her white shoulders gleaming out of a low-cut gown. Still she felt she looked very well, and her feet fairly danced to be treading city streets again.

"I just saw my brothers off on a clipper for China," she told Pete. "A fine ship that was unloading and short-handed when we got back to town. They signed on and sailed without time to see how the town has changed."

"Growing," Pete said. "Bounding up the hills like a runaway horse. Maurice told me you were back."

"He's a good friend. He watched my house and kept the rents for me."

"More you couldn't ask."

"Except a job. I'm ready to go to work."

Pete sighed and admired the polish on the glass before he looked at her. "I told you when you ran out that night, The Boss wouldn't take you back. He doesn't hold a grudge, but he doesn't forgive and forget, either."

"I had to go, Andy was in trouble, bad trouble," Poppy cried, shocked. She had not expected this. She brought in as much as two other girls. "Anyhow, now Andy's gone, so it won't happen again."

"Not here," Pete said definitely. "He laid down the law. You're through here."

"But I need a job."

"Try the Eureka. The girls aren't our class. Most of them do private work after hours, but that's their business. Nothing to do with working the floor."

Poppy did not like the sound of that. She shook her head.

"Phillipa's there," Pete encouraged. "I don't know why she left here, and maybe she doesn't, either. I always wondered how she knew what time to come to work and when to leave."

"Not many pretty girls are restful, too," Poppy protested. "A good man will notice that someday and take her home and keep her to ornament his parlor, like a wax doll in a glass bell."

"She never said, but she must have some family to watch out for her," Pete said. "The head bartender at the Eureka, Clyde, is all right. I know him. I'll tell him to watch nobody loads drinks on you."

"Who wants to work in a place where they load drinks?"

"Don't try to bust in and see The Boss here, Poppy," Bill warned. "You're poison, and he'll tell you so the whole town hears it. Take my advice. Try the Eureka."

"Even the Eureka, without a recommendation—" Poppy faltered, convinced, but appalled.

"I'll say you're the best but to tie you to a hitching post when you hear fire alarm bells." Pete polished a glass vigorously and did not look at her. "There's a certain fancy lady around town wearing some diamond earrings you may recognize. Mr. Dunbar didn't give them to her. I heard he sold them back to the jeweler."

"I'm not interested in Mr. Dunbar."

"He spends a lot of time in Sacramento. Good luck to you at the Eureka, Poppy."

The Eureka was five doors up the street from the Palace, but a steep drop down socially. The carpets were crimson, but brighter strips showed where places had been patched, not the whole replaced. The lifesize oil paintings of languorous ladies, nude and voluptuous, had frames as wide and elaborately carved and gilded as any in town, but the artists had favored bright pinks, blues, and yellows. The musicians were noted, even in a drinking town, for deep thirsts and loud music. The dealers were as immaculate in black and white and as soft-voiced as any at other tables in town, but strangers were warned their hands were as quick on their guns as on their cards. The gleaming bar was mahogany, and the shining mirror reflected rows of bottles, but rumor had it the expensive contents were not always the fine imported brands of the labels. The bartenders were deft and quick, but their skills were reputed to include magnificent mickeys.

The girls were young and pretty, but the men who wished their company only for a drink sought them out early. Later they disappeared one by one on the arms of escorts and did not return.

Only the two who had worked at the Palace were different. Pretty, lack-witted Phillipa drifted in, moved decoratively and slowly through the hours, and vanished as quietly as she did everything else. Poppy, too, stayed the long evening and was known to leave alone in the hired carriage that waited for her every night.

Poppy was unhappily aware she was not as *soignée* as she had been at the Palace. Her Paris wardrobe had been handsome, complete but not extensive, and a year's wear had left her with only two possible gowns for evening. Both were subtly dated in style and trim. She yearned over the new imports with the changed fashionable flare of skirt and cut of waist, but despaired at the prices.

Dressed in rustling silk, sipping champagne, Poppy smiled at the men who told her she was beautiful, deftly avoided their hands, sang snatches of the songs the band played, and chattered, watching, listening, waiting for something, but she did not know what. Casual-sounding questions, phrased as gossip, only informed her the English banker that the Pannet girl was so crazy about had been in town and had left again. Maybe he was coming back, or maybe he had sailed for home. Nobody really knew. If Jeremiah heard she was in town, he did not come to the Eureka. More miners straight from the diggings came in there than had at the Palace. They tipped lavishly when their pokes were full, but strikes were few in winter. The city men, except those who lingered with the more compliant girls, came in only to have a quick drink and a word with other businessmen.

Poppy listened to their talk. Some of it was about the new growing wave of lawlessness and whether it would be necessary to bring back the Vigilantes. More was of money, and much she did not understand, though as always real estate was booming.

She dared not sell her houses. That roof and the rent were her security, her assurance she could not end homeless and hungry. But her poke did not fill. It grew steadily lighter.

She could not cut expenses. The days were cold and gray, with pounding rains and thick fogs. The price of wood to heat the house dismayed her, but she bought. She could not afford to catch a cold. She had to hire a carriage to take her back and forth to the Eureka. Jobs were scarce and money tight, so the streets were not safe even in the gray daylight, if she had been willing to risk her delicate, wide-skirted dresses on the muddy streets.

That day started badly. The rain clogged the chimney, and the house filled with smoke. When she got out her best dress, the green silk with the silver-braid trim, she saw that the elaborate scrolls of braid around the hem had been ripped loose and the silk torn past all mending. She had been too tired the night before to know when or how it had happened.

The week before she had gone to her favorite shop. She had yearned over a brilliant blue gown with layers of overskirts that paled in graduated tones to a pale azure at the bodice, which was cut so it cupped her shoulders like the petals of a flower. She had disdained the yellow rep that was the only thing she could afford, and walked out without buying. Now she weighed her poke in her hand. She hated the yellow that faded the

360

gold in her hair and made the red tones look coppery. She could not afford the blue. But she would buy it anyhow.

This would be the first dress she ever had selected and bought for herself, with nobody at her elbow to censor her choice, and she would never own a lovelier one. So, smiling, she walked into the shop and described it.

"Oh, miss, that was perfect on you," the owner remembered. "Just yesterday, what a pity."

"You've sold it?"

"Miss Pannet. Usually she orders direct from Paris, but she saw that, and she would have it, though we had to tear it apart and are remaking it. She's so petite."

Petite but big enough to take everything she wanted, Poppy thought, choking, fists clenched. Dex first. Now the blue dress.

"You did consider the yellow?"

"No," Poppy cried and started to fling out of the shop. Then necessity drove. She had to have something. "What else do you have?"

"One dress, a special order rejected."

"By Félicité Pannet? Not good enough for milady?"

"Oh, no, you wouldn't mind that, I'm sure." The woman clasped her hands tightly in embarrassment. "By one of Madame's, the Frenchwoman's, girls."

Poppy laughed shrilly. "Let me see it. I'm not offended by that."

Poppy saw why the dress had been rejected. The layers of delicate embroidered white silk voile were unseasonable, but worse, the merest spark from a cigar would destroy its freshness permanently. She shuddered as she pictured a large brown burn on those skirts.

"Not practical," Poppy sighed.

"Not for one like that, in and out of her clothes," the woman agreed and touched the tiny gold and glass buttons. "Thirty of these, miss, and it takes patience, they're so small." Then she blushed. "If you don't mind my mentioning it."

"What else?" Poppy sighed.

"There's a purple velvet, the finest French velvet, but you're young for such a color."

"Purple's for royalty, isn't it?" Poppy said. She seldom remembered that. "Sounds nice and warm. Let's see it."

The purple was ruinously expensive, but it made her eyes look the same deep-velvety color and turned her hair into a glowing halo. Poppy took it and wore it to the Eureka that night.

The minute she walked in, she realized the place was tense as a fiddle string. Phillipa had painted a thick mask on her face, but it could not conceal that her face was swollen from long weeping. Poppy whispered a question but Phillipa, inarticulate as always, only shook her head and sidled away. Clyde whispered a customer had challenged a dealer's card, and the dealer had shot too quick and too straight. The customer was dead, and the dealer was in jail. The gambling tables were almost deserted. By tomorrow, everybody would have forgotten, but now the dealers handled the cards slowly, and the few players laid only small bets. Joe, the young Italian waiter, came up for an order, limping. The night before, some thugs had cornered him in an alley on his way home. Because he had not pulled out his poke fast enough, they had knocked him down and kicked him senseless. He was lucky to be alive, he confided out of the side of his mouth as he passed with the loaded tray. Later, when two businessmen came in and told how their stage had been held up, on their way back from a trip to inspect some mine machinery, nobody was surprised. Violence was in the air.

"Vigilante times are a'coming again," Clyde murmured to Poppy.

She shivered and gulped the champagne in her glass, wishing it were something as strong as brandy. She only wanted this night to end, but she had a role to play. She smiled and moved closer to the two men who had been held up, but the younger, red-faced one was staring over her head.

"Prettiest girl I ever seen, but all blubbered up from

crying," he said to his friend. "In the lacy ruffles over there. Say, pretty girl, come have a drink with us."

Even more slowly than usual, Phillipa joined them and stood looking pretty and saying nothing.

"Cat got your tongue, pretty girl?"

Phillipa's eyes widened. "It's a cold evening," she said uncertainly. Comments on the weather were the extent of her conversational powers, but she did try. "And turning colder."

"That isn't what I asked."

Poppy laughed and patted his arm. "She's too afflicted to tell you, sir. Just buy the pretty girl a drink, and that will help."

The man jerked his arm free. Plainly he had had several drinks to help him recover from the shock of being held up. "I didn't ask you. I asked her."

Phillipa looked terrified, and her lips began to quiver.

"Her kitten died, sir," Poppy improvised desperately. "Such a pretty kitten, and she loved it."

The man shoved her aside. "I don't think it was any kitten. Let her answer for herself."

Already shaken, Phillipa wailed and turned to flee. The man swore, then caught her arm and jerked her around to face him. Joe, again loading his tray at the bar, crashed it down. He caught Phillipa and whirled her around behind him.

"The lady is upset, sir," he said, breathing heavily. "She'd like to retire."

"I'll retire you, you two-bit tray juggler," the man said, and hit Joe hard on the jaw.

Joe sagged, his knees collapsed, and he crashed down. His head hit the brass rail with a dull, hollow thud. Remembering another hollow thud, Poppy bit back a scream and fought against a dizzying wave of blackness that left her blind and staggering for a moment. A piercing shriek jolted her upright.

Phillipa was on her knees beside Joe. "You've killed him, you've killed him," she wailed. "He was half killed already, and I was up nursing him all the night, and now you've killed him completely. He's dead, my Joe's dead!"

So she's Irish, and that's more words than I've heard her say in all these months, Poppy thought dazedly. And Joe's the reason she came to work here.

"I'm a doctor," a man said. "Let me look. Stand back. Everybody away, please." He knelt and prodded briefly and looked up. "I don't know. If somebody will call a carriage, I'll take him to the hospital."

"There's no money," Phillipa shrieked. "They took all his money and half killed him, and now he's killed completely, and there's no money, and my Joe's dead!"

Poppy shook her head free of the dizziness, snatched the tallest glass she could find, hoisted herself up on the bar, and scrambled to her feet. She fumbled her poke out of the placket where she had tucked it and held it up in one hand and the glass in the other.

"We're all sorry this happened," she called. "I'm sorry. You're sorry. We're all sorry." She chanted like an auctioneer. "I'm sorry this much." She poured the little that remained in her poke into the glass where it glittered. "Poppy's sorry that much. All she's got. How sorry are you?"

"Give that to me, I'll pass it," Clyde said and held up his hand and grabbed the glass. "Come on, boys. Fill 'er up, fill 'er up. We want to have this full up to give to the little lady to take to the hospital with her Joe. Fill 'er up before the carriage arrives. That's right, boys. Keep those pokes open and pouring."

Poppy moved through the rest of the evening in a numbed daze. She had learned with Dex how treacherous wine could be, and she always tried to be careful. But that night every man in the place, and every man who came in and heard the story, insisted on buying her a drink. Many of them pressed gold pieces into her hand as they murmured awkward compliments. By the time her carriage was due, she did not know whether she was dead drunk or only dead tired. She got her cloak and walked to the door, pausing to steady herself for a moment on the bar.

"Never mind," Clyde whispered. "Bad night, but the boss will have a little something extra for you at the end of the week."

Poppy swallowed sickly. "The men tonight, generous," she muttered. "Have you heard anything about Joe?"

"Nothing," Clyde said and shook his head. "But that's two, and these things go in threes. I wonder who the third one will be?"

Chapter Thirty-eight

*P*OPPY dreaded going to work the next day. She dawdled over her dressing, steaming invisible creases from the purple velvet and working her hair into a coronet of curls to form a crown above the short tendrils that framed her face. Formless fears shadowed her mind. When she finally forced herself through the door of the Eureka, she hesitated there as if balancing on the edge of a precipice before letting out her breath in a long sigh of relief. Everything was almost as usual.

The band was playing, the gambling tables were busy, and Clyde was working a full bar. Yet as she walked into the room, her step dragged. Everything seemed subtly damaged and sinister. She winced and moved away from the brighter strip of carpeting near one of the tables, doubtless replacing the bloodstained one. The brass rail of the bar was freshly shined and polished until it glittered as harshly as the barrel of a loaded gun. The girls were moving around too fast, as if they were trying to give the impression of being double their number. A young blond giant was working Joe's place, looking uncomfortable in a too-small white coat.

Poppy disposed of her cloak and strolled over to lean on the bar. Clyde eased toward her, polishing a glass over and over.

"Gone," he said, breathing on the glass and giving it another rub. "Before they ever got him to the hospital."

"Phillipa?"

"Everett G. Wilton came in this morning," Clyde said impressively.

"Wilton?"

"Everett G."

"Should I know him?"

"Big man. Very big. Mines. Other things. Everything. Quiet. The quiet one."

"Those two from the stagecoach? Oh." Poppy tried to recall the second man who had stood back while his companion blustered and bullied, but only had an impression of a middle-sized man in ordinary clothes with no-color hair and a face that was just a face. She said, "Oh, that one."

"The other's gone, long gone, and I don't think we'll be seeing him around these parts again. Mr. Wilton said it was an accident and best to handle it quietly. Mr. Wilton said he was taking care of the funeral, and he would let us know. Mr. Wilton said he had sent his own minister to Phillipa, but she asked for a priest." Clyde breathed and polished again. "That upset him some, yes, that upset him."

"Mr. Wilton said?" Poppy prompted.

"He got her a priest, of course. And everything else she wanted. But that tells a story, when a man's upset because a girl's of a different religion. He's serious, very serious. Phillipa may be weeping her eyes out now, but she's a lucky girl, very lucky."

Poppy remembered she had joked that someday a wealthy man would see Phillipa and take her home to keep as an ornament. The Prof had murmured more than once that many a true word was spoken in jest. "Did Mr. Wilton say anything else?"

"He did. He said he wouldn't forget a girl who was willing to give the last grain of dust out of her poke for a friend. And if you ever needed anything, ever, anything, and he meant exactly that, you were to let him know. He left this for you."

Clyde pulled something from his pocket and unobtrusively thrust it across the bar to Poppy. She looked down and gasped. The long elaborately wrought gold chain, made of half a dozen different fine chains intricately worked together into one heavy strand, ended in a nugget half as big as her fist.

"Fine man, Mr. Wilton, fine man. He wouldn't leave a tip, not for what you did. A tip's for something ordinary, and he's got fine feelings for what's proper. So he meant that to be a personal thanks, a free gift repaid freely a thousandfold in kind, and don't you insult him by refusing it."

"I wouldn't think of it," Poppy said, and put the chain around her neck where it hung warm and glowing against the purple velvet. "Anything else?"

"Pamette didn't turn up, Georgie sent word she had a headache, and Clara says her feet hurt and she wants to go home. What did they think they were working, a church supper? We've passed the word all over town that we need more girls—right now. But meanwhile, you do your best. Just keep moving."

"I'm moving."

The Eureka was at the same time quieter than usual and noisier. The regulars were quiet, dropping by for a glance at the papers or a fast drink with a friend and leaving quickly. An exceptional number of strangers, transients who must have heard this was the gaudiest, toughest spot in town, swaggered in, loud-voiced and rambunctious, looking for trouble. Oppressive looks from Clyde and the new giant waiter sent them out again after a single drink. The miners from the diggings gawked at Poppy's purple velvet and whispered together over the size of the nugget, but they were not inclined to waste the price of a drink. She smiled at them prettily. They were not troublemakers. That was the important thing tonight.

Still, as the hours passed, her smile grew strained. That deaths went in threes, that anything went in threes, was sheer superstition. She did not believe it. But all the strangers wandering in, eyes glistening in anticipation of seeing some violence, of having a tale to tell when they got home about the dangers of the wicked city of San Francisco while they swaggered in the glory of surviving such terrors, were fraying her nerves. She wished the night would end. She wished she could walk out and never come back. She half promised herself, touching the nugget warm on her breast, that as soon as the Eureka found a couple of new girls, she would see what the town could offer a girl with a little money to invest in a small business.

"A busy evening, Poppy."

She recognized the voice and whirled. "Jeremiah." Then she stiffened, eyes flashing. "I've been working here for some time."

"I heard you were back in town. I hoped you would drop me a note giving me permission to call."

Poppy gasped. "Invite you to call after the way you tried to hunt down Andy?"

"I half tore this town apart to try to take him into custody that night," Jeremiah admitted coolly.

"You were hunting us down like runaway slaves."

"People were in an ugly mood. I could have kept him safe until we investigated the fire and settled the cause."

"And if it had settled on Andy?"

"We're fair men, only seeking truth and justice," Jeremiah said. "As for the manufactory fire, that Cornishman told a tale about Andy."

"I heard it. And you believed it."

"I wanted to hear Andy's side."

"He's gone. Gone to England where he can get a proper education."

"That's good, but write that when he wants to come back to you, he needn't come in fear. We always wonder about a man who's too quick to accuse others, and I was satisfied in my own mind when the smith disappeared a couple of days after the fire. He hasn't been seen around these parts since."

"I think you have the right of it," Poppy said slowly. "We knew him in Cornwall. Knew him to be greedy and treacherous."

"And you still allowed your brother to associate with him?"

"Andy liked him," Poppy excused.

"A little woman with too much responsibility too young," Jeremiah said fondly and then frowned. "I still can't commend your judgment. Why are you in this place?"

"Because they gave me employment, and I need it. Why are you?"

"I am here as a citizen. I am investigating a report this is a center of violence and lawlessness."

"No more than any other."

"Let me buy you a drink. Please. We can sit over in those chairs. A bottle of champagne and an unopened bottle of brandy, waiter."

She did not want a cozy, intimate talk in a shadowy corner. "Let's sit over by the bar. We're shorthanded tonight, and I might be needed."

"You're too decorative to hide," Jeremiah agreed, looking at the dress and the necklace. "You've done well?"

Poppy laughed as she perched lightly in a chair close to the end of the bar. "I prefer it to the diggings."

"So that's where you were." Jeremiah settled himself and leaned close to her. "In confidence, what kind of a place is this?"

Poppy bent her head over the glass of champagne to hide the anger in her eyes. She was no spy to tell tales on the man who paid her salary. "Like any such place."

"With two men killed here yesterday?"

"The waiter was already half dead from a beating in the streets the night before."

"But he was killed here."

"An accident. Like dozens of others in this town every day."

"Accidents, violence, death. A terrible situation. Something must be done."

Poppy drained her glass. "I'm sure you'll do your best," she murmured indifferently.

"I always have. I always will. I don't change. I haven't changed about you. I don't want you working in a place like this. I want to marry you."

"I am content here," Poppy said sharply. She had not forgotten crouching in Madame's cellar while he searched for her, or washing those heavy, filthy shirts to buy food in the diggings. She stood up. "Clyde asked me to keep moving this evening."

"I'll wait."

"But you never stay in the evening."

Jeremiah's lips tightened. "This evening I want to observe. I'm sure nobody will mind if I sit quietly and read one of your papers. I haven't seen the newest ones from the east."

That was the final, miserable strain, the dark, quiet figure sitting with a paper in front of his face and watching every move in the room. Poppy wanted to go someplace and stamp her feet, pound her fists, and scream. Instead she moved around, smiling, whispering the words of the songs, always smiling, though she started at every sound—a glass dropping, a gust of laughter. Nobody was going to start a fight here tonight, she assured herself desperately. This was the last place, with every waiter and dealer and bartender doubly alert to stop trouble before it started again tonight. The whole place was on guard, and if she could only endure, even this night must end eventually.

She was standing by a back table, watching a man who had been gambling all evening, winning heavily and then losing and now winning again, when something made her look toward the bar. For a moment she thought what she saw was only a part of the whole nightmare mood of the evening. Then she knew it was Josie, in a garish green dress trimmed with cheap yellow lace, standing there talking to Clyde. The year had marked her, but she still knew how to tilt her head in coquettish appeal and move with a swaying, graceful lilt.

Clyde's face was impassive, but his pursed lips told he was considering Josie's attractions. Poppy's eyes widened. Clyde had sent out a wide-open call for girls. They were seriously shorthanded enough to take anyone not obviously off the streets. But not Josie, not here, never Josie, not in a decent place that was trying to avoid trouble.

Clutching an empty glass, she hurried to the other

371

end of the bar and called, "Clyde, here, please. Clyde, service, please."

"Minute, in a minute."

"Special order."

That was a signal. Clyde came with deliberate speed. Poppy leaned over the bar, smiling and holding out her glass.

"Special for me, Clyde," she said loudly and then mouthed, "Not that one. No, no," and looked up to see Josie had moved close behind her and was reading her lips reflected in the mirror.

Poppy froze and then whirled. "Why, Josie," she said with a high, artificial laugh. "I didn't know you were in San Francisco."

"No, you thought your friend Madame had finished me," Josie sneered. "Shipped me out to be pulled down and die in a dollar crib. But you don't do that to Josie, not to Josie."

"So you're doing well?" Poppy babbled.

The strange, close-set eyes were a little mad. "As well as you, if I could have got a job here. But that's too good for me. You won't let me have that. No, you told him, no, not that one."

"I meant, I meant my drink, the special."

"You meant me. I know you. Chunks of gold for you and the mud of the alleys for everyone else. I'll give you gold."

Poppy knew even before the knife flashed in Josie's hand. This had happened before, in the dark shadows on the waterfront. She was hemmed in, flat against the bar, but she flung up her hand. She felt the knife slash across her wrist and saw the bright blood spurt. With a shriek, she dropped her arm, and the knife stabbed into her side. She sagged as a long arm grasped Josie and flung her to one side, holding her at arm's length. Jeremiah shook her once, and her head cracked back, but she writhed in his grasp, slashing at the arm that held her. Then from the door, a gun cracked. She jerked upright on her toes and then collapsed like a rag doll. Jeremiah let her fall to the floor.

"Thank you, Deputy," he said to the lawman in the doorway. "Fortunately I realized there was likely to be trouble here tonight and asked to have a guard outside while I came in."

"She was attacking you," the man said slowly. "I never—I never killed a woman before."

"That's the third," Clyde whispered, and the words echoed loudly in the appalled silence.

"Remove the body," Jeremiah said. "I'll make a statement to your superiors about this. You're to be commended." Then he turned to Poppy, and his face went gray. "What is this? She's bleeding to death. Somebody do something!"

Poppy stood hypnotized, looking at the blood spurting from her wrist and soaking the front of her velvet gown. The lifeblood was pulsing out of her with every beat of her heart, but she was so numbed with shock and horror she could not move.

"I'm a doctor," said a voice she had heard before, and the man shouldered Jeremiah aside. "I'm going to start charging this place for standing night duty here. Stand back, gentlemen. Let me through to the young lady." He grasped Poppy's wrist, deftly wrapped his white handkerchief above the cut, twisted the linen tight, and the terrible pulsing flood stopped. "We'll have to take her someplace before I look at the other wound. My guess is it went into the lung."

"Home," Poppy whispered.

"You're alone there?" Jeremiah demanded.

"Maurice, next door," Poppy managed to say.

"You need care and not in a hospital ward," Jeremiah said decisively. "Doctor, this young lady is an old friend. I live in a respectable boardinghouse, and the owner is a fine woman with an ample staff. I'm sure she can find a spare room and somebody to nurse. Will you come?"

"Call a carriage," the doctor said, then looked around and shook his head. "Two nights in a row is too much. Hereafter I do my drinking elsewhere. Now let's go."

373

Chapter Thirty-nine

$\mathcal{P}$OPPY sat propped up in the big velvet armchair by the front window with the lace curtains pulled back so she could look down on the street. A thick fog, so thick she had thought it was snowing when she first looked out, obscured the row of fine residential board-inghouses, so she saw only an occasional maid or urchin scurrying along on an errand.

A lively fire crackled in the fireplace, and new books just arrived from London were stacked on the table at her elbow. A jingle of the silver bell there would bring her morning tea and sugared toast. She was so bored she felt like screaming.

When Dr. Armstrong had said she was stabbed in the lung, she had pictured herself, if not dead, as a lingering invalid, not quite strong enough to sit erect as she reposed on a chaise longue, useless limbs gracefully arranged under a silk coverlet, delicate hands barely able to raise a china cup, hair brushed around her shoulders because having it dressed was too exhaust-ing. She had thought she might linger thus for months, perhaps a year, while people smiled bravely when they were with her and went outside to weep and tell each other they would miss the sweet, patient little saint when she was gone. She thought she would wear white, with dainty blue ribbons drawn through the edging, and ask people to bring her only violets, as the scents of other flowers were too strong for her weakened sen-sibilities.

Instead it seemed a hole in the lung was no lethal

matter. If she rested quietly and gave the wound a chance to heal, the lung was capable of repairing itself miraculously and would soon be as strong as ever. Even the slash across her wrist, since it had been sewed promptly and young flesh was resilient, should show no more than a hairline in a few months.

Once she was certain of all that, her spirits soared. Only her body remained weak. She could picture a dozen amusing things to do with each hour if only she could leave this room in Jeremiah's boardinghouse. But she still trembled with weakness when she walked from bed to chair.

Maurice had come once to bring the rent, but she gathered from his quirked eyebrow and meaningful glances that professional gamblers were not welcome visitors in these respectable quarters. Madame, doubtless warned by him, had sent a fine French ivory fan, painted with lilies, and a note saying she hoped it might stir the air. Poppy had laughed at that until her side hurt. The Eureka sent a dozen bottles of their best champagne, and Everett G. Wilton a mass of red roses, but nobody called. Poppy decided they had been warned off and vowed to get herself home as soon as possible.

The days were long and empty. Jeremiah visited before lunch and before dinner, but he stayed only a short time. Mrs. Stander, the dark hawk-faced owner of the house, inspected the room briskly after breakfast and after dinner and spoke little. The small Irish maid, Mary, scurried around like an intimidated mouse and squeaked rather than spoke.

So Poppy sat alone by the window looking out at the fog and planned. Somebody had brought her night-clothes from home, but they were shockingly ragged. Only the blue satin robe and slippers were presentable. She could send home for a dress to wear when she left here, but she would still need a whole new wardrobe. She would have to sell the wonderful chain with the nugget and the jade earrings.

She knew that knock on the door. This was the hour of Jeremiah's before-lunch call.

He said, "Dr. Armstrong is as good as his word. He is doing his drinking at the Palace these days. I had a word with him there."

She never knew what to say to Jeremiah. He had saved her life, but she could not feel easy with him. "What did he say?"

"He hopes you are walking in the room, no further."

"Tell him I am doing exactly that."

"He will be in to remove your stitches in a couple of days. After that you may get dressed but do not attempt the stairs or to leave the house for another week."

"I'll remember. He's a good doctor."

"He said something about Edinburgh, if that means anything."

"The best medical education, I think."

"Indeed," Jeremiah acknowledged indifferently. "I'll speak to Mrs. Stander then."

"Don't you ordinarily speak to her?" Poppy laughed. "Or is she my guard?"

"There, that sounds more like my girl."

I'm not your girl, Poppy wanted to cry. "I'm better," she said primly.

"That's the reason I'm speaking to Mrs. Stander. I'll see you this evening."

Jeremiah was planning something, but she did not know what and could not stop him if she did. Still, only a week more here. By the time she had assembled a wardrobe, gone out to see people and hear the news, she would be strong enough to work again. The Palace would not have her, and she could not face the Eureka again, but she would find something. Perhaps Mr. Wilton could advise her.

The stitches came out one morning, and when she brought the lunch tray, Mary seemed puffed to half again her diminutive size with suppressed excitement. After she removed the tray, she began to bring in parcels, small boxes and large boxes, flat paper bags and large bulging ones. All Poppy's inquiring glances could not get a word out of her. She simply ducked her head and giggled behind her hand.

Mrs. Stander, arriving out of her usual time, came in and, hands clasped at her waist, surveyed the heap.

"Do you feel strong enough to consider these now?"

"What are they?" Poppy asked and succeeded in sounding mild.

"You'll be going out soon now. I didn't like to rummage too closely through the drawers and cupboards at your house when I went to get your bed gowns, but it appeared to me your wardrobe was in need of replenishing."

Poppy did not doubt Mrs. Stander had fingered every one of her worn possessions. "I'd planned to go to the shops myself."

"Mr. Dunbar thought you would need something when you first go out."

So this was what Jeremiah had been planning. "What have you found me?"

Mrs. Stander began unwrapping. Poppy could not fault the sizes, since Mrs. Stander had had her garments to measure against. The stockings, a half dozen each of silk and lisle, were of the finest. The slippers, black, brown, and cream, were of English leather and make. The undergarments and night robes were of plain white linen, fine as silk.

"Just the necessities," Mrs. Stander apologized. "I knew you'd want to make most of the selections for yourself."

Poppy nodded. These were the exact things she would have had to buy, though she would have hesitated and worried over every single item. She hoped she did not look surprised. Mrs. Stander's behavior had been impeccable, but she had felt an undercurrent there, a subtle attitude of condescension toward her and possessiveness about Jeremiah. Perhaps that was natural, since apparently he had lived here since the place first opened. Still, she would have expected Mrs. Stander to be less careful in her selections. She would not have been surprised if Mrs. Stander had produced, not these fine garments suitable for a gentlewoman's wear, but the sleazy, lace-trimmed, gaudy clothing of a street girl. Then Poppy told herself even if Mrs. Stander had not prided herself on her taste—and that showed in every appointment in this room—she might well fear Jeremiah's anger if she showed less than respect for this lady.

"I noted where you had purchased the purple velvet gown. She always labels her garments."

"Yes?"

"I'm sorry, but it could not be saved."

Poppy shuddered. "I hope you burned it."

"Only the bodice and front panels," Mrs. Stander said, looking shocked. "Such beautiful material, not worn at all. I saved yards from the back of the skirt, enough for a capelet, muff, and bonnet. Or even to upholster a small settee and chair."

"You are provident," Poppy gasped. "I could never endure to touch it again. If you have some use for it?"

"Thank you," Mrs. Stander said. "Waste not, want not, I was taught."

Where was that? Poppy wondered. And how did you come by the money to open this handsome house?

Mrs. Stander resumed, "Since she knew you, she was able to produce a quite satisfactory street dress and matching coat. A blue we thought would become you."

"I'm sure it is beautiful." She dared not question the cost. "Where is it?"

"Also a blue and gray stripe since you will want to begin to dress for dinner. Suitable for indoors, but it can be worn under the coat, also."

Poppy frowned. "I'm not sure what kind of dresses I'll need, and I must purchase carefully."

"Of course if these are not to your taste, they can be returned," Mrs. Stander said stiffly. "I selected only the bare necessities. You will need a morning dress and a wrap, too. I found a pretty rose print and a lavender sprig for the wrap." She gestured toward the large, unopened boxes.

Mrs. Stander had assembled, possibly out of honest

378

ignorance of other people's lives, a wardrobe for a married woman. "I am not a housewife," Poppy said, her tone sharp in spite of her intention.

"Your evening clothes are important." Mrs. Stander nodded understandingly. "I know. So we included another dress, one I was assured you had seen and thought most attractive."

But Félicité had bought the blue. "Let me see it."

Mrs. Stander lifted a lid. Poppy caught one glimpse of the white dress, and fury flared in her. Necessities she must have. That was the ultimate in unnecessary luxury.

"I saw that and said it was lovely," she said crisply. "I did not even consider it. Most unsuitable."

"So beautiful," Mrs. Stander murmured wistfully.

"I cannot think of any place I would wear it."

"Almost like a wedding dress."

"You don't like it?" Jeremiah asked from the doorway.

Poppy almost jumped from the chair. "What are you doing here in the afternoon?"

"The clubhouse can survive my absence for once." He came in and stood looking down at the boxes. "Did you include a second choice for the occasion I mentioned, Mrs. Stander?"

"What occasion?" Poppy demanded.

They did not seem to hear her. Mrs. Stander had opened the largest box, and they were looking at a gown of fawn velvet heavily beaded with brilliant brown around the low neck and down the panels of the skirt. Poppy caught her breath, knowing how that fawn and brown would bring out the brilliant colors of her hair and eyes.

Mrs. Stander held it up. "See the little train. Small, not enough to impede even for dancing, but it gives height and dignity."

"Beautiful," Poppy admitted. "Beautiful. But too expensive and too elaborate for any place I would go."

"But this is a command performance," Jeremiah smiled. "For Mr. Wilton. Everett G."

379

Poppy had to laugh. "Is there an Everett A or B?"

Jeremiah brushed that aside. "Phillipa is recovering but still low in her spirits and needs distraction."

"An unsuitably elaborate gown for me will hardly distract Phillipa."

"Mr. Wilton wishes to take her to the theater. To start accustoming her to such public appearances with him. She professes the idea throws her into a frenzy of fear." Jeremiah's tone was contemptuous.

"Phillipa is timid."

"She feels she could face it with you beside her, an old friend."

"I see."

"Accommodating Mr. Wilton is important to me," Jeremiah said, speaking as if Mrs. Stander were either a piece of furniture or an intimate so close he could reveal himself without restraint. "An appearance at the theater with him would make an excellent impression. He is an influential man, Poppy, and I have long wished to cultivate his acquaintance. I assure you the evening will be worth far more to me than the cost of the gown."

So she could earn the gown with one evening spent on Jeremiah's elbow and wear it usefully for dozens of other nights. "When?"

"Three evenings from now."

Poppy bit her lip. Having the stitches removed and watching these things unpacked had left her trembling with weakness. Dr. Armstrong had been emphatic that she should not attempt to leave the house for another week, and Jeremiah knew that. Perhaps he had forgotten, and she decided not to mention it. The gown was gorgeous, and three days could work a miracle.

"I'll accept the gown with thanks," she said demurely. "I cannot afford most of these other things."

"Select what you wish to keep, and Mrs. Stander will remove the rest," Jeremiah promised.

Poppy selected only what she felt she must have, but Mrs. Stander refused to give her the bills. She said that must be settled with Mr. Dunbar, and he said it could wait until later.

Three days later, as she dressed for the theater, Poppy wondered how she would get through the evening. Her hands were shaking by the time she started to brush her hair. But she needed that dress, and she had no other way of earning it. Besides, she owed Jeremiah more than this small favor for the great one of saving her life. She would endure the evening if she spent days in bed afterwards.

Mrs. Stander had brought her furs from the house. Though the weight seemed intolerably heavy, Poppy knew there were no finer in the city.

She and Jeremiah slipped into the theater as the curtain was rising. Phillipa and Mr. Wilton were already in the box. Poppy pressed Phillipa's hand and sat back gratefully. She would be all right if she had only to sit here through the play, though Shakespeare did run long, and then walk back to the carriage to be driven home again.

When the lights went up between the acts, Phillipa sat as if frozen. Poppy decided her gown of rich shimmering gray, with bands of tiny pink rosebuds at neck and around the hem, was a compromise between mourning and Mr. Wilton's wishes. The colors set off Phillipa's fragile beauty to perfection.

"I'm so frightened," Phillipa whispered. "I've never been in a theater before."

"Do you like it?"

"It's like magic. All those olden people that I thought were dead, walking and talking down there."

"Then sit back and enjoy it."

"Nonsense," Mr. Wilton boomed. "We can't have the two loveliest ladies at the theater and not show them off on our arms. Come now, just a short promenade to stretch our legs before the curtain goes up again."

That promenade was part of the payment for her gown. Mr. Wilton only wanted her to help support Phillipa, who was looking more terrified every minute.

He had no way of knowing Poppy was not fully recovered. Jeremiah certainly had not mentioned it, and he was not mentioning it now. Face averted from him to hide the anger in her eyes, Poppy smiled reassuringly at Phillipa and stood up.

"Just pretend you're walking across the floor of the Palace to the bar and back again," Poppy whispered. "Take Mr. Wilton's arm, and I'll stay on this side of you, and Jeremiah will be beside me. Come on. You'll see. It will be all right."

Phillipa was trembling as she stumbled to her feet, but Poppy put her good arm around her. Entwined like schoolgirls, she thought with a grimace, but she thought Phillipa might turn and run to hide if left alone. They went out into the carpeted corridor back of the boxes and slowly walked the length. As they turned back, Poppy felt Phillipa give a shudder of relief and relax.

This was not too unlike the Palace at a crowded hour, with men in severe black broadcloth, flourishing their long black cigars, except that each man had a lady on his arm. The ladies were not as pretty as the Palace girls, but their gowns were magnificent, and each of them preened and turned to show off her flashing jewels. The air was dense with cigar smoke and heavy perfumes, and the chatter of many voices seemed to reverberate off the walls.

All of them were too busy with their own parts in the flaunting parade to do more than glance at Phillipa and Poppy. The women did not recognize them, and the men would not speak in this company. Phillipa was realizing that and relaxing, but Poppy, after her long days alone in a quiet room, felt dizzy from the impact of odors, noises, and crowding bodies.

She turned her head to ask Jeremiah to return to the box and looked straight into Dex's eyes. On his arm was Félicité, exquisite in delicate lavenders and pinks with tiny violets framing her white shoulders and crowning her golden hair, diamonds sparkling at throat, ears, and wrists. Always before, she had seen Félicité at a distance, beautiful and perfectly dressed and groomed, a vision of loveliness. Seen close, her face was still beautiful but almost inhuman, cold and perfect as a china doll, with no hint the rosy lips could alter their slight pout to smile or the blue eyes change their calm, bored stare to a warm glance.

Mr. Wilton held out his hand to Dex. "This is fortunate. I heard you were back in town, and I've been waiting impatiently for another conference."

"I only returned yesterday." Dex made as if to move away.

"Then I'll see you tomorrow morning. My business won't wait," Mr. Wilton said. He boomed out introductions and did not wait to hear them acknowledged. "I'll be marrying very shortly, and I want the matter of this damn Mex thieving settled before I leave on my honeymoon."

"Perhaps it's best left until you return."

"Meanwhile you go down there again, and they spill their side of it into your ear?" Mr. Wilton demanded. "No, Mr. Roack. I don't trust what those people are going to do or say. You'll look at my papers first and see that it's rank theft, rank."

"Tomorrow morning then," Dex said, turning away. "And my congratulations."

Mr. Wilton's laugh boomed out. "Congratulations, yes, and thank you. Aren't we the lucky men with our two beauties? Phillipa is my lovely. I don't believe Poppy and Jeremiah have yet set a date."

Félicité's perfect lips parted, and she said, in a barely audible childlike whisper, "Yes, two beauties. I think I've heard. Similar backgrounds. Perhaps a double wedding. Have you settled the place?"

That was intended as an insult. She was telling them she knew they were gambling hall girls and their weddings could only be some vulgar performance, such as a double ceremony at a place like the Eureka. The men were beaming complacently. Men never understood such female clawings. They took the words at face value.

Poppy felt herself go white with rage. "Not yet," she

said. "Have you settled yours? The engagement has been rumored for so long." She hoped her tone made it sound like years, with Félicité sinking into spinsterhood.

"A wedding?" Félicité's perfect face almost showed expression. "In winter? But no. The trousseau alone. Winter clothes, so heavy, so dull. Impossible."

"As you hear, neither have we set a date," Dex said quickly.

Félicité's glance wandered in search of other company. "Such discussions, *je m'ennuie.*"

"Natural enough, if you have to travel," Mr. Wilton said, sensing something wrong and trying to inject a note of cordiality. "Not every lady enjoys traveling, even with a new husband and especially if he has his mind on business. She couldn't enjoy being left behind alone, either. Very understandable."

"Très boring," Félicité shrugged.

Poppy stared. What could Dex see in this painted china doll? Not one flicker of emotion touched her face or colored the voice that whispered only of *l'ennui.* Poppy bit her tongue to keep from blurting that obviously she must find the prospect of bed boring, too.

"Then you don't wish to marry?" Poppy said and shook her head as if in pitying sympathy. "Of course for some women, better, much better alone."

The faintest color touched Félicité's white cheeks. "A spring trousseau, quite pretty. Spring weddings, quite pleasant."

Rage burst in Poppy. So she did intend to marry him. Then Dex was a besotted fool. Remembering the surge and fire of his passion, the tumult and torrential cresting of his physical expressions, she was outraged that he planned to unite himself with this china doll. At best, Félicité would find his caresses barely pleasant, provided she did not decide they were completely dull.

Poppy knew she would walk out of the theater on the instant, without a word or backward look, abandoning everything and everybody, if Dex gestured her to go with him. She would throw herself into his arms, if he promised no more than the one night together. She would take it, without counting the cost and without regrets. Félicité was prepared to tolerate him, barely, for a lifetime. Fury, frustration, and jealousy bubbled up in Poppy until she could not stop herself from speaking.

"Insipid," she drawled, raising an eyebrow. "Spring weddings are for those who like infants for attendants, buds instead of flowers for decorations, and maidenly blushes better than kisses. Spring weddings are for children. I've chosen white for my wedding gown, but I'll have every fireplace burning at the reception and every dark red rose in San Francisco for decoration. I am a woman, and I love color and warmth and life. So perhaps you would not care for an invitation to my wedding to Jeremiah next week."

Then she stood there, head defiantly high, wishing she could die.

Chapter Forty

*P*OPPY was so exhausted the next day that she fell
to her knees when she tried to get out of bed. She
barely managed to pull herself back up into the bed and
ring the silver bell. Mrs. Stander took one dismayed
look at her white, drawn face and black-shadowed eyes
and sent for Dr. Armstrong. He came and told Jeremiah, hovering outside the door, that the theater ex-
cursion last night had been madness. The girl was young
and strong, but she needed time. Then, in answer to
Jeremiah's question, a wedding, that was something
else. A small, quiet wedding in a few weeks, no, a
month would be better, provided they did not contem-
plate a strenuous honeymoon trip, should be quite
possible. Mrs. Stander would take care of all the arrangements? Then they had his blessing.

Poppy listened, motionless, silent. She knew she
would not die. She was condemned to life. Out of spite
and jealousy, she had announced her wedding plans.
She was trapped by her own words. Her mind circled
endlessly through the long, sleepless hours of her nights
looking for a way out. She could find none. She had
the gold chain and the earrings, but they could not
buy her a new reputation. As Jeremiah's bride, she
would be that beautiful gambling hall girl who had
married the man who saved her life. As the woman who
had jilted the man who saved her, she would be a
notorious wanton. No respectable woman would speak
to her. No respectable place would employ her, not
even the Eureka if she could face it again, and she

could not. Only one profession would be open to her. Madame, for all her friendship, might think her too notorious to have in her fine house, especially at the risk of offending Jeremiah's powerful friends.

So she must marry. Jeremiah promised Sacramento after the next election, and she did not doubt that promise. That she might be the governor's lady in time was completely possible. The future could hold Washington as well.

There would be a certain bitter pleasure in receiving Dex in an official mansion. She literally would have killed herself before she let him see her sink into the gutter. Yes, she must marry.

Phillipa clapped her hands with pleasure like a child when Poppy asked her to be the only attendant. She would not be at all nervous, she promised, because all the attention would be for Poppy. This was wonderful, the perfect rehearsal for her wedding, because afterwards she could copy every detail of Poppy's and arrange her own without an anxious moment.

Jeremiah wanted an evening church wedding, even if small, with only their closest friends as guests. He asked his Fire Company. With a wicked secret smile, Poppy asked Maurice and Clyde and Pete and all the rest of her favorite people from the Palace and the Eureka.

Mrs. Stander said she would arrange everything for the reception at the boardinghouse. Remembering her bitter boast, Poppy asked only that fires be lit and the decorations be red roses, but she did not even bother to look at the room or inquire about the collation. Mrs. Stander and Jeremiah could arrange that to their pleasure. She left the guest list for the reception to them as well, except for one thing. She made sure invitations went to the Pannets and Dex. She anticipated their polite refusals, but regretted they did not send even token gifts. She had looked forward to dashing them to the floor and stamping on them.

She had no heart for shopping, and when Mrs. Stander said she had not yet returned any of her purchases to the shops, Poppy nodded indifferent acceptance. At another time she might have wondered at this selection of a wardrobe so suitable to her new condition in life and been angered that he had been so certain of her acceptance, but now she was too numbed with despair.

For the church, the white dress was as perfect as anything she might have found, ethereal as a cloud. She designed a wedding veil of layer after layer of finest tulle, falling only to her waist, and held by a wreath of pearls and gold leaves. That was Jeremiah's wedding gift. Mr. Wilton, as his gift to them, added the pearls to wear at her throat. Poppy knew his generosity represented his sincere gratitude for the perfect ease with which Phillipa was beginning to plan her own wedding.

When Phillipa and Mr. Wilton called to take her to the church, Poppy nearly panicked. Once in the carriage her eyes must have been frantic, for Mr. Wilton put a firm hand on her arm and held her back. By the time they arrived, she was numb, shaking, and half-blind as she stumbled down the aisle. She was dimly aware of her friends on one side of the church and the glittering uniforms of the Fire Company's full dress on the other. She stood trembling at the altar, fighting to stay upright and not whirl and run out of the building in a mad frenzy of escape. She heard her own whispering voice only as an echo from a great distance, faint as the last cold breath from a tomb as the door closed and locked.

Oddly enough, once the words were said, she began to recover so that she felt quite cool, detached, and weak. By the time they got back to the boardinghouse, she was able to notice the reception room had been made larger by opening the double doors to the dining room, forming one space the length of the deep house. At first she was aware only of the fires blazing at each end and the masses of dark red roses everywhere. Then she saw the long table along one side and the four waiters in red coats standing in front of it. She had assumed Mrs. Stander would provide a small collation of champagne punch and cake. Instead, she saw the white damask-covered board was heaped with silver platters of elaborately prepared hams, turkeys, roasts of beef and meat pies, with an enormous suckling pig in the center. Whole salmon and chafing dishes of seafood mixture were set out beside heaps of snowy rice and glittering jellies and aspics. Hot rolls, breads, crackers, and dozens of cheeses and bowls of fruit were set out on a smaller table.

The towering wedding cake and bowls of punch were on a table under the bay windows. The length of the house away, at the back, another table was loaded with bottles, glasses and ice, and standing beside it was a bartender who sometimes worked at the Palace.

"Do you intend to feed an army?" Poppy gasped.

"This is my one and only wedding," Jeremiah said sentimentally, patting her arm. "You wouldn't want me to give offense?"

"How many people do you know?"

"Dozens are coming from Sacramento," Jeremiah boasted. "With their wives. The highest officials. And the members of the legislature. And the judges, of course."

The rest was lost as the string quartet beside the living room fireplace began to play and the first of the guests arrived. As they walked in the door and she heard the deep, steady rumble of carriages outside, Poppy realized the truth. She had left everything to Jeremiah and Mrs. Stander, and they had turned her wedding into a political circus. Her husband was making a public demonstration of his friends and power.

Not only the men from Sacramento but the city officials and army officers from the Presidio had brought their wives. Poppy knew only one thing to do. She must carry this off with royal grace.

She stood nodding and smiling, trying to repeat and remember names. The Fire Company men were easy, as were the few San Francisco social figures. Most of them had been in the Palace at one time or another, though not with their wives. The Governor, the Mayor, and the General were simple to identify. For the rest, she tried to give the impression that seeing each of them was the greatest possible pleasure for her. She thought she was succeeding. Jeremiah's eyes were gleaming with satisfaction, and he kept patting her arm, not as much a caress, she thought, as the encouraging pats one gave a horse or a dog that was performing well. She came to resent that touch and moved as far away from his side as she could, without making it noticeable.

Within an hour, the room was so jammed it was impossible to move, and the air was thick with smoke and sultry perfumes. Poppy's stomach knotted up, and she felt herself swaying on her feet. She knew it would be a disaster if she tried to swallow one bite of the rich, spicy food. She could only be grateful for the long hours at the Palace, which had taught her to keep smiling when her feet were burning and to juggle a glass for hours without doing more than lift it to her lips now and then. People must leave eventually.

When the Fire Company's chorus, boasted as being the best in the city, grouped in front of the fireplace and began a concert, she almost broke down. How long would they sing? Her hands were so swollen from being pressed that she could hardly hold her glass, her cheeks were raw from affectionate dabbings, and her feet had stopped being twin throbs of agony and were now mere stumps.

By the time the carriages began to roll back to the door and the crowd to thin, she was in a daze. She only knew she must keep standing and smiling and not disgrace herself. Jeremiah was beaming and bowing, his eyes sparkling, alive as she had never seen him. When he personally closed the door behind the last of the guests, he half pranced back into the reception room.

He looked around, at the carpets stained and trampled, the flowers drooping in their vases, the tables a shambles of dirty glasses and dishes, and he nodded, eyes glittering, nostrils flaring wide with triumph. "We did ourselves proud, Mrs. Stander," he said, nodding again. "This is one wedding reception they won't forget. They've never seen anything like it in this town before, and it will be a long time before they see its equal again. Those that weren't here will regret it. Yes, siree, we did it up brown."

Mrs. Stander, in severe iron-gray silk, had hovered in the background all evening. Now she walked into the center of the room, hands clasped at her waist, and said expressionlessly, "Thank you, sir. We have to clean this now to be ready to serve breakfast in the morning."

Jeremiah nodded but did not move. He did not seem able to tear himself away from this scene of his triumph. "Yes, siree, that was some spread we put out. I said to lay out everything they could think of and then double it, and that they did. Did you see old Senator Coy? Skunk drunk. Skunk drunk." He slapped his thigh.

Poppy swayed on her stubs of feet. From far away she was vaguely grateful Dex had not seen her in the midst of this ultimate humiliation of vulgarity.

"You remember Mrs. Dunbar has not been well, sir," Mrs. Stander said. "She looks exhausted. I've prepared everything in your rooms."

Jeremiah glanced around indifferently. "You know the way. My rooms. I'll be along in a minute."

Poppy was beyond speech. She stumbled up the stairs and along to Jeremiah's suite. Earlier Mrs. Stander had showed her through the rooms, the finest in the house, especially designed for his use when the house was built, with tall windows overlooking the back garden. Now a fire burned in the sitting room, and vases of red roses stood all around. A large table was placed in front of the fire, set for two with covered dishes waiting and bottles in ice buckets, obviously just refilled.

Poppy stared numbly. She was exhausted from the strain of speaking to hundreds of people and half sickened by the memory of the masses of food downstairs. Jeremiah could not expect them to sit down to a cozy little supper *à deux* after that and at this late hour.

Jeremiah's feet thudded out in the hall, and he slammed into the room. He looked around, nodded with satisfaction, shrugged out of his coat, and tossed it on a chair.

"Now," he said with gusto, smacking his lips and rubbing his hands together. "I knew we'd be too busy with our guests to enjoy ourselves, so I had some of the best of everything brought up here. What will you have?"

Poppy's head was throbbing with every pulse beat. "I had plenty."

"Did you?" Jeremiah said absently, his eyes gluttonously looking over the food. "Oh, yes, my dear, I meant to tell you. You did very nicely. Received the whole lot of them pretty as a princess."

That was the breaking point. He did not see she was white and sick. He had not even noticed she had not eaten or drunk. The thing she seldom thought and had never said burst from her lips. "I am a king's daughter."

"Huh?" Jeremiah looked up, startled, and then burst into a great laugh. "Oh, sure, sure. We all can make up our ancestors out here, can't we? My family name is Bonaparte, and we all end up as kings, too. Now how about a little of the beef? Good and rare."

"I said I had plenty," Poppy whispered, white lipped.

"I didn't. I was too busy flattering the ladies and polishing up the gents." He picked up a tall glass and plucked a bottle of whiskey from the ice bucket, then poured the glass full. "Sure you won't? Might as well because I'm going to enjoy myself now."

Poppy gaped, wordless. Jeremiah did not drink. Ever.

He threw back his head, drained half the glass, and smacked his lips. "Ah, I needed that. Sure you won't have some? All right. Here's what I want. Rare beef, horseradish, mustard, fresh bread. Ah, now I'll have something worth putting my teeth into."

He loaded half a loaf of bread with blood-rare dripping beef, heaped on horseradish and mustard, then pushed the load into his mouth, and gave a strangled laugh as it smeared his face. He snatched up a linen napkin and scrubbed his cheeks and chin. He took another monster bite, grabbed another napkin and wiped again, and threw both on the floor. He was gorging like a famished animal and draining and refilling his glass between gulping bites. He was on his third glass now.

Poppy closed her eyes and swallowed convulsively. If she watched one more bite, she was going to be sick as she never had been sick before, even on shipboard.

"Ah, that'll hold me for a while," he said. Then he went into the bedroom, and she heard water splashing in the washbasin. He came back, toweling his face vigorously, and said, "Are you still just standing there?"

"I'm very tired," Poppy said weakly. Her mind was scurrying around in feverish circles. She had thought she was resigned and numbed to anything that might happen, but his animal greed had sickened her. In his expansive mood, would he listen if she pled exhaustion and asked to be allowed to return to her old room just for tonight? "Too tired," she began tentatively.

"Of course you are," he said. He dropped the towel on the floor and came over to her. Lifting her in his arms, he carried her into the bedroom, stumbling a little, and dropped her on the bed. He mumbled, "Too tired, very tired, I'll do it."

He tore the veil from her head, ripping out the pins that held the wreath to her hair, and ignored her shriek of surprised agony. Then he reached down and lifted each foot in turn and tore off the slippers. He broke the dainty ties so they lashed across her burning flesh like whips. Her swollen feet, suddenly released, ached as if they were thawing after being frozen.

She tried to struggle up. "My dress."

"I got it," he said thickly. He hooked his fingers under the neck of the bodice and jerked. The dainty buttons broke and flew in all directions.

The shop owner had said this was no dress to get out of in a hurry, Poppy thought hysterically, as he flipped her over and pulled the dress down as if he were husking an ear of corn. Then he caught the straps of her underbodice and jerked those away before he pulled at the waistband of her underskirts. He swore when the firm bands of silk did not break and grotesquely bounced her up and down on the bed as he tugged at them.

"If you'll let me up," Poppy gasped.

He staggered back. "Yeah, you do it. You get out of those while I get rid of these." He began to tear his clothes off, scattering them around him on the floor.

Poppy pulled herself off the bed and fumbled with the pearl buttons that held her petticoat waistbands. She did not believe this was happening. She was having a nightmare, and when she woke, she would know this was only a grotesque, distorted dream. But as always in a dream, she could not stop it. She could only let it go on and on, cringing as the horror intensified and carried her along, praying she would wake before the dreadful, shocking end.

Jeremiah tore the last bit of clothing from his thick-trunked body and slapped his sides triumphantly. "Here we are, and here we go, my girl," he said. He picked her up, threw her back on the bed, and fell on top of her.

She lay, gasping for breath, crushed under his weight, wondering wildly if she could tear free of this madman and run somewhere, any place, for safety. He was capable of any violence.

He slapped her knees apart and straddled her, fumbling with himself and grunting. She stiffened, clenching her teeth, ordering herself not to scream. This was happening, and she could not stop it. But she must not scream. She waited to be impaled, torn by this wild animal, but he only grunted and fumbled. Finally she realized he was talking to himself.

"Yes, you can," he was muttering. "Yes. You go on ahead, Jeremiah, you know you can do it. Go on. This is your wedding night. This is Poppy. Now here we are. Here we are. You can do it. You know you can. Wedding night. Poppy. Wedding night."

Finally she felt a soft dampness intruding into her as Jeremiah grunted and fumbled. Then after a moment, there was nothing. With a sob of gratification, he fell away and lay beside her, panting and patting himself happily.

"Did it, did it," he crooned with satisfaction. "Did it. Night. Goodnight. Li'l bride. Poppy. Did it. Did it."

She lay there more shocked than she would have been by the brutal animal rape she had expected. Her husband was impotent, or the next thing to it.

Chapter Forty-one

*P*OPPY roused dully. She had suffered a terrible nightmare, born of sickness and fever. She sat upright, trying to steady her whirling head, then slipped to the floor, feeling her legs giving under her. She was almost relieved that she was ill. It meant that the night had been only a nightmare.

Then she saw the torn shreds of her wedding gown. She gave a stifled cry, and the door to the living room opened instantly.

Mrs. Stander said, "I've cleared away in here so you can have breakfast in front of the fire."

"What time?" Poppy asked dazedly.

"Nearly eleven. Did you sleep well?"

"I was exhausted."

"Dr. Armstrong said it would be all right as long as the wedding was small and quiet." Mrs. Stander was worried about something.

Poppy glimpsed the new sprigged wrap laid out ready on a chair and turned to get it. "The *wedding* was small and quiet, anyway," she said.

"I've heard Dr. Armstrong has a temper when his orders aren't followed," said Mrs. Stander. "Used a horsewhip on one, they say, when he urged his wife out of bed too soon."

Mrs. Stander knew the wedding reception had been a brutal ordeal, and she worried for Jeremiah's sake. "I have no present need to consult Dr. Armstrong," Poppy said and decided to push her luck. "But until I feel stronger, I would appreciate having a breakfast tray up here."

"Of course." Mrs. Stander came into the room and

stood in her characteristic pose, hands clasped at her waist, and shook her head. "That lovely dress. What a pity."

"Don't tell me you can find some use for these rags, too?"

Mrs. Stander picked up the skirt. "Beautiful material. The finest embroidery and cutwork."

"It was."

"It still would make parlor maids' aprons and caps —for Sunday wear, of course. Or collar and cuff sets. Or jabots. With those lovely buttons."

Poppy tried not to stare. She could no longer doubt there was some old and close association between Jeremiah and this woman. No mere landlady showed such concern and interest. But last night had been the proof she could not be his mistress. Still Poppy did wonder. Where had Mrs. Stander got the money for this house? Where had she learned her skill at running a large household with comfort and economy? It could not be a happy story. Cosseted women did not learn to make aprons and caps from discards.

"Take it," she said, then collapsed in a chair in front of the fire.

She managed to nibble from a dainty tray Mary brought. Then she half dozed, dazed by exhaustion and shock. She was sure of only one thing. She had been pressed beyond her returning strength. She must give herself time to heal again and be completely well. Until then, she must endure as she was.

The days fell into a routine. Jeremiah woke, breakfasted downstairs with the other boarders, and was out of the house before she woke. Mary brought up a breakfast tray and cleaned the rooms.

Whoever had gone to get her night things and then her furs had packed all the rest of her clothes. Mrs. Stander had the trunks sent up, and Poppy sorted through them. Many of the things were so worn even Mrs. Stander could only shake her head and carry them away without any suggestions. Of all the Paris clothes, only a gray velvet skirt and cape were left unworn.

Poppy had a vague memory the beading on the matching basque had been unsatisfactory, but she had left before another was made. Now she pursed her lips over the cape and skirt. With a bright bodice, it still would give her a handsome walking costume.

The clothes Mrs. Stander had bought were sufficient as long as she and Jeremiah had no social life. Then she would need the changes expected of any young married woman. For the moment, she only needed gloves, bonnets, handkerchiefs, and a dozen other small necessities. But she could not quite rouse herself enough to make the effort to go shopping.

Jeremiah came home late in the afternoon, always with a full bottle of whiskey. She did not ask where he acquired it now on the pretext of taking it to the clubhouse. He started drinking immediately, but he was always sober enough to go down to dinner, and, since they ate alone at a table for two, nobody was able to remark on his condition. Back in their rooms, he quickly drank the rest of the bottle. Sometimes he was still sober enough when they went to bed to indulge in some of his fumblings. Sometimes he simply tumbled in, still in his underclothes, and lay, open-mouthed and snoring, until morning.

Poppy endured it. She took short walks and measured her growing strength each day. She was gaining but not yet strong.

One evening Jeremiah said, "Mr. Wilton wants to know when you will be able to help Phillipa select her trousseau. She is depending on you, but they didn't wish to interrupt our honeymoon." He snickered and gulped his whiskey.

"I can go almost any time," Poppy said slowly. "I need things for myself."

"What things?"

"Another wrap."

"You have two. Wash them."

"Gloves, bonnets."

"Are you barehanded and bareheaded?"

"Not completely," Poppy admitted, eyes flashing.

"Mrs. Stander squandered on you. You've got plenty."

"Your wife's appearance?" Poppy suggested, one eyebrow scornfully high.

"Handsomest woman in town," Jeremiah mumbled into his glass. "Much admired, much admired."

Another glass and he would be at the point where he understood nothing. "Shall I hire a carriage?"

"She'll call in his carriage. Shall I tell him tomorrow afternoon?"

"Ask if two is convenient. I'll be ready then."

Poppy told herself Jeremiah had been too blurred by drink to understand what she was telling him. She would explain and show him the things she needed when he was sober enough to comprehend her needs.

She and Phillipa had a delightful afternoon. Phillipa still did not talk much, but she glowed with happiness that made words unnecessary. She wanted a beautiful trousseau, but in her poverty she had never owned more than simple cotton dresses and her working gowns for the gambling rooms. Poppy mentally blessed the countess for her hours of meticulous tutelage in the Paris shops. Once Phillipa said Mr. Wilson wanted her to have everything possible, including clothes for a steamer trip down the coast on their honeymoon, Poppy threw restraint aside. They spent delicious hours fingering materials and discussing trims and agreed it would take them days even to complete their lists. Poppy would be the only attendant at the wedding, a wedding in Mr. Wilton's church since Phillipa's priest could not approve, but a dress for that was a small detail when they were envisioning orders by the dozens.

Then Phillipa in her artless way said Mr. Wilton had finally approved plans for the house he was building for her. He was even talking of sending to the east and Europe for some of the furniture. Poppy gasped and exclaimed, then began to make new lists of household linens. She wondered about rugs and samples for the draperies and upholstery, but when she saw Phillipa was becoming frightened and confused, she said that could wait.

They went out every afternoon. Twice, young matrons who had been at Poppy's reception recognized them in the shops and asked them home to drink a cup of tea. One evening at the end of the second week of this, Poppy actually found herself smiling as she changed for dinner. She was not happy, but life was endurable.

She would make an effort, she determined. She tensed, but always managed not to cringe when Jeremiah touched her, and he was always too far gone in drink to notice. If she steeled herself to put up with those few unpleasant minutes at night, perhaps in the other hours together they could build some kind of a companionship that would give them comfort and bind them together.

She waited, seated before the fire, still smiling, for once not dreading Jeremiah's appearance. He came in, tore off his hat and coat, and threw them over a chair. Clutching his bottle, he advanced toward the table where Mrs. Stander always had glasses and ice waiting. He stopped, staring.

"Who ordered that?" he demanded, pointing.

"The champagne? It's only a half bottle. I thought you might prefer not to drink alone."

"What are we celebrating?"

"Nothing in particular."

"You mean, every night?"

He drank his bottle every night. "Not if you prefer I didn't," Poppy said meekly. She honestly did not care. She had only meant to be companionable. "As you like, Jeremiah."

"Help yourself since you've ordered it and I'll have to pay," he grumbled. He wrestled his bottle open and splashed whiskey into a glass. "Go ahead. I'm not an expert waiter who will pop corks."

"Later," Poppy said warily.

He glared at her over his glass. "What's that in your hair?"

Poppy's hand flew up to touch the tiny nosegay of silk flowers. "From Paris. Phillipa and I were shopping, and they were just unpacking these. They were so charming all the ladies took at least one."

"How much?"

"I don't know," Poppy confessed. "They were just a little something pretty, and everybody loved them."

"If you don't know, how did you pay?"

"I gave your name."

"That dress," Jeremiah said, pointing again. "Is that new?"

Poppy smoothed the gray velvet over her knees. "I had the skirt and cape, so I only had to get the bodice. I can't always wear the same things, day after day."

"I looked in your wardrobe. I looked. You've got clothes, clothes, clothes, thousands of dollars worth of clothes."

"I have some fine furs, which cost you nothing," Poppy said slowly. "For the rest, I do not even have the necessities. I mentioned this to you before."

"You gave my name for that bodice too, I suppose," Jeremiah said and dashed his empty glass on the hearth. "I can't have this extravagance. I cannot stand this constant expense. It must stop."

"I can't return this. I've worn it."

"But no more, you understand, no more." He grabbed another glass and filled it. "No more giving my name. Understand?"

"You had Mrs. Stander buy those clothes for me before we were married."

"That was before I had you hobbled and haltered," Jeremiah said, gulping his drink.

Poppy's fists clenched. She remembered the promises he had made before they were married. Her own carriage. Now he ignored her hints for carriage fare. He always said they would be using Mr. Wilton's carriage. Her own house—he had vowed he would build her the finest in the best part of town. She might as well find out how sincerely he meant that, too.

"When we finished shopping, we went to drink tea with Mrs. Finney in her new house," Poppy said without inflection. "I have been in several of the new homes.

Now that they are laying the foundations of the Wilton house, everybody wants to know when we will be building ours and if it will be near theirs."

"A house? We'll be in Sacramento."

"That's certain? Isn't your residence here?"

Jeremiah colored darkly. "Do you know what houses cost these days? Do you know what my expenses are? That reception, the handsomest reception this town has ever seen, and for your wedding, don't forget. Do you know what that cost? Do you know how hard-pressed I am sometimes? Don't you realize a man in politics never knows when he may need funds available? Large sums, instantly available, and you dribble my money away on nonsense." He tore the flowers from her hair and threw them into the flames.

Poppy watched the pretty trifle char to ashes. "I didn't understand."

"But I'm happy you're spending so much time with Phillipa," Jeremiah said hastily. "Yes, that's fine, fine. Mrs. Everett G. Wilton-to-be. Good, very good. It's not that my business interests aren't sound, completely sound, but I'd hate to buck him as a competitor. He's a man that doesn't forget, friend or foe."

"Then he must notice we always use his carriage."

"That's good, good."

Poppy tried one last time. "If Phillipa ever was not able to call for me, I do not have carriage fare in my purse."

"He'll see she always has a carriage, always. He can't set her up with her own before they're married. Not proper, and he has delicate feelings, Mr. Wilton has," Jeremiah explained expansively. "But she'll never lack a carriage and pair. Generous to a fault, Wilton. Well, he can afford it. Not like some of us."

"I think I'll have that champagne now," Poppy said.

She knew exactly what she was going to do the next day. Pretending to be asleep, she could hardly wait for Jeremiah to leave the house so she could get up and dress and be off. She walked the whole distance to her house, sustained by pure rage, and pounded ruthlessly on Maurice's door until he stumbled, eyes still half shut, to open it.

"Put on the coffee," Poppy ordered. "Then go soak your head in water until you're awake enough to talk."

She waited until Maurice, wrapped in a wool robe, sat opposite her, blinking and sipping the black brew.

"How much rent have I coming, and what have you done with the other house?" Poppy demanded.

"I have your rents, all, we are not behind. But I was not certain I was a welcome visitor, even to bring them."

"That's what I thought."

Maurice stood up and fumbled in a drawer. "Here."

"Thank you. And the other house?"

"Vacant."

"Can you rent it?"

"Easily. Is it for rent?"

"If I did not occupy it, could you find a tenant and collect the rents?"

"Of course."

She could not tell even Maurice the complete sordid truth. "I have decided a married woman should have her own private funds, privately available." She added hastily, "Provided her husband does not inquire, of course."

"Of course," Maurice agreed expressionlessly. "I do not believe most people are aware you own these houses."

"Consider yourself in charge of them both," Poppy decided.

"Perhaps I could have a note to that effect?"

"Bring me the paper. I'll write it now." Poppy drew a deep breath. "One more thing. If you were selling jewelry, where would you go?"

"I wouldn't."

"Or having pieces duplicated?"

"Like the fine ladies of London and Paris who gamble too high?" Maurice laughed. "In Europe, I could help you. Here? Some Italians are reputed to do fine work."

"It's not important," Poppy shrugged. "Let me write you that note."

With money in her purse, she hired a carriage, drove to the boarding hotel where Phillipa was living, and left a note that she would not be able to go shopping that day. She thought of going to Madame. Of all the people in San Francisco, she would know best where jewelry was bought and sold at favorable prices. Still Poppy hesitated. She seemed to go to Madame only when she was desperate, and she was not proud of that. Madame would accept it as she accepted many things, but the thought of what she could say about the marriage to Jeremiah made Poppy cringe. Madame's tongue was a sharp weapon, and she did not hesitate to cut with it. As to what Jeremiah would say if anyone saw her entering Madame's and told him, Poppy chilled at the very thought.

No, Madame was her last resort. First she would try Josh Wiggins. Josh had been in San Francisco almost from the earliest days. He must know every merchant in town. It would be good to see Josh again, to talk to him about Andy, Jack, and Maurice and, painful though it was, to tell him of Josie's end and that nightmarish night.

"The waterfront, Josh Wiggins and Son General Merchandise Store," Poppy ordered. She counted over the wealth she would show him. One pair of jade earrings. One gold necklace and nugget. One gold and pearl wreath. One pearl necklace. One small lady's gun with elaborate inlays. They meant money and self-respect. She did not know what she would do with the money, but it was freedom to decide the path of her future, and she must have that, instead of being held like an animal in a trap. She played with the half dozen long cords and heavy tassels that decorated her reticule and stretched out her legs. "Don't fight the other carriages. It's a fine day. I'm in no hurry."

"A fine day for a fire, as usual," the driver grumbled. "See the smoke."

Poppy glanced out. "No trouble. We're going to the other side of the wharf."

Chapter Forty-two

$\mathcal{A}$S the carriage stopped where the street ended at the wharf, Poppy saw a small clipper, probably one designed for the coastal trade, tied up at the end. Even with furled sails, she was a beautiful thing, graceful as a dancer and bright with new paint, polished brass, and a laughing golden dolphin figurehead. Clutching the heavy reticule, she walked forward, feeling irresistibly drawn, until she was standing right beneath it.

Such a pretty ship. Such a clean ship. Such a fast ship, bound for unknown ports, beckoning ports where perhaps a young woman could make a fresh start. If she had the will. If she had a little money.

Poppy's lips parted, and she breathed quickly. Josh would not buy the jewelry, but he would tell her where she could sell it. She only needed to learn when the ship sailed. South or north, she did not care.

She put one foot on the gangplank. The words, "When do you sail, where are you bound?" were ready on her lips, when a tall figure moved to the rail above her and stood looking down. She shrank back, hands flying to her throat.

Dex. She knew he came and went. She had assumed he was away now because, in all the gossiping hours when she was shopping with Phillipa, she had heard no word of him or Félicité Pannet. Was he arriving? Or leaving?

Fixed by that steady look that held recognition but no welcome, the set face that did not smile and the lips that uttered no word, she gave a stifled cry, turned, and fled back along the wharf. Panting, she whirled around the corner and ran into Wiggins's store.

Efram beamed from behind the counter. "Miss Poppy, I'm pleased to see you haven't forgotten us."

"Never," Poppy said fervently. "Where's your father?"

Efram's face sobered. "There's a fire a couple of streets over, a man we've had some trouble with. Stocks his place at a discount from us, but he's always slow to find the cash on accounting day. Still, Pa went over to see if he could help."

"He'll be back soon?"

"Should be. If I can't help you."

Poppy looked around. Everybody had gone to watch the fire. They were alone in the shop. She opened her reticule and made a little heap of the jewelry and the derringer on the counter beside it.

"I didn't like to carry those things without some protection," she said, in case Efram was shocked. "I know you don't handle this kind of merchandise, but do you know who might give me a fair price?"

"All of these?"

"I don't know. I needed the advice of an honest man, so I came here."

"I'd think you should take them two or three different places and compare the offers."

That was sensible, but this was a small, gossipy town. If she went to even two places, somebody would see her and mention it to Jeremiah, if no more than to joke that apparently his bride shopped for her own jewelry. The thought made Poppy shudder. Perhaps she should go to Madame after all.

Josh's voice said strongly from the doorway, "That is all I have to say to you, gentlemen. I was there to see if I could help. Now if you will excuse me, I have duties in my own establishment." The scent of smoke heavy around him, he strode in and said with surprise, "My dear Miss Poppy, this is indeed a pleasure."

"Poppy?"

Jeremiah, fireman's hat pushed back above his smoke-smeared face, uniform dripping sooty water, burst through the door and stamped across to stand over Poppy and glower down at her. "What are you doing here?"

"Here?" Poppy put out a casual-seeming arm to try to conceal the heap of jewelry. "These are my old and good friends, the first people I met when I came to San Francisco."

"Such good friends you've never mentioned them and didn't invite them to our wedding?" Jeremiah sneered. "Lies, lies, everybody lies to me. What are you hiding there?" He swept her arm aside and glared down at the heap of jewelry and the derringer beside it.

She did not lose her head. "I was showing them how I have prospered since we met."

"Bribery," Jeremiah said darkly. "Or blackmail. You were playing the beggar with me last night, whining you didn't have even carriage hire, but I doubt you walked here."

He swung around toward the door, and Poppy saw the other men in the Fire Company uniforms crowding there. Jeremiah made a commanding gesture, and they began to seep into the shop until they filled every inch of floor space and stood silent, eyes alert, waiting to hear what Jeremiah had to say.

"A good man, a struggling hard-working man, a competitor of this Wiggins, a man who had endless difficulties combating false claims for bills owing, which this Wiggins insisted on pressing against him."

Josh yelled, breaking into the tirade, "He owed me that money, and I can produce the notes with his signature."

"This Wiggins, bent on destroying a dangerous rival."

"His business was failing," Josh shouted.

"This poor man, as he has told us, standing in the ruins of his enterprise, his hope of livelihood, his hard-held independence won by toil and sweat, fighting jealousy and false claims, was making a success. He was reluctant to point the condemning finger, but a ruined

407

man must ask at least for justice. His rival, this man Wiggins, could not endure to see him succeed. When all else failed, he set that poor man's business to the torch and stood by gloating while we risked our lives to save a few pitiful remnants from destruction."

"He burned it himself for the insurance," Josh said.

"Now they do not spare him even lies and false accusations to conceal their own guilt," Jeremiah intoned.

Poppy shrank back, eyes wide. Jeremiah needed only an accusation to set him off. Any excuse would do to unleash his rhetoric, and he would lash his followers into a frenzy to strengthen his leadership. Now she did not doubt he had spoken exactly like this against Andy. He was the one who lied.

"I was here in my store, waiting on a customer, and Efram was delivering the goods, until long after your company arrived at the fire," Josh said.

"You lie in vain, your guilt will find you out," Jeremiah shrieked.

"One moment, please, let me through," Dex's voice said from the doorway. He came pushing past the fireman to confront Jeremiah. "I couldn't help observing the turmoil here, and I'd like an explanation."

Jeremiah pointed a long, shaking finger. "These men are fire setters."

"The fire on the other side of the wharf? Impossible. I was in this shop for close to two hours, buying cabin stores and supervising their packing and delivery to the ship at the wharf, before the fire broke out. I heard the fire companies arrive before Mr. Wiggins finished his business with me, and I went aboard to watch the fire from the deck. By that time, it was nearly over."

Jeremiah's face worked, and then he said, "We have conflicting testimony here, gentlemen. I must investigate further. If you will get the engine back to the station, I will join you there."

The men filed out, shuffling their feet and muttering. They left a strong odor of burned wood and rubber behind them. Nobody spoke until the last one had tramped across the wharf.

408

Then Dex said, "They're ready and waiting to take up the gangplank. Is there anything I can do before I sail, Mr. Wiggins?"

"There were some substantial citizens in that company, and I am sure many of them recognized you and heard your statement," Josh said. "That should be all that is necessary."

"Not so quick there," Jeremiah said, pointing that accusing finger at the jewelry on the counter. "What about those? What are they doing in your shop?"

"Miss Poppy was showing them to me," Efram said. "Pa never saw them."

"And why did Miss Poppy bring them here, to her dear and good friends, friends she has carefully concealed from me?" Jeremiah sneered and reached his hand toward the jewelry.

"Oh, no," Poppy cried and pounced. She snatched, but he was quicker, and her hand lit only on the little derringer entangled in the strings and tassels of the reticule. She swept that into her left hand and held out her right. "Those are mine. The earrings and the chain I had before we were ever married. Give them to me."

"You're my wife, dear, and everything you have belongs to me," Jeremiah smiled.

"Not those," Poppy said, grabbing his hand and trying to open his fingers. She pulled with her whole body. Suddenly the little gun spat, and Jeremiah reeled back, the jewelry spilling to the counter as he clutched his side. She screamed, "Jeremiah," and dropped the gun and reticule.

He sagged against the counter and slowly slid to the floor, legs straight before him, back stiff against the counter, while a flood of red poured out over his fingers. His face was congested, looking doubly dark under his white hair, and his mouth worked violently. But he made no sound after the great grunting shout he had let out when the bullet hit him.

Dex leaned over, scooped up the jewelry and gun, and shoved them into the reticule. Then he looked at Josh. "Doctor?"

"Don't know. Hard to tell."

"Maybe not," Dex said. "Scandal."

"Handled things myself before now," Josh offered.

"He's not bubbling at the mouth," Efram said calmly.

"Of course not," Josh said. "He's hardly breathing."

"Small bullet, light load, hit the ribs," Dex said.

"We'll take care of him," Josh said. "Don't give it another thought. Nobody'll hear a word of this."

Poppy listened, frozen. Jeremiah was still alive, still conscious, and she could hardly believe it, but these three men were coolly discussing the disposal of his body. Whatever else he was, he was her husband.

"No." The word was a scream in her mind, but it came out as a mere breath. "No."

Jeremiah's eyes were alive, and his mouth was a gaping hole in his darkened face. Now he drummed his heels on the floor and flung out his bloody, dripping hands, clenching and unclenching the terrible fingers. He too knew what they were planning.

Poppy swayed and closed her eyes. She could not watch that dying convulsion.

"I'll leave him to you," Dex said and caught Poppy's wrist. "I think the lady is best out of this."

"Yes, indeed," Josh said. "I owe you, Mr. Roack, and I'll take care of it."

"The poor lady was so shocked she was taken with a swoon. And when she came out of it, in her distress she fled," Dex murmured.

"Vanished completely," Josh swore. "Out of my sight while I was taking care of the unfortunate gentleman."

"*À bientôt*," Dex said and yanked Poppy's wrist. "Coming? Or must I carry you?"

"Carry me?"

"They're holding the gangplank."

That beautiful clipper was sailing. She did not know where it was bound, but it was away from this horror. Any place would be better than this. Any people would be better than these. Dex had saved her jewelry. She would not be penniless and helpless. She could make a fresh start.

"I can walk. But you are a monster and beyond any words I have."

"And I don't doubt that I'll have to listen to many of them," Dex sighed and tucked her hand under his arm.

He walked her down the wharf to the ship, helped her up the gangplank, nodding to the sailors waiting there, and guided her back along the deck to the open door of a cabin.

"You had better stay in there until we're out of sight of land," Dex said. "The cabin boy will bring you a cup of tea."

Part Seven

On Board the
Golden Dolphin
Winter 1852-1853

Chapter Forty-three

POPPY was in a daze, hardly aware of anything around her, only able to sit quietly in a chair and force herself to look composed. When she found a tea tray at her elbow, she had no memory of anybody bringing it. She sipped from the transparent china cup, nibbled at the thin bread and butter, and slowly revived. She looked about her. This was a fine cabin, not large but comfortably furnished. A real bedspread matched the material on the screen, which hid the cabinet holding the washbasin and pitcher. The chest of drawers with bright brass pulls was of the same polished wood as the compact desk and chair. She was in an upholstered armchair beside a small table, conveniently close to the bookshelves built above the desk. The hanging brass lamp was adjusted to light them both.

Compared to her cabin on the *Bonne Irène,* this was palatial. Other things were different, too. The *Bonne Irène* had hummed and throbbed with the movements and voices of hundreds of people compressed into too little space. Their noise was never completely silent, and only the loudest roars or the shriek of a gale wind could be heard above it. Now she could hear the lapping of water along the hull, the creaks of timbers and ropes, the thumps of sails being raised, the thud of feet on the deck, and only an occasional quiet voice speaking a few words.

Now she recalled something. There had been none of the usual activity on the wharf. No carriages had rolled up, bringing passengers or coming to wait and wave farewell. Not even a sailor's girl had loitered nearby. She had seen no sign of stores or cargo being loaded. As Dex rushed her across the deck, she had seen nobody except a few sailors standing ready at the gangplank and the ropes.

This was a lovely ship but a strangely secret, almost ghostly sailing. She started to her feet, hand at her throat, as the door opened and Dex walked in.

"Not yet," he said. "We're still in the bay."

"What ship is this?"

"The *Golden Dolphin*. Sailing out of San Francisco in the coastwise trade."

"Where are the passengers?"

"The four who were able to join us in time are on deck marveling at the size of the bay. We decided only late last night to sail some days earlier than announced. Most of our passengers were not able to prepare so quickly. That is why I was buying cabin stores at the last minute."

"Ships don't change their sailing dates like that," Poppy said.

"Bankers sometimes have business interests other than banks," Dex reminded her. "Such as owning ships. So in case of urgent business, the owner's needs come first. Two of the passengers are bank employees returning to their foreign posts after being in San Francisco for consultation. Another is one of our most important customers, Señor Romero Riano. He owns one of the largest ranchos in Mexico."

"And the fourth?"

"A lady, but not quite your style. I find her a touch severe myself. A certain member of the diplomatic corps in Mexico City has been dissatisfied with the education his children are receiving. He wants instruction less completely Spanish, and yet he is reluctant to send his children home. As another of our bank's special services, I chanced to hear of this splendid young woman who was gravely dissatisfied with both San Francisco and the family she was attached to. I persuaded Miss Shillingforth to make a change."

With a long shudder, Poppy relaxed. "They sound most respectable."

"They are. You'll meet them."

"Do they know?" Poppy whispered.

"Only that at the last minute a rather impetuous lady decided to accompany me."

"Decided?" Poppy's eyes widened. "I was too thunderstruck to protest, sir. Shocked. I was fleeing, as you said. Only fleeing to get away. Did you think I would willingly accompany a man I heard discussing the disposal of my husband's body while he was still alive?"

Dex straightened. "Disposal? Body? What nonsense is this? You must have been keeping even lower company than I suspected. Your mind is tainted. Your thinking is corrupt. Can you possibly mean this unspeakable accusation?"

"I heard what I heard," Poppy protested, lips quivering.

"You heard us agreeing that a small bullet, weakly powered, had hit your husband's ribs and knocked the breath out of him. The breath, not the life, you ignorant numbskull. The skin was torn, and probably a rib was broken, but Wiggins agreed he could see no sign the lung was penetrated."

"And Josh is wonderful with wounds," Poppy cried with a gush of relief. "Of course. Of course. Maurice loaded the bullets just strong enough for target practice. I used them, not knowing, not thinking, just used them." She stumbled to a halt, blushing.

"Exactly," Dex said, quirking an eyebrow. "I judge this Maurice did not remind you of the difference? He was both discreet and correct."

"Oh, always," Poppy agreed.

"Loaded like that, the gun was enough to stop a man, but not enough to get you into serious trouble. Decidedly I must meet this Maurice someday. A good man to know, obviously."

"But Jeremiah," Poppy said and began to tremble. "What am I going to do about Jeremiah?"

"That is your decision," Dex shrugged. "As for Jeremiah, I hardly think he will want to advertise that his wife shot him. Or that his bride fled from him. I think you can depend that he will seize on Josh's hint and spread some suitable and respectable story to account for your absence. Does this ease your mind?" Dex shook his head, smiling. "So you pictured yourself a murderess?"

"I thought—" Poppy stammered, then buried her face in her hands, weeping helplessly.

Dex's hand touched her bright hair. "I'm sorry. I forgot. Such unfortunate accidents don't happen twice. You mustn't go through life fearing that every time you raise your hand to defend yourself, somebody will die. You mustn't be death haunted."

"After the Eureka," Poppy said. She raised her face and wiped her eyes, then said sedately, "I fear I was overwrought, sir."

Dex frowned. "If that is what you were thinking, and the only reason you came aboard with me, I assure you that you can return quite safely. Would you like me to pass the word to hail a small boat to take you back?"

"I—" Poppy began and got no further.

"Are you afraid of that man?" Dex asked sharply.

"I had my jewelry—" Poppy began with difficulty.

"It's safe in my pocket."

"I wanted Josh to tell me where I could sell it."

"I saw you walk down the wharf and look at this ship."

"Yes, I thought perhaps another town, a fresh start."

"So he's as offensive as he sounds," Dex said. "You are afraid to return to him."

"I was perhaps overly impetuous to wed him," Poppy admitted.

"As in everything."

"But I never intended to shoot him," Poppy cried. "Never. I only carried the gun to protect my jewelry. And perhaps to sell. Not to shoot."

"Indeed?"

"The trigger tangled in the strings of my reticule."

418

"We will grant that your reticule shot him," Dex said, his mouth twitching slightly. "Now as to this ship?"

"I did wish to leave San Francisco," Poppy said and remembered. "I have no clothes."

"You never do."

"And not with you," she added hotly.

"Nor did I mean to bring you," Dex said, smiling. "So shall we admit we are helpless victims in the hands of a relentless fate?"

"I'm not a child you can tease any more. I'm a woman with her way to make in—in—where are we going?"

"A quick passage to Mexico, we trust."

"That won't do."

"Then we must think and contrive another place."

"I have heard good reports of Oregon. Or Canada. That's English."

"This ship carries cargo all up and down the coast. Meanwhile, you are my most welcome companion. A gratifying addition to the ship's passenger list. The others are waiting to meet you, Mrs. Dunbar—no. Miss Smith—also no. Something more elegant, I think. Miss Parksmith, that's it, in honor of our first meeting. Do you agree?"

He drew her to her feet and to him. Poppy looked into his eyes and, as always, was lost.

"I agree."

"No," Dex said. "Let them wait. We'll plead fatigue, an exhausting race to reach the ship before it sailed. That should help conceal your identity. And we'll have dinner served in the cabin. Oh, Poppy, you are always such a beautiful fugitive."

She had been chilled, chilled to the bone, the cold of fear, of winter, of death, but as his arms closed around her, warmth flooded through her. She was uncomfortably warm, so flushed she longed to be free of her heavy outer clothes. As she realized what she was thinking and feeling, her face flushed, and her long lashes fluttered frantically.

His hands, his caressing, arousing hands, were as

swift as her thought. Deftly he removed her clothes and his own, and they fell across the bed. His body was young, strong, and purposeful, smooth skinned, hard muscled and in superb physical condition. His hands knew her body, the softnesses and tender, sweet hollows. She remembered the long, lean line of his back. His heavy head bent to her, and the warmth in her leapt into flame. She clasped him even closer and arched her body to fuse the two into one.

Chapter Forty-four

*D*RESSED in a skirt she had made from the finest white canvas in the ship's stores, and a blue cotton coolie jacket, Poppy sat in the small chair in the cabin and sewed. Among the Chinese goods the Captain was carrying to trade on his own account, she had found a bolt of white silk, and she was hemming neck scarves for the gentlemen and a handkerchief for the lady so that Christmas day on board the *Golden Dolphin* would not go unobserved.

Head bent demurely over her fine stitching, she wondered if The Rev would find her hopelessly irreverent if she dared to think this was paradise on earth. Paradise was perfection, and she had lived it every day of the past week. Although this was the stormy season, the weather had been warm, golden, and calm. She had not for one moment been queasy. The company was excellent. Señor Riano was the finest and most courtly gentleman she had ever met. His brown eyes expressed the greatest appreciation of her beauty, but in such a genteel mode that nobody could object. The two bankers, Mr. James and Mr. Phillipson, made up a most pleasurable table for cards each evening. Even horse-faced Miss Shillingforth, all six feet of her, had showed a great sweetness of disposition and had almost persuaded Poppy that with a little study a map could become something more than a patchwork of colors separated by those silly lines. Best of all Dex, except for a little refreshing conversation with the other gentle-

421

men or the Captain now and again, was always with her, all hers.

Now he was working on his letter box at the desk. He was debating with himself as he wrote and muttering answers to his own arguments. This new president, this Mariano Arista, the first ever installed constitutionally, was a good man. But could he last? A rumor of trouble, something about his having cut down on the army and the generals resenting it, had started Dex on this hurried trip. He wrote his letters and debated the other possibilities if Arista fell. Santa Anna was always there but at this time discredited. Later, perhaps. Alamán was a conservative, but there were stories he considered Santa Anna the only man strong enough to hold the country together. And the people in the cafés talked of the fine old days, the good days when there had been a viceroy from Spain. Whenever he muttered, "Viceroy," Dex shook his head, scowled, and sighed.

To make a companionable sound, to stop the scowling and sighing, Poppy asked, "Is there any real difference between these Mexicans? Don't they come and go, leaving the country much the same?"

"They have their little differences," Dex said drily. "For instance, Santa Anna sells tens of thousands of acres for millions of dollars and then throws the millions away like confetti."

"We bought them honestly, didn't we?"

"The United States did. Are you a Yankee now?"

She did not want to think about that. "Why is Mexico so important to you?"

"Mexico is a rich country, and our bank has its customers and interests, naturally. Mexico will be a great country someday. We want to be numbered among its friends when that day comes."

"So you must watch and walk carefully?"

"And if we can, avert trouble."

"Do you think you can stop a change in government?"

"Not this time or probably many times." Dex shook

his head. "We can be discreet, wait it out, assist where it seems wise. As long as the leaders are Mexican."

Poppy remembered the mutters. "Does Spain want to send a viceroy again?"

"Not Spain. Didn't I tell you once the royal houses of Europe have too many sons trained for thrones and too few thrones?"

"Yes. In Paris."

"They're prowling Mexico like hungry wolves. A rich country, abandoned by Spain, without a stable government as yet. So sooner or later, sooner or later. And it will be a disaster, bloodshed and bankruptcy, for everybody concerned."

Poppy caught her breath. "What can you do?"

Dex reached out and touched her hand. "I didn't mean to frighten you. I assure you it's not the English royal family or the French, and we can be grateful for that. Though the present French government is, shall we say, aware."

Remembering Dex's allusions to spies and the way he had hurried her out of Paris, Poppy nodded. She did not understand, but she caught a glimpse of the tangled webs of international intrigue and finance with which Dex dealt.

"When royal houses need money, they turn to the private bankers," Dex went on explaining.

"I know that."

"We finance their royal fights, flights, and fancies. Different banking houses for different royal houses. So our views and interests don't always agree."

Here in Mexico, did his and the Pannet interests run together or oppose? No, she would not make that excuse for him, that he danced attendance on Félicité only as a matter of business. He was besotted with her blond dullness. But he was here on the *Golden Dolphin* now, and all night his arms held her. She would not think beyond that.

"So it's more of the same, keeping a watchful eye out for the legits as well as the illegits." Poppy smiled.

"Right." Dex shut his box of papers. "I can't do

anything more until we touch at a Mexican port and get the news. The Captain predicts a record run if the weather holds."

"Mexico City," Poppy sighed with anticipation.

Once her dreams had not reached beyond a single night in his arms. Then even that dream had died. Now everything seemed to conspire to heap happiness on her.

For Dex had promised to take her to Mexico City with him, and the stay might last for weeks. He warned her the roads were poor, but with a well-sprung carriage and four sturdy horses, the trip was possible. Even if he had to ride ahead, she could follow. The distances were great, but she would see strange and wonderful things each day, massive ruins in the jungles left from the days before the Spanish came, small sweet valley towns with great cathedrals where she would stay at rustic adobe *posadas* and be quite safe. In a great valley like a cup, ringed round by magnificent mountains, was Mexico City. There she would see wealth flaunted as she had never dreamed. The palatial homes, the women's clothes, the jewels, the carriage promenades, and the balls were beyond description. He would buy her a fine wardrobe, see she had a smart little carriage, and they would live in the suite the bank maintained there. Even Paris could not compare with Mexico City, for life in Paris was set and circumscribed, hedged in by old rules and customs. Mexico City, for all its aristocratic, *hidalgo* tradition, was still young and colorful and raw in its wealth.

Mexico City, Poppy thought, would be like Paris and San Francisco, the best of both put together, and better than either. There with Dex, she felt, her destiny waited, glittering, alive, and incredibly rich.

"Tell me more about it," Poppy begged.

"An experience as highly spiced as its food," Dex warned.

"I've never met anything beyond my digesting," Poppy said demurely. "I'm counting the days and hours."

"We do not dine for two hours," Dex hinted.

Poppy widened her eyes innocently. "You had no tea?"

"You and Mexico City will understand each other," Dex said, shaking his head. "You are both shameless hussies, always thinking of a bribe."

"That is it?" Poppy demanded, not even trying to pretend. She looked at the cloth-wrapped package Dex had carried into the cabin before lunch. "A length of silk from the Captain's Chinese goods?"

"A length of silk? A bagatelle worth a few pieces of gold. This, I had to ransom. I thought he might ask a share of the ship."

He unwrapped the cloth and held up the dark blue silk robe. Poppy caught her breath as the sunlight from the window flashed on the magnificent embroidery in gold and peacock-bright silks. The pattern of rich reds, greens, and blues seemed to move and blend and burn together as if it were alive, with the gold glittering around and through the colors like licking flames.

"A mandarin's robe," Dex said with a little bow. "Almost as beautiful as the lady."

"Let me try it," Poppy gasped.

As she had known, as they had both known, the robe was forgotten once her clothes were put aside. Dex lifted her, swung her over on the bed, and gathered her into his arms, pressing her back against the pillows. In the old and yet always new magic that never failed to inflame her senses, his hands, lips, and body were molding her to his mastery. She put her arms around him, glorying in the strength of his hands on her flesh, of his strong body against her softness, his warmth heating her as she drew him closer and ever closer, eyes closing as his lips brushed her breast.

Suddenly the ship lurched, rolling heavily to one side with a force that tore Dex from her arms and flung him across the room, sprawled on the floor. The ship hung there while the two chairs, the screen, the china from the washtable, and the letter box edged free and rolled slowly across the cabin. Then all the books loosened at

425

once and rained down. Poppy clung to the bed, staring
at the slow progress of all the things as they slid neatly
down toward the far corner, at the impossible angle of
the floor that had hoisted her high above Dex, who was
scrambling now in the angle between deck and door to
try to get to his feet. Then with a long, groaning creak,
the ship settled slowly back on an even keel.

"But the sun's shining," Poppy whispered.

"That felt like a big wave," Dex panted, scrambling
to his feet. "From an earthquake somewhere."

Then once again the ship tilted, and he was flung
back with only time to wrap his arms around his head
before he hit the door with a cracking thud. Shocked,
Poppy loosed her hold on the bed and felt herself
pulled down and rolled across the cabin, until she slid
against Dex's shoulder and he caught and held her.
Again the ship hung as if it would never right itself,
hung in timeless suspense, until with an even deeper
groan, it settled back once more.

"Two big ones so close, that means if it was a quake
even underseas, it was a disaster somewhere," Dex said
grimly. "Let's hope that's all. Even this ship can't take
many more like that."

The ship was quiet with only the thud of feet and the
sound of quiet, urgent voices from the deck. Poppy
stumbled to her feet, dazedly righted the chair, and
fumbled for the beautiful robe. Big waves, Dex had
said. She could not believe anything could be so violent
and yet so slow. But she had felt it, had seen what it
could do. Then she realized something else impossible.
The living, burning colors of the robe in her hand were
dull and gray, not sparkling in the sun. Where was the
sunlight?

Then she heard a new sound, as incredible as all the
rest. There was a roar, which grew louder, until it was
a deafening torrent of sounds. It was all around them.
They were in the sound, and the ship hung there motionless for a few seconds before it corkscrewed violently from side to side, bow dipping and then rising high.
Poppy was flung back against the built-in desk, and she

clung to it. A great quiver went through the ship and then, as the ship reared then fell again convulsively, something thudded on the deck with a sound like thunder. The ship shivered from end to end and bounded wildly like a whipped horse.

"Hurricane?" Poppy whispered.

"Yes," Dex said, somehow already half dressed and pulling on his shoes. "That was the mainmast. They'll need help on deck. Get dressed, ready to abandon ship. I'll come back for you."

"No," Poppy cried, flinging herself on him and clutching him. "No, don't leave me. It's not true. It's not happening."

His hand slapped her sharply, first one cheek and then the other. "Stop screaming. It is happening. This is storm season, and the calm we've been enjoying was unnatural."

"This is unnatural."

"Call it unlucky, big waves and then a hurricane."

"Don't leave me."

"Our only chance is to cut that mast clear," Dex snapped. He freed her clinging hands and threw her on the bed. "I told you, get dressed and ready to abandon ship."

He fought the door open, and wind and water lashed inside like a living presence. When the door slammed behind him, the whistling roar of the wind and the deafening hiss of the rain, like whips cracking through the air, still filled her ears. Poppy clung to the bed, cringing. She must get dressed and ready to take a small boat, but with every crash of wind and water against the cabin window, she froze, unable to move. The seas were breaking right over the ship, and the ship was not rising to meet the waves but rolling sluggishly. The ship must be waterlogged, half sinking already. To take to a small boat in seas that were sinking a fine clipper? They would never get it launched.

Above the whistling and roaring, she could hear thuds, crashes, and shouts on deck. At least everybody had not been swept overboard. They would all go down together in the ship. She and Dex would die together. Since now she had nothing more to lose, she might as well do as he had ordered.

Staggering, clutching at the bed and the desk, thrown to her hands and knees more than once, she managed to get into her warm suit and put a padded Chinese jacket over that. She found her reticule with her jewels and put Dex's letter box close to her hand. She wished she could think of some noble sentiment for parting with Dex, but all she could feel was bitterness that she was being cheated of all the sweetness of life and love. She had barely tasted what they could be, and now there would be no more.

The door slammed open, and Dex braced himself and fought it shut again. "Towel," he said and began to tear off his jacket and shirt.

"Towel?"

"I'm soaked through. Any man can drown, but only a fool dies of pneumonia."

"Then we're not sinking?"

"Not in the next few hours, I trust. We cut the mast clear and only lost one man, swept overboard. There are a couple of cut heads and a broken arm, but they'll heal." Dex shed the last of his clothes, snatched a towel from the cabinet, and rubbed vigorously. "We've got a crack in our hull you could put your fist through, but our pumps are good. If we can ride out the night, we'll see in the morning what the damage is and where we are." He looked up and scowled. "Take off those ridiculous clothes and find me a clean shirt. Cook says he can manage some kind of dinner in half an hour."

In the dining saloon, the other passengers' faces made Poppy less ashamed she had panicked. Even stalwart Miss Shillingforth downed a surprising amount of the brandy Dex ordered for the table. Then he went to every cabin to supervise the lacing of straps on each bed and was adamant they must be buckled tightly. The danger of being drowned in bed was small. The chance of being thrown out and seriously injured was real.

The ship was still pitching in the morning, thudding

heavily, staggering through the heavy waves instead of mounting lightly over them. Poppy could hear nothing but the groans of the timbers, the wailing of the storm, and the steady thumping of the pumps. She could only glimpse ominous skies through the foaming crests of giant waves breaking over the rails.

On the second day, the storm abated its hurricane strength, but the rain poured down unceasingly. For Christmas, the cook produced fruitcakes put aboard by the Captain's wife, tarts made with her mincemeat, and roasted chickens. They made a small gala, with Poppy's gifts wrapped in thin red Chinese paper. Dex had two Chinese hairpins for her, enameled in blue, set with blue and green gems, and tasseled in gold.

Poppy knew vaguely they were far off course and some days they made almost no headway, barely holding their own against the wind and waves. The ship was sluggish, and a week passed before they even worked their way back into sight of shore. On New Year's Day, the Captain offered a prayer of thanks they were still afloat. More, Poppy knew, they now had a chance to make the shore in small boats if another storm widened that frightening gap in the hull.

Dex, even when he held her in his arms at night, was grim-faced and silent. The voyage was taking a week for every day he had planned.

She was awakened one morning by the sharp heaving of the ship and found herself alone. Tumbling into her clothes, she ran up on deck and saw they were anchored off a small fishing village. She could see a silver shore with crude huts scattered back of it under tall, exotic trees. Dex was already in a small boat, being rowed ashore.

When he returned, he and the three men passengers went straight to the Captain's cabin. Within minutes, the Captain came out, gave an order, and the sailors swarmed to the sails. With relief, Poppy saw they were still heading down the coast, not turning back to the States.

Dex's expression was bleak when he came to the cabin. "The government's fallen. I learned that much."

"What does that mean for you?"

"The ship is heading down the coast to a port large enough that the Captain can get the timber to jury-rig a mast and plug the leak. The others believe they will be safe enough from there if they can hire good horses and ride together. Miss Shillingforth assures me she was brought up in hunting country."

"And you?"

"I ride ahead immediately. Alone. I must get reports. Quickly. And return to meet the ship and send them back. She'll be ready to sail by then."

"And me?"

"I can't take you on a ride like that."

"But you are coming back?"

"Certainly. I'll know then what the situation is. If you wish to leave the ship, I'll hire a room for you in town."

"I'll wait here. This cabin is comfortable."

After his passengers left at the next port, the Captain was busy. He had cargo to unload. He had to see to repairing the storm damage to the ship, sufficient to get it back up the coast to a proper shipyard. He had his Chinese goods to sell, and cargo to load for the return.

A fresh-faced young sailor was assigned to row Poppy ashore and back again and to accompany her everywhere. She wandered around the town. She marveled at the shy women with their downcast eyes, Madonna-like faces framed in shawls, silent and elusive as deer on their bare feet. She liked the soft-walking men with their alert brown eyes and quick speech. The children seemed happy and loved, but they too ran from the strange foreign woman. She went to the native market and found a fleecy white shawl for her head and a pair of leather sandals. Tiring of the town, she found a beach deserted enough that she dared to take off her dress and petticoats and swim while the sailor stood guard. For dinners on the ship, the cook produced strange,

430

delicious fish doused in fresh lime juice, and crisp, flat cakes of a coarse corn meal.

The serenity and beauty of the place entranced her. The blue water, the silver beaches, the exotic flowering trees, the sound of singing and laughter drifting through the night air, all seemed perfection. More than ever she was sure this place was her destiny.

She did not count the days. Dex had urgent business, and he must ride far on it. He had said he would return, and whatever else Dex did, he did not lie. Three weeks passed before he returned.

He climbed aboard, looking brown and haggard, thinned down to bone and sinew. Pausing only to brush Poppy's lips with a kiss, he went straight to the Captain's cabin and stayed there, behind a closed door, for two hours.

By the time she was alone with Dex, she had already guessed. "The news was not good?"

"No. Alamán is taking over from the generals. I know what he advocates. A dictator, Santa Anna again probably, until a European prince can be found to accept a crown."

"That is everything you don't want."

"Everything." Dex dropped heavily into the chair by the desk and rested his head on his hand and stretched out his legs. "I can't do much, but I must stay and watch until this crisis at least settles for the moment. The great game is yet to come. That may take years."

Poppy bent her head to hide the happy smile on her lips. "When do we leave for Mexico City?"

"I start back within the hour. You sail with the Captain on the morning tide."

Poppy jumped to her feet. "No."

"This is a dangerous country, Poppy."

"Dangerous? These people? They are like sweet, gentle children."

"They are savages, Indians."

"You *do* lie," Poppy burst out. "You *do* lie! The one thing I always said you did not do. I have seen them, watched them. They are no more dangerous than a pet puppy dog."

"They can kill and tear and torture like mad dogs."

"You're lying," Poppy cried. "You don't want me. You're just looking for an excuse to send me back."

"I'm refusing to risk your life."

"You promised. You promised me Mexico City."

"A promise I must break."

"I won't let you. I'm coming ashore. I can ride. I can get there. I'll see you in Mexico City."

Dex stood up and pushed her into the upholstered chair. "Sit there and be quiet and listen to me. If I must, I'll lock you in this cabin and tell the Captain to keep it locked until he's at sea. You're sailing with the ship. So listen to me."

"You can make me listen, but you can't make me do it."

"Then listen. I must send you back with the ship. The *Dolphin*'s home port is San Francisco. Don't scream. Keep quiet. Listen. I'm not sending you back to the husband who arouses such dangerous impulses in your reticule."

"Then where are you sending me?" Poppy spat.

"Anywhere in the world you wish to go. You told me you wanted to make a fresh start. During the trip back, decide what you want. The Captain knows most of the ships that are in and out of port. He will arrange accommodations any place you want to go." Then hastily, "But not back to Mexico, of course."

"Are there any other places I'm forbidden to go?"

"I'd suggest you avoid the Continent," Dex said calmly. "Your unfortunate accident in the Vendée was unimportant, involving only minor figures in this network of intrigue. But the intrigue is still alive. In another year or two, it should be quite forgotten, but for the moment you might enjoy a more equable climate."

"You have suggestions?"

"The United States is a large country. Ships sail the Pacific to many interesting ports."

Out of sheer perversity, Poppy said, "Yes, I've heard many interesting things about Australia."

"Australia?" Dex grimaced slightly. "My sources of information do not reach that far. The choice is yours."

He was quite willing for her to sail away to a place where he would never see or hear of her again. Poppy stared at him, paling. Until then she had not really believed this conversation was taking place. The whole thing had seemed a grotesque joke, an unreal fantasy, a tease that only delayed the moment when Dex would take her in his arms and love her violently, fiercely, to make up for all the empty nights they had slept apart. Then there would be the weeks and months to follow, the dinners together in the small apartment, the carriage promenades, the balls, all the glitter of Mexico City spread out at their feet—their pleasure ground, their private festival of happiness. She had lived with that thought and dream for weeks, and now in minutes Dex was smashing it as casually as his hand might fall on a butterfly and crush it.

"I have been much impressed by the Australian men I have met," she choked.

"Indeed? The Captain will arrange your passage. I have also left money with him to give you for your needs while you are getting settled."

Poppy jumped up, standing tall. "He needn't arrange anything. I won't take your money. You gave me money once, and it nearly got us all killed, Andy and Jack and me. You won't send me on another voyage that's an invitation to murder."

Dex's eyes narrowed. "You complained once before about the gold, but you did not tell me you had trouble."

"Ask the Wigginses sometime. They saved us. And none of it need have happened if you had not been so ashamed of me or so careful of your reputation with sweet little Félicité that you wouldn't risk giving me a note of credit to the bank."

"I wouldn't risk it," Dex admitted blandly. "But not for the reasons you are giving. The Pannets are closely tied to the Austrians, and that matter in the Vendée was still rather widely remembered then. Besides, I sent a man to guard you. That went awry, and I had no way of knowing."

"Knowing what?"

"He suffered a fall before you were out a week, and was killed."

Poppy remembered Andy breaking into the cabin and asking if she wanted to go to a funeral. "That was your man?"

"One of my best. A tragic accident. For everybody apparently."

"Just the same, I want nothing from you," Poppy said stormily. "Except what you promised, Mexico City."

"And I only wish to see you settled and safe," Dex said. "The life I lead is neither. So you sail back with the *Dolphin*. You have only to let the Captain know your wishes, and he will do his best to provide all you need." He turned and walked out of the cabin.

Poppy took one impetuous step after him and then froze, realizing something. She tugged out the drawers of the chest and the desk. Then she was sure. Everything belonging to Dex was gone, had been removed probably while she was ashore this morning. Only her things were left. Dex must have sent a message to the Captain. Dex had known he was leaving her. The Captain had known it. She was the only one who had not.

He was gone. She heard the soft splash of oars as the ship's boat pulled away for the shore of Mexico.

Part Eight

San Francisco
Early Spring 1853

Chapter Forty-five

THE *Golden Dolphin* sailed into the bay that afternoon under a light, steady breeze and a brilliant
sun. The rains must have been heavy because the hills
and island glowed a rich green, lightened here and there
by great drifts of golden poppies. As they sailed through
the clear blue water, so unlike the gray English sea,
Poppy saw San Francisco was still spreading up the
hills from the valleys. The aspect was beautiful, but she
could have wept with helpless rage that the long arms
of land were closing around her like the bars of a cage,
a dreadful jail to which she must commit herself for
life, from which there could be no pardon.

She was not landing here only to find another ship,
on which she could sail away forever from all the old
ties and memories to a new and free life she could
make for herself. She was going ashore here, aground
forever, in this strange, beautiful, violent city. She must
go straight to Jeremiah and beg to be allowed to resume
her position as his wife.

When she first suspected she was pregnant, she had
gone to the Captain's cabin on the pretext of asking for
a calculation of their arrival date, and had feverishly
consulted his calendar. Back at the desk, she had jotted
down dates and confronted the inexorable facts. By the
time they landed she would be two months pregnant,
nothing noticeable, but she had not seen Jeremiah for
over three months. She could leave San Francisco again,
without seeing him, and go anywhere she liked and an-
nounce she was a widow, left with ample funds. She

could have Dex's baby in comfort and security. Except she knew too well the smirks and whispers that would follow them all their lives. A beautiful young widow? No sign of any family, paternal or maternal? The usual pathetic story. Everybody would be polite to their faces and whisper "illegitimate" behind their backs. She would not bear a child and have it labeled. She knew too well the price Andy had paid and would always pay, the opportunities for education and work denied, the social stigma. She would not have her child an illegit.

· Better to return to Jeremiah and beg. He might throw her out, call her a harlot and whore, and then she would have to find another place. But she did not think he would do that. His vanity, pride, and standing were all involved. If he cast her off and named her unfaithful, he was that pitiful figure, a man who could not hold his wife, and he knew better than any what his weakness was there. He would hardly risk that she might be brazen enough to whisper in turn "impotent."

If he took her back, his beautiful young wife was a social and political asset. He would be delighted to have a child as proof of his virility and proof to his public that he was a solid family man. He might pretend, even to her, that the child was his and accept it as premature. Once she was back with him, Poppy knew he would never let her go. This would be ignoble bondage for life. But she would fight to see that her child gained everything possible from it.

She did not want Dex to have any hint of this. He had cast her off, brutally, left her to find her own future. And she would. She would never let him know this child existed, that he had a child.

Because she knew he would report to Dex, she carefully measured her words to the Captain. "I have friends ashore I wish to consult before I make any decision about my future. Possibly one of them will have a suggestion I wish to accept. If that is so, I will have no need of your kind offices."

The Captain looked troubled. "You will let me know?"

"You will be in port a while?"

"The new mainmast, repairs, yes."

Once she was publicly reconciled with Jeremiah, nobody could do or say anything. "You will know," Poppy promised.

They were drawing close to the wharf. She must force herself to smile at the sailors and the Captain and speak a few words of thanks. They had done all they could to make the slow, halting trip pleasant. She could not tell them she had been grateful for every delay while they worked to plug once more the great break in the hull. They knew she had been languid and distressed, but she hoped they had put it down to grief at her parting from Dex. They could not know her sick dread of facing Jeremiah.

She could not bring a sparkle to her eyes or a lilt to her voice, but she kissed the Captain impulsively as she thanked him. She saw the concerned look on the face of the sailor who handed her down the gangplank and told her to wait on the wharf while he ran to fetch a carriage.

Waiting, her courage failed her. She felt too weak and shaken to walk up the steps of the boardinghouse and face first Mrs. Stander and then Jeremiah in those rooms with all their degrading memories. She was not ready, even now.

Even as she smiled and thanked the sailor when he handed her into the carriage, she heard herself, without knowing what she was going to say, blurting out the address of Phillipa's hotel. Then she knew sheer instinct was guiding her, and it was good. Phillipa must have married weeks ago, but the hotel was respectable. She could stay there and inquire if Mr. and Mrs. Wilton were in town. They were her friends. They could tell her what had been happening, what story had been told to account for her absence. With that information, she could face Jeremiah forearmed.

Thinking only that her suit was sadly wrinkled and her luggage makeshift, she got out in front of the hotel. To her surprise, the carriage dispatcher there recognized her and remembered. Her friends, he assured her before she could inquire, were within, taking tea in the blue room off the lobby. With a gasp of relief, Poppy motioned him to take her luggage and almost ran inside.

Across the red carpet, beyond a shield of potted palms, she saw Phillipa sitting in a small side parlor demurely pouring tea for Mr. Wilton. She sprang up when she saw Poppy, gave a soft cry, ran to meet her, and threw her arms around her.

"Glory be to God, you're home and safe."

"Glory be, you're here," Poppy breathed.

Mr. Wilton, hand extended, came to draw them back into the small parlor. "Welcome home. You've come for the dinner?"

"What dinner?"

"Ring for another cup, Phillipa," Mr. Wilton said. "Our guest has just arrived in town. She must be tired and in need of refreshment."

Poppy sank into a gilt chair beside the table holding the elaborate tea service on a silver tray. "Refreshment in many senses. I have been out of touch."

"Completely?"

"Completely." She knew Mr. Wilton to be an astute man, and she trusted him. "A long sea voyage."

"Some three months or more, I think?"

"Yes." Head high, Poppy looked straight into his eyes. "What was said about my absence?"

"That your health was poor, and you were staying in the country. A touch of lung trouble, in consequence of that old wound, I believe."

"Anything else?"

"Your husband was reported prostrate with grief and worry for a few days."

"Where in the country?"

"Would it be inconvenient if people checked the lists of ships arriving and departing on certain dates?" Mr. Wilton hinted.

Poppy went white. Shipping men knew who owned the *Golden Dolphin* and would recall her unscheduled departure and limping return.

Mr. Wilton needed no answer. "I believe then you have been at the hot springs for your health. I have a widowed sister-in-law who is sure to recall seeing you there." He wrote neatly on a small card and held it out. "This is her name and address."

"Now I am forever indebted to you," Poppy said unsteadily as she took it.

"Just as long as you're back to see me through my wedding," Phillipa cried. "Oh, Poppy, darling, I have been in a frenzy, but with you I won't have an anxious moment."

"I have been in fear I might never get her to the altar without your support," Mr. Wilton admitted drily. "Our house is sufficiently completed and partially furnished. We could move in, but I have not been able to persuade my bride."

"Once when he tried to press me, I went into a deep swoon," Phillipa admitted and leaned forward tensely. "I can't do it alone, Poppy. There's so much I don't know. Is it a dozen sheets for each bed or a dozen for all the beds? And the initials?"

Mr. Wilton patted her hand. "Poppy will help you with all that later. Meanwhile, there is this great dinner tonight, three hundred guests, I understand."

"Won't you be there?"

Mr. Wilton's lips thinned. "When you married Mr. Dunbar, I was willing to reconsider the opinion I formed of him in 1851 when the city was bankrupt. Then after the bond issue—but all this is beside the point. Since your departure and since he acquired the backing of the Pannets—no, I will not be attending this dinner in his honor. A fund raising, among other things, to promote his candidacy later this year."

To Poppy, one thing was of first importance. "You deal with Dexter Roack?"

"We do business together, yes." Mr. Wilton spoke so curtly Poppy realized he knew the ownership of the *Golden Dolphin* and who had been aboard at the last sailing but did not wish to discuss that. "Our relationship has always been highly satisfactory."

"The Pannets are another banking house entirely?"

"Rivals, in fact. As I understand their European connections, Mr. Roack's house deals mainly with the British government and the old regime in France. Mr. Pannet's bank is reputed to be closer to the present Emperor and the Austrian royal family."

"Of course there are mergers by marriage."

"And courtesies between rivals who sometimes need each other's good will."

Poppy nodded. This confirmed what Dex had told her.

"That again is beside the point," Mr. Wilton said. "Your appearance at this dinner would be a most propitious signal of your return to the city. And to your husband. If that is what you wish."

Poppy understood. Mr. Wilton thought it wise for her to appear with Jeremiah in public where he would be forced to treat her graciously. Then later he would not dare reject her on some pretext.

Phillipa, uninterested in either business or innuendos, had been wriggling with impatience. Now she burst out, "People will expect you to wear a grand gown, something splendid. Have you had anything new since you married?" She clapped both hands over her mouth and looked at Poppy with contrite eyes before she cried, "Oh, darlin', I said nothing to the other ladies, only to Mr. Wilton, but I couldn't help noticing you never put your hand in your pocket like everybody else."

Mr. Wilton said, "Phillipa is to have her own money and no accounting asked. A man should do no less for his wife."

There was another reason he did not like Jeremiah, Poppy realized. "The dress I wore to the theater is handsome."

"People will remember it," Phillipa said impatiently and turned to Mr. Wilton. "You recollect the blue, the one you said was too heavy and fussy, that you didn't like? The one I selected for myself?"

"A handsome dress, but a trifle matronly for a bride," Mr. Wilton said and consulted his watch. "The dinner begins in less than an hour, hardly time to go home, greet your husband, and change your apparel. You could appear in good time if you would permit Phillipa to dress you here. The gown will become you mightily, and I will never permit her to wear it. At least not when I am her escort."

"Which means never," Phillipa cried, clasping her hands. "Oh, Poppy, please do. It is a handsome gown, and it would be a pity to waste it."

"Most suitable for a young matron joining her husband at an important affair," Mr. Wilton approved and stood up. "I suggest you ladies go to Phillipa's rooms now. I'll send the luggage up to you, and I'll have a carriage waiting when you are ready."

He was again advising and guiding her strongly. He was right. If she confronted Jeremiah first in public, before his admirers and supporters, he must receive her warmly or make a degrading scene from which his reputation would never recover. If tears had not been a luxury she could not afford, Poppy could have wept in gratitude. They were making everything unbelievably easy for her.

While she pulled off her suit and washed, Phillipa produced the dress. Of dark blue taffeta, the skirt was all ruffles curled back to show the lighter blue linings, like the petals of a half-open rose. The bodice was heavily beaded in the same light silvery blue. Even holding it up to show, the heavy materials and colors almost wiped out Phillipa's delicate beauty.

"It's not for you," Poppy agreed. "But I must pay you for it." Then as Phillipa's lips quivered, she said, "We'll settle that another time."

Phillipa cried, "Oh, it's so good to have you back. Can you wear the matching slippers? You feet are smaller, but these tie around the ankles."

Poppy brushed her hair into a high coronet held by the jeweled Chinese pins. With those, the gold necklace, the jade earrings and pale blue gloves, she knew she would decorate any banquet table handsomely. Then for her entrance, she put on the mandarin robe glittering in all its barbaric beauty. What Jeremiah would do when she appeared, a regal shining figure, she did not know, but he was adroit at seizing his public opportunities.

"You're enough to win him the nomination all by yourself," Phillipa said naively. "They got up this big dinner, you know, because there's been so much criticism and public feeling."

"Public feeling? Because I haven't been at his side?"

"That wouldn't have made Mr. Wilton vow he would fight him to his last breath."

"Then why is Mr. Wilton being so good to me?"

"You are our friend," Phillipa said. "No, it was the shooting." Then she clapped her hands over her mouth again. "Oh, you didn't know that, either. I think I shouldn't have told you."

"What shooting?" Poppy said tightly.

"The editor, Amberson, the one who was always writing such editorials about Mr. Dunbar."

"Jeremiah shot him?"

"Met him on the street and dared him to fight."

"Not for the first time," Poppy remembered. "And Amberson did?"

"That's what was so terrible," Phillipa confided. "Mr. Amberson always said political differences could not be settled by guns. Only there he was with one in his hand. People say," Phillipa's voice sank to a whisper, "somebody shoved it into his hand, and the minute he saw it there, Mr. Dunbar shot. They had it all planned."

Poppy sank into a chair. "I can't go through with it. I don't care. It doesn't matter. I can't be married to a man like that."

"But you've got to go, Mr. Wilton thinks you should," Phillipa wailed. "He wouldn't have said about the dress and the carriage and everything if he hadn't thought you should go. It isn't as if Mr. Amberson was killed dead."

"Just killed?"

"Not killed at all. Just shot a little so his paper only missed a couple of issues. He's writing it right there from his bed in the print shop. Only I think he must be out of bed by now."

Poppy stood up slowly. She felt incredibly old and tired. "Then since my husband only planned a murder and did not succeed, perhaps I should join him." In a terrible way, she thought, they were two of a kind. She, too, had shot and had been fortunate she had not killed. "No, I'm all right, Phillipa, dear. You'll hear from me tomorrow."

All during the ride to the hall where the dinner was being held, Poppy thought it was as well she was too numbed with shock to feel anything strongly. She could only walk in, making her glittering appearance, head high, and wait to see what happened. Jeremiah would do whatever he considered of benefit to himself. She doubted he would point a finger at her and publicly label her a Jezebel. That would reflect on him too badly. More likely, as Mr. Wilton confidently expected —and Mr. Wilton was a shrewd man—whatever Jeremiah felt, he would force himself to welcome her back as his beautiful helpmate providentially returned for a gratifying and important occasion.

She walked into the building and stood for a moment by the great double doors, looking in without being seen. The hall was brilliantly lit and gaudily decorated in red and white, with streamers hanging from the ceiling and banners draped around the walls proclaiming "Dunbar, Duty, Democracy"; "Dunbar for Order"; and "Dunbar, Devotion, Decision." The air was thick with cigar smoke, heavy perfumes, and the stench from the flaring lights, so the bowls of red and white roses on the great horseshoe-shaped table were already drooping. Jeremiah was seated on a raised dais in the center of the horseshoe. Behind him, a band was playing deafeningly loud. Obviously dancing was intended later, for the vacant center floor was highly waxed.

Peering through the smoky haze, trying to hear above the thumping of the band and the clamor of voices, Poppy was tempted for a moment to turn and flee. She could see the men, some black-suited, some in brilliant

445

dress uniforms, and the ladies with jewels shining in their hair, but she could recognize nobody. Then a waiter saw her hovering and bustled forward officiously.

"Have you a ticket, miss?"

"I'll sit beside my husband," Poppy said clearly and swept into the hall.

She paused deliberately in front of the doors, a glittering regal figure, while every head in the room seemed to turn toward her. She fancied the music faltered for a moment. On the dais, Jeremiah rose to his feet, leaning forward tensely, supported by his hands on the table, staring through the smoke-filled air. Poppy swept around the side of the room, walking toward him, and now she recognized faces from her wedding reception. She smiled and nodded to them. She noticed a number of the men were there without their wives. Perhaps her absence, though smoothly explained, had hurt him. She walked steadily forward until she faced Jeremiah and looked at him with steady, level eyes.

"Have you saved no seat for me?" she asked in a clear, carrying voice.

"My dear wife," Jeremiah whispered. "My dear wife. How did you get here?"

Again she had knocked the breath out of him, Poppy thought grimly. "You did not think I would miss your great occasion? I only regret my coach was so delayed I had time only to change on the way and come directly here."

Jeremiah straightened, and color flooded back into his face. She had reminded him that this was his great occasion and she was his wife, come to do him public honor. "My dear," he cried strongly, "my very dear. I had given up hope you would feel you could come. Everybody, move down. Make a place for my wife."

Plates were pushed aside, and chairs shoved together to leave a space beside Jeremiah. A waiter brought another chair, placed it, and Poppy sank into it gracefully and smiled around.

"What a happy and handsome company you have here. I am well returned, indeed."

"Indeed," Jeremiah said, his voice sinking to a menacing growl for a breath before he smiled widely under eyes that regarded her with stony coldness. "Are you sure your health will stand this strain?"

Poppy turned her head and smiled again all around the room. She could not meet his look because she was suddenly cold with fear. In public, she was Jeremiah's dear wife. In private, she did wonder what her health would be. That had been a threat, and Jeremiah had meant her to understand it as such. Remembering the way he had torn her wedding dress to shreds, she knew he was capable of anything once they were alone. It would be, she thought, chilling even while she picked up a fork and pushed the food around her plate, something as deadly and as unprovable as the attack on Amberson.

"You are a brave woman to make this great effort, Mrs. Dunbar," the man on her other side said.

"My health is excellent, never better," Poppy said loudly.

"You are right, she is a brave little woman," Jeremiah said, catching her hand and crushing it in his. "You are here, my dear, that is enough. Do not strain yourself with the effort of talking."

"I will be listening to your speech," Poppy said, widening her eyes, and made one more effort to protect herself. "Mr. Wilton will be interested to have me report to him tomorrow what you have said."

"Why should Mr. Wilton be interested?"

"Because I have been much with his sister-in-law these last months."

Jeremiah's eyes were contemptuous and hate-filled above smiling lips. "I know the company you keep, dear lady. Now please give the appearance at least of enjoying this food."

Chapter Forty-six

*P*OPPY went on smiling, but she felt her face go
white. Jeremiah intended to punish her, every day
and every hour. In public, appearances would be maintained. In private, her life would be a hell of brutality.

"Mr. Wilton is not here tonight," the man on her
other side observed.

He was somebody from Sacramento, but she could
not remember his name. She tried to shore up the frail
timbers of the Wilton protection around her. "He is
much preoccupied with his approaching marriage. Phillipa has been insistent that I return to town for it."

"But he did not accompany you?" Jeremiah sneered.

"Since there is so much shooting in the streets, as
usual he was kind enough to loan me his carriage,"
Poppy said.

She had angered Jeremiah afresh. Now he was white,
and his lips were a thin line of barely controlled rage. She
would pay for that remark when they were alone.

On her other side, the man whispered into her ear,
"Is Wilton withholding his support because of that affair? He and who else? Many others?"

Poppy saw the red flicker deep in Jeremiah's eyes.
He had heard. "I have been out of town," she excused
unsteadily.

"Then it will reflect," the man said sharply. Just then
there was a stir by the big double doors.

They swung open, and the loud hum of conversation
in the room died down to a shocked silence as Amberson strode into the center of the empty, shining floor.

He was carefully dressed in a light gray suit with the coat slung over his shoulders. His right arm was in a sling, but a gun dangled from his left hand.

Beside her, the man from Sacramento pulled away whispering, "Under the table. He's a lefty. Last time the gun was in his right hand, and Dunbar never could explain that."

"So these are the people who think you worthy of public office," Amberson said, standing erect and quiet and letting his gaze turn slowly all around the horseshoe-shaped table. "I disagree. Bring up your gun, Dunbar. I'll give you the chance you didn't give me, a fair exchange of shots."

"I'm not armed. I don't carry a gun. Guards! Remove this man!"

Nobody stirred as Amberson stood waiting, his gun still hanging by his side. "Shall I give you a count?" he asked.

"I have no gun," Jeremiah shouted. "This is a respectable dinner, and you are disturbing the ladies. Please leave."

"I'll be happy to accompany you outside," Amberson offered.

"I have no gun. I won't shoot."

"You won't force me to appear the murderer here."

The company around the table stirred, and a sharp buzz of conversation rippled over the room. Poppy sensed somebody had moved close behind her, but she dared not turn to look. She could not look away from Amberson's slender figure, his brilliant eyes shining in his haggard face.

"You corrupt everything you touch, Dunbar. I see your fine mottos, but I am doing less than my duty as a citizen of this democracy if I do not protest openly and demonstrate by every means in my power that you are unfit for public office."

"If it's a debate you want," Jeremiah said, his voice loud with relief.

"You forced this manner of debate on me. Now you

are demonstrating you are a coward." Amberson broke off, his feverish gaze shifting past and above Jeremiah's head to somebody behind him.

"Now you mustn't say that about our brave Fire Captain," a voice drawled. A black-coated arm came over the table and laid a gun at Jeremiah's hand. "She's all cocked and set to go, Cap'n."

Jeremiah stared down at the gun as at a deadly reptile. Then with a convulsive backward jump, he overturned his chair and started to his feet, hands outflung to avoid touching the gun. But Amberson was slowly raising his, pointing it with lethal steadiness straight at the white shirt front.

"Shall I give you a count, or do you want to check the loading?" he asked evenly.

Jeremiah made a strangled sound deep in his throat, and his hand darted toward the gun, clutching it and shooting even as he raised it. Amberson's shot followed seconds later, and Jeremiah reeled back, his face dissolving in a blur of red, spattering blood.

"You know where to find me," Amberson said, then turned and walked out of the hall.

The black-coated arm jerked Poppy away and turned her face against his shoulder. "Don't look, Miss Poppy," said a voice she remembered from the Palace. It was Pete, the bartender. "Come on. Let me get you out of here."

"I—I—"

"There's nothing you can do," Pete insisted, still urging her along the wall of the building away from the huddle of bodies surrounding the heap on the floor. Then he said anxiously, pulling back enough to look down into her face, "You hate me to touch you, Miss Poppy, because I handed over that gun?"

"Why should I?" Poppy whispered through the long shudders that were shaking her from head to toe.

"I figured Amberson got dealt from a crooked deck last time, and he was entitled to a fair shootout," Pete said simply. "He's a good man, and he deserved it."

"Just get me a carriage," Poppy whispered.

"I'll see you to your boardinghouse."

The days that followed would never come clear in Poppy's mind. She had a mental picture of Mrs. Stander hurrying into the hall as if to bar and hold her there, and then her shocked gray face when the waiter explained the situation. She knew she stumbled up to the rooms of her wretched memories, and little Mary appeared to light the lamps and fire. She knew the next day she managed to talk to officials and lawmen and nod assent to something referred to as arrangements. She knew proper mourning clothes appeared from somewhere. She managed to get into them, ride alone in a carriage to the church, and then in the mile-long funeral procession to the cemetery. She knew she went back alone to the rooms, and time passed, and she saw nobody but Mary. Somehow she learned, perhaps Mary told her, perhaps she read a paper, that a hearing was held, and Amberson was released with a mild reprimand. Jeremiah dead had no supporters who felt strongly enough to come forward and demand vengeance.

Then Mrs. Stander was before her, hands folded at her waist. She said something about the rooms.

"Move?" Poppy said dazedly.

"I'm not running a hotel with fancy service, ma'am, and you've not been down to a meal in ten days. This is a boardinghouse, and I need these rooms for boarders. I've a long waiting list."

"Of course, of course." Poppy pushed the heavy hair back from her forehead. "I don't wish to stay here. Of course not."

"When will it be convenient for you to leave, ma'am?"

The woman's animosity, her dislike that was out in the open now that Jeremiah was not there to curb it, pulled Poppy to her feet. She looked around her, the daze clearing from her eyes. "All these things," she murmured.

"They can be packed and sent wherever you like."

"No, I couldn't live—I mean, I'll need only my clothes," Poppy said and then sharply, "Is there a bill owing?"

Some secret triumph flickered back in the cold eyes. "I can make up my accounts and communicate with your lawyers."

The woman hated her and literally could not endure her presence under this roof, Poppy realized. She had been right. There was some old association between Jeremiah and Mrs. Stander. They were of much the same age and, now that she thought of it, they had much of the same rigidity of manner and speech, and secretiveness about their pasts. She would never know what it was, and she did not care. She only wanted to be away from this place and its memories of misery and degradation.

"I'll have to see about other accommodations," Poppy said.

"Mr. Wilton and his lady have twice left cards and inquired when it would be convenient for them to call."

"Was I told?"

"Mary brought up the cards."

Mary had brought up many cards from calls of condolence, and she had barely glanced at them. She did not think Mary had delivered any special messages, and she wondered at the omission. "Please find a messenger to take a note and return with an answer. I am asking Miss Phillipa and Mr. Wilton to tea and will require a suitable collation."

"Yes, ma'am, thank you, ma'am," Mrs. Stander said, almost openly mocking now. "Immediately, ma'am."

Poppy pulled back the heavy curtains and had Mary run out and find flowers to freshen the room. Now she was once more almost herself, though she was surprised to find she was unsteady on her feet.

When Phillipa walked in, her face rosy under the frame of her fur bonnet, exuding an atmosphere of fresh cold air and happiness, Poppy flung her arms around her. "How good to see you," she cried. "How good of you to come. And you, Mr. Wilton, too."

Over her teacup, Phillipa spoke of the thing upper-most in her mind. "Mr. Wilton says he won't wait a year for you to be out of mourning, Poppy."

"For your wedding? Of course not. That would be nonsense."

"I should think it would be quite proper for you to attend," Mr. Wilton said.

"As a guest at the church, if I slip in quietly and leave again before the festivities, yes," Poppy agreed.

"I had so hoped for a state of perfection," Phillipa sighed.

For the first time since her return, Poppy smiled. "Not in this world."

"If you are there, where I can see you, I think I can go through with it in a mode designed not to disgrace Mr. Wilton," Phillipa admitted, long lashes fluttering.

"Of course you can. When will it be?"

"As soon as possible, within the month," Mr. Wilton said.

"I must find other quarters," Poppy said.

"Of course." Mr. Wilton looked around him with distaste. "Old associations, tragic memories, Mrs. Stander," he murmured.

"What do you know of Mrs. Stander?"

"Only that I understand she and Mr. Dunbar arrived in San Francisco together, and there was a distant but definite familial connection," Mr. Wilton said, raising an eyebrow. "You did not know? I could be mistaken."

"I knew there was some old association," Poppy nodded. "Distant. Not of importance now."

"Decidedly not," Mr. Wilton said. "Where do you propose to live?"

"I have a house," Poppy said. If Maurice had called and left a card, she had brushed it aside with the others. "It may be rented."

"Have you consulted with Mr. Dunbar's attorneys about your circumstances?"

"Mrs. Stander mentioned them, in connection with her bill, but I don't even know who they are."

"Let me inquire and send someone to you. You should talk to them before you make definite plans."

"Yes, please," Poppy said gratefully. "And soon?"

Mr. Wilton gave her a sharp look. "Very soon. Tomorrow, if possible."

As always, Mr. Wilton was as good as his word. A young attorney, a junior member of the firm, arrived before lunch, and after he had explained the basic facts, left a sheaf of papers for Poppy to study further. In answer to a message, Maurice called on his way to the Palace and spent an hour. After she was alone, Poppy realized her choices had narrowed and simplified. Maurice had good tenants in the house, a dealer at the Palace and his wife, a clever little woman who had made a new position for herself, one that left The Boss shaking his head and smiling with satisfaction at the same time, that of housekeeper for the Palace. It did shine these days, Maurice said. When it came to housekeeping there was nothing like a woman's touch. He urged her to keep them as tenants. They paid well and regularly. She agreed.

The sheaf of papers the lawyer had left required more thought. Jeremiah had spent money as if he had large funds at his disposal, but he had few assets, small pieces of property here and there, sure to grow in value, but they did not represent wealth. The lawyer frankly did not know the source of his income, although he was certain some of the money represented funds given in hopes of future political benefits.

She could live modestly on the rents from the various properties, Poppy decided. But she was not a woman of wealth. She would have to take careful thought to the future of herself and her child.

She was sitting by the fire, head bent over the papers, when someone knocked on the door. It burst open, and Phillipa stood there, glowing with happiness.

"Oh, Poppy, this is schoolgirlish of me to come without sending a note," she babbled. "But tomorrow, could you—would you—would it be proper for you to come to some of the shops with me?"

"Come in. Take off your coat. Let me ring for Mary to bring us some tea. Now what is this about the shops?"

"I need you," Phillipa said, throwing off her coat and bonnet. "I've looked and looked, and I know what I like but, Poppy, without you, I don't want to choose definitely. I'm not sure what's right." Her eyes grew wide with remembered dismay. "Like the blue dress."

"I think it would be quite proper," Poppy decided. "After all, I must select at least two mourning outfits for myself."

"Only two? But you'll be in black for a year."

"I needn't buy them all at once," Poppy said lightly. Because, she thought, the clothes she bought now would not fit her in a few months.

"We have it settled," Phillipa confided. "Mr. Wilton talked to the minister about the arrangements for the church today, and he'll have one of his clerks send out the invitations. Isn't it good of him to take care of things that other men put as a burden on the bride?"

Because he knows you could not do it, Poppy thought fondly, and if he hoped I could, he knows I have my own arrangements to make now. Though he cannot guess the whole of it. "He is very good," she agreed. "When is the date?"

"In three weeks," Phillipa said. "We have a choice of two steamships for our trip. Mr. Wilton will decide. We will be away a month."

Two months before they returned from their honeymoon. She would be five months pregnant, and everybody would know. If she had rejoined Jeremiah, people would have accepted a premature baby. But they would not accept one born so long after she had lived with her husband. That was obvious, but she had been too shocked and dazed to think of it until now.

"By the time we return, the ships from Europe should have brought the stained glass and marble Mr. Wilson ordered," Phillipa said. "The house will be so grand, with a ballroom and picture gallery. Even the servants' rooms upstairs are big as a house by themselves. Do you know there are fifteen bedrooms?"

"You told me when we were talking about sheets. A dozen for each room."

"Oh, Poppy, sometimes I can't believe it."

"I can, and I know you're going to be the happiest couple in town."

Though she said nothing, she knew her decision by the time Phillipa left. For the first time, she finished everything on the dinner tray Mary brought her. Then instead of Mary, Mrs. Stander knocked and came in. She stood looking down at the empty dishes.

"You are feeling better now that you have seen your friends."

"And decided what I am going to do," Poppy said. "I'll be leaving here tomorrow morning." She would be comfortable at the same hotel as Phillipa.

"You talked to the attorney?"

"Of course."

"It's all satisfactory?"

"I think I understand the situation, the various properties Mr. Dunbar held."

"You have the list there?" The woman's hand quivered toward the sheaf of papers Poppy had left strewn on a table. "Everything?"

"I hope so." She owed this woman no explanation. Yet perhaps something, because of the past, her clouded association with Jeremiah, should be said, and the truth could do no harm. "Four small properties, probably shanties from the size of the rents, and six or eight, I've forgotten, vacant lots. I've not seen any of them."

"That's all?"

"No debts, at least," Poppy said. "Or small ones only. Like yours. Do you know of anything else?"

"Nothing." The woman's face was radiant with relief for a moment and then darkened with suspicion. "Nothing about me?"

"You expected a legacy?"

"Nothing about me?"

"No, nothing."

456

"Then it's finished, it's finished," Mrs. Stander said and looked around the room as if saying goodbye to something, before she turned to Poppy, eyes hot with contempt. "For the suspicions I've seen in your eyes, I'll give you something to chew on. Jeremiah and me, we grew up together, I was trained to run a fine house in the hopes I'd make a good marriage. My part of the family had no money. Jeremiah, he was to have it all—the fine education, everything. We were too distant to be raised equal but too close for marriage. But when Jeremiah's folks died, he said goodbye to all that education and the rest, and we came out here with his money. He had his scruples about marriage. T'ain't good for the children to marry relatives, they say. Instead he built this house, and he swore it was in my name, and with the money it made, he built his career. If he hadn't decided he had to have a pretty doll, and things started going wrong from the day he saw you, he would have been one of the great men in this state. Great, the greatest. Maybe in the country!" Her voice had risen almost to a wail.

Poppy tried not to shrink back. The woman sounded half mad. So she might be, momentarily, grieving for the loss of the man she had loved all her life, and doubly bitter because she could not acknowledge it openly.

"I can see why you want me out of here," Poppy said quietly. "I can pack my clothes, that's all I'll be taking, and be out of here in the morning. I'll be staying in San Francisco only for the Wilton wedding. Then I'm sailing for England."

Part Nine

London
Summer 1853

Chapter Forty-seven

POPPY maneuvered her heavy body down the narrow stairs of the cottage at Pallminster Lane, burst into the living room, and threw herself into Jack's arms. He hugged her gently, then held her off and looked at her and shook his head.

"Widow's weeds and the child not yet born. Oh, Poppy, what tragedy is this?"

She could not dance a jig of impatience, but she settled herself in a chair and motioned to Jack to take one opposite her. "The tragedy is months past. Please respect my sensibilities and do not ask me to tell you everything. I have newspapers you can read if you must know the whole."

"I only want you to forget all unhappy things. You are here now. My carriage met you and brought you safely from the ship?"

"Thank you, yes, dear Jack. We were lucky we spotted that fast clipper two weeks back and were able to send letters to precede us to England. But I also wrote to Daisy. And why this house? And when did you get back? And where is Andy? I am yearning for news of everyone."

Jack held up a cautionary hand. "Gently, gently."

Poppy tapped her toe and tossed her curls. "I am in splendid health. Will you answer my questions before you drive me into a decline?"

"You wrote that your husband was killed in a political feud, and you wish to be with your mother at—er—at this time," Jack said fondly.

461

"I made a long, harsh trip to be here with her," Poppy sighed, eyes modestly lowered, and then flashed, "So where is she? And why is this house still furnished and in use with Mr. and Mrs. Peters still employed?"

"Your mother and her husband are entertaining in the country, a large party, including some minor royalty. You understand, she could not leave? She hopes to join you here Wednesday or Thursday."

"She wrote to you and not to me?" Poppy cried, outraged.

"Our places in the country are close. When your letters were forwarded to us there, I rode over to Redferns at once to see her. We agreed I should come to town and make arrangements for your reception."

"This house, this house?" Poppy demanded. "Mrs. Peters will say nothing. She regards me still as a *jeune fille,* supposed to eat my nice porridge and ask no questions."

Jack's mouth twitched slightly. "Perhaps she regards the subject as delicate. Since her marriage, your mother has interested herself in good works."

"Good works?"

"With fallen women. She feels she understands their difficulties."

"I see," Poppy murmured.

"Many fine, sincere, eminent men are engaged in urging such women off the streets," Jack said earnestly. "But that is only the beginning. They must have a haven while they are prepared to return to a self-respecting life."

Poppy nodded vigorously. "Of course."

"For a while, your mother considered the country air conducive to such a course. Unfortunately—" Jack did not seem to know how to phrase the matter—"Venus was too often in ascent for the experiment to be a success."

"Venus?"

Red-faced, Jack took the plunge. "Many young gardeners and stable hands are employed at Redferns and nearby houses. At one time, of the twenty young women your mother had there, half were found to be breeding."

"Oh, no," Poppy cried and giggled helplessly. "Oh, no. Venus indeed."

"Your mother still had this cottage, and she decided that Mr. and Mrs. Peters were in need of occupation. What better occupation than to house the young ladies here and have Mrs. Peters instruct them in the skills needed to go into good service?"

"Now that is sensible," Poppy cried. A girl who could go into service in a good house, prepared to be something more than a kitchen maid, was indeed better off than on the streets. "But where are they?"

"Temporarily, as long as you are here, I have lodged them in the servants' quarters of our townhouse. Your mother agreed to that."

"Oh, Jack, you are good," Poppy cried and looked at him, long and seriously. "Your skin is still darkened. You have not been back long? You did get to China?"

"And back again. All I ever dreamed it could be and more, a fascinating country, and if I were free I would return again and again."

She could not help him in that. He was an heir. "And Andy?"

"He is at the moment at our place outside Edinburgh with my old tutor."

Poppy felt shocked. "Daisy did not forgive him? She did not accept him back? Or is her husband difficult?"

"Sir Edward is amenable to all his wife's wishes," Jack said stiffly.

"Is he?"

"My family put forth that we had a prior claim," Jack said, and added hastily, "Without elucidating any details that might perturb Sir Edward. He could see for himself that Andy and I had developed a brotherly relationship during our years, yes, years together."

"I think you had better elucidate the details to me," Poppy said. "He really is *my* brother."

"This is an old history."

"For some weeks yet, I have only to sit and wait. And listen."

"My next older brother was no happier to leave the Army than I was to leave the Navy," Jack admitted slowly. "The news he must throw up his commission hit him hard. He was for some months in London, in a mood of deep despair, before he could bring himself to it."

"He rode a horse with four white feet?"

"The description, the markings, were well known. The same he was riding when he was killed."

"Then I can understand the resemblance between you and Andy."

"Our family excels in producing females. But we consider the males we produce to be exceptional."

Poppy groaned. "The British and their breeding."

"Are you then so much an American now?"

"I can decide that later," Poppy said hastily. "But surely you cannot consider you have bred a winner in Andy?"

"Our tutor assures us he shows unusual talent," Jack said, stiff again. "We agreed his background, while broad, of course did not prepare him to go into the usual educational channels."

Poppy stared at him. "Jack, I believe you are going to make a prime heir. You could not sound more in the proper mode if you had never left England. What is this talent you mention?"

A slight smile flickered on Jack's face. "This has been too much for your delicate condition. I will call again another day."

"You will tell me right now," Poppy said and stamped her foot. "What is Andy up to now?"

"He is with his tutor at our place in Scotland working with the stones that have been displaced from the battlements."

"What?"

"You remember he always wanted to construct things of iron. He enjoyed the heaviest labor if it involved casting. He carved in wood, too, if he could find nothing

464

else. You do not recall, but I do, his interest in the artists during our stay in Paris. His tutor reports he has a fine feeling for shaping stone. It is possible that in Andy we have produced a talented sculptor. At the proper time we will see he is sent to Paris and Rome to ascertain if he has such a talent."

"I can't believe it, but you may be right," Poppy said.

"If not, he still will be most useful in overseeing practical work around our properties," Jack said. "We care for our own, Poppy, and Andy is one of ours."

"I believe he is one of the luckiest boys in the world," Poppy cried with a gush of her old warm feeling for Jack.

He saw the look on her face, leaned forward, and caught both her hands in his. "This is not the moment to speak to you, but I have never changed in my regard for you."

"The widow of a man who died violently. A widow with a child."

"A woman who can produce healthy children is held in high regard by my parents," Jack said drily. "Now that your mother is our near neighbor, believe me, you need have no fears. My parents would regard us as well suited and wish us happy."

After Jack left, Poppy sat a long time in front of the fire. She would never know a finer man than Jack or one she liked better. He could give her everything she had ever dreamed of and more. Except she did not love him.

Alone here, all the old musings from her girlhood came back to her, the old wondering what would become of her, what shape her life would assume. Now far away in San Francisco, she had a dowry of sorts. She had arranged that Maurice and Jeremiah's lawyer should pay funds to the English bank, and the bank should manage everything for her. When she could see a little farther ahead, if she wished, she could write the bank to sell her holdings and send her the funds. Or she could let the bank manage everything and leave the whole to accumulate as an inheritance for her child. She had a shrewd idea that, in time, it would represent real wealth.

Once the baby was born, she could return to San Francisco. If she juggled the dates a little, people would think no more than that the child was small for its age. But her heart and mind cried out against such a move. Even if she could face all the memories of the violent and unhappy past, life for a widow with a child and too little money would be hard.

Life in London for a poor widow with a child would be no easier. She had seen women striving to maintain their gentility in conditions of near-poverty, and she shuddered from the memory. Daisy would be helpful, possibly even let her stay at Pallminster Lane, but then she would be a poor dependent. That was not a happy role, and the child would suffer a hundred small deprivations.

Poppy sighed. Jack loved her, and Jack could give her everything. He did not expect her to love him as he well might suspect she had loved Dex. He would be happy and ask nothing more, if she only married him. But she did not think she could be happy with herself. She would always feel she was cheating a fine and deserving man.

Mrs. Peters bustled in. "I've fixed you a fine, strengthening meal, aired your bed for you, and put in the warming pan."

Poppy frowned rebelliously and then remembered. "Do we still have the carriage?"

"Yes, and the horse growing fat," Mrs. Peters sniffed. "There's naught Peters can do about that with no daily driving, only hauling them trollops from station to here or there or wherever."

"Mmm," Poppy said, with a pang of sympathy for the women who were trained under Mrs. Peters. They would be trained well but not gently. "That's easily mended. Tell Peters I'll be driving at the usual hour every day."

Mrs. Peters looked scandalized. "In your condition, miss?"

"Mrs. Dunbar, if you please." She had deliberately left the newspapers, folded back to the account of Jeremiah's death, with her appearance and name recounted prominently, where Mrs. Peters must see them.

"Excuse me, Mrs. Dunbar, ma'am," Mrs. Peters said, with a glint in her eyes that told clearly she believed only half of what she read. "It's old habit, Miss Poppy, ma'am. But you know very well that ladies in your condition don't go driving, don't even step outside the house, you know that."

"Who's to know if I stay in the carriage with the robe over my lap?"

"You could be seen," Mrs. Peters protested, horrified. "On the doorstep here. By anyone. It's not done, ma'am."

Poppy got slowly to her feet. "Tell Peters I'll expect the carriage in front of the house at the usual hour."

Chapter Forty-eight

WHEN a summer day in England was perfect, nothing could be more perfect, Poppy thought happily as she settled herself in the carriage and let Peters tuck the lap robe around her. She sniffed the city smell of the air, caught faint echoes of street cries from around the corner and church bells in the distance, felt the familiar soft jolting of wheels rolling over stone, not planks or dirt, and laughed aloud. This was London. Until now, she had not known how homesick she had been.

She craned forward for her first glimpse of the park and gave an involuntary cry of satisfaction when they entered it. The green of the English grass was like no other green. The beds of flowers, the trees, the whole aspect was so completely England, not the wild, untrammeled beauty of California, nor yet the too-mannered perfection of the landscaping of France, but beautifully and naturally England, a land long loved and cared for and kept at its loveliest.

She leaned forward, hands clenched, greedily eyeing everything, trying to imprint on her mind all the things she had not seen for so long and had missed so bitterly without knowing it. The horses were so handsome, and the gentlemen rode so beautifully, not for travel, but for pleasure and style. The ladies in their light carriages were so beautiful, gracious, composed. And, oh, the clothes the women on the promenade were wearing!

She plucked resentfully at her black gloves and shoved her black bonnet farther back. For the child's sake, for custom, she must endure this hated mourning that was a mockery. Jeremiah's death had meant nothing to her except escape from degradation and terror. Still, she was his widow and his child would be legitimate. She pushed the thought from her.

Leaning forward again, she studied every walking costume. After the new year, she would have new clothes, beautiful clothes, whatever else she went scant on. Nobody here would question by a matter of a few weeks whether her year of mourning was up or not. That blue, the tailoring was severe, but it only made the lady appear more delicate and fragile in contrast. She must try something like that but perhaps in green.

When they returned to Pallminster Lane, Poppy almost danced up the steps for all her weight and ran into the house. Jack jumped up from a chair beside the fireplace.

"Dear Poppy, this is not California."

"So I have been observing, most happily."

"If you must go out, perhaps a closed carriage?"

Poppy pulled off her black bonnet, shook out her curls, and nodded to Mrs. Peters, who was hovering nearby for propriety's sake. "I enjoy the air and sunshine. I am neither an invalid nor a monster. Wrapped in the robe, nobody sees anything to shock them. So where's the harm?"

"It simply is not done."

"I'm doing it. You will stay for tea?"

"If you would care to come down to the country with me, the house is large, and you would be welcome."

"I have never met any of your family."

"I came today to ask if you would receive my sister-in-law if she calls?"

To meet his family was serious. To stay at their country place under the circumstances was almost a commitment. "I must wait on everything until I have talked to Daisy," Poppy reminded him.

She was thoughtful after Jack left. If Jack, who knew so well the freer ways of life outside England and seldom faulted anything she did, if Jack disapproved of her drives, Daisy would be outraged. Poppy knew she would writhe in the position of a child and a dependent in another woman's house. More than ever now, it would be intolerable.

Still, she had tomorrow and perhaps the day after, and she had had the barest taste of all a return to London meant. The park was too delicious to abandon after one drive, but the following day she would tell Peters to bring the carriage around early. They would drive through the streets, she would have at least one glimpse of the fashionable shops before they went to the park.

Mrs. Peters sniffed when she gave the order, and Poppy knew she was hoping Daisy would arrive to put an end to this brazen behavior. The day proved fine, and Poppy only smiled when Peters glowered as he helped her into the carriage. In minutes, she forgot him completely. She relished every sight, every familiar street corner and shop sign, every beer dray and grocer's cart, all the things she had missed so bitterly, though secretly. She knew now she had grieved she would never see or hear any of this again. Yet here she was, once more a part of London. Then she realized the carriage had stopped.

"Yes, Peters?"

"It's Her Ladyship's bank, miss. Since you're so independent these days, I thought as maybe you'd be stopping in to take care of some of your independent business."

Poppy's eyes narrowed. His tone was just this side of insolence. Still he might honestly think that, newly returned to England, she had urgent business she must transact. She glanced at the bank, Dex's bank, and went white. She was imagining things. She was fanciful, pregnant fanciful. That could not be Dex peering out the window straight at the carriage.

"Thank you, Peters," she said. "I have no business here. The park now. Quickly. We'll be late."

She forced herself to lean back and clasped her hands together to keep them from trembling. That could not have been Dex. He was still in Mexico or California. Even if it had been, he could not have recognized her

470

or the carriage or known that Daisy still held the cottage at Pallminster Lane. He could not guess she might be here. He probably had heard of Jeremiah's death, and he might know she had left San Francisco, but London was the last place he would expect her to be. He knew she would refuse to become a dependent child again. He could not guess the special, urgent reason for her return.

That glimpse had left her feeling faint. "The park, quickly, I need fresh air."

"That's all we need for a real scandal," Peters said dolorously. "A baby born in the park."

"Worse than a coachman dismissed without a character?" Poppy threatened, but her heart was not in it.

Daisy might be at the cottage when they returned. If she was, she might listen to an urgent plea of the need for country air. Poppy shuddered at the thought of staying in London and accidentally seeing Dex when she looked like this. When she was lithe and slim again, when she felt beautiful and seductive, then she would face him. And somehow she would tell him she was a respectable widow with family responsibilities and not a lost, lonely, frightened child any more. Oh, the things she would say, that things had changed, that now she had a mother married to a fine gentleman and a brother with the best family connections. And if Dex said he knew all that, she would tell him she had an offer for herself from one of the finest families in the country, one of the very finest as he well knew. He could not take advantage of her again and pay her off with a few shreds of clothing and promises that were worse than nothing. She would spurn him and leave him groveling, apologizing, but in vain, for all the wrongs he had worked on her.

Absolutely rosy with anticipation, as more and more words poured through her mind, things she could hardly wait to say to the man, Poppy let Peters drive quickly through the park and head back to the cottage. As he handed her down, she shook her head impatiently when he tried to point out something up the road. She had no time for flower girls or peddlers.

471

She opened the cottage door, burst into the living room, and realized too late, as she saw Dex standing in front of the fireplace, that Peters had been trying to point out a groom walking two horses, Dex's horse and his own.

Dex advanced two steps and growled, "What have you been doing to my child, madame?"

Dazed with shock, Poppy stared at him. "What child?"

"My child, my baby, my little girl," Daisy's voice called from the stairs. She ran into the room, gathered Poppy close in her arms, and kissed her fondly. "My little girl and in mourning weeds. Oh, my poor darling."

"I want to know what she has been doing to my child," Dex stormed.

Poppy drew back and looked at him over Daisy's shoulder. "As you see, I am a bereaved widow, sir, come to beg my mother's protection."

"I see that somehow, in a delicate condition, you have made a dangerous ocean crossing and endangered my child. What was your ship?"

"I am not a Vanderbilt, sir, to build my own steamship for a single crossing," Poppy said with dignity. "I am a poor but respectable widow. As you can see."

"I see that following a political shooting affray in which your husband was killed—" Dex began.

"Oh, no," Daisy shrieked. "Oh, that terrible California. Was it Indians? Was he scalped?"

"Only killed, Lady Redford," Dex said but his eyes never left Poppy. "Shot within minutes of your rejoining him in public, my courier reported. So I can see why his widow did not find it wise to remain in a town where it was well known she had not lived with her husband for some months."

Poppy bent her head over her clasped hands. "Daisy, I have come to you in deepest affliction. Can you not protect me?"

"Do you wish to retire to your room while I deal with this?" Daisy asked.

Poppy peeked up at Dex's blazing eyes. He was capable of saying anything. He probably would. And Daisy was capable of believing him. "I am no longer an infant," she said bravely. "I assure you, Daisy, I was honorably married to a man well regarded in the community. He was shot down, at a banquet given in his honor, while I was sitting at his side. Upstairs I have newspapers which will give you all the details."

"Came provided with proof, did you?" Dex asked. "Did they mention my ship the *Golden Dolphin* had docked only a few hours before?"

"Daisy, will you permit this man to make such accusations?" Poppy demanded.

"As the owner of the *Golden Dolphin,* I have copies of the log and manifests of the ship. They show clearly we were both aboard and give the exact dates."

"Together, and you have the dates," Daisy said thoughtfully and looked at Poppy with narrowed eyes. "Exactly when do you expect your baby, dear child?"

"Later," Poppy said. "Later."

"I assumed you did not know of the child when you embarked on this long trip, but I see that could not be so," Daisy insisted.

Poppy let an appealing tear drop. "I wished her to be British born."

"My son," Dex thundered. "I, too, wish him to be British born. And legitimate, with my name. We do not have illegits in my family."

"My daughter," Poppy repeated pathetically.

"It's a good marriage," Daisy said, with a nod of her head, her sweet voice at its most practical. "Of course in your condition, no, not a large wedding."

"All my life," Poppy cried, "I've known sooner or later you would attempt to force me into a marriage of your choosing. Time and again, it has driven me into a state of despondency, a marriage for the sake of marriage."

"My son will not be born with the slightest cloud on his name," Dex roared. "A small private wedding here at the house. It can be arranged before the week is out."

Poppy sank into a chair and burst into tears. "My baby, my daughter, my little girl!"

Daisy put a hand on her shoulder. "She wrote her husband was a man of substance, and nobody here is likely to question a small discrepancy in dates, Dex. There is no need for Poppy to make a marriage that will reduce her to a state of despondency."

"I assure you I have yet to see her in such a state in my company," Dex said, biting off his words. "I suggest you ask her, Lady Redford, if she was ever forced into my bed."

"I was in a state of despair and affliction," Poppy vowed.

"Her reticule had unfortunately shot her husband," Dex explained. "Only lightly, but he was a man who seemed to bring on a looseness in triggers."

"Her reticule?" Daisy said thoughtfully. "I see. And you feel she perhaps has some small affection for you?"

"Except at times when I have been forced to send her away from me, for her own safety. Personally, I have always held her in high regard. As I said in Paris, I've wanted her from the first moment I saw her, and every moment since."

"I see," Daisy repeated, even more thoughtfully. "Poppy, my sweet, exactly what is your objection to this marriage?"

Poppy jumped to her feet. "Do you think I want to spend my life with a man who thinks he has only to be in the same room for me to run and throw myself into his arms?"

Daisy nodded. "If that's it, I think you had best be married so all your children will be legitimate. As your mother, and speaking to you as a young woman under my protection, I think I may urge most earnestly that this marriage take place as soon as possible." Then she pursed her lips and murmured, "For myself, I've always had a fancy for the name Lilly."

"His name will be Dexter, combined, of course, with other family names about which I will be happy to consult you," Dex said.

"Rose is one of my favorites," Poppy said shyly.

"I think Blossom is a little common but there's May," Daisy mused.

"Violet?" Poppy suggested.

"Women!" Dex thundered. "I assume you are not forgetting there is also a jade plant?"

"Mr. Roack," Lady Redford said, drawing herself up.

"His name will be Dexter. Then we might consider Wolfington."

"Or perhaps Amaryllis?" Poppy said.

Her eyes met Daisy's in a gaze of perfect harmony.